WORST Nanny EVER

ANGELA CASELLA

ALSO BY ANGELA CASELLA

Hideaway Harbor shared universe

The Holiday Hate-Off (November 2025)

Babes of Brewing

Best Served Cold

Worst Nanny Ever

Best Kind of Trouble (January 2026)

Worst Liars Ever (Spring/Summer 2026)

Unlucky in Love

The Love Fixers

The Love Bandits

The Love Losers

The Love Destroyers

Spin-off Standalone

The Thief Who Saved Christmas

Finding You

You're so Extra

You're so Bad

You're so Basic

You're so Vain

You're so Phony (coming soon!)

Fairy Godmother Agency

A Borrowed Boyfriend

A Stolen Suit

A Brooding Bodyguard

A Reluctant Roommate

Bringing Down the House (Nicole and Damien's story)

Highland Hills
(co-written with Denise Grover Swank)

Matchmaking a Billionaire

Matchmaking a Single Dad

Matchmaking a Grump

Matchmaking a Roommate

Matchmaking a Player (novella) by Angela Casella (May)

Bad Luck Club
(co-written with Denise Grover Swank)

Love at First Hate

Jingle Bell Hell

Fraudulently Ever After

Matchmaking Mischief

Asheville Brewing
(co-written with Denise Grover Swank)

Any Luck at All

Better Luck Next Time

Getting Lucky

Bad Luck Club

Luck of the Draw (novella)

All the Luck You Need (prequel novella) by Angela Casella

To all the women out there who love DILFs.

Because we know there's nothing sexier than a man who shows up for everyone in his life.

CHAPTER ONE

TRAVIS

A scream rips through the house, loud enough that the noise-cancelling headphones I'm wearing don't do jack.

I hurl myself out of bed, forgetting the rumpled blankets wrapped around my legs and plunge headfirst onto the floor, face-planting hard enough that my forehead bounces off the wood flooring.

Yup. That really hurts. But I can't focus on the pain because my son is still screaming. It feels like the sound is inside of my head. It's the wind powering my anxiety tornado.

Is there an intruder?

Or...is Ollie dying? Maybe he has some awful medical diagnosis his mother didn't disclose to me when she dropped him off on my doorstep a month ago with nothing but a single suitcase.

Is he homesick?

Does he miss his mother?

Then there's the other, more persistent, thought—I've known I'm a father for all of a month, and I'm already failing.

I stagger to my feet, my head aching, my headphones askew. The sound of my band's music is still blasting out of them. I throw them onto the bed and charge out the door with renewed determination and the beginnings of a really awful bruise just beneath the birthmark on my forehead.

A few seconds later, I burst into Ollie's bedroom.

It's not pitch dark, because there's a night-light in here, purchased after he woke up weeping on his first night in my house. I'd felt like a jackass for not realizing most kids his age are afraid of the dark. Though I work with children in my after-school music program, The Missing Beat, they're all older than Ollie. Teenagers. I've discovered there's a world of difference between seven and thirteen.

Thanks to that night-light, I can see my son's wide eyes. His serious little face. For a second there's no recognition in his gaze, but at least he stops screaming.

"Oh, it's you, Travis," he says after a moment. He sounds disappointed, like he'd really hoped an intruder would have come in instead.

My head is throbbing, my breath coming in pants.

"Are you okay?" I ask in a gush, leaning over to catch my breath.

"No," he says, his little cheeks pink, his eyes shining. "I just had a nightmare that my mother left me at a stranger's house, and I woke up *here*."

Well, shit. I don't know what to say to that. There's no denying it's true. Up until just over a month ago, I didn't know I had a son, and Ollie thought he had a different father.

"This is your home," I say, because it sounds comforting.

It's also true. Right now, my house is the only home he has.

Years ago, his mother Lilah left me for a very rich, very old record producer before she realized she was pregnant. Her solution was to marry him and pretend Ollie was his child. He and Ollie had both believed it up until last month. The truth had come out thanks to one of those home DNA tests and a justifiably suspicious family who hadn't wanted his millions going to Lilah.

The geezer had thrown them both out, as if all of the years he'd spent with Ollie had meant nothing.

Asshole.

I did one of those DNA tests too, after Ollie came to live with me, and it confirmed that he's my son. I didn't really need the test, though. He could have stepped out of my childhood photos. Looking at him stirs up memories I'd thought I'd made peace with years ago.

"This definitely isn't my home," he says, folding his knees up and wrapping his skinny arms around them. He looks so painfully small like that, wrapped up like a pretzel. It hurts to look at him, to want to protect him but not know *how*.

I sit at the end of his bed. The spare bedroom still looks the same as it did when he first arrived—a double bed with a white comforter, a nondescript bureau, a desk with a chair, and a framed photo of the Blue Ridge Mountains.

"Why don't we go to the store and get some stuff for your room?" I suggest, not for the first time. "Wouldn't that be nice?"

"No," he says, tightening his arms around his legs. "My mom's going to come back."

Not anytime soon, she's not. She made it very clear it was my turn with Ollie—*indefinitely*—and then boarded a plane to Australia to follow her new boyfriend's band.

She has called all of twice to check on him.

A lawyer helped me secure emergency temporary custody, and I plan to seek sole custody as soon as Ollie has been with me for sixty days, which would legally qualify as child abandonment in North Carolina. While I might not know what to do with him, at least I would never abandon him.

"Sure," I say. "But while we're waiting, we might as well have a little fun, huh?"

"You're not fun," he says flatly. "You don't have any toys, or anything interesting in this house besides your drums, and you won't even let me play them. This place is a prison."

Ouch.

I bought him a train set the week he got here in mid-September, nearly a month into the school year, but he insisted it was a boring baby toy. I asked if he wanted anything else, and he told me he wanted nothing from me. The only toy he's accepted is a stuffed sloth my best friend Rob gave him. He also calls Rob "Uncle Rob," while I'm still just Travis.

"What about Winnie?" I ask, referring to the new nanny. "She's always got that cool fun pack with her."

We've had three nannies. Three, in five weeks. That has to be some kind of record.

The first nanny quit because Ollie asked her not to sing to him anymore, and when she pressed him for a reason, he said her voice sounded like a dying parrot's.

I told him not to be rude and found a new nanny.

She quit because he didn't say a word to her. Not one word in two weeks.

He admitted he'd only given her the silent treatment because I'd told him not to be rude.

Now we're on Nanny Number Three, Winnie, and she seems perfect. She's young, pretty, and has a degree in early childhood education. Better yet, she's got that fun pack of activity books, markers, bubbles, and other kid-centric crap like stretchy hands that probably leave stains on the walls. (I would have worried about that last month; I couldn't care less now.) Ollie smiled the first time he saw her stash of goodies, which I figured was a good sign.

"I don't think she's coming back," he says flatly.

The ache in my head instantly gets worse.

"What happened?" I ask, massaging my forehead. My band has a show at a brewery tomorrow night, and Winnie was supposed to watch him.

"I didn't do anything," he says.

"I didn't say you did." Although, let's be honest, he totally did. Ollie is smart—his teacher, Mrs. Applebaum, told me he's several grade levels above his peers—and he's devoted his considerable intelligence to his new goal in life: making me miserable.

Let this be said for my son: he is very goal driven.

In addition to driving away two—possibly three—perfectly good nannies, he has written his math homework on the walls (to check if the markers are actually washable; they're not), destroyed ten of my vinyl records because he "thought they were frisbees," nearly burned down the house by microwaving metal, and stuck spiky dried sweet gum balls beneath the sheets of my bed (he denies it, but how else would they have gotten there?). Don't even get me started on how he keeps calling his teacher Mrs. Applebottom.

Rob says Ollie's just acting out to get attention. I get it. His world has imploded, but my world has imploded too.

For years, I've been keeping my anxiety at bay by closely controlling every aspect of my environment at home, and now I'm in control of nothing. I've barely slept. I stay up for hours, waiting for Ollie to scream or to start roaming the house in the middle of the night. My mind is a constantly whirling tornado of intrusive thoughts.

"I know you hate me," Ollie says, glaring at me with burning eyes.

"I don't hate you," I say softly.

What I do feel for him would be harder to put into words. I didn't have any time to wrap my brain around the idea of him before I was dealing with the reality. He's my son, and I love him, but it's not like any kind of love I've ever experienced. My feelings for him ache, and they're awful—protectiveness wrapped in worry, encased in a shell of inadequacy.

"If you cared about me, you'd ask Hannah to be my nanny."

Oh, Christ, not this again.

Hannah is Rob's girlfriend's friend. They brought her over here once, on the day Ollie was first dropped off. Honestly, I barely remember that evening. I was struggling to process the fact that I was a father, not of a baby, but of a fully formed seven-year-old boy who is probably smarter than I am.

Rob and his girl Sophie took off, but Hannah volunteered to stay behind and hang out with Ollie for a while. She watched some cartoons with him and made him mac and cheese. Everything seemed to be going well—she has a knack for talking to kids—and she said she was cool with me leaving them alone for a while. I needed to play the drums in the (mostly) soundproof music room. It's one of the only things that helps me work through my emotions so I can feel like a functional human being.

When I came back, Hannah was playing Cards Against Humanity with Ollie, both of them laughing hysterically.

"What are you doing?" I asked, horrified.

"We're having fun," my son said, giving me a dark look. The first of many.

"Oh, relax," she said, rolling her eyes at me. "I took out all of the bad cards."

"But they're *all* bad," I stammered. "That's the whole point."

I mean...who plays Cards Against Humanity with a seven-year-old kid?

Ollie might be a genius, but he's still a child.

I announced it was time for her to go home, Ollie told me he hated me for the first time, and now he asks about her every few days, like clockwork.

"Hannah's not a nanny," I remind him for the hundredth time.

"She doesn't have another job right now. She told me."

"That doesn't make her a solid employment prospect. And, again, she has no relevant childcare experience."

"She helped raise her little brother," he counters. "Now he's a chef in Boston, so he must have turned out okay."

"Every chef I've ever met is mentally unbalanced."

He gives me a hard look. "That's not very nice, Travis. You told me not to make assumptions about people."

After he'd told another boy he mustn't be very smart because he thought the *Teenage Mutant Ninja Turtles* were real.

I massage my temples again, which doesn't help at all.

"Why don't I have one of those?" Ollie asks, pointing at my forehead.

I rearrange my hair over the port-wine birthmark, which is small enough to be hidden. "Genetics works in funny ways. Consider yourself lucky you inherited my fingers instead."

"You can't inherit fingers, Travis," he objects.

But he did. His hands are tiny versions of mine. It filled me with awe the first time I noticed, a more profound kind of wonder than when I first heard a song I'd recorded broadcast on the radio.

"Well, you'd know. You're the brains in this operation, Ollie."

"I didn't get those from you either."

I sigh.

"Or from my mother. She doesn't care about facts."

That's for damn sure. Lilah is wild. The time we'd spent together was fun, but it had felt like riding a roller coaster with no exit or ending.

This is a guess—an assumption, if you will—but Hannah is a bit like that too. She's the life of every party she goes to, but bright lights can be blinding.

I'm a man who believes in learning from the past, so I've tried to stay away from her.

It's hard, and not just because Ollie is so fixated on her. She's Rob's girlfriend's best friend, and Sophie goes to a lot of our shows. So Hannah does too. And whenever she's there, I find myself watching her. Soaking in the details of her, even the slight look of contempt she seems to reserve just for me.

But I don't want to think about Hannah right now. I don't want to think about anything but my pillow....and whether it'll hurt to lie down now that I've bruised my forehead.

"Will you be able to get back to sleep?" I ask.

"I'm going to read my science facts book for a while," Ollie says, flicking on the small lamp next to his bed. "And then I'll try. Are you going to call Hannah?"

"I don't know," I mutter, feeling defeated.

"You didn't say no!"

He sounds so excited that I'm positive he won't be going back to sleep. He'll probably wander around the house again, knocking things over. Watching TV. Waking up the neighbors.

"Good night, Ollie," I say, leaning forward to hug him.

He's wooden in my arms, but he doesn't pull away.

"I want you here, kid. I'm glad you're here."

Not true. Also not a lie.

"Okay," he says. Which is better than if he'd told me I was full of BS, I guess.

I go back to my room, feeling beyond exhausted.

Which is when it occurs to me...

I can't bring him to the show tomorrow. So, if Winnie is planning on ghosting me—

Oh, what am I talking about? Ollie made it clear he drove her off, so yeah, I have to assume she's gone for good. Which means I might really have to get in touch with Hannah. I've burned every nanny bridge I've come to.

CHAPTER TWO

HANNAH

Being unemployed is fantastic. Seriously! I get to do whatever I want, whenever I want. Today, I'm doing special event makeup for Tallulah, who's getting hitched to two dudes who run a goat farm.

Yes, she's marrying both of them. (Well, symbolically.)

Tallulah used to come to Big Catch—the brewery where I worked as the evening floor manager—to buy the occasional keg for events at the goat farm. Goat yoga with microbrews is their big moneymaker. We got to talking, and I mentioned that I was a professionally trained makeup artist. So she reached out to me a few weeks ago and offered me a trade: all the goat milk soap and cheese I could possibly want in exchange for doing her bridal makeup.

I'm lactose intolerant and iffy about goat soap, but you can bet your butt I said yes. I mean, I had *questions*.

For one, why would a woman bother getting symbolically married to two men? Isn't one man enough of a burden?

It looks like I'm about to get my big chance to interrogate her, because event makeup takes time, and we just finished cleansing and moisturizing her face in one of the bathrooms in the *delightful* cottage on the goat farm. The farm is between Asheville and Black Mountain, and it looks like it was plucked out of one of those German cautionary fairy tales my dad used to read to us, where someone always loses a hand or an eye. It's especially lovely at this time of year, with the leaves on its many trees turning gold and orange and red. Even the bathroom is delightful. There's a deep copper tub and plenty of room for a chair in front of the sink and mirror, which is making my job a lot easier.

"Sooo," I say as I start to apply primer on her smooth cheeks. "Isn't it a bit hard to juggle two men? Men are *so…*" I make a face to indicate I don't even have words for them.

"Oh, they're both lovely," Tallulah replies with a pitying look. "Very in touch with their emotional selves. I love them, and they love each other. There's a lot of hate in the world, but there's so much love to go around."

I have to snort. Literally have to.

"Sorry," I say, continuing with the application. "I was just thinking about my ex, Jonah. He had plenty of love to go around too. He was seeing four of us at the same time, but none of us knew."

"Really?" she asks hungrily. So at least I'm not the only nosy bitch in the house. (I say this with the utmost respect.)

"Yeah, but we flipped the script," I tell her. "Three of us got together, and we became best friends, because *screw* him. We hang out all the time."

I feel a warm fondness bloom in my chest whenever I talk about Sophie and Briar. They'd walked into my life at a time when I'd needed a friend, badly. I found two. Losing Jonah had barely been a blip on my radar.

"What about the fourth woman?" Tallulah asks, souring me on her the slightest bit.

"She doesn't seem too interested in our girl gang." I pause to dot some color corrector beneath her eyes. "But I haven't given up. I reached out to her again last week."

Truthfully: I *don't* give up. I've been compared unfavorably to a bulldog by more than one person. When I was a kid, my father drilled a *no one left behind* philosophy into my brothers and me, and it's stayed with me.

"What about the bed?" I ask, ready to change the subject. "Doesn't it feel crowded with all three of you?"

She gave me a tour of the cottage before we got started, and it's a double bed. A DOUBLE. Unthinkable with three people.

"Sometimes. When the goats sleep with us," she says with a careless shrug.

"The goats sleep with you?"

"Oh, sure," she says. "But they're not housebroken, so it can get rough."

Damn. I wish I'd thought to bring a notebook. I'm not sure what I'd be cataloguing the information for, but I kind of like the thought of being a modern cultural anthropologist. Self-taught and self-appointed, obviously.

I desperately want to ask if one of her grooms is better at sex, and if that is a subject of embarrassment and sensitivity to everyone, but even I know better than to ask that.

I'm kind of hoping she'll just offer up the information.

"You're very good at this," she says dreamily, staring in the mirror as I move on to the foundation. I've barely done anything yet, but she already has a bridal glow.

I smile at her reflection. "You're beautiful. You make it easy. Just wait until I'm finished. They'll both want to get into your pants at once."

This is what I love about makeup—bringing out people's natural beauty. Everyone has beauty. *Everyone.*

The proper use of makeup is to highlight what makes a person special. To give it a crown.

That's what I'm doing with Tallulah.

"I'm going to send you home with some of our goat cheese ice cream too," she says, beaming at me.

Well, I'll certainly be giving *that* away.

THE SERVICE IS HELD outside on a well-shaded corner of the farm. The officiant is a woman named Stella—a fellow goat enthusiast and the godmother of one of the goat farmers—and her husband is sitting in the front row weeping. From joy, everyone insists, patting him on the back.

It's bizarre but kind of sweet, and I can't deny there's something compelling about the adoring way both of Tallulah's husbands-to-be are watching her. It's been a while since anyone's looked at me like that.

My car is constantly just on this side of being junkyard ready, so I hitched a ride to the farm with someone I know on the catering staff. I opt against riding home with her after the ceremony, deciding instead to stay for the after-party. I'm hoping to witness some weird shit: a tantric sex party, some cultist chanting, dancing around a bonfire, that kind of thing.

Now, don't judge me. I've known Tallulah for long enough that I can reasonably expect not to be murdered—and if anyone tries, I have pepper spray and brass knuckles on my person. I'd like to think I'd take my killer down with me or at least leave them with a bloody nose to remember me by.

To be honest, though, the party ends up being a bit of a disappointment. The dancing only lasts until dark, and everyone left funnels inside to play Settlers of Catan. We divide into three separate groups.

I suggest strip Catan for my group, and a guy lectures me on how I don't understand the "true spirit of the game."

I also, apparently, don't understand the "true spirit" of marriage, because shouldn't the happy throuple be having wild sex, or at least dancing to mellow eighties songs?

I'll admit, after a few too many hard kombuchas, I flat out ask Tallulah why she isn't getting freaky with her husbands.

She gives me a pitying look and says, "This is foreplay."

I don't see it. Nothing about trading for grain or rice makes *me* feel hot and bothered. And the gaming goes on for hours. *Hours.*

By the time my phone buzzes at two in the morning, I'm more than ready for the distraction.

"Oops, so sorry, gotta answer this," I say, lifting it up to show everyone at my table.

"That's a text alert," says the player sitting next to me, a guy whose name I didn't catch. "You *can't* answer it."

"It's probably super important," I respond, already on my feet. "You can skip me this round."

I'm guessing most of the people at my table are happy to get rid of me, probably because I don't actually know how to play Settlers of Catan, even though three separate people have given me long-winded explanations.

I shut myself in the bathroom with my latest bottle of hard kombucha before checking my phone—and then do a double take.

The texts are from Travis.

> Hi Hannah.
>
> I was wondering whether you're busy tomorrow night.

Oh, you have *got* to be kidding me.

After my friend Sophie started dating his friend Rob, Travis and I exchanged a few fun, flirty texts. Okay, several. Mostly about our friends. But our enjoyable back-and-forth exchange ended abruptly after I babysat for his son.

The poor kid had just gotten dropped off by his mother as if he were a mis-delivered package. My own mother had abandoned me at around the same age, so I knew exactly what he was going through. He was terrified. He needed a distraction, some fun...so I'd pulled out the only game that looked remotely fun in Travis's cabinet.

And, sure, it isn't precisely meant for children, but what kid doesn't love being allowed to do something they shouldn't?

Travis made it very clear he doesn't approve of my parenting skills. *I* don't approve of the drumstick he has firmly wedged up his ass. Nor do I want lectures on "proper behavior" from someone who's my age.

It's incredibly amusing that Travis would try to sidle into my phone using such a casual approach when we've barely spoken all month.

Based on his opening, there are only two things he could want. Option A: a booty call. Or option B: a favor.

It's not hard to figure out which one he's after.

Travis is a good-looking guy in a popular local band. He has a *very nice* house and an attitude that suggests he grew up rich, which is appealing for some women. In other words, he's not the kind of man who needs to plan ahead to cinch a booty call.

I also happen to know that his band, Garbage Fire, is playing at Big Catch Brewing, my former place of employment, tomorrow night.

Which means we're definitely dealing with option B.

The guy's got *cojones*, I'll give him that. It's almost admirable.

I shake my head at my phone for a solid five seconds before responding:

> Ohhh, are you asking me out?

> Because sorry, not interested.

> You're not my type.

As I wait for his response, I catch a glimpse of myself grinning in the mirror across from me.

No getting around it, messing with Travis is way more fun than Catan.

He doesn't keep me waiting long.

> Very funny, Hannah.

> I thought so too.

> I also think it's very funny that you're texting me at two in the morning.

> I didn't think you'd answer.

> A fantastic reason for getting in touch.

> So, let's have it. What do you need? A makeup artist? My rate is $125 an hour.

> I'm starting to regret texting you.

> Only now?

I have a pretty good memory of his house's layout, so I try to visualize where he is. Is he sitting in his music room, at his drums? Nah. He wouldn't want to keep Ollie up with the music. The soundproofing in that place is the best that money can buy, but Travis is the cautious type.

So he's probably in his bedroom, maybe even lying in his bed. Would he be wearing a T-shirt?

It's my imagination, so no T-shirt. Just his toned arms and chest...

My phone buzzes, and I stop salivating for long enough to pick it up.

> I have that show tomorrow night.

Boom, there it is.

> Everyone at Big Catch is probably still pissed at me for quitting. They won't do you any favors on my account, unless you want free beer. My brother can hook you up with that.

> This isn't about Big Catch.

My mouth puckers, because suddenly I know what he's going to say next, but I can barely believe it.

> Our nanny quit, and I was wondering if you'd be willing to sit for Ollie tomorrow night.

> Look, I know what you're going to say.

> I was a little harsh about the game, but I'd like to keep things age-appropriate.

> I can pay you fifty an hour. It's not makeup, but I hope it's still worth your time.

I drop my phone.

Fifty dollars an hour to watch cartoons with Ollie?

Most babysitting or nannying jobs offer about half that.

Hot damn. He must be wealthier than I realized and *very* desperate. Suspiciously desperate, which automatically makes me curious.

Still...I'm a woman of principles.

And, by that, I mean I'm stubborn.

So I respond:

> Nope, sorry. Wouldn't want to poison young minds.

> You're going to make me grovel, aren't you?

> You might want to start by apologizing.

Five seconds later, my phone rings.

My grin spreads wider. Yup, no denying it. I'm enjoying myself.

"Yes, hello," I say, "Hannah's babysitting services. Nothing but the best neglect for your kids."

"Hannah," he says, his voice gruff and very tired. "I'm exhausted."

"That definitely sucks, but I fail to see how it's my problem."

"Ollie likes you. He's...he doesn't like everyone."

"Then he's the rare man who has excellent judgement."

"Please, Hannah. Will you do this for me? I need you to do this for me."

I pause, letting him sweat, though I've already decided I'll do it. Truth is, I've been worried about Ollie and want to see how he's faring. But while I'm doing it more for Ollie, I'd be lying if I said the bone-deep exhaustion in Travis's voice didn't move me—or the gravelly purr of his voice saying please.

I'm not immune to the appeal of making a big, strong man beg.

"Yeah, okay," I say after another couple of seconds. "But I'm really bummed to be missing Garbage Fire's fourth show this month. It's going to hurt my psyche not to get to hear the same songs over and over again."

"We always play a different setlist," he says with a touch of annoyance, and I nearly burst out laughing.

He's right, they do. They're good, too. And Travis is so touchy right now that a puff of wind against his skin would set him off.

"Oh, my bad," I say. "But yeah, I'll do it. Do you need me to bring some fun stuff with me?"

"No," he replies quickly. "Not necessary. We'll have everything you need."

"You're going to hide all the fun stuff in the house, aren't you?" I ask, leaning against the sink. "Say, what are you doing awake at two a.m.? Sophie said you didn't have a show tonight."

"Ollie hasn't been sleeping well."

I think of that little boy from last month, so small against Travis's massive sofa.

When my mom left, I was Ollie's age, and my little brother Connor was a baby. Just three months old. I never forgave her, and I'll never forgive Ollie's mom either.

"What a cunt," I mutter.

"Excuse me?" he says.

I roll my eyes at my reflection in the mirror.

Travis isn't as much of a prude as he likes to pretend. He's a sexy guy in a band. He plays the drums, for goodness' sake, a sensual instrument if ever there was one. All that banging around. All the sweating he does under those hot lights after moving his arms for an hour...

Sweat's sexy when you know a man's worked for it.

I really have attended a lot of Garbage Fire shows over the last month, so I can honestly say I'm not the only person who's noticed the allure of Travis. He's a tall, fit man with hair that's too long up top and shorter on the sides, and dark eyes that remind me of black holes. Even more intense when he's lost in his music.

Sophie, obviously, only has eyes for her boyfriend, who's the lead singer. Briar claims she's disinterested in all men at the moment, but the band is popular, and there's a group of women who show up for every single show. Admittedly, so do we, so I'm not judging. Just...noticing. Partly for Sophie's sake, because if any of those women try to make a run on her man, I'm gonna cut a bitch. Metaphorically.

There's this one woman who's always front and center, though, and she seems fixated on Travis. All the guys in the band know her, but I haven't asked who she is...I don't want them to misinterpret my question and think I'm interested.

"Hannah? Did you just call Ollie—"

"Oh, no. I wasn't talking about Ollie, obviously. He rocks. I was talking about his mother."

"I'm not sure that's much better," he says, firmly back on his high horse.

"I didn't call her a cunt in front of him," I say, annoyed. "And I wouldn't. But I think you and I can solidly agree that she's a cunt."

"I don't think I should answer that," he says, but I can hear a thread of humor in his voice.

"Plausible deniability. I got you. So what time do you need me tomorrow night?"

"From seven until ten thirty, maybe eleven? Is that okay?"

"Yup. Great. It'll help make up for doing makeup in exchange for goat cheese and soap tonight. Do you like goat cheese?"

"I'm suspicious of anyone who'd give you goat cheese in exchange for doing makeup, so I'm going with no."

"All right, you barrel of laughs, I'm going to go see if I can convince someone to give me a ride home. If not, I'll have to find a goat to snuggle up with so I can sleep off this hard kombucha."

He groans, and I can practically feel his judgment radiating over the phone.

I'm not gonna lie.

It's energetically feeding me.

"Good night, Hannah," he says.

"Good night, Travis. Don't be a hero. Take a few Benadryl if you need them."

"They're for—"

"I know what they're for. I can read instructions. I just choose not to follow them."

"Delighted you'll be working for me," he says, his voice all husky, and there it is again—that trace of humor that saves him from being intolerable. And then he's gone.

I stare at myself in the mirror. "This is probably a terrible mistake."

"Are you still talking to yourself in there?" asks a guy from behind the door. "I need to pee."

"Oh, come on. Isn't the whole point of being a man that you don't have to wait?"

CHAPTER THREE

TRAVIS

A knock lands on the front door. I take a in a slow, deep breath and let it ease out. That's got to be Rachel, right on time for her interview.

"If you scare this one off, no Hannah tonight," I tell Ollie, feeling like a jackass for negotiating with my son like he's a terrorist. But desperate times call for bribery. He wants Hannah to be his nanny, but I had to beg to get her to babysit tonight. This isn't a job she'll want permanently, and I need someone who's actually a trained childcare professional. The nanny who raised me had a degree from Norland College, which my mother liked to tell her friends was the "gold standard." Nanny Grace was kind of frosty and a stickler for rules, but there was no denying she knew her shit.

I managed to schedule three interviews for this weekend—one today, two tomorrow—with people who can start on Monday. I'm a bit concerned that anyone who'd be available to start within a couple of days won't be the best and brightest, but hopefully one of the three will be responsible and have references who actually like them.

Rachel works at a daycare but said she'd "leave them in a

heartbeat" for fifty an hour. Her attitude suggests a lack of loyalty, but at least she has childcare experience.

"Hannah's the one who should be my nanny," Ollie says sullenly. He's standing by the couch, staring at the door with open hostility while he picks at the blanket splayed across the back of the sofa—a gift from my sister. "I'm going to ask her tonight."

"You're not the one who'd be hiring her," I tell him, moving his hand. "That would be me."

"Yes, we all know you're the one with the power, Travis, and I'm your prisoner."

"Oh, Ollie," I groan. Is this what a seven-year-old is supposed to sound like? I realize he's several grade levels more academically advanced than his classmates, but he's still a kid. Half the time he sounds like a grumpy old man. I said as much to Rob, who laughed and told me the apple doesn't fall far.

"Behave yourself," I say one final time, then rake my hands through my hair before taking a step toward the door.

"Your birthmark's showing."

Pausing, I give him an incredulous look. "Really, man?"

"I'm not saying it to be mean," he tells me, his face surprisingly earnest. "I just know you don't like strangers seeing it."

I nod stiffly, feeling a tightness in my throat, and adjust my hair. I head into the foyer and open the front door.

It takes me a solid five seconds to square the woman in front of me with the professional headshot Rachel Lynn has on LinkedIn.

She has long blonde hair like the woman in the photo, but everything else about her is different. Instead of wearing a sweater set and pearls, she has on full-on glamour makeup and a very short red summer dress with spiky heels.

"You must be Travis," she says, her voice low and throaty. "I'm Rachel."

It's a mark of my desperation that I wave her inside instead of pretending to be someone else. I know when a woman's done her research, and she's obviously done hers. The greater concern is how she found out who I am—and whether she's going to tell anyone else.

"Here's Ollie," I say, leading her into the living room and gesturing to my son, who's still standing by the couch. He looks unfazed. Then again, Lilah's the kind of woman who wears clothes like this to the grocery store. Maybe he thinks nothing of it.

She plants her hands on her thighs and leans down to talk to Ollie, giving us both an unwanted view of her cleavage. "Well, aren't you just the sweetest little thing. We're going to be the very best of friends. I can tell."

She glances up at me, giving me an overdramatic wink before shifting her attention back to him.

Ollie watches her clinically for a moment, then says, "I don't think so. You don't have to pay your friends, and Travis isn't looking for a friend for me. He wants to keep me out of trouble. I don't think you could."

She looks pissed for half a second, but then she forces a laugh. "Oh, how funny. Isn't he funny?" she asks me, still leaning down with her cleavage on display. As if I could have still failed to notice she has C or maybe D cup breasts.

"Why are you crouched over like that?" Ollie asks.

She stands but crosses her arms just under her chest, pushing her breasts up. "What a nice house you two have," she comments, glancing around. "We're gonna have such a good time in here, Ollie. What do you like to do? Do you enjoy playing music like your dad does? You're *so* lucky to live with a professional musician."

Ollie glances up at me as if to say, *Really, Travis? Is this the best you can do?*

Then he turns to face her and says flatly, "I don't know."

Her grin is as sweet as saccharin. "Well, you know what, Ollie? It just so happens that I have a fun little music set I can bring over here, and we can make our own music together."

"Are you talking about one of those plastic kids' sets?" he asks with withering contempt. "I'm a little old for that."

"I have recorders," she says tightly. "Lots of grown-ups play recorders."

Ollie and I exchange a quick glance—he'd complained about the recorders used in music class at school, and I admitted I still have nightmares about the shrill plastic recorders handed out at my private school when I was a kid. He gives me a half smile, and I return it, feeling a surge of affection for him.

"No, thanks," he says. "Do you like doing science experiments? I *love* chemical reactions. The messier, the better."

"Um, like baking soda and vinegar?" She looks down at her dress in quiet dismay and dusts off the skirt with her hands. "Sure. I've done that before."

"And making gooey things. I *love* gooey things. We could get into a goo fight. That might be fun. Would you like that? Playing catch with goo?"

She gives him a simpering smile. "I'm not much for playing catch, but you can throw it to yourself or your dad. We could read together, though. Do you know how to read?"

"I'm seven," he says flatly. Without missing a beat, he looks up at me with a gaze that's all innocence. "Hey, Travis, can I please go read quietly in my room by myself?"

I nearly laugh.

Instead, I nod. "Sure. Thanks for asking."

No point in having him hang around. I've already decided this one is a no-go.

I watch him head to his room. Before entering, he casts a

pointed look at me and mouths, *No!*—which Rachel must notice.

She wraps her fingers around my arm, stroking my bicep, and I barely resist the impulse to pull away.

"You poor thing," she says, batting her lashes up at me. "It's not easy being a single father, but I'll take care of both of you, you'll see. Do you need a live-in nanny?"

I remove her hand. "No."

"Wouldn't it be nice to have someone get little Paulie ready and out the door in the mornings?"

Yes, dammit.

"Ollie," I correct.

"Of course. Well, I'd be happy to live here if you change your mind. We could be true partners in Ollie's care."

The sad thing is that it's tempting. It would be so easy to hand over the reins to someone else—and if Rachel's after my father's fortune, she'd be more likely to put up with Ollie's antics than Nannys One, Two, or Three. But I don't want her to be nice to my kid because she thinks she can get something from it. Screw that.

"No," I say tightly. "I don't want a stranger living in my home."

She looks taken aback. "But we wouldn't be strangers for long. We'd have plenty of time to get to know each other while Ollie's sleeping—"

"He doesn't sleep much."

"I can help with that."

I shudder at the thought of her force-feeding him melatonin like Nurse Ratched so she can make an unwanted pass at me in my living room.

Sure, she's hot, and I haven't been with a woman for months, but nothing turns me off more than a woman who'd use

Ollie to get to my father's money. I don't like being used either, but this is many orders of magnitude worse.

"No, that's okay," I say. "In fact, I don't think this is going to work out."

She pushes her bottom lip out, which isn't as sexy as she probably thinks it is. "He'd like me if he got to know me better." Her fingers wrap around my bicep again. "You'd *really* like me."

I make a show of removing her hand. "I don't think I would. How'd you find out?"

"Find out what?" she asks, suddenly all innocence.

"About my father. It's obvious you know who he is."

I have his last name, sure, but it's a common enough last name.

"I don't know what you're talking about," she says, lifting her eyebrows in a mockery of innocence.

"I think you do."

Her expression hardens. "The only thing I know about you is that you're in that band with the awful name and your son's a horrible little brat."

"Nice," I say with a pissed-off nod. "The truth comes out. He's a good kid, actually, and very talented at seeing through artificial people. Speaking of...would you have worn that outfit for your interview at the daycare?"

She gasps in outrage. "How *dare* you comment on my clothing!"

"Yeah, that was kind of a crappy thing to do, but I guess I take offense at people walking into my house and insulting my son. Have the day you deserve, Rachel."

Rage flashes in her eyes, and she grabs a bouncy ball off the side table next to the couch—there are hundreds stowed all around the house now—and hurls it at me. I catch it easily, my reflexes honed by years of drumming.

"See, you *can* play catch!" Ollie says, swinging open his door, which must've been slightly ajar this whole time.

She grabs another ball, but before she can even aim it at him, I wrap my fingers around her wrist. Not hard enough to hurt, but no, she will not be throwing a ball at my son.

"Go," I say firmly.

"You're an *asshole*."

"And you shouldn't be swearing in front of children."

She stalks off but looks back at us before rounding the corner toward the front door. "I'm going to warn all of my nanny boards about you."

Oh, fucking fantastic.

Then she leaves and slams the door loud enough to shake the house.

Ollie comes running out of his room, a huge grin on his face. "That was awesome, Travis."

And, just like that, my kid gives me a high five.

It's the first time he's touched me on purpose since he got here. Emotion swells in my throat. He's looking at me like he's actually glad I'm his father.

It's because I was rude to someone, but at least she deserved it.

"Why does she care about your father, though?" he asks. "Hasn't he been dead forever?"

I laugh under my breath at his typical candor.

"No, not forever. He died just before you were born, though, so I guess for you it has been forever."

"Did he have an accident?"

"No, he was sixty when my parents got married. Older, like your d—"

Like your dad, I almost said.

The look on his face says he knows it, and my instant regret is so thick I nearly choke on it.

That man is not Ollie's father in any way that matters. He abandoned him without a backward glance.

"He's not my dad," he says, his voice hard. "And neither are you."

He turns back toward his room, and I want so badly to stop him. To tell him that I'm trying. That I want to be his dad, but I don't know how yet...

"Ollie," I call, my voice full of all those things I can't seem to say. "I'm trying," I manage.

"I know," he says, pausing without turning around. "Thank you for letting Hannah come tonight and for being nice to me."

I watch him disappear into his room. The warm moment between us is already slipping away, and I'm not sure what to do about it.

HANNAH ARRIVES in yoga pants and an oversized Asheville Tourists baseball T-shirt tied at the waist. She looks like she's hungover from whatever alcoholic kombucha she was drinking last night. Still hot, though, because she's a redheaded spitfire with wild green eyes and a dusting of freckles across the bridge of her nose. I've always liked freckles—like constellations on a face—but I don't want to like *her* freckles. Or her perfectly rounded ass, cupped by her yoga pants. Or the sassy smile on her face that seems to challenge everyone around her to war.

She looks good, but I've seen her out enough times to know she likes clothes and makeup. Short, bright dresses and pants that hug her every curve. I wouldn't be surprised to learn that she changed into this outfit specifically to send the message that she has no desire to impress me.

This is her way of saying she's here for Ollie, and Ollie

alone. It's the complete opposite of what Rachel did, and it's honestly a huge relief.

Unfortunately, it's not having the intended effect. If anything, it's making me more aware of having a sexy woman in my house, when it's been so long since I had one in my bed.

"Hannah!" Ollie says, running up and wrapping his hands around her waist. Hugging her as if they're long-lost pals. "Thank goodness you're finally here."

She laughs and hugs him before pulling back and whirling him around. "Look at you! I swear you grew half an inch since I last saw you. How's school treating you?"

"It's very boring," he says. "They keep teaching us about things I already know, and the other kids don't talk to me because Mickey told them I sleep in the sewers."

"You didn't tell me about that," I say, stricken.

Ollie's being bullied, and Mrs. Applebaum didn't say anything? She sure as hell has been communicative about everything he's supposedly doing wrong.

I'm having an ongoing conversation with both her and the school's principal about *what to do* with Ollie. He's in second grade, but the work is much too easy for him, and when he gets bored, he finds "unproductive" ways to entertain himself.

"I tried," he says hotly, his arms still wrapped around Hannah. "He's the one who thinks the Mutant Ninja Turtles are real."

"He probably only said that to convince your teacher he thinks it's a compliment to say you sleep in the sewers," Hannah says, her eyes alight with fury. "I think you should offer *him* the compliment of a nickname like Turtle Boy. Or better yet, we can get some turtle costumes from one of those Halloween stores and scare the—"

"*Hannah.*"

She turns toward me, her expression a five-alarm fire. "You're seriously telling me to let this go?"

"No." I rub my temples, which suddenly ache. I'm tempted to ask why she cares so much, but Hannah seems to throw her entire being into any cause she decides she believes in. "I'm going to have another talk with his teacher."

"They call people who tattle to teachers snitches," Ollie says with a sigh.

"In second grade?" I ask in disbelief.

Damn. Our middle school students at The Missing Beat are like that, but I was expecting kids this young to be kinder, or maybe hoping they would be.

"I can get my brother Liam to walk into class with you a couple of times," Hannah says. "He's an amateur boxer, and I bet that little assh—jerk..."

"You already said the bad part of the word," I mutter.

Ignoring me, she continues, "He won't know what hit him."

"What about me?" I ask. "Why don't I just walk him in?"

Technically, I'm not supposed to. I drop him off in the auditorium, and the kids walk to class from there, but I have every intention of talking my way into it.

She gives me a weighing look, head to toe, her eyes blazing fire through me as she studies me and finds me inadequate.

"I mean, you're tall and strong, sure," she says. "And I'd be pretty intimidated if I were a twerpy little second grader who makes up lies, but Liam takes it to a whole different level."

"Do you think he'd do it?" Ollie asks, buzzing with excitement at the thought of some other guy defending him.

Shit, I feel like I'm failing again.

"Of course he would," Hannah says. "He's desperate to get on my good side." Her gaze falls on me, though. Lingers. And I feel her eyes shoveling past my barriers. Seeing what I wish she wouldn't.

Turning back to Ollie, she says, "But, you know, your dad probably has a supercool plan for humbling this kid. You should give him a shot first. Travis can be very crafty when he wants to be."

I'm grateful. I'm annoyed. I'm a little turned on by her, which is ridiculous. She's been here for all of five minutes, and she's already causing trouble.

And yet, Ollie is talking more than he has in weeks, and she just gave me an opening—and is now giving me the most obvious *don't mess it up* eyes I've ever seen.

"I'd like that, Ollie," I say. "Are you okay with letting me handle it?"

I expect him to say no. Or to point out that I haven't handled any other aspect of parenting well, so why should this be any different? But he nods. "Okay. But shouldn't you leave, Travis? It's seven o'clock. Uncle Rob's probably waiting for you."

"His bedtime routine starts at eight o'clock," I say, brushing my hair back, then promptly forward again when I remember Hannah's here. "I left a few pages of instructions in the kitchen."

"A few pages about how to get a kid to bed?" she asks, her eyes dancing. "I think Ollie and I can manage." She thrusts a plastic bag with a goat printed on the side at me. "Will you give this to my brother?"

"Sure, no problem."

"Now, go bang it out. We'll be waiting for you."

This woman's going to kill me.

CHAPTER FOUR

HANNAH

"I think there's something weird about Travis's father," Ollie says.

It's getting late, and we're in his bedroom. He's been reading a painfully boring book about earth science in bed while I sit beside him, being companionable and texting Sophie and Briar about the band's performance.

"Oh?" I say, glancing up from my phone.

"Yeah." Ollie sets the book down as he warms to the subject. "He was really old when Travis was born, and he's been dead forever. I think he must have been famous or something, because this woman came here earlier to interview to be my nanny, and she acted like she was going to kiss Travis. You know...*adult*-kiss him. And Travis asked if she knew who his father was. So he must have been someone important, right?"

"Huh, did you ask him?" I say, setting the phone aside and trying to remind myself that I should not get gossip from a child. Definitely not.

"I did, but he didn't really answer me. We're basically strangers. I guess I have a new aunt and a grandmother, too, but they're *definitely* strangers. We're going to meet them at Christmas, but I'm not sure how much I'm going to like them. His mom has a scary stretched-out face, plus she sent me a bunch of picture books that are for toddlers." He sighs. "Travis doesn't like me."

"Totally not true," I say, feeling an ache for him. He's so little, tucked into his bed. "I can tell he's crazy about you."

"I drive him crazy, that's for sure," he says with a huff.

"Yeah, but I think Travis only gets himself wound up about people he cares about. Otherwise, he wouldn't bother, you know? Has he brought you to any of his band performances?"

"No," he scoffs, "and he won't. Travis says it's for adults."

"What about to his after-school program?"

He sticks out his lip. "They're all middle schoolers. I'm too young to go. But Mrs. Applebaum says I practically read at a middle-school level."

"Did you tell him you want to go?"

"I told him it was dumb that he wouldn't let me."

Men. The failure of communication starts early. "Would you like me to talk to him for you?"

"Would you?" he asks, his little face transformed by happiness, and I feel my heart swelling.

I hold out my fist for a bump, and he reciprocates. "Consider it done, little man. Are you good to go to bed?"

We completely ignored Travis's two pages of instructions.

Okay, I'll be honest. We didn't just ignore them; we made them into paper airplanes and had a competition with them. Ollie's was way more aerodynamic, and it surprised neither of us when he won by a long shot. We also made a supersized batch of slime and got it all over the armchair. I turned the cushion over, and we threw away the evidence.

"Yeah, but Hannah?"

He pauses, giving me the kind of look that makes people donate fortunes to sad dog-rescue charities. "Would you be my nanny? I know you're not really a nanny, but you're my only friend. Uncle Rob's nice, but he's Travis's friend, not mine. Sophie, too. I want someone who's mine."

Well, stick a javelin in my heart and call me a kebab.

"Your dad hasn't asked me about that," I say, feeling a bit like a jerk for saying it, even though it's technically true. Travis is obviously struggling to make inroads with Ollie, and it won't help if Ollie sees him as the only obstacle to his goal.

"He's going to ask," Ollie replies. "I think he's desperate. He doesn't know what to do with me." He's quiet for a second. "Travis thinks I miss my mom, and I guess I kind of do, but the person I really miss is my nanny. Nanny Rose is the only one who cared about me. My mom doesn't even like it when I call her Mom."

"Do you think your old nanny would move to Asheville?" I ask, temporarily excited by the idea.

He shakes his head. "She writes me letters, and she says she'll come visit sometime, but she just had her first great-grand-child. Can you imagine? She's in her seventies. Maybe eighty. I think her traveling days may be done."

Inspiration strikes, and I feel like a genius. Sophie's next-door neighbor is this gorgeous woman in her eighties who runs a tea shop, and she's in a club with three other delightful elderly women. They'll fawn all over Ollie and make him feel loved, no question. "I have some friends you'd love. We're gonna get with them, pinky promise."

I extend my pinky, and he hooks it with his, shaking.

"But what about *you* being my nanny?" he asks, so hopeful it hurts.

I hadn't intended to tie myself down. This time was supposed to be about figuring out what I'd like to do with my life, about detaching my tether from my brother and having fun

—accepting weird jobs and unexpected opportunities. But the way he's looking at me...

"I'm not saying no, and I'm not saying yes," I tell him. "We both know I'm not a real nanny like Nanny Rose. I'll bet she had one of those magic bags that always held the right amount of snacks and sunscreen and water, and she probably made color-coded schedules and did laundry and stuff, right?"

He nods.

"I'm not like that. I enter rooms and forget why I went in, and I'm pretty sure your dad would have a heart attack if he ever saw my apartment. It definitely doesn't look like this place."

"This place is boring," he says, puffing his lips out.

"I totally get why you'd feel that way, but hey, your dad's a drummer. That's pretty cool. Don't you like listening to him play?"

"I wouldn't know," he says bitterly. "I've only heard recordings of his band. It's like I told you. He won't let me go to any of their shows."

It's hard to keep silent. Because, honestly. Travis is trying so hard to connect with Ollie, but he can't see the obvious solution sitting right in front of him.

What better way to connect with his son than through something he loves?

"I'm sure he has his reasons."

He pauses. "I don't want to talk about Travis right now. We were talking about you becoming my nanny."

"To be perfectly honest with you, I'd be an awful nanny."

"I don't care," he replies, and the stubborn set of his jaw reminds me sweetly of Travis.

"Okay, but your dad might." I lift my hands to cut off the protest I know is coming. "And he'd have every right to. I think I ruined that chair, and I've only been here for a couple of hours."

"I'll get the stain out," he says. "It's simple chemistry."

"But you shouldn't have to clean up after your nanny, Ollie. That's not how this is supposed to work."

He gives me a long, serious look. "Parents aren't supposed to leave either. A lot of bad stuff happens. It doesn't really matter whether it's supposed to or not."

There he goes again with those heart javelins.

"No, parents aren't supposed to do that. But we're like the heroes in fairy tales, aren't we? They all had crappy moms or stepmoms. So let's just say we're super-duper, extra special. I'll talk to your dad about all of this, though. I promise."

"Thank you, Hannah." He flings his little arms around my neck and hugs me, and I'm shocked by the burning in my eyes.

It's just...

The man and woman who abandoned this child deserve a special place in hell. I truly hope they have to spend an eternity listening to a dry British narrator read a thousand-page manual about steam cleaning carpets. No, that's not enough. They should have their eyelids peeled back and be forced to—

"Hannah?" Ollie asks.

"Yes?"

"You can go now. I'm feeling pretty sleepy."

I tuck him into his bed, then hand over the big stuffed sloth next to it. Something super suspicious happens to my heart when he wraps his little arms around the sloth and snuggles into the blankets, his tiny body barely a blip under the covers.

"Sleep well, little man," I whisper.

I head into the living room, feeling restless, driven by the same curiosity that's steered me into half of the bad decisions I've made. Except this curiosity runs a little deeper, with a metaphorical current I feel pulling at my toes. It's because Travis is so closed-off, I decide. A mystery of a man.

I check out his music room.

I look inside his refrigerator, taking in the shocking and kind of sexy orderliness.

I tiptoe into his bedroom, feeling less guilty than I should, and look around. There's nothing much in here other than a big, king-sized bed with a black satin comforter.

It's easy to imagine Travis pulling off his shirt and falling into that bed, the covers draping over him.

There are a few framed album covers on the wall, a couple of floofy throw pillows that suggest he had a girlfriend at some point, but there's a conspicuous lack of family photos.

I run my fingers over the books on his nightstand, feeling a tug on my heart when I see a well-thumbed copy of *The Single Dad's Handbook*. I pick it up and flip through it, smiling when I see that he's written notes in the margins.

"Hannah?" a little voice says.

I glance back and find Ollie standing in the doorway, his hair sleep mussed.

"What are you doing?" he asks, yawning. He says it with such perfect innocence, I feel a lurch in my heart. A need to protect him.

I lift up the book, showing it to him. "Learning how to be a single dad." I don't want to lie to him, and it's a better explanation than saying I was nosy about his mystery-wrapped-in-an-enigma father, who plays the drums with complete abandon but is so set in his ways.

"Can you teach Travis?" he asks, rubbing his eyes sleepily.

I laugh and set the book down, then join him in the doorway, resting my hand on his little head. "If he can teach me how to be a nanny, we'll call it an even trade."

CHAPTER FIVE

TRAVIS

Text conversation with Hannah

> If he won't sleep, he can have some chamomile tea.

> Oh, he's fine. I let him smoke a joint, and he was out like a light.

> I know you're joking. But can you just confirm for my anxiety that you're joking?

> Oh, Travis. You're the wind beneath my wings.

Two minutes later...

> Fine. Confirming: it was indeed a joke. He got out of bed, so I made him some hot chocolate, and he read that boring science book until he conked out for real.

"That was banging," says Bixby, the bassist in our band, as we pack up our equipment.

I roll my eyes. "You sound like one of our kids at The Missing Beat."

"He *is* a child," Rob teases, ruffling Bixby's hair, then making a face as he pulls his hand away because we're all covered in sweat. Bixby's the youngest of us, at twenty-nine.

"Yes, the couple of years of experience you have on me made all the difference," Bixby says. "But come on, it *was* banging. One of our best sets in a while." He waggles his brows at Rob. "You know it, front man. You don't get panties thrown at you on just any old night."

Rob snorts. "Maybe she was throwing them at you, but she had bad aim."

He's making jokes, but I can tell from the zen look on his face that he feels it too. Bixby's right. We were perfectly in sync tonight—*all for one and one for all*, the way Rob and I tell the kids at The Missing Beat to play when they're having trouble meshing. It's been a while since we've sounded so good.

Small wonder, since I've been more present tonight than I've been over the last several weeks. Even though I'm desperately worried about what Ollie and Hannah might be getting up to, I know he must at least be happy.

It makes a difference, surprisingly.

"It was a good set," I agree, "but something feels a bit off about this place tonight, doesn't it?"

"Ah, here we go," Bix says, already laughing. "Travis and his endless vibe checks."

"Yeah, but he's usually right," Rob says, nodding to me before glancing around, his eyes unsurprisingly settling on Sophie, who's standing with Briar.

Bixby huffs a laugh. "Yup, he's really good at reading a room. That's why he keeps getting back together with Karen, when everyone who's met them knows the violin music started playing on their personal *Titanic* years ago."

"Oh, come on," I say. "That's over for good this time."

He shakes his head. "Is that why she comes to all of our shows? Hell, she was here up until fifteen minutes ago. That woman's like a dandelion. Give her a bit of sun and water, and she keeps popping up."

"Don't jinx us," Rob says, rubbing the penny he wears around his neck—something to do with an in-joke he has with Sophie.

Rolling my eyes, I say, "She just likes the music. I haven't even talked to her for weeks. Maybe months."

I scan the area, trying to put my finger on what I'm sensing....

Big Catch Brewing is one of the best-looking breweries in town, slick and shiny and devoted to its fishing theme down to the nautical décor. You won't find a lot of people willing to say so, though, because the owner sold out to Bev Corp, one of the big beverage conglomerates, which pissed off locals.

We've played here a few times before, including back when Hannah was the second-shift floor manager. It's funny to think about that now. I'd seen her, noticed her, but we'd never had a casual conversation. She'd existed on the periphery of my life, not unlike the black-haired woman staring slack-jawed at her cell phone in the background of one of my beach photos—a forever mystery.

Then Rob got with Sophie, and suddenly the loud, outspoken floor manager at Big Catch became loud, outspoken Hannah.

Wait...

That's what's different. Hannah's not here, and the whole vibe of the place has shifted. Before, Big Catch had the friendliest staff of any of the breweries in town. Now, most of the staff seem exhausted and annoyed.

"It's the staff," I muse. "They're..."

"Are you done up here yet?" asks a sullen-faced man with a knit beanie pulled all the way down to his eyebrows. He's wearing the Big Catch uniform but not the old Big Catch smile.

"Uh, almost, man," I say, nodding to my kit, which I've already packed up.

He glances at his watch pointedly, then sighs. "I'll have Liam come out and help you move your stuff."

I'm not sure what the big hurry is, given that we were the last act tonight and they don't close for another hour, but I'm too caught on his last sentence to say so.

"You mean Hannah's brother?"

He was already walking away, but he pauses. "You know Hannah?"

I gesture to Sophie and Briar, who've just walked up to the stage to join us. "Yeah...so do they. Hannah's babysitting for my son tonight."

His glower deepens. "We all thought she'd be here until she texted Liam earlier."

"Yeah, he's *definitely* not passing the famous Travis Thomas vibe check," Bixby says, sounding amused.

The guy looks at Bixby, shakes his head ruefully, and says, "Sorry, it's been a long month. It's just...anyway, I'll get Liam." And he takes off as if herding dogs are nipping at his heels.

"They all miss her," Sophie says, watching him as he disappears into the back. "Of course they do. I'll bet they replaced her with someone truly repellent."

"And I missed *you*," Rob says as he pulls her close.

Briar crosses her arms, looking a little uncomfortable.

"I'll hug you if you want," Bixby tells her with a grin. He has at least half a thing for her. She isn't the slightest bit interested in him, but I'm not worried about his feelings. He has half a thing for every woman he comes across.

"No, thank you," she says. "But if you'd like me to help move your stuff, I can carry up to a hundred pounds."

He whistles and hands her a case that weighs twenty, max.

"Let's get 'em out to Travis's truck, Rapunzel," he says, tugging gently on a lock of her long blonde hair.

"I want to help too," Sophie says, pulling away from Rob.

He gives her his guitar with a grin, which, for him, is like entrusting another person with his child.

Ollie.

I'm about to tug out my phone to text Hannah again, when her brother comes lumbering over with Beanie Guy. I'm six-one, but Liam's got at least four inches on me, and he's broad, with reddish-brown hair and a short beard. There's a bruise on his cheekbone, and I'd hate to find myself on the wrong side of the man big enough to have given it to him.

I consider what Hannah said earlier, and I have to admit she has a point. It would make more of a statement for Ollie to walk into school with this guy than with me. But I'm grateful she reversed course and gave me the chance to make a stand for my son.

"You need help getting your stuff out?" Liam asks.

Not really, but I nod. I need to give him the bag she gave me earlier, for one thing, and I'm also curious about Hannah. Maybe he'll give me some insight. "Sure, thanks, man."

My kit is already packed into cases, and we both grab a load and start maneuvering through the crowded room, crossing paths with Rob as he heads back in from packing up his load. My buddy reaches out for a fist bump, and I oblige.

Moments later, Liam and I are out in the cool night air. I didn't put on my coat before stepping out, but I don't miss it. The mountain breeze feels good after the performance.

"Hannah mentioned she's watching your son?" he asks, glancing at me.

"Yeah." I smile. "She's really good with him."

As soon as I say the words, I feel a strange yearning bloom in my chest. *I* want to be good with Ollie. To be easy with him. But from the beginning, nothing between us has been easy. Maybe it never can be, given the way we began—a thought that's depressing as hell.

"She has a way about her," he says enigmatically as I pause next to my truck and unlock it.

"She certainly does."

We stow the cases inside, working companionably enough, but there's a reserve about him that seems at odds with Hannah's uninhibitedness.

Before he can turn back toward the brewery, I say, "So what's going on here? Why does everyone look so pissed off?"

He shrugs. "Like I said, Hannah has a way about her. The new second-shift floor manager has a different way." His mouth twists into a sardonic smile. "We're supposed to have the stage cleared within five minutes of an act ending."

"Five minutes? Does Hannah know about this?"

Another shrug, this one weary. "She doesn't want to talk about it."

"Seriously? I'm surprised she didn't ask you for this guy's social security number and cell phone history."

His laughter has an edge of bitterness. "Usually she would. She's not too happy with me right now."

I nod in sympathy. "Actually, she asked me to give you something."

I unlock the cab and pull out the bag with the goat on it, handing it to him.

He opens it and laughs. "That's Hannah for you."

"Oh?"

"A goat headbutted me when I was six. I've hated them ever since. Her little way of reminding me."

I have to laugh.

That *is* Hannah for you. I haven't known her long, but there's no denying she has a unique sense of humor and justice. It's the kind of gift that tells him she still thinks he's a shithead, but she's thinking of him all the same.

We head inside together, but I only make it a few steps, because Rob's waiting for me by the door.

"There's a guy sitting in the back booth who wants to talk to us," he says, acting a bit jittery, the way he gets after too many cups of coffee. "Travis, he's a producer who caught our set. Frank Jacobs. He came all the way from Nashville to listen to us."

It feels like he just poured a bucket of ice down my back.

Producer. Nashville. Us.

This was what Rob wanted, years ago. Before we met, he'd had an up-close-and-personal brush with fame. The band he'd formed with his high school buddy, Bad Magic, went platinum… after Rob had been forced to drop out because his asshole little brother broke his hand right before the band went on tour.

He'd seen his friends and former bandmates achieve all of his wildest dreams, knowing he would have been with them if just one thing had gone differently for him. So I understand why he's still hungry for it.

My throat constricts, and it's suddenly hard to breathe. But I take a slow, deep breath, let it out.

"That's awesome, man," I say, almost sounding like I mean it. "Just let me finish up. We're supposed to have the stage cleared five minutes after we play, apparently. New rule. I'm not going to risk them throwing the rest of my kit away."

"Who made up that dumbass rule?" Rob scoffs.

"I did," says a gruff voice.

I shift to look at the speaker—and find a wizened man in a Big Catch T-shirt and corduroy pants. He has a full head of hair the color of tarnished silver, a bushy mustache the same color, and rheumy light-blue eyes behind enormous double-bridge wire glasses.

"*You're* the new Hannah?" I ask in disbelief.

No offense to this guy, but going from him to Hannah is like swapping crisp french fries for a shriveled, uncooked potato. I have no idea what the hiring managers were thinking. He's got to be in his late sixties, past the normal age of retirement, while the majority of the people who work here are in their early to mid-twenties.

He sniffs. "I'm Eugene. I was brought in to restore order. You have no idea what it was like before I came on board. People fornicating in canoes, outrageous parties, and bands leaving their kits out *overnight*."

"Sounds fun," Bixby says as he breezes past us and heads out the door. Liam's with him, and they're both weighed down with cases.

"Hardly," the old guy scoffs, then rubs his chin. "Still...I suppose she had a way of connecting with all of these hooligans." He hesitates, playing with the end of his mustache like a cartoon villain. "Actually...I've been thinking of reaching out to her. Having an official handing over of the torch."

"Yeah, I bet she'd like that," I say, knowing this guy would entertain her. Another thing I know from observing Hannah is that she likes a good story. "You want her number?"

CHAPTER SIX

HANNAH

I feel someone pulling a blanket over me.

"Liam?" I ask, still mostly asleep.

"It's me," a familiar voice says, and I open my bleary eyes to see Travis leaning over me, his hair brushed back enough to reveal his strawberry birthmark. He probably hates it, but I'm fascinated by it. It's his special beauty—everyone has one, if you ask me.

"Jesus, how late is it?" I ask, sitting up, the blanket pooling around my lap.

"I'm sorry." He sits beside me, not close enough that our thighs are touching, but enough that I feel the whisper of him. "It's two. There was...it was an interesting night. We went somewhere else for a little while after the brewery closed."

His vague explanation suggests I'll be getting information from Sophie and Briar about it, not him. So noted.

I turn to get a better look at him. He's wide awake, his eyes full of worry or maybe excitement.

"An expensive night for you," I point out. "If you intend to bankroll my nap."

He laughs, a low, husky sound that my mind stores away. "A deal's a deal. I already Venmoed you. Did it go okay?"

Ah, worry, then.

He scans the room, searching for disaster, and I make a point of not looking in the direction of the stained chair.

"Like I said over our *many* text messages...it went great. He's a good kid." I pause. "Why don't you ever take him to your shows? Sophie, Briar, and I would be happy to look after him."

He gives me an incredulous look. "They're all at bars or breweries."

"As if other people don't bring their children to breweries."

He shrugs. "But the music's for adults. The lyrics..."

"You're worried he'll realize 'Hot Honey' is about Rob going down on Sophie? I doubt it. He may be too smart for his own good, but he's still seven."

He gives me a wry smile and leans back into the sofa. "I'm not comfortable with it. Some woman threw her panties at Rob tonight."

"Dammit," I say, instantly bristling. "I wasn't there to defend Sophie's territory."

"What if Sophie was the one who threw them?" he asks, his smile widening.

"Come on. We both know she wasn't."

"It's okay," he promises. "Rob threw them back and said there was only one person whose panties interested him."

"Did Sophie go bright red?"

"Yeah, and so did Briar."

I pucker my lips, wishing I'd been there to see it. At the same time, I don't regret having been here instead. Besides, I have mixed feelings about returning to Big Catch. I worked there for years, and going back as a visitor would feel bizarre, like seeing a dude you dated for months out on a first date with someone else.

Granted, I know my ex, Jonah the Super Tool, went out with Sophie, Briar, me, and the elusive Nora Leigh aka Ginger-BeerBabe at the same time, but I didn't see it go down. I also never cared about Jonah the way I care about Big Catch. I'd felt no sense of ownership toward him. He'd claimed to be single. I was always more or less single, and I'd figured we might as well have some fun. I know it was different for Briar, who genuinely cared about him, and of course for Sophie, who was engaged to him.

But I *do* care about Big Catch. It was never mine, but for a long time it had felt like mine. Even the way it smelled, like malt and hops, had reminded me of my childhood home. Because Liam and my dad had brewed beer together for years, starting when Liam was at least ten years too young to drink.

All of the over-the-top nautical touches are super dumb, given we live in the mountains, but also really dear to me—like Christmas displays in July.

I loved leading the second shift team. Figuring out which of the employees loved each other, which of them hated each other, and which of them wanted to bone. Helping them. Holding their hands as they figured out what they wanted to do for a living. What their passions were.

So, no, I don't really want to watch anyone trying on my old job for size, whether they like the fit or not. I have a feeling it would piss me off and make me want to defend my territory, even though I left willingly.

Travis studies me, then says, "You're dying to ask what it was like there, aren't you?"

"No," I say tightly. "If I'd cared, I would have gone. I had *way* more fun here."

He gives me a knowing look. "Okay, but I'm going to tell you what you supposedly don't want to know. The new evening floor manager sucks, and everyone misses you."

I search his face for lies and see none, but I can tell he's holding something back. "I had my doubts, but you *do* know how to improve a woman's day," I say. "Still, I think Ollie would like to feel included. You should bring him to one of the daytime shows."

He leans a little closer, maybe only half an inch, but I feel the distance between us shrinking. "My parents brought me to things I shouldn't have gone to when I was a kid, and I don't want to subject Ollie to that. Kids should be allowed to be kids."

I'm reminded of what Ollie said about Travis's mysterious parentage, and my natural curiosity kicks in. "Like what kinds of things?"

His lips quirk up at the corners. "You're imagining live sex shows or coke dens, aren't you?"

"Just trying to get a mental picture."

"Fashion shows. Concerts. Red carpet events."

"Sounds *terrible*," I say, pressing a hand to my chest in mock outrage. "You poor dear."

"It *was* terrible. My mother treated me like a purse dog. My suits always matched her outfits. The kids at school eviscerated me."

"Ouch. Okay, maybe I can share in your outrage over that. But Ollie wants to feel like he's part of something. What about your after-school program? I bet those kids would go crazy for Ollie."

He messes with his hair, covering the birthmark again. "I'd worry about not being able to keep an eye on him. Thinking about it makes me anxious. Maybe once I have a steady nanny."

I tell him quickly about Nanny Rose and my idea about introducing Ollie to the little old ladies from the tea shop.

By the time I finish, he's shaking his head.

"No?" I ask incredulously. "This is a slam dunk, Travis. You just don't want to admit I'm brilliant."

"That's not it. You're right. It's just…I should have thought about that. I didn't even ask follow-up questions about his old nanny. I'm so bad at this."

There's something earnest and sad in his eyes, and I think about that marked-up book sitting on his bedside table. A surge of affection has me reaching for his hand and squeezing it.

"You care about him. You're *trying*. That means more than you think."

"Oh shit," he says, giving me a slow smile that's frankly a bit devastating, "you're being nice to me. I must seem more pathetic than I thought."

I pat his hand, and he turns it around to clasp mine for a brief squeeze. The gentleness of his touch shocks me. This is a man who can slam those drums. I know. I've watched. I've noticed every flexing muscle.

I clear my throat and pull away. "You do. Very pathetic. How dare you make me be nice."

His eyes, dark and bottomless, are still holding mine, and I'm newly aware of how close he is, of his body inches from mine. He's dressed in the clothes he wears for concerts—a black T-shirt and jeans, distinct from the preppier look he goes for otherwise—and I'll bet he's still salty with sweat from playing…

I clear my throat. "Speaking about nannies…there's no sugarcoating this, so I'm going to come out and say it. Ollie wants me to be his nanny."

He gives me a look he'd probably describe as droll. "Do you honestly think I haven't heard about this every day since you were here last month?"

I snort-laugh. "He's good for a girl's ego, too."

"Not so great for mine. But he gave me a high five earlier, so maybe all hope's not lost." He pauses, studying me, his gaze digging deep again. "Do you *want* to be a nanny, Hannah?"

"Honestly, no."

"Would you prefer to return to Big Catch? I get the sense they'd carry off a full-on rebellion to get you back."

I smile, imagining my former colleagues holding pitchforks. "No, not right now, anyway." I hesitate. "I care about Ollie. Would you let me take him places? I'm not much for sticking around in someone's musty old living room for hours on end—"

"You know it's not musty."

I lift my eyebrows. "But it *is* boring. Honestly, would it kill you to get a PlayStation?"

"You're only supposed to let kids use screens for an hour or less a day."

"Oh, please, I must have watched thousands of movies when I was his age."

He casts a wry glance at me that's totally asking for the shove I give him.

He laughs, then gives the room a thorough once-over as if taking it in with new eyes. "Look, I know. His room is a blank slate too. But he won't go shopping with me. He insists he isn't going to be here long enough for it to matter."

"But he will be, won't he?" I ask, all humor slipping away.

He nods slowly, watching me. Probably waiting for me to ask the dozens of questions dancing in my head. After a moment, he says, "I think so. I hope so. But I can't tell him that yet."

I nod. "I get it. But kids shouldn't sit around twiddling their thumbs. You ask me, that's why he's getting into mischief. He's smart, and he's probably super bored. Which is why I like the idea of taking him places. Look how we circled back around to that."

He sighs and rubs his temples. "I like knowing where he is."

"So put that find-my-friends thing on his phone."

"Hannah," he says. "He's seven years old. He doesn't have a phone."

"You can put it on mine, if you want to keep tabs on *me*." I didn't mean it to come out like that, a little sultry, or...you know what? Maybe I did. There's something about Travis that makes me want to tap-dance all over his buttons. Maybe because I want to see what it takes to unleash that other side of him, the one that takes over when he's sitting at the drums. I know I can't go there—not only is he my potential boss, but also his best friend is dating my best friend—but that just makes me want to more.

He laughs. "Maybe. But no strip clubs until he's eighteen."

"Damn it." I snap my fingers. "There go my plans for Monday afternoon. I'll have to think of something else that's educational."

"We could maybe put together a list of approved places. If we do this."

"Like with the little old ladies?"

"Like with the little old ladies," he agrees. "I'd have to install a car seat in your car."

"I could do it."

"I'd want to do it," he insists, which makes me bristle. He might as well have said he wouldn't trust me to water a cactus without supervision, let alone his son.

I consider this for a moment. "Fine. I don't like following instructions anyway."

He gives me a wry look that prompts me to roll my eyes.

"I'd nanny for you for a little while, if you want, especially if you're going to keep overpaying me. It's not like I have any super important career plans to run back to."

He size me up for a long moment and then frowns. "Why'd you really quit Big Catch?"

"I was sick of working with my brother," I say, leaving it at that. It's true, at least. "I love him like crazy, but it was too much."

He nods. "I get it. I'd never work with my sister. But you might want to check on your old staff. They seemed seconds away from mutiny. The new floor manager accused you of encouraging public fornication in one breath, and in the next, he said he wants to give you a call for the official passing of the torch. So you can look forward to that."

"What's his name?"

"Eugene," he says with a smile, as if he somehow knows this will delight me.

"An elderly man named Eugene replaced me?" I ask.

"How do you know he's elderly?"

"Can you be named Eugene without being elderly?"

He inclines his head as if to concede the point, then adds, "He wears corduroy pants."

"You *do* want to make my day," I say, grinning back at him. "Where did they even find him?"

"I'm sure you can use your delightful charm to get the whole story out of him," he says, his arm pressing against mine with the slightest pressure.

"Oh, you just bet I will. That old geezer won't know what hit him."

He shakes his head as he laughs, revealing his birthmark for a half second before his hair slides back into place, hiding it from me again. I want to find it with my finger, trace it, but I'm grateful to report that I have some self-control left.

"Your brother seemed pretty nice, though. He helped us move our equipment."

My scowl deepens. "Of course he did."

"I know, that bastard, right?"

I shove his arm again, feeling the delicious muscle he's honed by banging rhythmically against those drums.

I whistle and slide my hand up and down his bicep. I do it to tease him, I think. Or maybe to tease myself. I had a few one-night stands after the whole Jonah mess, but I haven't slept with anyone for months—a near record for me. Haven't really wanted to. "Will you look at that? All that banging pays off."

He gives me another headshake, but the corners of his mouth lift. "You're pretty good at evading questions."

"So is Ollie, and I'm guessing he gets it from you. The three of us could spend a cozy evening evading questions."

"That sounds kind of nice actually," he says. "Would you like a drink?"

"Hoping it'll loosen my tongue?"

"Maybe," he replies with a smile.

"It probably would, so no. I'm not staying here tonight."

"I wouldn't mind if you did," he says, his dark eyes on me. I feel a quake of awareness. Is he asking what I think he's asking? Or is he just offering me his couch?

Either way, I know what the answer needs to be.

"*I'd* mind," I say.

He gives me a solemn nod, his gaze still hot on my flesh.

"So, what's the deal?" I ask. "Am I working for you? Are we doing this thing?" I feel almost excited. Bopping around from one odd job to the next has been fun, but I suddenly realize I've been missing a sense of purpose. The satisfying feeling of helping someone. Human connection.

Travis's gaze catches on something on the floor, and he gets up, his leg brushing mine. He stoops, gifting me a view of his very toned butt, and rises with one of the paper airplanes in hand.

Lifting his eyebrows, he unfolds it, then immediately rolls his eyes when he realizes what it is.

"I just aced this interview, didn't I?" I ask, kind of enjoying myself. But also a little on edge. I need him to say yes. It was the way Ollie looked at me earlier, like his happiness was on the line...I don't want to disappoint him.

I've definitely already disappointed Travis.

He rubs circles between his eyebrows. "I don't know, Hannah. I set up a couple of interviews for tomorrow. They're with people who have a lot of childcare experience."

"And I'm guessing they wouldn't make paper airplanes out of your instructions?"

He has the grace to smile. "Yeah, something like that."

I get up and make finger guns at him. "You didn't say no, drummer boy."

One corner of his mouth twitches upward. "That's because you're a hard woman to say no to."

CHAPTER SEVEN

TRAVIS

Text conversation with Daphne, applicant #2

> I withdraw my candidacy.

> Shame on you.

Text conversation with Rose, applicant #3

> I won't be available to watch your son.

> This is a small community, you jerk. You burn one of us, you burn us all.

"Fuuuuuuck," I say with feeling, setting my phone down hard on the coffee table.

At least Ollie's in his room. Still, I should probably still stick a buck in the swear jar I bought for myself.

I haven't told anyone about said swear jar. I know Bixby, for one, would have a field day.

Both of my candidates cancelled their interviews, and I just discovered why. Rachel has smeared me on every single nanny board I can find on social media—

WARNING: Travis Thomas is a disgusting, sexist jerk who commented on my outfit and tried to make unwanted advances on me. IN FRONT OF HIS SON. And his little boy is an absolute nightmare, too. A chip off the ole sexist block. He THREW something at me.
DO NOT INTERVIEW.

Bullshit, obviously, but at least she didn't mention my father. I want to reply and defend myself, but if I do, it'll only get messier.

The comments are already thirsty for my blood.

I tap my fingers against the side of the table, my anxiety spinning up. Before long, people will be saying they should cancel my band. Maybe even my after-school program.

Fuck...I *need* to play the drums.

Hannah would say I have to "bang it out," and she'd be right. The need is thrumming through me like a low-level electrical current. I've felt it constantly, for weeks now, but more so this morning.

I also need to do some major damage control.

I text Rob and Bixby, sending the link for the post, and ask them to meet up. They probably won't get back to me for a while. I figure Bixby, at least, was up late celebrating.

Last night, we had a casual meeting with Frank, the producer who came to hear us play. He was impressed with what he saw, and he's coming to our Saturday afternoon show at New Belgium Brewery in a couple of weeks. But he gave us a to-do list to finish in the meantime. Number one is finding a rhythm guitarist. We were told to get on that stat, preferably before the New Belgium show, which is ridiculous. A little less than two weeks won't be enough time for us to find someone, given we've already been looking sporadically for months.

Rob seems to be all for working with this guy, and Bixby's definitely a fame whore. He's already been blowing up our group chat, blathering on about famous bass players, saying he's going to be the next Roger Waters or Flea.

Me? I want to play my music. I want to run my after-school program with Rob. I want to figure out how to be a parent. My life might not be big, the way my parents always wanted their lives to be, but it's mine, and I won't let anyone take it from me.

At the same time, I don't want to ruin things for my buddies. Rob's like a brother to me, and I know how much he struggled after losing his place in Bad Magic. It took him years to find himself again. And Bixby...he burns for this. He didn't grow up with wealthy parents like Rob and I did—he was raised poor in rural North Carolina. Money means something to him.

So, yeah, I can't just say no thanks.

Maybe I don't want to, either.

I had a dream once, too. It fell apart the summer before I moved to Asheville, but it never fully left me. I still hear the call of the music. The songs that want to be heard.

The spiral inside of me needs to be vented, so I head to the music room, pausing on the way to knock on Ollie's door. "I'm gonna play for a minute."

"Okay," he says after a long pause.

I linger there, wanting to say something else. Wondering if I should invite him to listen. But I feel wrong-footed, so after another second, I leave.

I play.

I pound.

I sweat.

I think about Hannah touching my arm.

Hannah, asleep on my couch.

I play louder, faster, and when I feel better, I set down my drumsticks and head to my room and take a quick shower.

Only then do I pick my phone back up. I'm not surprised Rob is the only one who responded. Bixby is probably still asleep.

> Want me to hop into those nanny boards and defend your good name?

> Wouldn't they question why you're in a nanny group?

> We got this. Let's meet at Tea of Fortune. Thirty minutes.

> I don't have a babysitter for Ollie…for obvious reasons.

> What about Hannah?

My mind skips back to last night as if it's one of the grooves in my best-loved records. To Hannah, asleep on my couch, her legs tucked up, her cheek pressed to the cushion, her hair a riot of red curls.

I'd felt something when I saw her like that.

Something I'd probably be better at putting into music than into words.

Maybe what I'd felt was simple relief. Because even though I'm not sure I trust Hannah to make the best decisions, I do believe she cares about Ollie's welfare.

Or maybe I was moved by the innocence of her asleep, all her sarcasm and hard edges blurred away. I like her hard edges, but I liked her like that too—the smooth expanse of her cheeks, her eyelashes brushing the skin, and the sweet sounds she made as she changed her position to be more comfortable.

Truthfully, part of my resistance to the idea of Hannah

taking care of Ollie is that I'm attracted to her—fiercely attracted, the way a man only can be to a woman who has the power to destroy him.

So maybe I should hire her, if only to make her completely off-limits.

I rub my eyes, feeling very tired indeed, and text her.

> Are you free for an hour or so? I have to meet up with Rob for an important discussion.

> This is just like you, Travis, to ice me out for a month and then ask me to jump and expect me to ask how high.

> Six inches.

> Disappointing.

I swear under my breath, then write: *I wasn't talking about my dick. You definitely wouldn't be able to jump that high.*

Okay, not sending that. I delete the message, then write:

> Can you come?

> How much coffee do you have?

> I'll make a pot just for you.

> Now you're speaking my language.

> Does this mean you want to hire me? Should I buy myself a Mary Poppins bag?

> Maybe, if you're still up for it. But there's something you should know.

She doesn't reply, but ten minutes later, there's a knock on the front door.

I open it to Hannah.

She's wearing a loose long-sleeved shirt, paired with gym shorts and a headband that's doing fuck all to tame her hair.

"Don't look at my hair," she practically growls. "It's way too early for this."

"It's ten."

"Exactly. I didn't get to bed until past four last night."

I nod in the direction of the kitchen—and the coffee scent emanating from it.

"Don't mind if I do," she says, striding in that direction.

I follow her, wondering how she spent the two hours after she left my house. Did she head straight over to some guy's house for a booty call?

It's none of my damn business, but I'd still like to know.

Once we're in the kitchen, I fill a mug with coffee for her. She takes it, then dilutes it with cream from the fridge, pouring until it's barely coffee colored. Then she finds my sugar pot and dumps in two spoonfuls.

She snorts without looking up. "I can feel the judgment emanating from you. I'm guessing there's a proper way to make coffee, and this isn't it?"

I laugh, although I'm not sure if it's at her or at myself. "No. I don't care how you drink your coffee. I mean, it's an abomination, but I had every intention of keeping that to myself."

She glances up at me, and I realize her eyelashes are a golden red when she's not wearing makeup. It's hard to look away now that I've noticed. It's like I've been let in on a secret.

"No one actually likes the taste of coffee," she says. "It tastes like dirt soaked in water."

"You have a lot of experience drinking dirt?"

"I swallow lots of things," she says with a smirk.

"Christ," I mutter. "Am I wearing a sign asking nannies to hit on me?"

Her hand finds the swell of her hip. "Who else flirted inappropriately, and why are they doing my job for me?"

I didn't intend to tell her about the Rachel disaster, but the words come flying out. I explain what went down yesterday and then about the cancelled interviews, the nanny boards, and my emergency meeting with Rob.

Within seconds, she's shaking her head. "Nope. We are *not* letting this go."

"It's a shared problem now?" I ask, amused.

"Yes. I'm going to take care of this, and then I'm going to do the kindest thing in my life and accept the job no one else wants now that you've been blackballed."

"But if you solve my problem, other people will be willing to take the job," I point out.

"And you'll have to tell them you've already hired the baddest bitch you know."

I can't help but smile as I take in her fierce expression. "You are, you know."

"Of course I am." She raises her eyebrows and then lifts the abomination coffee for a sip. "So you don't need me to babysit today anymore, I guess."

"Why not?"

She sets the coffee cup down on the counter with enough force for it to splash. "Keep up. The Rachel problem is in the bag. You can't play any part in fixing it. If you try to respond, it'll make things a whole lot worse. Same goes for Rob and Bixby, because they're connected to you, and Sophie, because everyone knows she's with Rob. But this situation *definitely* requires a woman's touch."

"Yes, because you handle everything with such delicacy."

She rolls her eyes. "Who said women are delicate? Honestly, you and your stereotypes, Travis. You should be ashamed of yourself."

I grin at her, enjoying myself. Not even caring that there's a growing circle of coffee around the spot on the counter where she sat her cup. "All right. I'll give you that. I also shouldn't have lost my temper yesterday, but—"

"Oh, you *definitely* should have lost your temper." She lifts her mug up and toasts me with it. "But, like I said, the situation is going to be handled."

Something about the way she says it leaves me with little doubt that she's going to either miraculously fix this situation or screw it up beyond any shadow of redemption. And here's the danger of Hannah: I should be worried enough about the second possibility that I'm not willing to hand my problem over. But I want to see what she does. The way her mind works intrigues me.

"I'm a little afraid of you right now," I tease.

"You should be."

I pause, weighing what I should say, then figure I might as well go for it. "I think this woman knows who my father is. It's not a secret, really, but I don't want everyone around town talking about it. Especially right now. So maybe don't piss her off too much."

"Aren't *you* mysterious..."

I drop my gaze, never eager to talk about my past, but I know Hannah's not going to treat me any differently if she knows. So I admit, "My dad was a famous actor. Back in the day. Like seriously back in the day. By the time I was born, his career was basically over. He did a few made-for-TV movies and some producing but nothing else that hit it big."

"What was his name?" she asks, her eyes flashing with excitement. "You know I have to know now."

"I don't want this getting around, Hannah."

"Not even to Sophie and Briar?"

I sigh. "I don't care. Sophie might already know. It's not really a secret, just not public knowledge."

"Ooooo-hoo no, she doesn't. She would definitely have told me something like this. It's in the girl code."

A smile ghosts across my face. "My father's Evan Thomas. You know, from those *Ships Ahoy* movies."

There were six of them, all about a nautical detective. They were insanely popular, and genuinely terrible. I had to watch them almost weekly, because my father was an aging narcissist who thought his children should grow up quoting him.

After the last *Ships* movie came out—the worst reviewed by far—his career took a nosedive and never recovered. He spent the rest of his life dreaming up how he could bring back the success he'd lost.

Hannah whistles, her gaze skating over my face. "I can see the resemblance now. I can't *believe* you've hidden this from me. This is big."

"I wasn't hiding it. My dad and I were estranged. We barely had anything to do with each other. He never forgave me for not wanting to follow in his footsteps." I smile at her, because I know she'll like this part. "He had this idea for a TV series called *Ships Ahoy Junior*. Had a script written and everything. He made me read for some producers."

"You could have been a star?" she asks, her eyes bright with humor.

"Some would argue that I am."

Her full lips lift on one side, the motion making her freckles shift slightly. "Oh, Travis, no one would argue that."

"You wound me. But, yeah, I had no interest in being *Ships Junior*. My father found a producer who was interested in making it, but when it came down to it, I had to tell him no. I didn't like everyone staring at me."

She nods. "So naturally you became a musician."

I smile at her, which is shocking, because these memories aren't exactly warm and fuzzy. "It felt different. They were watching me be someone else. When I play with the band... that's me being me."

"I get that. So they wouldn't do the show with anyone else? You were just that good?"

I laugh. "Let's go with that. I think they were banking on the nostalgia factor. The screen tests were released before my dad died—by him, of course—and they got a lot of attention. There was even this dumb petition with twenty thousand signatures to bring the show back. I don't think his fans realized I'd already grown up."

"Why didn't I hear about this?" she asks, lifting her coffee for a sip without taking her eyes off me.

"Because you're not a superfan, thank God."

As if she can tell this conversation isn't putting me in my happy place, she says, "I'm guessing you hate it when people say, 'Maritime law is mine,' to you."

"Loathe it," I say with a half-smile. "His catchphrase didn't make sense then, and it doesn't make sense now. But for some reason, I don't think that's going to stop you."

Her pauses for a moment, her gaze lingering on my face. "Does Lilah know about all of this?"

"We can talk about that later," I say, glancing at the doorway. No sign of Ollie, but he's got super hearing that hasn't been dulled by years of band practice. "But no, she doesn't."

Understanding flashes in Hannah's eyes, followed by a spark of anger. "And Ollie?"

"I haven't told him yet, but I will."

She nods. "Okay."

"If you're good with hanging around, I should still meet with Rob at the tea shop. We have some band business to discuss."

She nods a few more times. "Do you have to-go cups?"

"Excuse me?"

"To-go cups. I know Dottie makes all kinds of tea, and tea is all well and good, but I've yet to try a tea that makes me feel like I'm buzzing."

"I thought you were going to stay with Ollie."

"I am. It turns out I'm bringing him to the tea shop. You *did* say it could be on our agreed locations list."

I shift on my feet. "I don't want him overhearing us."

"He's not going to. Dottie's going to love him. She'll probably introduce him to every single person there as one of her hundreds of adopted grandchildren and great-grandchildren."

I should probably protest some more, but I suspect it would be like arguing with a brick wall.

Of course, that's when Ollie opens his bedroom door and calls out, "Hannah, is that you? Did you come back already?"

"It's me, little man!" she calls back, her green eyes full of challenge as she gives me some side-eye. "And we're going on a field trip."

CHAPTER EIGHT

HANNAH

"Have another," Dottie says, smiling at Ollie, who's already eaten three cookies. "A young man needs plenty of fuel."

Maybe Travis will be pissed off by the astronomical amount of sugar that's currently being pumped into Ollie's bloodstream —he's drinking sweet tea on top of all those cookies—but I figure that'll be a problem for later. A problem for *him*. It may be a mark of evil, but the thought of Ollie zooming around the house while Travis scratches his head in confusion amuses me.

But that's not why I'm being an accessory to excessive sugaring.

Ollie could use some pampering, and there's no better pamperer than Dottie Hendrickson, who in addition to being the owner of Tea of Fortune is also Sophie's former next-door neighbor.

She's eighty or so, with dyed purple hair and a seriously enviable collection of dresses. The woman still works at her dream job—a tea shop that offers tea-leaf readings. The woman's a true boss, and a perfect Nanny Rose stand-in for Ollie.

But it would be pretty messed up of me to hang out with Sophie's former neighbor without inviting her to join us, especially since I knew Sophie's boyfriend would be here, so of course I asked her to come too. She's sitting across from me, beaming at Ollie as if eating cookies were an Olympic sport and he's about to bring home the gold.

I didn't want Briar to feel left out, so I asked if she could duck out of work to come, too. She hates playing hooky—she's a bit like Travis when it comes to rule following, but she's here anyway, sitting next to Sophie and watching the door as if her father—who's also her boss—might storm in any second and say, *Where have you been, young lady?*

Travis is sitting at the farthest table from the door with Rob and Bixby, the bassist for Garbage Fire, who showed up several minutes after the other two. Of course, Travis being Travis, he took the seat facing us so he could keep an eye on me and Ollie.

The lack of trust would be devastating if I didn't have the strong impression he wants to keep his eye on everyone, all the time, and not just me.

Also, if it weren't deserved.

"Can anyone at this table read lips?" I ask casually.

"Oh, it's too bad my friend Ann isn't here," Dottie says, glancing around as if Ann might pop out from behind a corner. "She's nearly deaf without her hearing aids, poor dear, but she does have a talent for reading lips. You know, I was practicing it with her the other day, so I *could* give it a try."

"I want to do it!" Ollie says, practically bouncing in his seat.

"I don't think we should spy on them," Sophie says hesitantly. "They're just talking about finding a new rhythm guitarist for the band."

Sophie's already filled me in on what happened at the brewery last night. Apparently, there's some producer who's interested in them, but he insisted they need to have a fourth band member because threesomes aren't as bankable.

Yeah, that's not quite how she said it, but it's how she should have said it.

It's a promising development, so I wonder why Travis seemed a bit down when he came home last night. Maybe Big Catch's new evening floor manager is bad enough that he brings everyone down, a thought that probably shouldn't delight me as much as it does.

"If it's not a private conversation, then there's no harm in practicing our skills," Dottie says, surprisingly into the idea. "Let me switch places with you, Hannah."

We get up and shuffle around, and I notice Travis angling his head, watching us. His expression says, very clearly, *What the hell are you up to?*

I give him a jaunty wave.

"Now, the trick is to watch the shape of their lips, Ollie," Dottie tells him. "Can you see the shape your dad's lips are making right now?"

I twist in my seat to watch Travis's lips move.

Huh, he has nice lips. Nice lips that are forming what looks like...

"Did he just say my name?" I hiss, turning toward Dottie.

She gives me an encouraging smile. "Oh, I should think so, dear. More than once. How exciting!"

"I certainly hope he said something like, 'Thank God for Hannah,'" I mutter. "'My ship would really be sunk if not for Hannah.' 'Hannah is a goddess among women.'"

"I don't think that's what he said at all," Ollie says, going for gold and grabbing another cookie. "It looked like he said trouble or maybe bubble."

"Hm." Dottie peers intently at their table at the back of the shop. "Rob just said your name too."

I sigh dramatically. "Fantastic."

"This is what you get for spying on people," Briar says

stoically. "Two weeks ago, I eavesdropped at my dad's office door, because I was hoping he might say something about when he's moving on from Silver Star, but I overheard him telling my mom that I have no backbone, and the only way I'm going to learn how to swim is if he throws me in the deep end. It was a mixed metaphor, which somehow only made it worse."

Briar's father is an obscenely wealthy man who enjoys opening businesses every five to six years, only to sell or shutter them and start the next "big" thing. He started Silver Star Brewery five years ago, and according to her, he got bored with it a year or so ago, around the same time her handmade jewelry business folded. So he suggested handing over the brewery to her. But as with most things in life, there are conditions.

She sighs. "So he said he was going to put me through—" She darts a glance at Ollie and lowers her voice, "—h-e-double-hockey-sticks—"

"I can spell, Briar," Ollie says.

She mouths *sorry* at me, then tries again, "Through...you-know-what...to toughen me up. He called it Briar Boot Camp. He thinks it's the only way I'll become strong enough to run a successful business."

"God, Briar, that's horrible," Sophie says.

"And very untrue," I add.

"But it *is* true," she says, playing with a lock of her hair. "My jewelry business failed because my business partner was embezzling. Like, not even being terribly subtle about it. I thought something was weird, but the accounting wasn't one of my responsibilities. So I let it slide, and the next thing I know, she's in Jamaica drinking mai tais on the beach, and all the accounts were drained." She twists her mouth to the side. "She told me she was really sorry, but she had to put her needs before mine."

"Holy shit," I say, then glance at Ollie. "Sorry, Ollie."

He shrugs. "Shit and poop mean the same thing. It's kind of a dumb swear."

"I still shouldn't have said it in front of you."

Sophie reaches for Briar's hand. "Briar, that's awful. I'm so sorry that happened to you."

"It's mostly embarrassing."

"More embarrassing than dating Jonah?" I ask.

Briar heaves another sigh. "The fact that I dated an engaged man without realizing it *after* my business partner stole all of our money right under my nose makes me think I really am naïve. I've been doing all of this yoga and meditation to try to clear my mind, but my inner voice is too loud."

Dottie clucks her tongue. "We just need to try different types of meditation. There's one that works for everyone."

"Not me," I say with a snort.

"Or me," Ollie says, but I have a feeling he has no idea what meditation is and is just being loyal. I reach over the table and ruffle his hair.

"Thanks," Briar says with a tight smile. "I'm sure you're right. Anyway, that's why my dad's so hard on me. He thinks he can trick me into being tough. It comes from a good-ish place."

"You're already plenty tough," I say. "He should have seen you TP Jonah's house."

"You threw toilet paper all over someone's house?" Ollie asks, his eyes shining. "I saw that happen in a movie."

"It was Uncle Rob's brother," I say, "and trust me when I say he deserved it. But you're not supposed to TP houses or listen in at doors."

There, that's a good lesson. Take that, Travis. I can totally be a good influence.

"I know all about listening at doors," Ollie says, returning his gaze to the back of the tea shop. "That's how I found out Travis was my father. My dad—Roland, I mean—he said he didn't ever want to see me again, because I wasn't really his son and he'd already wasted enough money on me."

I grit my teeth, knowing better than to tell him exactly what I think of his mom and his not-a-dad.

"Have another cookie, dear," Dottie says, cupping her hand over his. "You have as many as you like. They were baked with love, and you can never have too much love."

He smiles at her, and I feel another strange sensation in the heart region of my chest.

"Hey, Ollie," Sophie says, with a slight smile. "Hannah told us you're going to be spending time together in the afternoons, and I was thinking we could try out some crafts together. You can be the test audience for my crafting business."

"Only if they're not lame," he says with typical honesty.

She gives him a serious nod. "You'd help make sure that doesn't happen. It's an important job. Friends don't let friends be lame."

He seems impressed by this, and I smile at Sophie, who obviously is way better with kids than I'll ever be.

"We'll take you up on that," I say.

"Yeah," Ollie says. "Thank goodness Hannah is finally my nanny now." His face creases into a frown. "I think Travis just said your name again, Hannah. He's frowning."

"Dammit," I say, then catch myself. "Sorry. I meant..."

"That's okay," he says. "I know all about swearing. Roland produced a lot of rap music, and sometimes rappers would come over and freestyle."

"That's really cool."

"Yeah," he says with a slight smile. "It *was* cool. They didn't invite me, or anything, but it was a big house, and Nanny Rose took plenty of naps. A lot of times no one noticed if I was in the room."

That's it. I want to *destroy* these people. I want to vanquish them so thoroughly there's nothing left behind but a scorch mark.

Sophie, who reacts in more normal ways to sad stories, looks like she's about to burst into tears. "Oh, Ollie," she says, "I know exactly what that feels like, but it'll never happen again. I promise."

He grunts, shaking his little head. "I wish it would. Travis always knows exactly where I am. I can't get away with anything."

"That's okay. I'll teach you how to get away with stuff." I extend my fist for a bump, and as he gives it to me, Briar gives me a disapproving look.

I'm tempted to point out that some rules are stupid and shouldn't be followed, and that building Ollie's confidence is more important than making him into a rule-following sheep, but I'm not sure she'd agree.

Dottie pats Ollie's hand, and I'm not at all surprised when she says, "Dear boy. I have a few things I *must* give you. In fact, come with me. We need to figure out which of the stones call to you."

He glances at me before meeting her gaze again. "Stones don't talk, Miss Dottie."

"Oooh, but they do." She presses her hand over her chest. "They talk to us *here*."

This time he gives me a look that requires no body language expertise to interpret. *Is this woman crazy?*

"She doesn't mean it literally," I explain, "but if you'd like to go look at some cool rocks, it's okay with me. Your dad knows Dottie's good people."

Ollie shrugs. "Okay. I *do* like rocks."

"And I'll tell you all about them," Dottie promises, beaming.

"Promise?"

"Oh, yes." She looks like someone just baked her a triple-decker birthday cake.

The two of them take off toward the back room of the shop.

I glance over my shoulder at Travis's table. He is, of course, staring at me, so I give him a thumbs-up and a huge grin.

I expect him to stomp over to demand an explanation, but he settles for giving me a severe look.

"So they'll be gone for at least six hours," I say, turning back toward my friends. "You guys, I have something really life-changing to tell you, but you have to promise to keep it to yourselves. Like, it's very important not to tell anyone. Even Dottie. I love her, but I get the sense that she's not very good at keeping secrets."

"What is it?" Sophie asks, her eyes widening. "Are you and Travis together?"

Shock ripples through me. "No, absolutely not. Why would you say that? Why would you even *think* that?"

"She thought so too," Sophie whispers furtively, gesturing to Briar, who shrugs, still playing with a lock of her long golden princess hair.

"Seriously, guys?"

"You're suddenly taking care of his son," Briar says. "And you've been checking him out for months."

Sophie nods slightly in agreement.

"Oh my God, I have not," I insist. "I check out every thirst trap equally. Except for Rob, obviously, because you've got that locked down."

"We've been to a lot of band performances with you," Sophie says hesitantly, "and you're always looking at Karen and her friends or Travis."

"Who the hell is Karen?" I ask.

"Travis's ex-girlfriend. The one who's always at their shows with her friends. I thought you knew."

"How would I know?"

My stomach twists a little at this new information. So it's Karen who's always checking him out, watching him sweat. Karen in the low-cut outfits.

Of course her name's Karen. She probably lives out the stereotype unironically, complaining about her brunch orders and other people daring to take up space around her.

Obviously I don't like or dislike people based on who they've dated—my present company is proof of that—but I don't have a lot of checkmarks in Karen's pros column. She annoyed me before I knew her name. It's the way she looks at Travis, like she thinks he belongs in her back pocket.

"I *didn't* know," I double down, "and I don't care. I was only watching those women because they act like groupies, and I will absolutely defend your claim if I need to. Up until a few days ago, I hadn't even spoken to Travis for over a month. He's *way* too uptight for me, and besides, he's Rob's best friend. I only agreed to help with Ollie because I care about Ollie. I know how hard it was for Connor after my mom left."

"He was a little baby," Sophie says in her usual empathetic way. "It was probably harder for you and Liam." For a second, it's enough to transport me back to that time. To the gut-wrenching feeling of being left alone with barely a backward glance.

"Maybe at first," I say. "But Liam and I are built from stronger stuff. Connor's a big softie."

"You were going to tell us something," Briar prompts.

"You kind of took the wind out of my sails," I pout, but I have to laugh at my own turn of phrase. "Wind. Sails. That's on point." I glance around again, making sure no one's paying attention to us. Even Travis seems otherwise engaged, so I lean forward and say, "I just found out that Travis's dad was the star of the *Ships Ahoy* series."

"Oh," Briar says, nodding. "Cool. I sort of remember those movies."

Sophie seems a little more interested, but it's obvious neither of them consider this news to be earth-shattering.

"Come on, guys." I wave my hands over my head. "This is huge. Travis's dad was the guy who always said, 'Maritime law is mine,' in that epic voice. Can you believe it?"

They exchange a look.

"Are you doing okay, Hannah?" Sophie asks. "We've been a little worried about you. Liam mentioned he hasn't talked to you much since you left Big Catch."

I rub my arms. "He knows why. I'm mad at him, but we'll be fine with each other eventually. We always are."

They exchange another of those silent but knowing looks that are way more fun when you're included in them.

"Liam said you really loved your job, Hannah," Sophie continues. "Everyone else at Big Catch seems to love you too. They honestly seem desperate to have you back."

"I'm not going to pretend hearing that doesn't feel good."

"Are you sure you don't want to go back?" she asks. "This isn't..." Worry fills her eyes. "You didn't leave because of Jonah, did you?"

I met Jonah, who used to work as a beer distributor, at a networking event Big Catch threw for beer professionals. His job in the beer industry is how he met all of us—Sophie used to work in the tap room at Buchanan Brewery, Briar works at Silver Star, and GingerBeerBabe, aka Nora Leigh, is the head brewer-slash-part-owner of The Ginger Station.

Nora helped us reveal Jonah's true nature to the whole town in a public reckoning a few months ago, but she hasn't exactly seemed eager to buddy up with us. Still, I don't know the meaning of the words "give" and "up" when they're grouped together, so yes, I emailed her a week or two ago and made the mistake of telling my friends about it. No doubt they're worried about that too.

In all honesty, they have more reason to worry about Nora rejecting me than freaking Jonah. He had nothing to do with me quitting my job, and I never give him half a thought anymore, now that we'd served up some well-deserved revenge. He is irrelevant.

"No, it wasn't because of Jonah," I say. "And yes, I loved my job for a while, but I couldn't work with Liam anymore. We were codependent for too long. I don't need some expensive therapist to tell me that."

"Are you being purposefully vague?" Sophie asks, raising her eyebrows.

"Yes, but now I'm going to be very specific." I glance between both of them before my gaze settles on Briar. "Do not, under any circumstances, date my brother. You have to promise me."

She looks taken aback by the out-of-left-field question, but she recovers quickly. "That's an easy promise to make. I've decided to never date again, and I doubt I'll ever hang out with him by myself."

"Good, that's settled then." I glance at Sophie. "Same goes for you if it ever falls apart with Rob."

She looks scandalized by the thought. "It's never going to fall apart."

I sigh. "I believe you. It's just..." Hell, it was past time to tell them. "I had other friends before we met."

"How dare you," Sophie says, giving me a slight smile. Encouraging me in a way she knows will work.

"I know, right?" I pause, gathering myself. My heart starts thumping faster. "One of those friends worked with me at Big Catch. She and Liam started seeing each other, and it fell apart catastrophically. I had to fire her."

"Goodness," Sophie says, taking my hand. "I had no idea."

"I don't like talking about it," I say. "It sucked. *Really* sucked. And all of our mutual friends took her side. They thought I'd chosen my brother over her, which I guess I did, but honestly, I didn't have a choice. She tainted a whole kettle of Big Catch beer by throwing his boxing gear into it."

Briar cringes. "Oof."

Sophie shakes her head. "Sounds like something you'd do."

"It probably is," I say with a half-smile. "I told you we used to be friends."

"When did this happen?" Briar asks.

"A couple of months before I met you. I lost everyone in my circle except for the other people at work. They all witnessed how unhinged she acted." I hesitate. "He didn't cheat on her. It wasn't like that. I don't want you guys thinking my brother's some kind of asshole."

"You tell us frequently that he's an asshole," Briar says, amusement ringing through her voice.

"Sure, but not like *that*. Not a Jonah-level asshole. He's just …emotionally unavailable. I warned her, and she didn't listen, and…" I shrug. "Anyway, please don't date him. Ever. Don't even be *nice* to him."

Briar laughs. "Yes, I'll ridicule him and throw rotten fruit at his face."

"Good. Start with bananas. He hates bananas."

"I'm glad you told us," Sophie says, her eyes finding and holding mine. "You should know you can tell us anything."

I feel my throat tighten with emotion. "I'm okay, though. I swear. Maybe I'll go back there someday, or get a different full-time job, but I'm not ready. I need some time to—"

"Heal," Sophie interjects, her eyes full of a sweet understanding.

"I was gonna say take some time off and chill, but sure, we'll go with your answer."

"I'm not sure being a nanny is such a chill job," Briar says. "You'll have to be the bad guy sometimes. Like, you'll have to make sure Ollie does his homework."

"Nah, that's his dad's job. Besides, he's reading a science textbook for kicks. He's some kind of genius. What I'm going to teach him is how to have fun. Hell, maybe Travis will even learn a thing or two in the process."

Briar gives Sophie another of those looks.

"What? What revealing thing did I say this time?" I ask, rolling my eyes.

"You *sure* there's nothing between you and Travis?" Sophie asks.

"Give it up, you guys. I'd never consider messing around with Travis. Besides the fact that I'm Ollie's temporary nanny, He's Rob's best friend. No way would I risk our friendship for a guy."

"I don't care if you sleep with Travis," Sophie says with a shrug. "I wouldn't even mind if you threw his drumsticks into a kettle of beer, as long as it's not at Buchanan Brewery."

"I bet you wouldn't, you unicorn of a woman, but I said what I said."

I grin at her, but my heart is thumping a little faster as I think about the way Margaret looked at me when I fired her. I'm glad when my thoughts do their usual chaotic jump, landing on another pissed-off woman who decided to get revenge. One whose feelings were much less justified.

I clear my throat. "Actually, I could use your advice on something." I quickly explain the Rachel problem. "I told Travis I'd take care of it, but to be totally honest, I don't have a plan yet."

"Easy," Briar says, surprising me with her quick response. "We'll have someone write her a cease and desist letter."

"Oooh," Sophie interjects excitedly. "I know a lawyer. She's really nice."

"Exactly what we're looking for," I tease.

"But also a tough customer. I bet she'd do it as a favor, so Travis wouldn't have to pay anyone."

"Probably not an issue for him, but I'm sure he'd appreciate it." I grin at them. "We make a great hive mind."

The conversation moves on to the band, and Dottie finally returns with Ollie, who's lugging a seriously enormous cardboard box. He sets it down on the table, his eyes gleaming with excitement. "Miss Dottie said I get to keep all of them."

She cradles the back of his head with her hand. "Yes, my dear," she says. "I'll tell you more about them the next time Hannah brings you by, and I'd *love* to introduce you to a few of my special friends. But first let me give you a box of sweets."

Yeah, Travis is definitely going to murder me. I catch him watching me again, this time with a small smile on his face. His hair is swept to the side enough that I can see a hint of his birthmark.

I feel something—a zip of awareness, of *appreciation*—that I shut down by mouthing at him, *Maritime law is mine.*

He surprises me by grinning. I'll be damned if I don't grin back.

CHAPTER NINE

TRAVIS

It's Thursday night, four days into Hurricane Hannah.

So far, she's broken three of my mugs, made slime with all of my baking soda, and turned two cushions over to hide stains she doesn't want me to see. They've been inexpertly cleaned, so either she put in the effort or Ollie's covering for her.

They've also acquired a collection of pumpkins with the emergency credit card, from one so big it could have doubled as Cinderella's carriage to a tiny, pocket-sized one. They're all carved with horrifying faces. Seeing them on the stoop made me feel a little blue, because I kind of wished they'd included me. I've never carved a pumpkin. My mother always said it was too messy, and my nanny agreed.

Hannah also helped Ollie put together his Halloween costume. He's going as a scientist, not a ninja turtle, thankfully. He looks cute, and when he dressed up in it to show me, a deeper sense of regret settled inside of me. Because I don't know what he dressed up as for his first Halloween, or what it sounded like when he said "trick or treat" for the first time. I tell myself I'll make up for it by being there this year, but it still hurts.

Kind of like stepping on one of Dottie's crystals—I can only conclude Hannah and Ollie must have played hide-and-seek with them, because they're literally all over the house, nestled between couch cushions, hidden in drawers, and on one memorable occasion, wedged into the floorboards. This morning, I found one in a cereal box.

Hannah has, for all intents and purposes, turned my life upside down. I can't take a step without being reminded of her, and everything in my house smells like her. Even my pillow. I have no idea how that's possible unless she rubs her head against it just to torment me, something I wouldn't put past her, but Ollie swears they've never gone in my bedroom.

Of course, it goes without saying that he'd lie for her.

I got home early on Monday and Tuesday, just after closing The Missing Beat, but last night we auditioned someone for the band—a definite no, because the guy was high on mushrooms and thought the walls were closing in on him. We spent more time cleaning the trash can he puked into than we did listening to him play.

When I came home, Hannah was softly singing to Ollie in his bedroom. I sat on the couch and listened, feeling a big emotion I couldn't put into words. All I knew was that listening to her sing to him shook my foundation.

She emerged on tiptoes and then screamed in surprise when she saw me sitting in the living room, which had led to Ollie getting up and asking if he could have a second dessert.

We all ate a scoop of ice cream on the couch together, which had felt good and bad—good, because it was almost like we were a family; bad, because we weren't.

Afterward, I walked her to the door like a dog trailing its owner, feeling like a dumbass but needing to see her get safely into her car. Ollie stood in the doorway with me until she drove off, and then I tucked him back into bed.

"Want me to sing to you?" I asked.

"Uncle Rob's the singer. And Hannah." He paused. "But I think I'd like it if you would."

So I sang him one of my favorites, "Here Comes the Sun"—a song that made me think of Hannah—and he said sleepily, "I didn't know you had a good voice."

I felt a deep ache settle in my chest. There was still so much we didn't know about each other.

Tonight, Rob, Bixby, and I auditioned someone else, but it didn't go much better. The candidate showed up seventeen minutes late, called Rob "Bob," and suggested we do a group colonic cleanse to bond.

So I'm feeling pretty spent as I approach my front door, bracing myself for...anything, I guess.

When I turn the corner into the living room, I see Hannah sipping a beer while she watches something with a very familiar soundtrack on TV. She's snuggled up on the couch beneath a throw blanket.

An unopened bottle of beer sits on the coffee table across from her.

I shake my head as I approach her, but can't help smiling as the cheesy soundtrack crescendos. "Really, *Ships Ahoy*?"

"The OG," she says with a grin, pausing it. "What can I say? You stirred my nostalgia."

I nod at the other bottle on the table. "I hope that's for me and not for Ollie?"

She rolls her eyes. "Seriously, Travis? If you think I'm irresponsible enough to offer alcohol to your seven-year-old, then you shouldn't have hired me to be your nanny."

"Fair point." I sink down next to her, keeping a few inches between us, and grab the beer, sighing with pleasure at the feeling of the cold bottle against my skin. "This doesn't look like anything I have in the fridge."

"I brought them. Liam made it. I thought we could catch up. Do you want some blanket?"

She lifts a corner of the throw, motioning for me to scoot closer. And even though my whole body still feels overly hot from practice, I do exactly as she suggests, moving in close until I can feel her softness pressed against me. She tosses the end of the blanket over me, enveloping us in it together. I'd sooner die of heatstroke than complain, because it feels good to be this close to her.

"Oooh, you're warm," she says, snuggling closer.

I shift my focus to the beer bottle, needing to latch onto something other than the feeling of her body against me. Lifting it, I ask, "Does this mean you've been talking to Liam? He said you'd had some kind of disagreement."

It's none of my business, but I can't deny that I care. My sister and I aren't close, but we were stuck in the trenches together, bonded because of it. I don't want Hannah to lose her connection with her brother.

She shrugs. "We've texted. He dropped it off at my place yesterday while I was over here. I got to it before my neighbors did."

I pause, digesting this. "What happened between you two?"

She grins. "Look at you. My nosiness is rubbing off."

"So you only have yourself to blame."

Sighing, she says, "Okay, fine. He was seeing one of my friends who worked at Big Catch with us. I warned Margaret it was going to end badly, and it did. She did some not-very-professional things, and I had to fire her. It was this big, awful mess. It's been hard to move on."

"She blamed you," I conclude, feeling her hurt, even though she's clearly dug it down deep and refused to put up a makeshift gravestone. I feel pissed at this woman I've never met, and also at Hannah's brother, for putting her in such a twisted situation to begin with. Not my place to care, but there it is. She deserved more from them.

"Yeah," she says with a sigh, running a finger distractedly around the mouth of her beer bottle. "So did all of our mutual friends."

"Mustn't be very good friends. You know, I have this theory about friends…"

She turns to get a more direct look at me, her knee brushing against me. "Oh yeah? Enlighten me, Travis."

"Some of them are meant to stick around, and others pass through our lives to teach us something."

"Sounds narcissistic."

I can't help but smile. "Maybe. But it's true for everyone."

"So what should I learn from what Margaret did?"

"That you're fair, but not everyone is. Anyway, sometimes bad things lead to good ones. You met Sophie and Briar just after that. You might not have become as close if you were still spending all your downtime with Margaret."

She opens her mouth to speak, then shuts it again before she gives me one of her big grins. "Admit it. Did you steal your wisdom from a fortune cookie factory?"

She's not the only one who recognizes deflections, but I go along with it, smiling. "You caught me." I nod to the bottle in her hand. "So you want us to drink from these unlabeled bottles that may have been made by the brother you're fighting with or a stranger with a thing for strychnine. Either way, we could be in trouble."

She looks at me as she lifts her bottle to her pink lips, wrapping them around the opening. I watch as she drinks deeply and then lowers the bottle. She gestures to the other beer. "Live dangerously, Travis."

I'd like to pull her to me and taste the beer from her lips.

This attraction is becoming…uncomfortable. While she was

off-limits before because of her friendship with Sophie, now she's *extra* off-limits.

By Norland College standards, Hannah Moroney might be the worst nanny ever, but she's exactly what Ollie needs, exactly what both of us need, and I'm not going to endanger that. Not for anything.

Especially not for sex, even though I'm certain it would be incredible.

I shift away from her slightly. "Thank you for getting Rachel to take down that post, by the way. I should have thanked you sooner."

She smiles mischievously at me. "I have my ways. And you're welcome. She messed with the wrong nanny."

"So it would seem," I say with a laugh. "I'm still getting the odd message accusing me of being an asshole, but it's possible it's related to something else."

"Oh, you'll always get those," she says, bumping her shoulder against mine. "Now, try the beer so I don't have to die alone if it's poisoned."

I lift my eyebrows. "You make a terrible argument."

"I was president of the debate club."

I twist the cap off and take a sip. The beer is smooth and delicious with a note of citrus. "Not a bad way to potentially die."

"I'll recommend that to Liam as the name." She studies my face, her eyes lingering above my hairline, and without a thought, I lift my hand to rearrange my hair.

"I don't know why you always try to hide it," she comments. "It's fascinating."

"I hate it," I say more vehemently than I intended—but I *do* hate it. It's always felt like a defect. A sign that I'm not what I'm supposed to be.

"It's in the shape of a heart."

"Doesn't make me like it any better. My mother used to make me spend an hour in her makeup chair before every event so it could be covered up with foundation."

Hannah's eyes light up with rage. "I'm a makeup artist, and I'd *never* cover it up. Never. They'd have to kill me first."

My lips curl up higher. "Who would give you an ultimatum between covering up my birthmark and death?"

She shocks me by reaching over, beneath my hair and tracing it—just one finger, the slightest touch, but it vibrates through me.

"A true sadist," she says, pulling her finger away.

My eyes hold hers for a moment too long before I look away. "I guess. So are we finishing this terrible movie or what?"

She stares at me in shock. "You really want to watch *Ships Ahoy* with me?"

"Not really, no. But it amuses me that you like it. Maybe you can help me see it through new eyes."

"Seriously?" Enthusiasm hums off her in an electrical cloud. Damn, I'd like to absorb it. To become an energy vampire so I can taste her excitement.

Of course, that puts an intrusive thought in my head about other ways I could taste her excitement, but I bury it and hand her the remote. "Do the honors, Hannah. I have a feeling I'm going to need this beer."

She watches me with a playful glint in her eyes. "You're surprising."

"I thought I had a drumstick shoved up my ass."

She lifts her eyebrows. "I've never said that in front of you."

I laugh. "You're not nearly as subtle as you think you are. Now, what part were you watching?"

She gets the movie cued up, then gives me a sidelong look. "How many times have you seen these movies?"

"Probably more than you."

I start humming the theme music, and her delighted gasp is more soothing than the beer.

I expect her to hit play, but instead she pauses, tapping a finger to her lips. "I'm about to be nosy."

"Do you ever stop?" I tease.

"No. So...did you ever want to be a lead singer? Ollie told me you sound like some singer whose name I've never heard of. I assume he meant it as a compliment."

That part makes me smile. At least I've done something to impress my kid. "No, zero interest."

"Why?"

"I like playing the drums." That's true, but the explanation feels small and inaccurate. I like plenty of things, like soft sheets and an organized refrigerator. My need to play is different. "I crave it."

Her lips part, and for a second the only thing I can focus on is the fullness of her bottom lip and the small freckle at the corner of her mouth.

I look away, my eyes coming to rest on the screen—it's paused on an image of my father in a Hawaiian shirt with what is very clearly a stuffed parrot perched on his shoulder.

"I didn't want any of that, Hannah." I gesture to it. "There were six of these movies, and they became his whole life. Twelve hours of film. It was all he wanted to talk about, all he wanted to be. His entire life can be summed up by them. It didn't matter to him that there were other people who needed him, other opportunities he could have pursued. So, no, I don't care about being famous or being recognized. I'd rather not. No one really recognizes the drummer. Rob's not into that kind of thing either, but it doesn't bother him."

I feel her studying me, her green eyes full of curiosity, the way Ollie looks when he actually meets an equation he can't immediately solve.

"You're more interesting than I thought you'd be," she finally says.

I laugh, shaking my head slightly. "Interesting *and* surprising. What a banner night for me."

"Yeah," she says thoughtfully. "I guess it is."

There's a buzzing awareness between us, and our bodies are still sealed together beneath that blanket I didn't want, which is quickly becoming my favorite blanket in the world. She's already right next to me, so close I'm breathing in that maddening scent, feeling the press of her, but it's not close enough. I want to pull her onto my lap and feel the silk of her hair against my face—and, yeah, the pressure of her body against my dick—but I'm not an idiot.

She's not here for me.

Still, it's the kind of night that can make a man forget reality.

So I take the remote from her, our fingers brushing, and turn on the movie—waking myself up.

CHAPTER TEN

HANNAH

"I'm definitely not into Travis," I tell Sophie, glowering at her and Briar across the table from me. It's Saturday, and we're having breakfast at Tea of Fortune. It's like they're presenting themselves as a united front to grill me. "He isn't my type, and I'm guessing I'm not his."

Sophie shrugs, clearly ready to play peacemaker, but Briar says, "I thought we promised not to lie to each other."

"I'm *not* lying," I insist, even though I keep thinking about the other night. Watching that movie snuggled up next to him...

I fell asleep with my head on his shoulder and woke up during the final credits, practically in his arms. My hand was on his chest, so I could feel his heartbeat thrumming through me. I looked up at him and found him looking down at me, the longer hair at the top of his head brushing my face.

"I guess you don't like the movie as much as you thought you did," he'd said.

"Maybe it was the company that was lacking," I'd replied, but it took me several seconds to find the will to move. I liked being there, cocooned with him. I felt safe.

I'd wanted to stay in a way that scared me.

I definitely wasn't ready to tell my friends about it, though. Not after I'd pledged never to touch anyone connected to Rob.

But Sophie's still staring at me, as if she can will me into confessing.

"I'm not lying," I repeat, feeling even more like I might be.

"So maybe he's not your type, but you *do* like him," Sophie says.

"It doesn't matter," I insist, which is obviously not the same as a no.

My phone rings, and I'm happy to pick it up, even though it's a number I don't recognize and probably a scammer on the other end who wants to grill me about my car's extended warranty.

I lift a finger as I answer, signaling that I'll just be a second. "Hello?"

"Yes, hello," says a man with a monotone voice. "This is Eugene Peebles. Have I reached Hannah..." He pauses, then adds, "Moroney?"

I grin at my friends as I say, "Yes, you absolutely have. I've heard you'd like to get together and discuss your position at Big Catch?"

"Yes, I thought a passing of the torch would be in order. I was wondering if Friday would suit you. Perhaps at nine a.m.?"

"It would suit me perfectly."

"At Big Catch?" he asks.

Panic unleashes inside of me.

No. Not yet. I'm not ready to see it yet.

"We'll meet at Tea of Fortune," I say, then give him the address. "I know the owner, and she'll take excellent care of you."

"I wouldn't want to put anyone to any trouble."

"It'll be no trouble at all," I say. Then we exchange super polite goodbyes and hang up.

"Your replacement?" Briar asks with raised eyebrows.

"Yes, I'm excited to meet him."

"Isn't he that unpleasant old guy who wears all the corduroy?" Sophie asks.

"Yes," I say, grinning at them. "I'm going to enjoy messing with him, and hopefully I can get him to calm down so he stops bugging my friends."

"You have a strange idea of fun," Briar says with an indulgent smile.

Dottie, who was passing by, stops near our table to give my shoulder a squeeze. "How's our young man doing?"

"Ollie's doing fine," I say. "We've had a lot of fun together. I'm seeing him this afternoon while the guys' band plays at The Ginger Station."

Sophie and Briar glance at each other.

"Are you going?" I ask them, trying to sound like I don't care about GingerBeerBabe and haven't given her half a thought.

The second part is somewhat true—my mind's been busy with other things—but I definitely haven't forgotten her.

"We're not going," Briar says. "I have to work."

"And I'm going to the Buchanan Brewery Halloween party," Sophie adds. "I invited you."

"Travis definitely wouldn't want me bringing Ollie there." I glance at Dottie. "So I guess we're never going to be friends with the illustrious GingerBeerBabe."

Dottie gives me one of her patented knowing smiles. "The time isn't right yet, but it'll happen."

"Of course it's not," I joke. "Maybe we'll all be in the same retirement home together, accidentally sleeping with the same old dude with dentures. That would be so us."

"Nope." Briar shakes her head. "I don't think I'm ever going to start dating again. Staying single has been way better for my mental health."

This time Dottie directs her patented knowing look at Briar. "Don't give up on love yet, my dear. It has plans for you."

"You make it sound like some kind of stalker," I say, laughing. "Is it going to hit her over the head in the library with a candlestick?"

"No, I don't think it *is* going to happen in the library." Dottie glances around as if she's worried about being overheard. "I'll admit I got a little tipsy last night, and I tried pendulum dowsing with Penny."

"My aunt?" Sophie gasps as if scandalized, while I say, "What the fuck is pendulum dowsing?"

"Oh, it's wonderful fun," Dottie says, squeezing my shoulder. "You hold an activated crystal suspended on a string, and it moves in response to yes and no questions."

"And what did this pendulum tell you about Briar's love life?" I ask, trying not to laugh.

"It seemed to think she was going to fall in love at Silver Star Brewery," she says, starry-eyed.

"There you go," Briar says, waving a hand. "I'm going to fall in love with my work."

"Oh, that wasn't my interpretation at all," Dottie says. Then she glances at me. Uh-oh.

"You did it for me too?"

"*Of course.*"

"Let me guess. I'm going to fall head over heels in love with Eugene Peebles, and we're going to have a May-December romance for the ages."

"I'll be sure to send you a tea basket when it happens," Dottie says with an amused expression, and then she walks away without saying anything else.

"She didn't tell me what my pendulum thingy said," I complain.

"That you and Eugene are sitting in a tree," Sophie teases, while Briar stares after Dottie.

"Now, that's a woman who knows how to work a room," she says with an admiring smile.

SEVERAL HOURS LATER, Ollie and I are sitting on the couch in Travis's living room.

He's stuck in a funk so deep he's refused to do anything, including going to a trunk-or-treat that has gift bags. Gift bags full of *candy*.

"So why don't we just sit here and make funny faces at each other?" I ask, pulling my mouth dramatically to one side.

"Nanny Rose says your face will get stuck like that if you do it, so you'd better not. I think she was kidding, but it's better to be safe than sorry."

"Uh-oh," I say, keeping my mouth twisted up. "It's too late. I'm going to have to spend the rest of my life like this, Ollie. Will you be embarrassed when I pick you up at school?"

I arc an eyebrow to complement the weird mouth thing I have going on, and he finally cracks a smile. "You're teasing."

"No, I swear, it's really happening," I say, "but I think it's going back to normal. I can feel it." I let my mouth slide back into its neutral position, then dramatically twist it to the other side. "Oh no, it shifted!"

Now, he's laughing in a steady stream that has me grinning back at him.

"Thank goodness," I say. "I was worried you were going to frown forever, and then we wouldn't be able to get ice cream, because everyone knows you can't frown while you're eating ice cream."

"I don't think I'm supposed to eat ice cream before dinner."

"What Travis doesn't know won't hurt him."

He smiles and nuzzles his face against my arm. "You don't talk like any of the other nannies."

"We can both be grateful for that."

I'm about to ask him if he's ready to go, but something gives me pause. My intuition's telling me he's not pissed off at the world in general. Something specific happened today.

"Ollie, why are you so upset today?"

He sighs and meets my gaze. "Don't tell Travis."

"I only will if I have to. What happened?"

"I have this iPad that Roland gave me, and I've been using it to play games in my room sometimes. Travis thinks I only read in there."

"Oh, I won't tell him about that," I say. "Consider this record sealed."

"Well...there was this game subscription service on it, and Roland cancelled it." His eyes look glassy, and I can tell he's trying not to cry. "I think he hates me."

Oh, that *fucker*. That absolute maggot. It wasn't enough that he completely abandoned the kid he'd helped raise—a kid who'd played no part in his wife's deception—he seriously had to do *that*?

I inhale a deep breath before slowly letting it out. "Do you know this joker's address?"

"Of course, I do, Hannah," he says practically. "I used to live there."

I pull out my phone. "I'm going to send him some presents."

"Why would you send him presents?" he asks, his forehead furrowing in the exact same place Travis's always does. "He has everything he needs."

"Halloween's on Tuesday. This guy took away your treat, so he's getting a bag full of tricks. He asked for it."

"What? You're really sending him tricks?" he asks, his face lighting up.

"Sure. Plus, I'm guessing you're wrong about him having everything. He probably doesn't have a glitter bomb. Or catalogs for every major store. If you know his email address, we can also get him on dozens of spam lists, which would be fun. And that's just for starters. I have all kinds of inappropriate ideas I can't share with you."

His smile widens but then slips. "My teacher says we're supposed to treat other people like we want to be treated, even if they're not so nice to us."

"This is a special occasion," I say. "It's almost Halloween! Besides, it might make you feel a little better, and it's okay if it does. You don't have to be a little ray of sunshine all the time."

He studies me for a moment, then takes my hand. "Is my mom coming back?"

"I don't know, Ollie," I say tightly, because let's be honest, Lilah's even worse than Roland. She's the one who lied to everyone, and now she's off in Australia, chasing a good time and letting everyone else fix her mistakes. Still, I can hardly go Rambo on her given there are custody issues to sort out. This producer guy, however, is fair game.

I squeeze his hand. "What your mom did sucks. My mom walked out on us too, so I know what it feels like. But she didn't do it because *you* suck. Because you're the coolest kid I know."

"I'm glad you're here." He bites his lip. "I know boys aren't supposed to admit it, but I was really scared when she left me here. And not just because I didn't know Travis. I'd never left Nashville before. Whenever they went on trips, I stayed home with Nanny Rose."

I take a deep breath, burying my anger, and say, "You feel however you want to feel, Ollie. It's okay to admit you're scared. Only psychos don't get scared."

"Thanks, Hannah," he says with a soft smile. He pauses, his eyes lighting up with mischief. "Can we send a glitter bomb to Travis too? Not because I don't like him. I just think it would be kind of funny."

I laugh at the mental image of Travis covered in glitter.

"So do I, and I'm an easy customer right now. I'd do just about anything to make you smile."

We go on an online shopping spree for tricks, then go out and get ice cream sundaes with all the toppings, an indulgence guaranteed to ruin his dinner and probably my stomach. Worth it.

Travis gets home at around six, wearing a dark T-shirt and jeans, looking like a snack, if I'm perfectly honest. He's got a bit of a glow, the kind he gets when he played well and knows it.

When he sees the smile on Ollie's face, he lights up and shifts his smile to me. He mouths *thank you*.

His approval means nothing to me, obviously, but when he insists on walking me to my car, I don't object.

"I knew you'd cheer him up," he says after opening the door for me.

I slide into the driver's seat and look up at him. "You're a smart man."

One corner of his mouth lifts up higher than the other. "I *am* an expert at maritime law."

"Look at you, cracking jokes about your birthright."

He hesitates, then says, "I realize I should have asked you this inside, but would you like to stay for dinner?"

I can't think of the last time a man offered to cook for me, but I have to set firm boundaries. I can't slip into any more dangerous behavior with him. "No, thanks. We already got huge ice cream sundaes."

"You're messing with me again," he says with a slow smile.

"Nope."

"And you didn't get me one?" he asks, still leaning into the car.

"Nope, but maybe next time I'll save you my cherry."

Dammit, Hannah. Bad Hannah!

He smiles wryly, shaking his head at me. "You have a good night, Hannah."

When I get home, I do something I'd promised myself not to do and google Ollie's mother—Lilah Santiago.

The woman has a Wikipedia page because her (now) ex-husband produced one god-awful single for her. She's also some sort of "influencer," with an Instagram page full of artsy shots of her face, a grapefruit, and some kitchen implements I doubt she's ever used, and has an IMDb page for a few roles as an extra in TV shows and movies.

I purse my mouth to the side, studying her face. Of course she's pretty. She looks like she comes from a long line of models on both sides, with her perfectly sleek, waist-length black hair, and big almond-shaped gray eyes. Her boobs are also freaking huge, although I'm guessing they're too perky to be one hundred percent natural.

I snap a photo of her and text it to Briar and Sophie.

> This is Ollie's mother.

> Briar: Are we going to put up STD posters of her too?

I laugh out loud. After we figured out Jonah was a creeper who was four-timing all of us, I started putting up posters of him all around town, warning women he was infested with STDs. There are still a few he hasn't tracked down, including in the bookstore bathroom, which amuses me to no end.

Sophie: No, that wouldn't work. She doesn't live here.

Me: I love that we've awakened Sophie's dark side, but no. I'm just showing you this so you can see I'm totally not Travis's type. THIS is what he likes.

Briar: Tall, dark, and evil?

Me: Not me, basically. Karen's tall and brunette too, so he probably has a thing for brunettes.

Me: I mean, from what little I remember about Karen.

Sophie: Do you WANT to be his type?

Me: No, I was proving a point.

Briar: Yes, you're doing internet searches on his exes. We can all tell you're definitely not into him.

Well, shit.

CHAPTER ELEVEN

TRAVIS

Every day, the house feels more and more like it's Hannah's as much as mine. It still smells like her. The furniture has been pushed out of alignment, and my Netflix profile has been skewed so badly it's recommending dating shows about couples who meet in darkened rooms and, worse, tacky movies inspired by our watching history, i.e., *Ships Ahoy*.

On Halloween, we have a thin crowd at The Missing Beat since most of the kids were out carousing, but we have ourselves a little party and teach the kids who showed how to play "Monster Mash."

When I get home at around six, there's a note waiting for me on the counter:

> *He couldn't wait anymore, so I'm bringing him in search of full-size candy bars. JOIN US. –H*

I text Hannah, and she sends me a pin of their location and a warning:

> You better be in a costume.

I glance down at my outfit. Black button-down. Jeans. I'm tempted to just meet them as I am, maybe bring my sticks and say I'm a drummer, but I don't want to disappoint her. So I head into my room and rummage through my drawers until I find the red-striped fisherman sweater my sister gave me for Christmas last year. With the addition of the black-framed glasses I wore all of twice before switching to contacts, I'm the guy from *Where's Waldo?*

Ten minutes later, I jog around a corner, toward the latest pin she sent, and there they are—

For a second, I stop in my tracks and stare at them. Hannah looks like she flew out of a fairy tale. She's wearing a blue dress with petticoats beneath and iridescent wings, and her face is made up with sparkly makeup. Her arm is wrapped around my son, who's in his scientist outfit. They're both laughing, and he's holding an enormous pillowcase weighed down with candy.

My pillowcase.

But I don't even care.

They're beautiful, and for a second I think about turning and blending into the night. Because I don't want to do anything to destroy their fun. But then Hannah spots me, and her whole face lights up in a way that radiates through me, like some chain reaction Scientist Ollie should study.

"We found you," she says, laughing and hurrying Ollie toward me. "We found you!" she repeats, her face alight and gorgeous, and for a second, it feels like those words have a deeper meaning. But the moment slips away as she bumps my shoulder gently, her sparkles attaching to me. "You'll need to do better than that to evade me, Waldo."

As if anyone would want to run away from her.

We keep trick-or-treating, even though Ollie has more

candy than he can probably eat in a year, because there's a look of pure happiness on his face I want to keep there. I want to forget that later I'm going to have to hide the candy and parcel it out so he won't go into a sugar coma. But right now, at this moment, all I want is to live in this magic place.

Of course, the night ends, as all nights do, and the next day streams past, afternoon bleeding into evening. I get home late, after Rob, Bixby, and I auditioned a fourth guy. He didn't play well with us, and Rob called the producer, Frank, to let him know we're getting nowhere and won't have a fourth in time for the New Belgium show on Saturday. He gave us a one-week extension, which wasn't as much of a comfort as he seemed to think it should be.

To top it off, my anxiety seems to be popping off in new and unpredictable ways. I saw someone in a sailor suit earlier, and for a minute, I had myself convinced they were following me around, as if one of the extras from a *Ships Ahoy* movie stepped out of the TV to stalk me. The obvious explanation is that Halloween just passed, and someone's trying to make the party last a little longer, but it still gave me goose bumps.

Sighing, I walk inside the house as noiselessly as possible. Ollie must be in bed by now, given the hour, and I can hear one of Hannah's dating shows playing quietly in the living room—the guy's asking the woman if she likes French kissing, as if anyone calls it French kissing anymore instead of just regular kissing.

A stack of mail is waiting on the hall table, but it all looks like junk other than a thick manila card envelope—probably some kind of greeting card from my mother. I grab it and slide a finger under the seal as I head toward the living room.

Just as I'm rounding the corner, Hannah laughs at the TV, lifting a Sprite toward it. "You, sir, are a dipshit."

I laugh as I finish opening the envelope—and stop laughing

abruptly when it explodes glitter into my face. I shout a word that rhymes with duck, Hannah drops the can, spilling soda all over herself, and I throw the exploded letter.

"What the hell?" I sputter as she sets the can on the table and switches off the TV.

She turns to face me, and my mouth practically falls open like a cartoon character's. The soda must have been nearly full, because her white shirt is plastered to the red bra beneath it.

"You're . . . wet," I say thickly. I only find the willpower to look up when she starts laughing

"And you're covered in glitter." She laughs harder, leaning forward, which only presses her tits harder against the wet shirt, as if they'd like to break through it and say hello.

Damn it. I make myself look away and reach down to pick up the offending envelope, which is still full of rainbow glitter. A paper note is tucked inside it, along with the clever mechanism that attacked me with glitter.

If it makes you feel any better, we sent one to Roland too. –
XOXO Hannah and Ollie.

Annoyance slices through my Hannah haze.

"You did this?" I ask, shaking the envelope at her. Another handful of glitter comes trailing out of it like snow. Great. I'm going to have to clean this up, and it's going to take forever to get it all out of the rug.

"Hannah," I growl.

"I'll clean it up," she says and gets up off the couch, lifting both hands in the air. "I promise." Glancing back, she takes in the trail of spilled soda on the couch cushion. "And that."

I shake my head, and glitter sprays from me like I'm a unicorn. "The way you cleaned the undersides of all the cushions? Because, if so, I'll have to turn down your very generous offer."

Her lips teeter upward as she fights a smile and loses. "I thought you hadn't noticed."

"I notice everything you do." I didn't mean it to come out like an accusation, but she's closer now, her bra so vivid against the white of her shirt. I want to nuzzle my head against her chest to give her some of the glitter she wanted, but I shove that thought down and say through clenched teeth, "Let me get you a towel."

"I can get my own towel." She reaches out and runs her finger over my eyebrow, coming away with glitter. "You're probably going to need to take a shower. It's too bad you already opened it. I was hoping Ollie would be around when it happened."

First she flooded my house with her scent, making me think of her anytime I do anything. Then she messed up my Netflix queue instead of using her own profile. And now she's annoyed because I got blasted by glitter at the wrong time? Anger pushes through me—the kind of anger that usually steers me straight to the music room to play. "You're upset because I opened the glitter bomb you ordered for me, *your boss*, at the wrong time? I should fire you."

She stands her ground, holding my gaze. "Just when I thought we were becoming friends."

Her words prick my anger like it's a thin balloon, but I try to press a finger over the puncture and hold onto it. If I'm pissed off, at least I won't do something totally insane like kiss her. "You work for me."

She raises her eyebrows. "Would you like me to call you boss man from now on? Or maybe Mr. Thomas?"

"How about sir?" I ask, part joking and part pissed.

"Why, Mr. Sir, all you had to do was ask." She brushes some glitter off my shoulders. "I *am* sorry. Ollie was feeling low, and I wanted to cheer him up, but I went too far. If it makes you feel better, I paid for it. I didn't use the emergency credit card."

"You sent one to Roland too?"

She nods, her gaze holding mine. "Along with some other stuff."

I gesture for her to go on.

"I didn't do anything bad. There was the glitter bomb, of course, and I got him some shitty magazine and catalog subscriptions, signed him up for spam mail, and sent him insulting cookies."

"Insulting cookies, huh?" I ask, trying not to smile.

"*Very* insulting. I have high hopes that they'll destroy his self-confidence forever."

"That's a big ask for a cookie. You think he'll need to put on reading glasses to read the messages?"

"Hopefully not before he gets an eyeful of glitter."

"And you did this out of loyalty to Ollie," I ask, my feelings still on a roller coaster. I'm pissed that my house looks like a twelve-year-old's Pegasus party just ripped through it, but I appreciate her devotion to Ollie. Truthfully, I want to rearrange Roland's face—senior citizen or not, he's a pox on humanity and deserves to be treated like one—but I've held myself back. I need to look squeaky clean if it comes down to a fight for custody.

"Of course," Hannah says. "That asshole cancelled Ollie's game subscription on his iPad."

"iPad?"

"Oh, shit." She lifts her hands to her face and speaks through them. "I wasn't supposed to tell you about that."

"Hannah," I say, frustrated again. "You're my nanny, and he's a minor. You're supposed to tell me everything."

She lowers her hands. "How's he ever going to trust me if I do that?"

"You work for me, not Ollie."

Heat flashes through her eyes. "Yeah. So noted. Roland was paying for some kind of game subscription service on this iPad he gave Ollie, but he cancelled it. It sent Ollie spiraling, so I decided to make him feel better. And yes, all of this is very juvenile, but it's also harmless, and he's a kid. Juvenile is his language. But he didn't want me to tell you about the iPad, because you already told him he's too young for screens."

"He doesn't trust me," I say, feeling deflated. I already knew that, but it doesn't feel great to have my fear validated.

"So show him you won't overreact to every little thing."

"I'm starting to think you just enjoy giving me a hard time," I say tightly. "Go ahead and get that towel. I'll get you a shirt to change into."

"You don't need to—"

"I'm getting you a different shirt, because yours is transparent, and we're not done with this conversation."

Her eyes widen slightly, and I can't help it. My gaze lowers to her tits again, taking in the sweet curve of them under her shirt. I'm still worked up, and right now I want to push her against a wall and take that shirt off myself. I want to lower my head and lick off the soda.

I feel her staring right back, and the urge pulses stronger as blood funnels down to my dick.

"Your shirt is covered in glitter," she remarks, reaching over and skimming the hem of it with her fingers. "Are you going to change too?"

I grab her hand, and her gaze immediately darts to mine, full of the same kind of heat that's pulsing through me. I should drop her hand. I need to. But I hold on and edge closer.

My ringing phone pierces the moment, which is probably for the best, because it's the ring tone I assigned to *her*.

To Lilah.

Gold Digger.

I release Hannah's hand.

"You should get that towel," I say. "I have to take this."

"Do you want me to leave?"

I consider it for half a second, even as the phone keeps ringing, then shake my head. "No. I'd like you to stay." I pause, letting myself take one last look at her before she leaves. "You can grab a shirt from my dresser."

She surprises me by lifting onto her toes to kiss my cheek, her full lips soft against my skin. Before I can say or do anything, she turns and walks back toward my bedroom. I'm still watching her swaying ass as the ringer stops. Then starts again. My bedroom's going to keep smelling like her...

I'm surprised by the little voice in my head that says, *Good*.

I check my phone and am annoyed to discover it's a video call, and even more annoyed to see Lilah's in a sparkly red dress, calling me from a restaurant. I answer the call as I head over to the couch and lower down.

"Is Ollie awake?" she asks.

"No. It's past ten."

"Tell him I'm sorry I missed him," she says, but she doesn't look particularly surprised or sorry. "But I actually need to speak with *you*."

"Oh?"

She plays with a strand of her hair, drawing this out. "Someone sent Roland a glitter bomb and some other unwanted deliveries, and he thinks *I'm* behind it."

I hear a stifled laugh and glance back to see Hannah standing in the threshold leading to the back end of the house. I do a double take at the sight of her. She has swapped the soaked T-shirt for one of my Garbage Fire T-shirts.

Does she know what she's doing to me?

Probably.

I'll bet she likes it too. Not in the way Lilah would—because a man's desire gives her power—but because she loves to tease and laugh.

"Travis?" Lilah says shrilly, recapturing my attention. "Were you behind this?"

"Are you seriously asking me if I sent your husband a glitter bomb?" I ask, sounding pretty convincing, if I do say so myself. "Does that sound like something I would do?"

There are other things I'd like to say to her, an ocean's worth of anger I'd love to unleash, but I don't need more drama with her. The only thing I want from her is her continued absence. She's already been gone for six weeks. Only two and a half more, and she'll meet the state's threshold for child abandonment. So I don't want to do or say anything that's going to piss her off enough that she decides to end her little hiatus early and try to take Ollie away to spite me.

She narrows her gaze on me. "Is that *glitter* on your clothes?"

A strangled sound issues from behind the couch, but I manage to keep a straight face. "It's from a school project I helped our son with."

"Oh." Emotion flits across her face. I'd like to believe it's guilt, but after everything she's done, I doubt it. "Well...I'm sure Roland pissed someone else off. Of course he wants to blame me for it. Anyway. I also wanted to tell you that I'm going to be traveling through an area with some spotty reception. So you probably won't hear from me for another couple of weeks. Maybe three."

As if that would be any different from her usual calling schedule.

"Okay," I say, ready to end the conversation. "I'll tell Ollie."

She smiles. "And I'm going to send some photos from this koala sanctuary I went to. He'll love them. I got him a stuffie too, even though it takes up a lot of space in my bag."

My rage spikes, and I want to tell her to go fuck herself or say something about koalas having chlamydia, so hey, they have something in common with her, because she gave it to me eight years ago...

Instead, I smile, squeezing the phone, and say tightly, "Great. Have a nice trip."

Then I hang up and throw the phone so hard it bounces off the rug and slams into the wooden flooring beyond it, probably spiderwebbing the screen. I run my hands through my hair, dark emotion pounding through me.

A warm hand descends on my shoulder, squeezing, and I smell her. My animal side recognizes Hannah. The beast in me feels desperate to pin her to the wall and claim her. To sink my emotions into something that feels good.

"I've tried not to hate her," I say in a low, thick voice. "But I fucking *hate* her. I don't want anything bad to happen to her, but I wish she'd never come back."

"Go play for a few minutes," she says softly, her hand massaging my shoulder. "Get some of it out."

"I'll wake him up if I do that."

"If he wakes up, I'll put him back to bed. Go play."

I suck in a deep breath full of her scent and then let it out slowly, hissing like a punctured tire. "Thank you."

Then I head into the music room, and I play, hitting harder than I should, letting all of my anger stream into music—not one of our Garbage Fire songs, but a long freestyle solo that says what I'm feeling. The anger. The shame. The feeling of being so lost, I don't even know what map I should be looking for. The deep well of need that's a black hole inside of me.

When I finish, my hands hurt, and I look up to find her standing in the open doorway, her lips parted. I don't know how long she's been there.

I set my sticks down. "Hannah," I say in a low voice. "I'm not trying to be a dick right now, but you should probably leave. I'm struggling tonight."

She steps into the room. "I thought we were almost friends. Friends help each other."

I rise from my chair and take a step back, feeling too big for the space suddenly. "Right now, I'm not interested in being your friend, or being professional. I want..." Damn. How do I say this without making it awkward? I guess there's no way. "I want things I have no business wanting, and it would be better if you just left until I regain control over myself."

"You want to fuck me?" She sounds almost surprised by it, which is a joke, because I assume most men want her, although I might be the only one who's made a practice of counting her freckles.

"Can't you tell?"

"I didn't think I was your type," she says, putting a hand on her hip. "I don't look anything like Lilah."

"Thank God."

She smiles but adds, "Lilah's gorgeous."

"So are you," I say, frustrated, not wanting to hear their names in the same sentence or even the same paragraph. "Look, Lilah's the one who pursued me in the beginning, not the other way around. I got caught up in the current, but she wasn't what I wanted. I'm working through some things right now, and I'm not in a position to date anyone. But, yeah, I'm attracted to you. *Very* attracted. And it's been..." I pull my hair, hoping the pain will give me the jolt I need. "It's been a while since I've been with anyone, so it's getting harder to ignore it."

She pads farther into the room, wearing that shirt that's mine, her pupils dilated. Her curls sway as if they're dancing. "So you've wondered what it would feel like between us?"

She says it as if it's been a casual thing for me, no different from wondering about the weather, or what the specials are at a favorite restaurant.

"*Yes*," I admit, my voice practically shaking. "But you should go. This is a line we can't cross."

But even as I'm telling her to go, I take a few steps toward her. I stop in front of her, wanting her to walk away. Also wanting her to reach for me.

"Probably not." She tips up slightly on her toes, bringing her lips closer, more kissable. So tempting I feel myself leaning in just the slightest bit more, my body vetoing my brain.

"I've wondered too," she says. "I love watching you play. You put your whole body into it. It's...fascinating."

My dick is rock-hard, and I'm struggling to hang on to sanity. "We can't."

"But don't you think we should at least know what we're missing?"

That'll only make it worse, *so much worse*. But playing didn't release all of the emotions boiling inside of me. Most of the rage Lilah awakened has slipped away, but not the need.

"Maybe just one kiss," I say, my voice hoarse.

"Only one," she agrees.

"A *French* kiss?" I ask, surprised I still have the capacity to make a joke.

She laughs in surprise, and that's the moment I lower my mouth the rest of the way to hers, my whole body thrumming with the strength of my desire for her. My mouth brushes against hers, tentatively at first. Then she parts her lips to welcome me in, and it's like something else takes over.

Our mouths move together, clashing almost violently, all tongues and teeth and desire. The next second I'm backing her into the wall of the music room. She tastes like wild honey, and even though it feels like there's a risk of being stung, I can't get enough.

My need for her eclipses everything.

It sure as hell eclipses what's left of my sense. So much for the single sip of sin we promised ourselves. All I can think about is getting closer, getting more. I lift her up so I have better access, and she wraps her legs around my waist, her thighs surprisingly strong, which has me pulling her closer. Taking more of her. She buries her hand in my hair, pulling, and kisses me as fiercely as I'm kissing her.

I break away, but only so I can kiss down the side of her jaw and neck, which tastes of sugar from the soda. A sigh eases out of me as she grips my hair tightly.

I push closer, and she's got to feel my dick as she presses into me with a breathy little sound that I swallow. I want that sound to be mine. In that moment, I want everything about her to be mine.

Then I hear a shaky little voice out in the hallway, audible because we didn't even close the door all the way.

"Hannah? Travis?"

I jerk back reflexively and set Hannah down on her feet. What in the ever-loving hell am I doing?

Hannah is here for Ollie. She's the only one who has the slightest clue what she's doing with him, even if her methods are unconventional. I can't take one more thing away from my son, not when he has a mother who thinks the only thing he needs from her is a dumb souvenir.

My horror must be written on my face, because Hannah gently traces her fingers down my cheek, mouthing, *It's okay*.

It's not, but I appreciate the sentiment.

She brushes her fingers through my hair, fixing it, and calls out, "Ollie, we're here in the music room. I was just listening to your dad practice before I head home."

She collects herself well enough to swing the door wide. Ollie's standing quietly in the hall, so small my heart breaks at the sight of him. His hair is mussed from sleep, and he's wearing pajamas with penguins on them.

"I couldn't find anyone," he says, his voice hitching. "I thought you were gone."

I'm shocked that he says this while looking at me. He was worried *I* was gone—that I'd left him like they did.

Emotion clogs my throat as I span the distance between us. "I will never willingly leave you," I say, stooping to hug him. "You're stuck with me."

To my surprise, he hugs me back. The backs of my eyes heat as I pull back enough to meet his gaze. "Hannah told me about your iPad."

He gives her a look of such complete betrayal, I can only laugh.

She lifts her hands, palms out, in the universal *I come in peace* gesture. "Your dad's like the grand inquisitor. I didn't have any hope of holding out."

"I don't know what that means," he says gruffly, his bottom lip pushed out, "but I'm mad at you."

"It's okay," I say, smoothing his hair. "I wish you'd told me directly, but if you want this gaming thing, or whatever, I'll get it for you. Me. You don't need to depend on that guy for anything. I don't want you to."

He looks up at me in surprise. "But you said screens aren't good for me."

"There will be limits, obviously. But I want you to be happy here, Ollie. I want you here."

He studies me for a long moment, his brow furrowing. "Travis, did you open the glitter bomb?"

His gaze darts to Hannah.

"Did he—" He pauses, staring at her with narrowed eyes. "Why are you covered in glitter too? And you're wearing Travis's garbage shirt."

It's not really funny, but I'll be damned if I don't laugh.

CHAPTER TWELVE

HANNAH

"I spilled soda on my shirt," I tell Ollie, my heart still racing, very aware of Travis standing inches away from me. "So your dad let me borrow one, and the glitter got all over *everything*, not just us."

"Really?" Ollie says, perking up. "Was it rainbow glitter?"

"Yes. And you and I are going to clean it up tomorrow afternoon. I promised your dad."

I can practically feel Travis rolling his eyes at me, because there's no way that man will leave all this glitter sitting around in his living room until I report to work. But when I glance at him, he's watching me in a different way, and I have to break our stare-off.

He looks...*hungry*. He's wild tonight—Travis the drummer, not Travis the domesticated single dad—and my body wants more of him. No one's kissed me like that for a very long time. Maybe ever. And I could feel him against me when he backed me into that wall, so hard and needy and big. But I know without asking that he regrets what happened. He's obviously going to tell me it can never happen again. Knowing him, he'll even apologize.

Which sucks, but it's probably for the best.

I made promises, too, after all.

Ollie says something I don't register, then shakes my arm. "Hannah, can I see the glitter?"

"No, Ollie," Travis says. "It's getting late. Hannah's probably ready to go home."

I dart an annoyed look at him. I don't want Ollie to think I'm in a hurry to get away from him.

"No," I insist. "In fact, why don't you go ahead and shower that glitter off, Travis. I'll get Ollie to bed, and then we can catch up. There are a few things I wanted to talk about."

Travis gives me a hangdog look, as if he thinks I'm going to beat him over the head for daring to kiss me, even though I basically threw myself at him.

"About Ollie's school," I add. "I would have mentioned it earlier if not for..." I make a sweeping gesture to indicate the glitter bomb, the call with Lilah, and the kiss. Although to call it a kiss would be doing it a disservice. He ravaged me with his mouth. Undid me with his lips. Rewrote desire with his tongue. He...

Travis runs a hand through his hair, a few flecks of glitter flying off. He forces a smile and nods. "Yeah, sure. That would be great."

I lead Ollie out, leaving Travis in the music room, and smile as I notice a trail of glitter leading back toward the living room.

"It's like in Hansel and Gretel," I say, pointing it out to Ollie.

"What do you want to talk to Travis about?" he asks, giving me a sidelong look. "Are you going to tell him I got in trouble for calling Mickey the s-word?"

"What's the s-word, anyway? I meant to ask you earlier."

"Stupid," he says warily like he thinks I might fly off the handle.

I almost laugh. I'd figured he'd called him a shithead or something, especially since his teacher, Mrs. Applebottom, had made such a stink about it when I picked him up earlier. Which is something I *do* need to talk to Travis about, because it seems like this feud with Mickey should probably be addressed sooner rather than later. Ollie is also bored and under stimulated by school, but I know that's something Travis has been working on with Mrs. Applebottom.

I force myself to look stern. "We shouldn't call people stupid, even if they are. They tend not to respond well."

"Yeah, you're probably right. But if you tell Travis, make sure you mention Mickey called me a sewer rat first."

"It'll be more of a general conversation," I say, wrapping an arm around his shoulders.

I steer him into his room, but he still seems wide awake after he climbs into bed.

"Want me to sit with you for a minute?" I ask.

"Yeah, can you rub my back?"

My heart swells as I settle in beside him and start rubbing his little back. I start humming and then singing, and when his breathing evens out, I kiss the side of his head and leave the room.

Travis's bedroom door is open a crack, so I stop beside it. I hear the pattering of water in his shower.

An aching awareness settles between my legs. He's in there naked. The water is pounding down on him, his body bared to the tiles and shower stall. Will he touch himself after what we did in the music room? Is he running his hand over himself right now, thinking about me?

I stand in the doorway, well aware that I should go sit in the living room like a normal person, but not quite able to move.

Then the shower switches off, and I still don't move. I'm waiting. For what, I don't know...until it happens.

Travis opens the door and leaves the bathroom with a towel tied around his waist, revealing the vee of muscles leading down to an area I've grown very curious about.

His hair is a wet tumble, his eyes dark and determined—until they land on me.

For a long moment, we just stare at each other, and then he straightens. In a voice that's full of authority, even though he's wearing nothing but a towel, he says, "You can wait for me in the living room, Hannah."

I raise my eyebrows. "Yes, *sir.*"

The dark look on his face says he doesn't appreciate me flirting with him right now. Fair enough. I'm teasing myself too.

I return to the living room, which is infested with glitter. The vacuum would risk waking Ollie again, but I feel a little guilty about the joke now, so I grab the broom from the kitchen to sweep up the worst of it.

I'm about to load up a second dustpan with glitter when I hear Travis emerging from the back hall. He approaches me and gently removes the broom from my hands. I take in his damp, toweled-off hair, the fresh smell of him, and the T-shirt he has on, which matches mine.

"I was trying to help," I say, suddenly feeling short of breath.

"Please don't feel like you need to help with any of the housework." He smiles at me, but his eyes are dark and unreadable.

"Something tells me you're not saying that because you value and respect me so much as a nanny."

"You're pushing the glitter into the rug," he says, "but yes, I do value and respect you. Even though I will absolutely lose it if you bring another glitter bomb into this house. Actually, I'm instituting a no-glitter-ever-for-any-reason rule."

"That's fair."

He props the broom against the coffee table and gestures to the sofa. "Let's sit for a minute."

I sit first, and I notice he settles onto the other end of the sofa—a far cry from the other night when we were snuggled under that blanket together.

He gives me a long look and then says, "I'm sorry, Hannah. That was beyond inappropriate. I don't know what got into me. I'd understand if you don't want to work here anymore, but I'm begging you to stay. Ollie needs you."

I scoff, "*I* know what got into you. It got into me too. And I don't regret kissing you. It was good."

"It was better than good," he says darkly, as if he resents that truth. "But it can't happen again. I've taken enough from my son."

I'm tempted to press him on that. He hasn't taken anything from Ollie. If anything, he hasn't given Ollie enough of himself. So much of Travis is tucked away, hidden in a lockbox no one's given access to, Ollie included. But I know he wouldn't appreciate it if I told him that.

Instead, I say, "You're right. It shouldn't happen again. Because of Ollie, and also because you and Rob are friends. I won't let things get weird with Sophie."

He surprises me by smiling, although there's a sharp edge to it. "If you can get over the fact that you both slept with that dumbass Jonah, then you could probably get over anything."

"Does it bother you that I slept with Rob's brother?" I ask with interest.

"I just don't like him," he says. "I've never liked him. He's a little shithead."

The firm set to his jaw suggests otherwise. He *is* jealous, and I *like* that he's jealous, which isn't usual for me. But I can tell his emotions are already like a poorly bandaged scab, so I'm not going to pick at them any more tonight.

"You can't go into my room anymore," he says. "We need to set that boundary."

I lift my eyebrows. "Okay, boss man. You *did* leave the door open. I thought you wanted me to see you in that towel, and I can't say I minded. You must work hard for those muscles. It would be a pity not to let people see them."

"Hannah," he groans. "You're killing me." He rakes his hands through his hair, looking like he means what he's saying.

"I really did want to talk about Ollie's school stuff," I say.

He nods, and I launch into the whole s-word, sewer rat story. I finish by saying, "So we should probably do something about this situation before they get into some kind of kiddie cage match."

"I know," he says. "I'm bringing donuts to Ollie's classroom on Friday morning. When I asked Mrs. Applebaum, she acted like I'd suggested bringing crack cocaine for them to share before morning circle." He twists his mouth to the side. "I don't think she likes any of us. She refers to you as 'the young lady' in a disapproving tone."

"Wait. Her last name's Applebaum?" I ask, laughing. "I've been calling her Mrs. Applebottom since she asked to speak to me last Tuesday. No wonder she hates us."

The school has pickup and drop-off in the auditorium, but Ollie's teacher has asked to talk to me a couple of times after some "unfortunate incidents."

He laughs, and some of the tension seems to lift from his shoulders. "You know, she actually reminds me of the nanny I had growing up."

"Oh, you poor thing."

His lips tip into a smile. "Nanny Grace used to say 'back in my day' every five words. And whenever I talked back, she rapped my knuckles with a wood ruler. I don't even know where she found it."

"This is explaining a lot," I joke.

"I guess so," he says, his expression falling a bit. "But her nephew's the one who taught me to play the drums, so I'll give her a pass. I just wish Ollie had a teacher who valued his strengths more."

"He has us," I say tightly, wanting to push closer on the couch but knowing it's not a good idea right now. "And donuts are a smart move, *Mr. Thomas*—" I bite back a grin as he shakes his head with mock dismay. "But I'm surprised you didn't opt for something healthy like bran muffins."

"You make me sound like a constipated old man." He pauses. "Speaking of constipated old men, have you talked to Eugene? I keep forgetting to ask."

"I did," I say, beaming. "I'm meeting him for breakfast at the tea shop on Friday morning. He sounds like a complete psychopath, so I have high hopes for our meeting."

"I have no doubt he'll come away from it a changed man."

We laugh and then lapse into a heavy silence.

It's probably time to leave. I glitter-bombed my boss, then kissed him, then nearly walked in on him naked. That's a solid day's work for any nanny, but I don't want to go. It feels like something precious will slip away from us when I leave.

"I'm sorry about the glitter bomb," I finally say.

He actually laughs, the corners of his eyes creasing. "No you're not. I saw the look on your face when it happened."

"It was hilarious to watch, I'm not going to lie. But I'm sorry the room's a mess, and that I'm terrible at cleaning it."

"That's okay." He glances around the room, as if taking in a disaster area, then says, "Maybe you can make up for it by going shopping for Ollie with me. I still don't have enough kids' stuff around here."

"You want to go shopping?" I ask, delighted.

"Yes, if I had the slightest idea of what to get, I would have already done it."

"*The Single Dad's Handbook* hasn't been helpful?"

A wry expression twists his mouth. "Had a look around while I was in the shower, did you?"

I don't want to admit I'd been in his room before, so I shrug and say, "People's bedrooms say a lot about them."

He shifts a little closer, cutting the distance between us by a few inches. "What does mine say about me?"

I grin at him. "That you need someone to remind you how to have fun."

"And what would your bedroom say about you?" he asks.

"That I need someone to remind me to pay my bills and go through the mail."

"So we have opposite problems," he says thoughtfully. "Maybe I can organize your apartment and you can have fun for me."

I reach over and shove his arm. "You may be good at playing the drums, but you're terrible at making bargains."

"I don't know about that. There's a certain joy to finding order in chaos. That's what playing the drums is all about, riding the line between the two and hoping you don't crash out."

"And you like that?"

"I love it. I'd live in that place if I could. It's the only place I've ever felt totally at peace."

"You don't look like you're at peace when you're playing. You look like you're fighting. Especially tonight."

He pauses, and for a second I'm sure he's going to end the conversation, which has probably been skirting the nanny-boss line we already jumped across once today. But then he says, "It's like I'm unleashing something. Rob calls it the beast. It feels good. Necessary. But it didn't totally work tonight. Obviously."

A pulse of awareness flares through me, but I shut it down,

nodding. "My brother's a boxer. Liam's most at peace when he's smashing someone's face in."

"And you?"

Suddenly, I realize the distance between us has been eliminated. There was a foot, then eight inches, and now there's nothing. Our legs are pressed together in a seam of heat.

"I get involved in other people's business, obviously. Being nosy is my superpower." I hesitate, then figure I might as well go for broke and add, "Which is why I'm going to say you should share your music with Ollie. Show him what you love, and teach him how to play. Give him something real. It's pretty obvious Lilah and Roland never did."

His expression shifts, the lightness drifting away. But he doesn't seem pissed exactly. "Yeah, maybe."

A kiss-off if I've ever heard one.

"My dad didn't know what to do with us after my mom left," I push. "But one of his buddies said to share what he loved, so Dad taught us to brew beer. Now look at Liam. He made beer for the first time when he was ten."

He gives me a pointed look. "This should go without saying, but no teaching Ollie to brew beer."

"Yeah, yeah, *Mr. Sir Thomas*. I know. But that's not why I told you the story. Liam didn't *drink* the beer. It was about doing something together. 'Sharing is caring' is a cliché for a reason."

"I'll give it some thought."

I'm tempted to tell him to do it quickly, so he can hurry along to the conclusion that I'm right, but I'm wise enough to know that tactic would never work for either of us.

I sigh heavily, then ask, "What was Lilah like when you dated?"

He looks off in the distance. "She was wild. Fun. All in for going on tour with the band I was playing with at the time. We were only together for a month, maybe, before she found a better option. Roland came to our show in Nashville, and he invited us all to his house for drinks afterward. It was this huge mansion with a full staff. Lilah climbed onto his lap half an hour in, then told me she was staying."

"What a bitch."

He shrugs. "I felt pretty low about it for a while." He smiles self-deprecatingly. "Okay, really low. I was young and stupid and thought it was love. Drank myself stupid. But the next city we stopped in was Asheville. I went to a karaoke bar with one of the other guys on the tour, and I met Rob. This was before he got sober. He was drunk off his ass that night, but it didn't matter. When he sang, everyone in the bar stopped what they were doing to listen. He had this...star power, I guess you'd call it. We clicked, and I knew we could build something together. The rest is history. It didn't take long for me to see Lilah leaving as a good thing."

"Because if she went for the old guy's money, she definitely would have gone for yours."

He sighs. "I didn't have any back then. My dad and I hadn't talked for years, but he died not long after I left the tour. He left me some money, yeah. Enough to get us started with The Missing Beat and for me to buy this house and have a good chunk left over to invest. But it's not as much as Lilah would think. About half his fortune went to establishing a *Ships Ahoy* museum in Upstate New York that no one goes to."

No shit.

"Can the three of us go sometime?"

He smiles. "Absolutely not. I'd rather set off fifty glitter bombs."

"So you don't want Lilah finding out who your dad is."

"Not before she's been gone sixty days," he says, glancing back to make sure Ollie's not listening in. His gaze has taken on an intensity, a depth of purpose, that makes his eyes look like black holes. "My lawyer says we'll have a good case for child abandonment if I can prove she left him here that long."

"You have a lawyer?"

"I hired one to get emergency temporary custody as soon as she left him here. He's a hard-ass, and he's got a kid of his own, so he gets it."

My heart swells. Travis might think he doesn't know how to be a father, but he's already making important moves to take care of Ollie. I reach for his hand, and he gives it to me. Instead of holding it, I trace his fingers, letting my touch linger on his calluses. "I understand why you hate Lilah. It must drive you crazy to know Ollie was in Nashville all that time, and you had no idea."

"I'll never get that time back," he says darkly. "I'll never see him as a baby. I don't even know what his first words were."

My fingers tighten around his hand as he speaks, and for a moment the heaviness of his loss is a weight in my own chest.

He releases a tired sigh. "And he thinks I abandoned him. He'll never forgive me for not knowing about him."

"We'll see about that."

He smiles at me, and suddenly I'm hyperaware that I'm still holding his hand, cradled in my lap like a promise. "Are you going to defend me, Hannah?"

"No, but I might want to hold your hand to guide you through single fatherhood."

"Like this?" he asks, weaving his fingers through mine.

"What strong, rough hands you have, Travis," I say, rubbing my thumb across his palm. "They don't fit this whole gentle-man-about-town air you usually have going for you. Neither does the way you play."

"I'm glad you think I have something going for me."

"You *know* you do," I say. "And even though it's probably

inappropriate to say so, you kiss like a man who wants to make it his life's greatest achievement."

He leans in closer, and I'm sure he's going to vault across that line and kiss me again. Right now, there's nothing I want more than to feel his lips and hands on me. But then I think about that scared little boy I just sung to sleep, and I'm the one who pulls back.

Even though I know it would be good with Travis—mind-blowingly good—I don't know what would come next. What I do know is that Ollie doesn't need any more complications in his life. None of us do, really.

Clearing my throat, I say, "I'll see you tomorrow."

"You're leaving?"

"Yeah." I nudge him with my arm. "I don't have the best self-control tonight either, so I think I'd better go home and get out my little silicone friend."

"Come on," he groans. "This is hard enough."

I reach over and trace his birthmark with my finger. "It can *always* get harder, Travis."

Then I kiss him on the cheek and make my exit, stepping over the glitter mess.

"I actually don't think it could get any harder," he calls after me.

I smile, but I don't let myself look back.

CHAPTER THIRTEEN

TRAVIS

After Hannah leaves, I sit on the couch for a long time, watching the door. Remembering how good she felt against me —how right.

I'd take a cold shower to forget it, but the knowledge of what she feels like isn't something a cold shower can cure. It's in my bones. In the flesh that's aching for her.

I grab one of the beers she left in the fridge last week and sit back down, sighing. Trying to decide if I want to jerk off or if that would only make me feel worse.

Worse.

Definitely worse.

So instead, I do something that's rare for me. I grab a pencil and a pad and sit down and write a song. I consider sending it to Rob when I'm finished, but I hold back. I knew Rob was crazy about Sophie because of the music he was writing. Each song was like falling in love.

If he knew I was writing again, something I haven't done for years, he'd know I'm having feelings about Hannah that no man should have for his nanny. That's not something I'm ready to admit. For one thing, Ollie needs her. If I mess things up and she decides she can't be around me—or Ollie—anymore, he'd never forgive me, and I'd never forgive myself. For another, I'm in no place to start something with a woman. I'm still trying to find a balance with Ollie, and for all I know, I might end up in an ugly court battle with Lilah.

I don't sleep much. In the morning, I get up early and spend at least an hour vacuuming the house to try to suck up all the glitter.

"There's still a lot of glitter around," Ollie observes as he eats his whole wheat toast at the breakfast table.

"It'll probably be around rest of our lives," I say with a sigh.

"That's okay," he says, munching on his toast. "I like glitter."

His innocence makes me smile. Then it hits me that I should probably tell him something about Lilah, and the smile drops like a stone. "Your mom called last night."

"After I was in bed?" he asks through a mouthful of toast.

"Yeah. She was sorry to miss you. Sounds like she's heading to a part of the country that doesn't get much cell service. So she's not sure when she'll be able to call again."

He sets the toast down. "Oh."

"She sent some photos of koalas," I say with forced cheer. "Do you want to see them?"

"No, I don't think so. I'm not really hungry anymore. Do I have to finish this?"

"No," I say, feeling another wave of fury on his behalf. "Maybe we can go to the zoo or something this weekend. See some real koalas."

"I don't really care about koalas," he says seriously. "Hey, Hannah said if it's okay with you, Sophie and Briar might come over during your concert on Saturday so we can have a spa day party. She got a box of animal face masks and everything. Can we do it?"

"Yeah, buddy," I say, still feeling heated. "Save me a face mask, will you?"

"Do you want a koala mask? You seem to really like them."

I can't decide whether he's messing with me, but given how much time he's been spending with Hannah, all signs point to yes.

The day passes in an exhausted blur, and by the time our last kid gets picked up from The Missing Beat, Rob has asked me at least three times what's wrong with me. Probably because I snapped at two of our students, a pair of twins, when they swapped places to trick us—a game they still think is hilarious after doing it a hundred times.

I get him off my back by telling him that I had a video chat with Lilah last night and she accused me of some crazy shit.

Rob lifts his hands. "Say no more."

Which is a convenient invitation because I have no interest in telling him why I'm really on edge. The truth is, my mood has very little to do with Lilah. It's the natural consequence of knowing Hannah wants me to touch her but not being able to do anything about it.

When I get back home from The Missing Beat, Hannah and Ollie are playing a complicated tag game where they spray water at each other. I'm obviously not a player, but that doesn't prevent them from joining forces and spraying me with their water bottles at the same time, forming two enormous wet spots on my shirt.

"I look like I'm lactating," I say with a sigh.

Hannah laughs so hard her nose wrinkles.

"Are you going to stay for dinner, Hannah?" Ollie asks, jumping up and down with his spray bottle still in his hand. "Thursday is Chinese takeout."

She gives a surprised laugh, seeking out my gaze with those

dancing eyes of hers, and I know it's at my expense. "Each day of the week has an assigned meal?"

"There's nothing weird about meal planning. Lots of people meal-plan."

"I'll stay if we don't have Chinese," she says, waggling her brows. "What do you say, Travis? Want to live dangerously?"

Not really. I was looking forward to Kung Pao chicken, but I want her to stay, God help me, even if it would be smarter to avoid her. "What'll we have instead?"

"I'm going to make dinner."

"I'll just go get the fire extinguisher," I say, taking a step toward my room.

She shoves a hand at my arm, her fingers curling around it for just a second before she pulls away. We exchange a loaded look.

"We could all cook together?" I suggest.

"Really?" Ollie says, more excited than I thought he'd be. "You'll let me use a knife?"

"Absolutely not," I say. "But you can rinse off the vegetables."

"And what will we be making with those vegetables, pray tell?" Hannah asks.

I grin at her. "Stir-fry."

She pokes me in the chest, her touch sending a sizzle through me. "You, *Mr. Sir*, are a hopeless case."

Probably for the best if she thinks so, but I'll be damned if it isn't fun cooking together. With all three of us crowding the kitchen, it feels lived-in. This big house is a home in a way it never was with just me and my drum kit.

We sit down to dinner. Ollie's way more talkative than he ever is when it's just the two of us, and tells us all about Mickey's latest crimes and the evaluation tests Mrs. Applebaum's been giving him. He's not a fan of those, but he is excited about bringing the donuts to class tomorrow.

After we eat, Hannah and I deal with the dishes while Ollie reads in his room.

"You know he's probably playing on his iPad in there," she says as she hands me the last fork to put in the dishwasher.

I shrug. "Maybe. Let's let him feel like he's getting away with something. I always make sure it's out of his room at night."

"Good thinking. I'd better head home. I promised Briar I'd watch *Matchmaking Small Town America* with her."

"The French kissing show?" I ask, shutting the dishwasher so I have something to do with my hands.

"Yes." She grins. "You must have really enjoyed that part. You've mentioned it twice now."

I glance at the exit to the back hallway, and seeing no signs of Ollie, I say in an undertone, "No, I just liked the kissing part."

"I'll let you watch it with me sometime if you're lucky."

"Then I'll be sure to never get lucky."

She laughs, her eyes dancing with humor. "Why don't you circle back and consider what you just said there."

"I'm going to pretend I did it on purpose to make you laugh."

She smiles and surprises me by leaning in for a hug. I hug her back tentatively, drawing in her scent, and she whispers in my ear, "Good luck with the donuts tomorrow."

I pull back with an impressive force of will. "Thanks. I'm pretty sure I'll need it. This morning Mrs. Applebottom—Jesus, you've got me doing it. Anyway, she told me that I have very interesting parenting methods." I pause. "I'm going to want to hear all about your meeting with Eugene, obviously."

She smiles at me. "I was hoping you'd say that. Text me when you're ready to go shopping."

Look at that. She just gave me permission to text her socially again. Something tells me I'll be abusing that.

ON FRIDAY MORNING, Ollie and I pick up the goods at Vortex Donuts, and I drive him to school, the sweet scent filling the car. When I park in the lot, he stays put, gazing out of the window.

"Actually, this might be a bad idea, Travis. It's probably only going to make things worse with Mickey. What if he hates donuts?"

"It'll be great. Even if he hates donuts, this little Mickey—" I swallow the word *asshole*, "—kid will realize you've got people in your court." I pause. "What's he look like anyway?"

"He has brown hair, and he wears a lot of T-shirts."

"So he looks like you."

He glowers at me. "That's not very nice, Travis."

I lift my hands. "Sorry. I'm just not getting a good mental picture."

"How about I say a code word when I see him? They do that on that show *Odd Squad*."

"Okay, what about..." My mind's sluggish, but I plug in Mickey and it comes up with, "Mouse."

He nods. "Okay." Then he glances at me, taking in my button-down shirt and jeans. "You don't look very tough. You should have worn one of your band T-shirts."

"Excuse me if I didn't want to come into your classroom wearing a shirt that says 'Garbage Fire.'"

"Maybe your old leather jacket, then. It makes you look like you have big arms."

"I *do* have big arms, but it's not like I'm going to beat this kid up, Ollie," I say, frustrated. "He's seven years old."

"Would you beat him up if he were eighteen?"

"If an eighteen-year-old were following you around and messing with you? Yeah, he'd definitely regret it."

"Really?" he asks, sounding excited about the prospect. "What would you do to him?"

I tap the wheel with two fingers, hesitating, then turn off the ignition. "You don't need to physically intimidate people to get them to leave you alone. You're smarter than this kid is. Intelligence is a strength."

He gives a world-weary sigh. "My mom told me people don't really like you when you're smart."

"Other smart people do," I say tightly.

I can practically hear Hannah saying, *and what would you want with stupid friends anyway?*

The thought would probably have made me smile if I weren't so pissed at Lilah. How dare she make Ollie feel like being smart is something to be ashamed of?

Ollie sighs again. "Okay, let's get this over with."

"*Everyone* likes donuts," I say, making eye contact in the rearview mirror and holding it. "You'll be the class hero." Because I'm weak, I add, "You know, Hannah thinks this is a good idea too."

"Really?" he asks, leaning forward to look at me from his booster seat in the back. "I wish she were coming."

It feels a bit shitty hearing him say that. Clearly he thinks coming through those doors with Hannah and the donuts would gain him more social currency than going with me. But I can't deny he's probably right. She'd step through those doors and within five minutes she'd be friends with the custodian, half the kids, most of the teachers, and maybe even sour-faced Mrs.

Applebaum. Hannah has a gift for drawing people in. For dazzling them.

If I'd had that same gift, maybe I'd have wanted to be the front man instead of the drummer.

Maybe my son would be more impressed by me.

"I wish she were here too, bud," I admit.

We leave the car together, the bribery donuts in hand, and enter the school. The building's neither new nor old, with whitewashed walls and the slight unwashed funk all schools seem to have. Some of the teachers give us wistful looks as we pass them, and Ollie seems to notice. I can tell from the new pep in his steps that he's realizing the donuts are their own form of gold.

We step into his classroom and are immediately mobbed by kids and questions—

"Are those donuts?" one kid asks.

"Is this your dad?" another wants to know.

I feel Ollie looking at me, and I prepare myself for another long explanation like the one he gave the clerk at the bookstore a couple of weeks ago. *Biologically, but we barely know each other. I thought someone else was my dad up until a couple of months ago.*

But he nods, his eyes still on me. "Yeah, he's the drummer in a band."

My heart swells and feels stretched.

Mrs. Applebaum, who was waiting behind her desk at the front of the class, heaves a heavy sigh to let me know I'm inconveniencing her. She's a stout woman who could be sixty or six hundred. She has a rounded ageless face but iron gray hair bound into a low, tight bun and a pair of spectacles so small it's impossible they could actually improve her eyesight. Her sweater, covered in little knit pumpkins, is the only cheerful thing about her.

I privately suspect she chose those glasses just so she could deliver that perfect withering stare. She's doing it now, and I smile broadly at her, pretending I don't notice.

"You might as well set them down on my desk," she grouses. "Children. Line up if you'd like one of these don—"

But the box is already being attacked. Two children go for the same donut at the same time, ripping it in half, and then get into an argument about it, even though there are plenty of other whole donuts.

I glance at Mrs. Applebaum, who studies me with another of her masterful withering stares.

"Thank you, Mr. Thomas. What a *treat*."

"Travis," Ollie whispers in a very audible undertone, standing behind the two kids who are each holding half of a mangled donut, glaring at each other.

When I turn to look at him, he says, "Mouse" pointedly, nodding at one of the kids, a dark-haired boy wearing a T-shirt.

As soon as the boy—presumably Mickey—hears the word "mouse," he shrieks.

CHAPTER FOURTEEN

HANNAH

To be totally straightforward, I've been having trouble sleeping.

I can't stop thinking about Travis. He told me he loves drumming because he likes riding the line between control and chaos, and that basically *is* him. So super self-controlled that each weeknight has a specific dinner and his laundry is always done immediately after his bin is full. So chaotic that he can play like he did the other night, like his soul would leak out of his body if he stopped. And the way he kissed me...

I can't stop thinking about how it felt to be his complete focus, if only for a few minutes.

Lust isn't the problem though. I *like* him. My whole body reacts whenever I hear him opening the door to his house, like I'm one of Pavlov's dogs.

I positively live to tease him, but also to make him smile.

It's disconcerting, because I've never felt like this before with anyone I've dated, and Travis is supposed to be my boss. Obviously he's more than that, but I wouldn't exactly call him a friend. I don't want to fuck my friends.

Shaking off all thoughts of Travis, I head into Tea of

Fortune five minutes early to meet the one and only Eugene Peebles.

I feel like patting myself on the back for getting the jump on Eugene, especially since I'm more of an accidentally-five-minutes-late kind of woman. But when I walk in, he's already there, sitting solemnly at the table in the back where Travis and the band sat a couple of weeks ago.

How do I know it's him?

Every bit of him screams the name Eugene. He's got these double-bridge glasses and a bushy but entirely unhip mustache, plus a dishwater-gray button-up shirt. Honestly, his parents knew what they were doing when they named him.

And, sure, I *might* have looked up his photo and asked a few Big Catch staffers some questions about him.

Dottie, who's sitting at one of the tables at the front with her friends—Ann, Constance, and Sophie's Aunt Penny—practically leaps out of her chair when she sees me. Since she's way past retirement age, Dottie treats the café as more of a gathering place than a job and only works when she feels like it.

"I thought your Wise Women Group only met on Wednesdays and Saturdays," I say, giving them a wave.

"Usually," she says, "but Ann asked for an emergency session so she could show us her rash."

"Shouldn't she go to a doctor?"

"Oh no, I had just the salve for her. Your friend Eugene is sitting in the back already, dear, but I wanted to have a word with you. That poor man's aura is *very* gray."

"You know, I actually believe that," I say as we meander toward his table, walking past other groups sipping tea.

Dottie places her hand on my arm, gently stopping me on the plush rug.

"Do you understand what I mean by that, dear?" she asks,

fully aware I'm not much of a believer in her favorite things—i.e., auras, crystals, and luck.

"That he's boring?"

She shakes her head, her lips pursed. "No aura is boring. Gray is actually *very* interesting." Her eyes pierce into me. "Yours has some shades of gray."

"A morally gray aura." I grin at her. "That's kind of cool."

"It means sadness, Hannah," she says, cutting me to the quick. "Both of you have experienced great sadness. Be gentle with him."

I glance at Eugene again. He looks like a pissed-off gym teacher who gives instructions from a folding chair.

"Are you sure about that?" I don't need to question her about myself. I know I've been in a funk. The mess at Big Catch has weighed on me for months. Jonah's behavior didn't exactly restore my faith in humanity, even though he did unwittingly lead me to Sophie and Briar.

"Quite so," Dottie says. "I already gave him a hunk of smoky quartz, but he might also benefit from stroking some rose quartz."

I laugh under my breath. "Looks like he'd definitely benefit from stroking something."

Her gaze narrows on me. "Are you wearing your necklace?"

After Sophie, Briar, and I realized we were dating the same lying loser, Dottie gave us each hunks of rose quartz, and Briar, who loves to give herself extra work, made us pendants out of them. The rose quartz is supposed to make us believe in romantic love again, which feels like a dangerous gamble right now. I might not believe in Dottie's stones, but I figure a girl should hedge her bets. So I took it off the night Travis kissed me and haven't put it on since.

"I'm not here to make a romantic connection with Eugene, Dottie," I say, rolling my eyes. "And it didn't match my outfit."

"Love matches everything," she insists. "And there are many different types of love, my dear, including self-love. You need to remember how to love yourself. Now, I've taken the liberty of ordering a *lovely* breakfast for you and your friend, but if you'd like to join me and the ladies later, you're more than welcome. We can help you determine how to help dear Eugene."

"What makes you think I want to help him?"

The woman sitting at the table next to us gives me a pointed *move on* look, and I smile sweetly at her and wave.

Dottie, who either doesn't notice or doesn't care, smiles at me. "Because that's your talent, dear. You're a fixer. I don't think you'll be able to resist."

She gives my hand another hand pat, then turns back to join the other ladies, leaving me in a mind storm.

That's Dottie's talent—acting like she's a sweet little elderly lady and then coming out with bits of wisdom that bite you in the butt and make you question everything you thought you knew.

Shaking my head to clear my thoughts, I continue the rest of the way to Eugene and sit across from him.

He checks his watch as soon as I sit.

"Oh, come on, I'm not late, and we both know it."

He meets my gaze with a sniff that rustles his glorious bottlebrush mustache. "I'm Eugene."

"And I'm Hannah, the old you." I reach into my purse and pull out the mini flashlight I brought, handing it to him from across the table.

He takes it, his brow furrowing, and turns it over in his hand.

"I'm passing the torch," I say. "Get it?"

He drops it like it's a hot potato, and it rolls down the length of the stable and stops next to a vase full of crystals. "I can't possibly accept gifts or bribes."

"You must be fun at parties," I say.

The very sight of the flashlight on the table seems to make him anxious, so I tuck it back into my bag.

"You must be wondering why I asked you to meet me here," he says, steepling his hands and then pulling them apart.

I can't resist the urge to mess with him a little. "I thought you wanted me to pass the torch, but now I'm starting to wonder. Is this supposed to be a *date*, Eugene?"

"No," he barks. From the look on his face, I suspect he would have taken off running if a dark-haired server didn't choose that exact moment to come by with a pot of tea and a tray full of pastries that makes me wonder how those donuts are working for Travis.

Eugene peers at the server, perplexed. "We didn't order anything. I haven't even seen a menu."

"Oh," she says. "The owner asked me to send all of this over. It's on the house."

"That's completely unnecessary," he says. "I can't accept gifts or bribes."

"It's for her," she says, pointing at me. "She's a friend of the owner."

He puffs out his lips, as if waiting for me to echo his sentiments, but I grin at her. "I'm very open to both gifts and bribes."

"Well...I don't eat anything without knowing what's in it," Eugene says in a stodgy tone. "What if I'm allergic to whatever's in there?"

"Do you have a food allergy, sir?" she asks intently.

"Well...no..."

"We're good," I tell her with a grin. "Thank you for bringing us breakfast. That was supercool of Dottie, and we'll be sure to go by and say hey before we leave."

"Oh, she'll definitely be coming by the table to read your

fortunes," the server says, glancing at Eugene as if he's a strange creature she can't wrap her head around.

"Fortunes?" he echoes.

I nod to her, and as she walks away, I say, "Yes, Eugene. This is a place where they read your fortune in your tea leaves. What do you think about that?"

"I think it's preposterous," he says, getting a bit worked up by the idea.

"I know, right? But the woman who runs this place is a friend, and she's into it, so I let her have her fun." I raise my eyebrows, hoping this will be a teachable moment for him.

He sighs. "You think I'm a stodgy old man who should just let you young people have their fun. I've heard plenty about the way you used to manage the tasting room at Big Catch. But I'm running a workplace, Hannah. Workplaces shouldn't be bacchanals with everyone sleeping in each other's beds and having... inappropriate relations *at the office*. Nor is it acceptable for people to drink on the job."

I pour us each a cup of tea, then grab a chocolate croissant. Waving it at him, I say, "You don't work in a tax prep office, Eugene. You work in a brewery. You can't run a brewery the way you'd run a tax prep office."

"I disagree," he says with a passion that tells me disagreeing with people is his true calling in life. "Any successful enterprise is run based on the same template."

"What's your background in?" I watch him over the rim of my cup as I take a sip. "I'm guessing you were an accountant, or maybe a teacher."

His eyes widen with surprise. "A principal," he says after a moment. "An elementary school principal."

"Which elementary school?"

He chews his lip in obvious reluctance.

"Oh my God. What could I possibly do with that information?"

"Lakeshore," he says, and I gasp.

"You just gave me that goose-over-a-grave feeling. My friend goes there."

"You have a friend who's a minor?" he says with a thunderous look. "That's highly inappropriate."

"Oh, relax, Eugene. I'm his temporary nanny."

He waves a hand at me. "See, this is the problem with your method of doing things. This child is supposed to be a client, but you're calling him your friend."

I gesture back at him. "And this is the problem with you. *No one* you work with would call you their friend. If you want people to listen to you, you need to gain their respect. You have to treat them like human beings."

He surprises me by sipping his tea thoughtfully. He pauses, twitches his mustache, then sighs and says, "Who's the boy's teacher?"

"Mrs. Applebottom," I say, delighted. Is he going to give me the inside scoop? Mrs. Applebottom's Achilles' heel? I'd love to pass his hot take on to Travis.

A surprised look crosses his face, followed by a smile, which looks even stranger on him. Like suddenly he's not Eugene Peebles, professional Debbie Downer, but somebody's grandpa.

"You mean *Moira Applebaum*, I suppose," he says. "You're very lucky. The boy's in good hands. The best."

I stare at him in wonder, because I'm picking up on some nonprofessional interest in Mrs. Applebaum. Yup, I *have* to tell Travis all about this. Instantly. The need to share this information with him practically hums under my skin.

"Did you get it on with Applebaum?" I ask.

"Of course not," Eugene says, nearly dropping his teacup. "I just finished telling you how I feel about inappropriate, unprofessional conduct."

"But you *like* her."

He bristles. "I think highly of her ability to run an organized, well-disciplined classroom, yes."

"I'm starting to think we have different values, Eugene."

"That much is obvious..." He trails off, looking down at his hands, and when he speaks again, his voice is plaintive. "How do I gain their respect? At Big Catch, I mean. I'm fairly certain Mrs. Applebaum and I have a strong feeling of mutual respect."

"Oh, Eugene," I say sadly.

He adjusts his posture before taking another sip of tea. "I didn't want the employees to dislike me," he says, and now I hear it, a strain of loneliness threading through his voice, of existing on the outside and looking in. "I knew it would benefit everyone if things were run more efficiently. My hiring manager told me he was going for the ultimate customer experience."

"You know what they say, buddy," I tell him. "Happy wife, happy life."

He scowls at me. "I don't know what that has to do with the situation."

"Okay, fine, Mr. Literal. Happy staff, happy customers. If you want the customers to have the 'ultimate' experience, then you need to make sure your staff isn't on the verge of quitting."

He takes another sip of tea, his features a little crumpled, as if they're collapsing in on themselves. Then he says, "What would make them happy?"

"Well, I'm glad you asked." I grin at him. "The answer's simple. Drinking, flirting, and fornicating. So I'm going to suggest you have a staff party."

He heaves a heavy sigh, and I can't help but ask, "Why'd you get into this line of work, Eugene? Shouldn't you be on a fishing boat somewhere, glowering down at the fish? My dad retired as soon as he hit that sweet six-five. He basically lives at my brother's restaurant now—as a guest, not an employee."

Eugene surprises me by serving himself one of the possibly allergy-laden pastries and taking a big bite. From the brief look of pleasure he allows to pass across his face, I can tell he's not completely a lost cause.

Once that bite of goodness is headed down his gullet, he says, "My son suggested I get a job after I retired from the school. I thought I would enjoy retirement, but there were some...problems."

"Problems?" I ask, because nosy bitch, reporting for duty.

He takes another bite of the pastry. "I made a schedule, so my days were highly structured, but I got a little..."

My heart suddenly aches for him. "You were lonely."

"My wife divorced me fifteen years ago, and my son has very little use for me. I'm used to being alone," he says, with a tone that suggests he's offended by the very notion that he might have sought out human companionship.

"I'm sure you're very good at being alone, but no one wants to be totally alone. Why didn't you join a seniors' group?"

"I tried," he says stiffly. "But it was poorly organized, and the leader didn't appreciate my suggestions for improvement. I was asked to leave."

I sigh and crack my knuckles, thinking Dottie must be psychic after all, because she completely foresaw what I'm about to say. "I'm going to help you, Eugene."

"You are?" he asks, surprised.

"I'm afraid I have to. You've given me no other choice."

Just then, Dottie swoops in with a ready smile. "Are we ready to read some fortunes?" she asks, beaming.

No one can talk smack about her sense of timing. Briar was right—Dottie really does know how to rule a room.

I give Eugene a sharp look, trying to telepathically remind

him of the beginning of our conversation, but he must be immune to telepathy, because he frowns at her. "It's dishonest to tell people you can read their fortunes from a clump of wet leaves."

"*Eugene*," I say.

"Oh, it's fine," Dottie says, seeming genuinely undaunted. "This dear man hasn't been given any reasons to believe lately." With that, she sits down at our table as if invited. She's wearing a pretty blue dress that makes me think of a sunny summer day and a crystal hair clip that probably has some deep symbolic meaning.

"Don't you work here?" Eugene asks her uneasily.

"I do," she says sweetly. "I also own the place. I like to connect with everyone who pays us a visit.

"She didn't know how to retire either," I joke.

His sighs are a language all their own, because this one is almost empathetic. *I know how that feels.*

His eyes linger on mine for a moment, and I feel another pulse of sympathy for him. This man is so lost in the weeds when it comes to making the connections he needs. *Just like Travis.*

I smile and nod and try not to think about Travis anymore.

"Okay," he says. "Why not. You can look at my wet leaves."

"First you'll need to finish the tea, my dear man," Dottie says. "Bottoms up."

He slurps down the rest of the tea, wetting his bottlebrush mustache, then passes the cup to her.

She does her tea-leaf routine, and Eugene and I watch with healthy skepticism. Smiling down at his teacup, she says, "Yes. Yes, indeed. This is exactly what I was hoping for."

"Well?" Eugene says.

"You're going to fall in love again, my dear man, deeply,

madly, and truly. Oh, I'm so excited for you. Your whole life is about to be transformed."

He gives me a quizzical look, and I nearly burst out laughing, thinking about what Briar said the other day.

"Don't look at me, Eugene," I say, lifting my hands. "I'm not the lucky lady. I have commitment issues, not daddy issues."

His cheeks go scarlet.

"Oh, it won't be with Hannah, of course," Dottie says. "Hannah's already met her great love."

"Excuse me?" I say, my heart pounding even though I know it must be BS.

"All of you girls are going to find new love. Sophie's already found Rob, of course, but you, Briar, and Nora will all be happily settled before long. I've known that from the beginning of our journey."

"Nora?" I scoff. "She wants nothing to do with us."

Dottie gives me a knowing look. "She's going to be part of your little group before long." She pats her chest. "I feel it here."

Eugene gives me a pointed glance, reminding me of the whole *let's be tolerant of other people's weird quirks* speech I gave him.

She beams at us. "Now, why don't you finish your breakfast? I'm meeting with my Wise Elders group this morning, Eugene, and I would simply love it if you'd join us once you're ready. We're having a riveting conversation."

"Eugene would be thrilled," I answer for him, because I can already hear he's gearing up for a no.

"Splendid," she says, then gets up to return to her friends.

"Why'd you have to say that?" Eugene grouses.

"She changed the name of her club just to include you. It's usually the Wise Women Group. Besides, you're looking for connections, and I'm guessing they won't kick you out for being a rigid..." I let my worlds trail off, because I can't think of a kind word for *prick*.

"She did?" he asks, clearly perplexed by the idea. "But why?"

I gesture toward her. "Because she genuinely wants to include people, and better yet, she's good at it. You could learn a lot from her."

He heaves a sigh. "It sounds like I have a lot to learn in general."

"Lucky for you, old dogs *can* learn new tricks."

My phone buzzes, and I pick it up, smiling when I see Travis's name.

Travis: *Are you free for shopping?*

Me: *Yes, please. DYING to hear how it went with the donuts.*

Travis: *Poorly.*

Me: *You know how to leave a girl wanting more.*

Travis: *Very poorly.*

Me: *Meet me at the tea shop.*

I set the phone down with a click and find Eugene staring at me.

"Who was that?" he asks.

I raise my eyebrows.

"I was just trying to take an interest," he says, gazing into his empty teacup. "You told me I should take an interest in people."

I didn't mean me, but it would be hypocritical to say so. "It was my boss, technically."

He gives me a look I can't interpret. "And do you have a strong feeling of mutual respect?"

I find myself smiling at him. "What do you know, Eugene, I think we do."

We eat the rest of our breakfast, and I manage to get a few salient facts out of him.

Eugene is sixty-seven. His birthday is on Flag Day, whenever that is. His ex-wife is an accountant, and his son is some kind of computer genius. His spirit animal is a hedgehog, and he has very strong opinions about cheese, which scheduling app is "superior," and basically everything.

When we're finished, the dark-haired server comes by to grab the dishes, and I tell Eugene, "It's time for you to join the elder brigade. We'll talk later about the kick-ass staff party we're going to plan together."

He adjusts the bridge of his glasses unnecessarily. "I'm not convinced a party's necessary."

"Oh, it's necessary. Give me your phone."

He shoots me a distrustful look.

"I'm just going to plug my number into it."

He passes it over, and I save my number under THE OLD EUGENE before calling myself so I have his number too.

"Very funny," he says when he sees it.

"I thought so. Now, come on. Be sociable. Consider it practice. I'm sure they're having a perfectly normal conversation."

He grumbles but stands up to join me. Of course, as we walk up to the table of four older ladies, one of them, whom I've nicknamed No-Nonsense Constance, says, "I told my granddaughter that I'd like to be cremated, and I want her and her boyfriend to sneak me into the Biltmore Estate and toss my ashes in the Italian Garden."

"Wouldn't the fishes eat you?" asks Penny, Sophie's aunt. She's not religious, but she makes the sign of the cross on her chest. "I'd rather eat fish than be eaten by them."

"I *want* them to eat me," Constance says. "I've always loved the phrase sleeping with the fishes. I figure this is my big chance."

Dottie catches sight of us. She gives us a luminous smile as she tugs over a chair, the feet screeching. "Join us, Eugene, please. We're all eager to get to know you better. Right now, we're discussing what we'd like our loved ones to do with our remains after death."

Eugene gives me the pleading look of a man on the gallows. I could save him, but what better way to force him to practice his social skills than to push him into the middle of an impossible conversation with a few strangers?

"You'll do great, Eugene. I'll be in touch."

He clears his throat. "Uh...ah..."

But then the door to the tea shop open, and Travis walks in.

He's wearing a button-down shirt, the sleeves rolled up to reveal his muscled forearms. There's a smear of powdered sugar on his cheekbone, and he has the look of someone who just survived a battle...barely.

"Who's *that* hot hunk of heaven?" asks the fourth woman, Ann, famed for her lip-reading abilities.

"He's my boss."

"Sign me up for your employment agency," she adds with an appreciative look.

"Ann, you've got to stop taking all that ginseng," Constance says with an eyeroll.

"Ginseng?" Eugene says as Travis reaches us, coming to a stop beside me. I can feel him there, his presence sturdy and unshakable. I have an insane urge to wrap my arm around him and soak up some of that energy, but I restrain myself.

Dottie pats Eugene's hand. "It gives a wonderful kick start to the libido. I'll be sure to make you a nice tea blend so you can prepare for meeting your lady."

"Well, this has been fun and all," I say, "but duty calls."

"Aren't you going to introduce us to your friend?" Ann asks.

Ginseng, Constance mouths to her.

"Of course." I gesture to him. "This is Travis. He enjoys playing the drums, making rules and schedules, and...actually, I'm drawing a blank, Travis. Do you enjoy anything else?"

He gives me a dark look, then says, "Walks on the beach and piña coladas, naturally. And glitter." He turns to face the Wise Elders' Club. "I've already met Penny, Dottie, and Eugene, but who are you lovely ladies?"

I smile at him, impressed by his hustle. Without thinking, I reach up and swipe away the sugar on his cheek. His skin is warm, and even though it should have been a lightning-quick maneuver, my finger lingers on his cheek until his gaze tracks to me, deep and searching.

"Are you smearing something on my face, Hannah?" he asks, deadpan.

"I was wiping something *off* your face. It's these new nanny instincts. They're impossible to turn off. Anyway, we should get going. We have a lot of work to do."

"Is that what they're calling it these days?" Ann quips, making it perfectly obvious what she means.

Eugene's mustache twitches. "I have a lot to learn about the modern working world."

"Goodbye, dears," Dottie tells us. "Don't worry about Eugene here. He's in excellent hands."

He shoots me a slightly panicked look, and I feel a bit like Travis probably did when he dropped Ollie off at school that first day.

"You'll do great, Eugene," I say. "I can tell you're someone who has a comprehensive body disposal plan."

Travis smiles at me, shaking his head slightly, and then we turn to head out of the tea shop.

I'm not sure whether I imagine it, or feel it just because I want to, but it feels like his big, callused hand is hovering just over my lower back as we leave.

CHAPTER FIFTEEN

Hannah's wearing a yellow-checked dress today, with a thick, fuzzy purple sweater instead of a coat. She was the brightest thing in the room at Tea of Fortune, which is saying something, because Dottie has never met a color she didn't like.

The color alone didn't do it, though. It was Hannah herself. She draws other people in without trying. To be with her for five minutes is to want to talk to her forever. To tell her things you haven't told your oldest friends. To stare at her and soak her in.

She calls herself nosy, and she absolutely is, but I'm starting to realize it's because she's interested in everything. She finds life exciting and full of possibility in a way that I only do when I'm playing the drums. And she makes me wonder what it would be like to live the rest of my life that way.

That's crazy, obviously.

All of the reasons for us to stay away from each other haven't changed over the last two days. Still, as we leave the tea shop, I feel my hand trying to settle on her lower back.

"We're not going to Target or one of the other big-box

stores," she declares as we walk down the sidewalk toward where I parked.

"No?"

"Definitely not," she says. "We're going to a real toy store. There's one off Tunnel Road that has Willy Wonka vibes."

"You mean the fictional man who made chocolate? Sounds like a much better bet than a well-organized store with labeled aisles."

"It looks fun." She gives me a sidelong glance. "More stores should put on a show. You, of all people, should know the importance of showmanship. You have that T-shirt you wear to all of the shows."

"They're different T-shirts. I'm not some guy who never changes his jockstrap because he thinks it's lucky."

"But they're all the same brand." She pauses as we reach a street corner, waving to an older woman who waves back with a bright smile. I'll bet everyone she's ever met remembers her, even if it's just as *the woman with all that bright red hair and that smile.* "I can tell," she adds, glancing back at me.

I shrug. She's right, and I'm kind of pleased she noticed. "I like keeping my street clothes and my performance clothes separate."

"Shocking," she says with a teasing smile.

"All right, Hannah." I pull her back because she clearly intends to rush across the street so she won't have to wait for the light to change. "We'll go to the Willy Wonka toy store. Have it your way." I'm pleased she cares this much, honestly. I know it's above and beyond the call of duty for her to come with me at all.

"Sooo, tell me what went wrong this morning," she asks when the light finally changes and we cross the street to my car parked on the side of the road. "The donuts plan seemed solid."

"It should have been," I agree, walking around to the passenger side. I unlock the car with my key fob and open her door for her, and she gives me a grin that looks half teasing and half pleased. "Why, what a gentleman you are, Ships Junior."

I roll my eyes as I circle around to the front of the car and then slide in behind the wheel. After I look up the store's address on my phone, I drive us toward Tunnel Road and tell her the whole sorry story.

"The kids thought there was a real mouse?" she asks, clearly delighted.

"It's not funny," I say, although I can feel the corner of my mouth trying to hitch up. "All the kids stampeded into the hallway like wild animals, and they were so hyped up on sugar it took a team of teachers twenty minutes to track them all down. And someone broke Mrs. Applebaum's prized pencil holder. A painted clay hedgehog. Someone who used to work at the school got it for her, apparently. If she didn't like us before, she's definitely not our number one fan now. Of course, that Mickey kid's embarrassed too. I mean, I think he might have wet his pants a little, and—"

Gasping, Hannah claps her hand around my bicep in a burst of excitement, and I nearly plow into the Honda Civic in front of me. I give an apology wave; the driver gives me the finger.

"Hannah..." I dart a sharp look at her. "What the hell? I nearly hit that guy."

"Sorry! Yeah, I shouldn't have done that, but I had a good reason. I'm pretty sure I know who gave her that pencil holder. This is crazy!"

"And that's a good reason for almost killing us?" I resume driving, white-knuckling the steering wheel, because my pulse is still elevated.

"It was *Eugene*," she says dramatically, pushing her seat belt down under her arm and fully turning in her seat to stare at me.

Anxiety blasts through me. She shouldn't be sitting like that. It's not safe.

"Come on, Hannah, sit properly."

She seems taken aback, but a second later she fixes the belt and scoffs, "Okay, *Dad*."

I feel ridiculous for letting anxiety get the better of me, so I shrug. "Sorry."

"It's fine."

I force a laugh. "At least someone wants to call me dad."

"I'm guessing there are plenty of people who'd be willing to call you daddy," she says with a sidelong glance that lights me on fire. Just like it's supposed to, no doubt.

I tighten my hands on the wheel. "You're right. But there's only one person I'd like to hear it from, and it's not them *or* you."

I resent her flirting, especially since I get the sense she talks to everyone this way.

Lilah used to speak in innuendos and compliments because she loved having every man she met wrapped around her finger.

It's not calculated like that with Hannah. I get the sense that she's barely aware she's doing it. She flirts because she likes to flirt, not because she wants me. While she may have kissed me back the other day, I was the one who started it. I'd do well to remember that (on top of all the other reasons I need to stay away from her).

To quote my least favorite film franchise ever: *Don't let yourself get carried away by the tide.*

It's the only useful advice my father ever gave me, and he didn't even come up with the words. Or say them to me.

"I'm sorry, Travis," Hannah says softly, and I steal a quick glance at her before returning my gaze to the windshield. "That was a shitty thing for me to say. I know Ollie cares about you."

"Thank you," I say with a stiff nod, feeling flustered. "Now, go ahead and tell me your theory about Eugene. I know you're probably dying to."

She grins at me. "Eugene is the ex-principal of Lakeshore Elementary, and he already told me that he thought very highly of Mrs. Applebaum. *And* he told me that the hedgehog is his spirit animal. So I'm thinking he's the one who gave her the pencil cup. She treasured it, which means there's a chance that she might have a thing for Eugene. Do you think it's possible?"

I consider Eugene, with his thick glasses, mustache, and complete lack of interpersonal skills, then Mrs. Applebaum with her contemptuous looks and stern voice.

"No," I say.

But Hannah's face falls, and I don't want to be the one to cast doubt on her pet theory. If she wants to think two disagreeable old people can secretly be in love, then who am I to take that fantasy away from her?

"Maybe," I amend. "But if they're into each other, what does that have to do with us?"

"I'm glad you asked," she says as I turn onto the winding side street leading up a hill to the toy store. "We're going to set them up."

I laugh with genuine amusement as I turn into the parking lot and maneuver through it, searching for a spot close to the store.

"You'll be flying solo for that one, Maverick," I say as I park the car.

She's out before I can even think about going around to open the door for her.

"No way," she says. "This needs to be a joint effort, and I'm going to tell you why."

"I'm listening." I reach down to touch her arm without thinking, guiding her toward the store. Her pretty lips curve into a smile. I force myself to look away, only for my gaze to fall on her freckles, dotted across the bridge of her nose with such precision it's as if someone took a makeup pencil to her face.

"Do you draw them on?" I ask before I can regain sense and stop myself.

"Excuse me?"

"Your freckles," I say. "It's just...they're perfectly spaced."

She laughs. "No. But thank you, I think."

"Oh, it was definitely a compliment. But go on. Tell me why I should want to help two disagreeable people fall in love."

She beams at me, barely seeming to notice as we step through the automatic doors. I claim a shopping cart at the front, and she trails after me, saying, "If they fall madly in love, it'll benefit both of us."

"I look forward to hearing how," I tell her, pushing the cart slowly past the first shelves, which are geared toward babies and toddlers. Many of the displays are interactive, allowing kids and adults to test the wares, and there are a couple of toddlers playing with a toy xylophone. The sound is overwhelming, but the sight of them connecting with music makes me smile.

"If Mrs. Applebottom—sorry, Applebaum—is getting some," she says loudly, prompting the toddlers to glance up and their mothers to give us disapproving looks before nuzzling their kids close, "she'll be way more chill in the classroom. That'll benefit Ollie."

I nod to the mothers and mouth *sorry*, before asking Hannah, "And what do you stand to gain?"

"The joy of being helpful. I'm going to help Ollie *and* Eugene."

I stop pushing the cart and just look at her for a second, trying to get a handle on this woman who has taken over so much space in my brain and my life. "I understand why you'd want to help Ollie, but why Eugene?"

"Because he's the new me," she says. "I don't want him to terrorize the people I worked with. Or my brother."

I raise my eyebrows, waiting.

"Fine," she says, rolling her eyes. "He's also super pathetic. He made me feel bad for him."

I don't fully buy it, but I can tell she's explained as much as she intends to.

"I don't know how I can help," I say. "If I invited Mrs. Applebaum over for tea, she'd probably file a restraining order. The mouse thing really put it over the edge for her."

She reaches over and idly pets a huge stuffed animal—a fluffy yellow dog. I reach for it and toss it into the cart.

"You think Ollie will like it?" she asks.

"It's for you."

Her lips part as if she's going to object, or maybe make a big deal out of it, so I change the subject, saying, "I don't know how we'd even get them in the same room."

Her brow furrows as she considers the challenge. "What if we ask Eugene to intervene on Ollie's behalf?"

"Would he?" I move the cart along. "He doesn't even know Ollie."

"So, maybe he can tutor him or something first."

I give her a pointed look. "Ollie doesn't need tutoring, and from what I can tell, Eugene doesn't have the manners or social skills to help him with what he does need."

She sighs dramatically. "All right, twist my arm. We're going to have to Parent Trap Eugene and Mrs. Applebaum."

"This is important to you." I come to a stop so I can get a better look at her.

"It is," she says.

"Will you tell me why?"

"I don't know, Travis," she says with a frustrated laugh. "It just is. I mean, what are the odds that you'd be having trouble with a grumpy teacher today while I'm having a meet and greet with that teacher's grumpy former principal, who quite clearly had a thing for her. It feels like..."

I grin at her. "Well, well, were you about to say that setting them up feels like fate?"

She blushes. I didn't know Hannah *could* blush. "Take that back." She nudges my shoulder. "You're going to ruin my reputation as a hard-ass."

"I'm not so sure you have one."

"Are you going to help me or not?"

Against my better judgment, I nod. To do anything else would disappoint her, and it seems very important not to disappoint her. "Okay, sure. You tell me how to help with your ill-advised plan, and I'm there."

A tired-looking brunette woman with a basket slung over her arm passes us, giving me a strange sidelong look. I could have sworn she's already passed us, so maybe we're standing in front of some must-have toy she wants for her kid.

I start moving the cart again. "Now, what are we going to get?"

"What kind of budget are we working with?" Hannah asks.

"An I-didn't-even-know-my-kid-existed-until-he-was-seven kind of budget."

"Then we're getting everything," Hannah says with a grin. "Can you imagine what his face is going to look like when he gets home?"

I smile back at her, but I'm not convinced Ollie's going to be so easy to please after Mousegate. In fact, I'm pretty worried about what the rest of his day is going to look like. Will the other kids blame him? Will Mickey be humbled after screaming like a baby and pulling a runner, or does he now have a deep-seated grudge against my son that'll last through high school?

"You're worrying," Hannah says. "You get this really

distinct expression on your face when you do. There's a tiny crease right there." She reaches out and rubs the pad of one finger between my eyebrows, and I instantly feel the furrow she mentioned being smoothed away.

"Does my face look like that all the time?" I ask. "Because I've done nothing but worry since Lilah dropped Ollie off in September."

She shocks me by layering her hand over mine on the handle of the shopping cart. I meet her eyes, feeling a fresh burst of awareness. Her eyelashes have been blackened with mascara today, and she's perfectly made up, with bright red lipstick. She looks good like this too, but in some ways I prefer the Hannah who's undone—the one only Ollie and I and a few other lucky people are allowed to see.

She comes over like that because she wants you to keep your distance, dumbass, a voice in my head whispers.

"You're staring at my lips," she says with her typical candor.

"I'm waiting for whatever wise thing you're about to say next," I tell her, because I'm not ready to confront the elephant following us around on a tether.

I'm attracted to her, which is a problem. I really enjoy spending time with her, which is problem number two. I can't stop thinking about that kiss the other night, which is worst of all.

"If you want wisdom, then you're really in for a treat," she says with a knowing look, as if she sees right through me. "Because I was going to give you some truly excellent advice."

"I'm waiting with bated breath."

She smiles at me, grabs a science experiment kit from the shelves full of DIY and crafting kits, and adds it to the cart. "Buy him a ton of shit."

"Retail therapy?"

She picks up a solar system crafting kit, gives it a cursory glance, and tosses it into the cart. "We have to try something, and you won't let me make beer with him."

I laugh as I check out a painting set that comes with an easel. "You think he'd like this? Sometimes my sister and I painted together when we were kids."

"Who knows, but if he doesn't want it, you can use it."

I give her a skeptical look. "I'm an adult, Hannah."

"Who gave you the crazy idea that adults aren't allowed to have fun?"

She picks up the paint set and holds it out to me expectantly. I feel like I should make more of a rebuttal, but anything I could say would feel like a schoolyard argument.

I do so have fun.

Or *I always have fun when I'm playing with the band or at The Missing Beat.*

"I won't let you become Eugene, Travis," she insists, staring me down. "I'm going to set you down a divergent path if it's the last thing I do."

"Let's hope it's not the last thing you do," I say, accepting the painting set and adding it to the growing pile in the cart. "Although I'm sure you'd take comfort in knowing the Wise Women have all planned their own funerals and would probably be happy to help your surviving friends and relatives with yours."

"Ha. Ha."

We move through the aisles, accruing a chemistry set, a telescope, some Lego sets, a few STEM toys, and posters from a couple of the shows Ollie likes.

While we're shopping, I catch sight of the woman from earlier a couple more times, giving us interested glances, peeking around aisles, meeting my gaze, and then swiftly turning around.

Maybe my anxiety's working overtime, but it feels like she's watching us, maybe even following us.

I'm about to say something about it to Hannah, but then we turn a corner into a music section arranged in a cozy nook in the back of the shop. There are a variety of instruments, including a small drum kit.

Hannah turns to me, her eyes sparkling. "Are you thinking what I'm thinking?"

"I don't think I am," I say, feeling an uncomfortable burning sensation spread across my chest. "We've got what we need." I start to turn the cart away from it. But she doesn't budge, so I only make it a couple of steps before I step away from the cart and turn back toward her.

"You won't let Ollie play your drums," she accuses, her gaze turning fierce. "Why won't you let him get his own set?"

"He said that?" I ask.

Ollie *did* ask if he could play them once, but it hadn't seemed like a big deal, and I'd thought he'd forgotten all about it.

"He said that," she says tightly. "More than once."

I consider this, my heart thumping faster and harder in my chest. "Look, I heard you the other night when you said I should teach him, but I don't think it's a good idea for me to do that yet. He's too young."

Hannah bristles. "Why wouldn't you want to teach your son how to do something you love? Something you need?"

She might as well have blown fire in my face.

I lift a hand in a halting motion. "Whoa, Hannah. That's not your place."

I'm not surprised when she lashes out. "You asked me to be his nanny. It *is* my place to advocate for him, even with you."

"Sure," I say, getting worked up too. "But I'm his father. I want that to mean something, dammit."

She holds my gaze, unflinching. "I think you have to ask

yourself why you won't give him the part of yourself you love the most, when you give it to other people's children every weekday afternoon. How do you think that makes him feel?"

Fuck, that's harsh.

I feel like my head is going to explode.

I'm tempted to walk away so I can cool off, which is my usual way of dealing with anger when my drum kit's not around, but I'm guessing she'd follow me. Besides, I can't let this lie.

I don't like the way she's looking at me right now, like I've disappointed her in some vital way there's no coming back from.

"Look, Hannah," I say. "My father didn't give a shit that I wasn't interested in his movies or in acting. He and my mom dressed me up in their little outfits and paraded me around and made me practice what to say like I was a trained parrot. It fucked me up. There's no way I'm going to pressure Ollie into liking the drums. If he wants to learn to play when he's older, I'll teach him then. But I won't influence him to be another Ships Junior." I gather my thoughts before adding, "And what if...what if he rejects music, the way he has everything else I've tried to engage him with? That's a major part of my life, of *me*. I'm worried I'll be disappointed, the way my father was. I don't want to take it out on him."

The look in her eyes changes, some of the anger leeching out. "I'm sorry, Travis. Of course I don't want you to force him into anything. That's not what I meant. And I'm guessing you're nothing like your father."

She takes a step toward me, accidentally stepping on a floor piano, which squeaks out a note.

Her eyes widen, but I abandon the cart and step onto the key next to hers, and she steps back onto the original key, and suddenly we're playing "Hot Cross Buns" and laughing.

She smiles at me, her curls sweeping around her cheeks as

she jumps on her final note with both feet. And isn't it just like Hannah to jump in with both feet?

She makes me want to do it too.

Damn, I want to kiss her again so badly. I want it more than I've wanted anything for a long, long time. The need is burning through my veins. Painful and sweet. Inevitable.

She reaches up and grabs the collar of my shirt, pulling me down toward her. Shocking me. Because I've been trying to convince myself I made an unwanted advance toward her, but there's nothing ambivalent about this. Our lips are inches apart, the musical notes are still curling through the air, and I lift my hands to her cheeks, tipping her face up toward mine. I need to taste her again, to have a sip of sin like I took the other night.

Then someone says, "Bless my soul. It *is* you."

It's the brunette woman, whom I'd never seen before we entered the store.

"Who are *you*?" I ask.

CHAPTER SIXTEEN

I almost kissed Travis. Again.

I'd decided I wasn't going to do that, but it feels like he just opened up his lockbox of secrets and invited me take a peek. Nosy bitch that I am, I want to burrow deeper and learn everything.

And, yeah, I suppose I've been obsessing about what happened between us on Wednesday night...

I took that first step toward him without meaning to, but I *definitely* pulled him closer on purpose. I fully intended to ravage him with my mouth, but the brunette woman who's been following us around put a stop to that.

I noticed her checking Travis out earlier, but I figured she was staring for the same reason his ex-girlfriend keeps going to his shows and pushing her way to the front of the crowd. Namely, he's pleasant to look at. But now she's giving off superfan stalker vibes, which is strange because I've been to a lot of Garbage Fire shows recently, and I've never seen her before.

"You heard the man," I say, bristling. "Want to tell us who you are?"

"Oh, sorry," she says, then stuffs a hand into her purse with intent.

"Whoa, what've you got in there?" I ask, trying to shield Travis by stepping in front of him. He frowns at me, then side-steps the motion, trying to place his much bigger body in front of *me*. It's like we're doing a dumb slapstick dance, which proves totally unnecessary when the woman pulls out a crinkled receipt and a child's marker.

"Can you give me your autograph?" she asks Travis, her eyes alight.

Travis gives me side-eye before glancing back at her. "Why? Are you a fan of Garbage Fire?"

"We're going to your afternoon performance tomorrow," she gushes. "We can't wait."

"Is that the royal we?" I ask, trying to maneuver in front of Travis again because the stalker lady is still holding out the marker and receipt. "Or are there other people who are obsessed with Travis?"

She flushes. "I wouldn't say *obsessed*, but we're all avid *Ships Ahoy* fans. We couldn't believe it when we heard Evan Thomas's son is living here in Asheville." Her smile widens. "Ships Junior himself. We'd been saving up to go to the museum in Upstate New York, but when we found out you live here, in our very own state, we decided it would be a better use of our funds."

I look over at Travis. He seems to be at a loss for words as he studies the woman, but after a moment, he collects himself enough to ask, "Who told you that?"

She squints at him. "It *is* you, isn't it? I recognize you because of the birthmark. You were so cute in those little sailor suits you used to wear. I loved that outfit with the suspenders too."

He clenches his jaw, because that was obviously the worst

thing she could have said. "Yes, but I won't be signing any autographs. I wasn't in those movies."

Her mouth purses into a disappointed pout. "But you're Ships Junior!"

"They never made that show," he mutters.

"But we came all this way..."

"How far?" I ask, letting curiosity take the wheel.

"Well, I'm here from Charlotte, which isn't very far, but Garrett's from Raleigh, and Jeanie came all the way from Wilmington. You know, Jeanie met your dad at a fan event back in 1990, and she said there were some real sparks. Maybe she could have been your mother if things had gone differently. Wouldn't that be something? It was right before he met your mom."

"It sure would have been," he murmurs. "And you are?"

"I'm Alice," she says brightly.

"Four of you drove all the way to Asheville because you heard a rumor that the son of an actor you like was living here?" I ask in disbelief.

She looks a little embarrassed now. "We're superfans," she says. "Those movies changed our lives. We just wanted to show Travis our appreciation." Turning toward him, she adds, "And we were hoping you might be willing to tell us some stories about Evan. You know, the inside scoop that fans wouldn't know about the great man."

Her gaze shifts to our shopping cart, abandoned just in front of the floor piano, before rising again. "Do you have a family?" she asks, then turns to me. "Are you his wife?"

"No," I say with a snort.

Travis's entire body looks tense, his hand curled around the handle of the shopping cart. "That's none of your fucking business, Alice, if you'll excuse my language. My father might have enjoyed parading his family around, but I don't allow other people access to my family or my friends. I realize you came a long way, and I'm sorry for that, but I didn't ask you to. I'd prefer to keep the past where it belongs. Let's go, Hannah."

He grabs the cart and heads toward the front of the store without pausing. Without grabbing the adorable drum set either, not that I'm surprised.

I hang back and ask, "How'd you hear that Travis lives in Asheville?"

Alice is watching him with a slack expression as he walks away, either because he just ripped her a new one, or because the man *does* have a very fine ass. I snap my fingers in front of her face, and she jolts out of her trance.

"Who told you?" I ask again, keeping my tone pleasant. She's vaulted over several boundaries, but I don't think she has bad intentions.

"Oh," she says. "Do you think maybe he'll change his mind?"

"No," I say, "he's a pretty private person."

"He's in a band," she protests.

"I know, but I think that's because he likes playing music, believe it or not. Look, I need you to answer my question. Who told you about this?"

She nearly fumbles her phone onto the floor in her haste to get it out of her purse. After pulling something up on the screen, she gives it to me, her hand shaking a little.

"Someone new posted in our online community. She had a photo of the band, and she said she was pretty sure the drummer was Ships Junior. So we did some poking around, and sure enough..."

I peer at the screen, taking in the photo, which has a drawn-on arrow pointing at Travis's junk and this caption:

Y'all, this guy is Travis Thomas, the would-have-been Ships Junior. He lives in Asheville, and he's in this band Garbage Fire.

GODDDD, *he looks just like a young version of his dad, don't you think? Let's give him the appreciation and attention he deserves.*

The poster has a generic name—MaritimeLaw69.

A sneaking suspicion itches at the back of my brain.

Rachel knows who Travis is.

Rachel holds a grudge against him.

Rachel is exactly the sort of petty bitch who'd go online anonymously and distribute his personal information to a bunch of possible stalkers, knowing he's a man who values his privacy.

Alice and her friends sound pretty innocuous, but what if someone dangerous shows up?

Not cool.

Very not cool.

No one messes with Travis but me, and both of us are protective of Ollie. Which means I'm going to have to shut down Rachel, or whoever else was behind this.

I take a screenshot of the post and text it to myself. Then I save my number on her phone: NOT TRAVIS'S WIFE.

"Text me if you or any of your friends hear from this person directly or see more posts, okay?"

She wrings her hands. "Will you tell him we don't mean any harm?"

"I'll talk to him," I say, then pat her shoulder because she seems legitimately upset. "But no more following him. It's super creepy, Alice. How would you feel if someone was following you around, spying on you from down the aisle?"

"You *saw me?*" she asks.

"Oh, yeah, I did, and I'm sure he did too. So no more stalking. You're not very good at it, which is probably for the best."

She nods, her eyes a bit shiny, like she's on the verge of tears. "He doesn't sound like he liked his father very much."

"This is why you should never try to learn more about your

idols. It almost never ends well. Now, promise me that you and your friends aren't going to show up at the performance wearing sailor suits."

Her lower lip wobbles. "We got them dry-cleaned."

"No sailor suits. And don't pull a paparazzo He doesn't want his face splashed over any *Ships Ahoy* websites."

"We don't mean any harm."

"Then don't cause any," I say. "Go and enjoy the show if you'd like, but be respectful. Take it easy."

I hurry to the cash register, where Travis is standing stoically as the clerk rings up the enormous stuffed dog. I flinch, because it's ninety bucks. Ninety bucks for a stuffed animal? He definitely doesn't have to get that for me. I mean, sure, my apartment doesn't allow real animals, and I love petting soft things, but ninety bucks is absurd.

"I don't need it," I whisper to him. "I'm thirty."

"Just like I don't need that painting kit," he says dismissively. "We're getting it."

The cashier has paused, noticing our exchange, but Travis nods at her. "We're getting it."

She keeps ringing up the purchases. When she finishes, the total is staggeringly high, enough to make me queasy, but he doesn't so much as blink when he hands over his credit card.

I didn't think that kind of thing would do it for me, but it sends a little shiver down my spine. Or maybe it's Travis himself who's doing that. His usual self-control has shattered, and I feel like he could do anything right now. Push me against a wall and ravish me. Rip into someone. Play a riff that will go down in history...

"You're staring at me," he comments, his voice low and ragged, as he returns his credit card to his wallet and nods his thanks to the cashier.

"I am," I agree. "I'd like to do it some more if you don't object."

"I do," he says roughly. "When you look at me like that, it makes everything…"

"Harder?" I ask with a hint of teasing in my voice.

He shakes his head almost savagely. "You're not going to make me laugh right now, Hannah. There are some things not even humor can fix."

I take possession of the cart, so I have something to do with my hands. "I disagree. Besides, I don't think Alice and her friends are dangerous. Just misguided. She told me she'd found out about you from some recent post she'd seen in her superfan community. I got her to show it to me on her phone."

He dips his head and stalks toward the doors, which open for him. I know they're automatic doors that open for anyone, but the way they open makes him seem like royalty.

Focus, Hannah.

I follow him out to the car with the cart. "I'm going to figure out a way to verify my theory, but I think Rachel might be behind the post."

He swears and raps his knuckles against the back of his car. Then he looks at me, his eyes a little wild. "If Lilah finds out about this before the sixty days are up…"

I swear too as the truth settles heavily on me.

He runs a hand through his hair carelessly, tousling it. Then, as if realizing what he did, he smooths out his hair to hide the birthmark. It makes me sad, seeing him hide who he is. But I understand, especially after what just happened in the toy store.

"We're going to fix this," I insist. "You said Lilah doesn't have access to the internet, and at the moment the problem is contained. We have to keep it that way. I have an idea for how we can figure out if Rachel was behind this."

He studies me. "We?"

"*We.* I might have pissed Rachel off when I got her to take down that post about you and Ollie. We had Sophie's lawyer friend reach out to her, and I guess she was pretty rattled. Anyway...Eugene's son is some super-nerdy computer whiz. So maybe he can help us get to the bottom of it."

He shakes his head. "Why does it matter? The damage is done."

"It matters. Because if she did it, she's going to answer for it. In the meantime, you're going to get in touch with this fan group and tell them to take the post down because it's a violation of your privacy. I'm guessing they'll do anything for Ships Junior."

He groans but stands up straighter, pinning his eyes on me. "I'm glad you're on my side."

"Remember that the next time you try to argue with me." I squeeze his hand. "You need to go home and play the drums."

Surprise registers in his eyes, but he nods. "Yeah, you're right."

"Do you want me to call Rob?"

He gives me a ghost of a smile. "I can still operate a phone, if I choose to."

"I think you should ask him to come over and jam with you. Maybe tell him what's going on."

I have two brothers and a single dad, and all three of them need help figuring out when they should lean on their friendships. Something tells me Travis is the same way. He'd offer help but never ask for it.

"I'm fine, Hannah," he says, then circles around to open the passenger door for me.

"I can open my own door, if I choose to," I say.

"Glad to hear it, but I got to it first."

I climb in, brushing against his arm as I get into the seat. Then, to my bafflement, he reaches in and secures my belt.

"I can do that too," I tell him.

"I figured. But I wasn't confident you would."

He gets around and climbs into the driver's side before taking off. Of course, Travis being Travis, he goes the speed limit. But I don't miss the way his eyes keep flitting to the mirrors, as if checking to see whether Alice is following us in some VW minibus full of *Ships Ahoy* fans.

He relaxes after a few minutes, so I say, "You can drop me off at my car, and I'll meet you at your house to help hide all of this stuff for Ollie. That way you can be there for the big reveal later."

"There's no need for that," he says gruffly. "I'll leave it all out on the dining room table, and you can have fun checking it out with him this afternoon. I'd rather not make a huge deal out of it."

I consider what he's told me about his dad. "Your father liked showboating?"

He laughs. "He liked every kind of boating. It was his defining characteristic.

"Then he would have really liked Big Catch."

He gives me a sidelong look. "Please don't tell me you took that job at Big Catch because you love *Ships Ahoy*."

I grin at him. "I won't tell you, but that doesn't mean it's not true."

He groans theatrically. "I can't believe there are still fan groups. I mean, those movies came out so long ago."

"But the bad lines have enduring staying power."

"Yeah, I guess."

"I'm just glad you can joke about it. That tells me you're doing better than you were twenty minutes ago."

"It's because of you," he says softly.

A rush of warmth fills my chest.

"Oh," I say, which is probably the least I've ever had to say about anything.

Travis smiles out the windshield, probably having that same thought. Then he says, "I shouldn't have lost it on her. I just don't like getting that kind of attention. You know, when people think they know you because they've seen your face online."

"That happens to me with online dating sometimes."

He darts a quick look at me, his expression serious again. "Are you dating anyone?"

"Not really an HR-friendly question, Mister Sir Thomas."

He swears under his breath. "You're right. It's none of my business. I was just...curious. I should have asked before...you know..."

Before he kissed me against a wall.

"No, I shut down my profiles months ago. Too much trouble. Too many dick pics. Why haven't *you* been dating anyone? I'm sure Alice would love to break your dry spell."

"No offense to Alice, but I'm not interested in her, or anyone else who may have thought about getting a *Ships Ahoy* tattoo."

"That counts me out."

His shoulders shake a little with repressed laughter. "No, it doesn't. I knew way more lines than you did when we watched the movie the other day."

"Because I have a shit memory." I steal a look at him. "Does it bother you when people are superfans of the band?"

"Sometimes," he says, his eyes facing front.

Interesting...

I've suspected for a while now that he's not as into the idea of going big with the band as Rob and Bixby are, and no wonder. He knows what it's like to get cornered in toy stores by women who know what he looked like in a sailor suit. Sure, it's probably the first time it's happened to him for a while, but it's obviously not his first run-in with fame.

"Just one more question. Does it bug you that Karen is still a superfan of the band?"

He shoots me a surprised glance. "What do you know about Karen?"

I shrug. "Just that you were in an on-again, off-again relationship *forever*, and she still likes to watch you sweat under the bright lights."

"I'd prefer it if she'd stop coming, but I'm not going to tell her what to do. I already feel like enough of a dick for leading her on." He rubs his cheekbone, making her wonder if Karen had slapped him there. "She said I did, anyway. I didn't mean to. I was honest." He hesitates. "I still have a hard time imagining you with Jonah. He's so full of it, and you have a good BS detector."

"Will you think less of me if I admit that I knew he was full of shit, and I didn't care?" I lift a hand. "Now, obviously I didn't know he was engaged. He made a big deal about being single. But I wasn't invested the way Sophie and Briar were. I didn't really want to be invested in anyone. I was dealing with enough heavy stuff at the time with Liam. Besides, I've made a lot of bad decisions. Dated a lot of bad guys. Sometimes it's easier when you go in knowing something's not going to stick."

He smile looks self-deprecating. "No, I don't think less of you."

And I can tell, without him saying so, that he basically felt the same way about his ex. He was lonely, but he didn't want to be broken down by anyone else, after what happened with Lilah, so he found someone who couldn't break him. I shouldn't care, but I do, and frankly, I'm glad.

He pulls up outside of the tea shop, then turns toward me. "I'll see you later."

"Are you sure you don't need help unloading the car?"

He gives me a lingering look before saying, "I don't think it would be a good idea for you to come back to the house with me right now. I don't have the best handle on my self-control."

His words shiver through me, because I can see the dark intent in his eyes. Now I'm imagining what he would do if I *did* go back there with him.

I'm thinking about those silky black sheets and wondering if we'd even make it to his room...

I remember the way his callused hands felt against me, pinning me to the wall, and the heat of his lips as they moved over mine, playing me like I was an instrument.

"I don't want to...snap at you or anything," he says, pulling me out of my fantasy.

But from the way his eyes are glued to me, I know that's not what he's worried about.

Desire jumpstarts my pulse, filling me with warmth and giving me a new awareness of my body and what it wants. What it hasn't gotten in too long...

But I've made promises to myself, and I'm a woman who keeps my word.

I blow out a stiff breath. "Please. You don't scare me."

He smiles at me, then reaches out and tucks my hair behind my ear. "That makes one of us, because you definitely scare me."

I feel like I should make a joke, deflect, anything. But I can't. Not at the moment, with my mind stuck on what-ifs.

He reaches into the back seat and pulls out the huge, fluffy dog he got for me. It's ridiculous, and it makes my heart happy. "Don't forget to bring Fido home with you. We're playing with another rhythm guitarist today, but I'll be home by eight thirty."

I salute him and wrap my arms around the dog before getting out of the car. I stand there watching as his car pulls away and blends into traffic.

CHAPTER SEVENTEEN

HANNAH

When I arrive at the school to pick Ollie up a couple of hours later, a tweed-wearing male teacher asks me to come inside because Mrs. Applebaum needs to speak to me.

My first thought is: *holy shit, this matchmaking gig is going to be way easier than I thought.*

Then again, there's no way she knows about my connection to Eugene. So I'm guessing either Ollie did something objectionable or she's still pissed about the imaginary mouse.

Tweed Teacher guides me through the halls of the school, looking half asleep from boredom. He looks middle-aged, and from the way he's guiding me, tapping into muscle memory honed by years of walking the same hallways, he's very familiar with this school.

"Hey, did you know Eugene Peebles?" I ask on impulse.

At the sound of Eugene's name, he glances back with a bemused expression behind his reading glasses. "You know Principal Peebles?"

"I do," I say. "He's a close, personal friend of mine." He clearly thinks I'm BSing him, so I add, "I had tea with him just this morning."

He glances around, then adjusts his glasses before asking in an undertone, "Is it true that he's working at that crappy brewery with all the nautical décor?"

"I love Big Catch," I say frostily.

"Yeah, sorry." He hesitates, his feet planting on the linoleum, and makes a scrunched-up face. "I mean...you know...I'm glad he landed on both feet after the nervous breakdown."

"Excuse me?"

"I've said too much." He starts walking again abruptly. "Principal Peebles is a great guy. Very...uh...organized."

"What nervous breakdown, exactly?"

"Oh, man, there have been multiple?" He glances in both directions, but no small children or wandering teachers are there to distract him.

"Which time are you referring to?"

He does his glance-around move again, then whispers, "I'm talking about when he drank all that hard seltzer and drove the groundskeeper's golf cart around the school to correct spelling mistakes on all the posters with a Sharpie. You know, they had to have the vending machine professionally serviced after he crashed into it. 5B wouldn't work, and everyone knows the flaming hot Cheetos are the best."

Oh, Eugene.

My heart melts for that hot mess of a man, and I double down on my determination to help him get his shit together.

The teacher doesn't say anything else to me before we reach the classroom, and he raps twice on the door.

"Come in," a woman says in a voice that drips with dissatisfaction and reminds me of three-fourths of my own grade school teachers.

To be fair, it sounds like both of my guys have given her the runaround today.

I open the door and see Ollie sitting at one of the front desks, one hand pressed to his head.

"Are you okay?" I ask, bounding forward, my heart racing. "Did someone hit you?"

"Now, now, it was nothing like that…"

I shoot Mrs. Applebaum a hostile glare, because it sure as hell seems like it was something like that. She's an older woman with iron-colored hair coiled into a bun at the base of her neck and blue eyes so light they look like ice behind rectangle-rimmed glasses, with a chain dangling from them that's surprisingly rainbow-colored.

Ollie has tears in his eyes, a rarity for him, and he buries his face into my dress.

"What happened, Ollie?" I ask, wrapping an arm around him.

Mrs. Applebaum begins, "One of the boys—"

"I asked *him*," I snap.

"Mickey put gum in my hair," he says into my chest.

"Why did he even have gum at school?" I ask, glaring at Mrs. Applebaum again.

"For the same reason he had a donut this morning," she retorts. "Parents see fit to send in whatever they wish without any regard for how it affects the learning environment."

Well, she and Eugene certainly have similar world views.

"We'll take care of it, Ollie," I say, rubbing his little back. "But why don't you go wait in the hallway for a minute so I can have a nice, cozy chat with your teacher."

"She says chitter-chatter is a waste of time," he says into the folds of my dress.

I pull my phone out of my pocket and hand it to him. "Here, you can use that coloring app you like."

"Thanks, Hannah," he says, taking the phone. One of his little hands lifts again to check if the gum is still there—*roger—*

but he steps out of the classroom without any further argument, shutting the door behind him.

"You shouldn't allow a child unobserved access to your phone," Mrs. Applebaum says primly.

"I trust Ollie more than ninety-nine percent of adults. Now, why are you letting him get bullied? I'm told that's frowned upon in schools these days."

She gapes at me. "Well, I never. If you'd bothered to ask me what happened, I would have told you that Mickey stuck gum in Ollie's hair as retaliation after Ollie shoved him. Now, obviously neither behavior is acceptable, and both boys will be missing recess on Monday, but this is hardly a cut-and-dry case, young lady—"

"I'm Hannah."

"All right, *Miss* Hannah. Ollie has struggled to make friends in the classroom, and this morning's little stunt didn't help."

"That was an honest mistake," I say tightly.

"I don't see how. The boy lied about seeing a mouse, and it caused chaos. His father didn't so much as reprimand him."

I don't see the point in explaining the code word misunderstanding to her. Something tells me it wouldn't soften her. So I settle for saying, "Maybe he *did* see a mouse."

She gives me a withering glare. "A mouse would never *dare* enter my classroom."

"Rodents don't pay attention to invisible territory lines." I pause, trying to remember this severe woman might be Eugene's secret beloved. "Did you know Mickey has been bullying Ollie? I'm guessing he said something to him."

"I struggle to believe that."

"Are you *kidding* me?" I snap. "Did you hear about the whole *Teenage Mutant Ninja Turtles* thing?"

She sighs and folds her hands. "Mr. Thomas told me about it, yes. What you must realize, *Miss* Hannah, is that Ollie's reading level and comprehension are several years ahead of the rest of his classmates. Mickey genuinely believed the *Teenage Mutant Ninja Turtles* were real. When Ollie told him the truth and wrote down a list of facts about sewers, Mickey was embarrassed and upset."

So the kid's not some master manipulator, at least. He's just a fan boy, kind of like Alice and the other *Ships Ahoy* obsessives. Maybe we can work with that.

"I'll have a talk with Ollie," I say.

I'm about to leave, but I pause, remembering that I'm supposed to be sugar-talking her for Eugene's sake.

I check out her folded hands and don't see a ring on her finger, but there *is* an indent where a ring used to be.

"Do you have any children of your own, Mrs. Applebaum?" I ask, changing tack with an ingratiating smile.

"If that's quite everything, *Miss* Hannah, I'll be leaving. We're not paid to stay overtime."

"Oh, do you want to get back to your husband? I totally get that."

"I'm not married," she says. "Not anymore."

That's good news for Eugene, but I try to keep a neutral expression as I ask, "Was he a jerk?"

She actually smiles for half a second. "I have a policy not to discuss my personal life with any of my students' parents or guardians."

I lift my hands up, palms facing outward. "I get it. I was just curious."

She makes a shooing motion with her hand. "Right now the only thing you need to be curious about is what that young man is doing on your phone."

"Wait," I say, desperate to make greater inroads for my new friend. "Travis told me there was a casualty after this morning's...misunderstanding. A hedgehog pencil cup? We'd love to replace it, of course."

Her lips flatten. "It's irreplaceable. A colleague made it for my Secret Santa gift one year."

Hot damn. There's our in. If Eugene made the pencil pot, he can remake the pencil pot. Maybe he can even write his invitation onto it!

Slam-freaking-dunk.

I consider my subject and come to the conclusion that he will also need a little more coaching before I send him back into the dating world with a pat on the back and a Hail Mary.

So I tip an imaginary hat to Mrs. Applebaum and head into the hallway. I figured Ollie would be playing on my phone, but he's waiting outside with a solemn look on his face.

"How good is your hearing?" I ask.

"It's normal, I think," he says, "but you're pretty loud."

Out of the mouths of babes.

"Let's get that gum out, Ollie. I know someone who's aces at getting gum out of hair. In fact, he's done it for me on more than one occasion. We're gonna go see my brother Liam."

I text Travis, filling him in on the situation, and ask him to head home before band practice to hide the spoils of our toy store trip, so they're not all sitting out on the table when we get back. I may not be the best nanny ever, but I'm guessing it's a bad idea to give a kid a dozen presents on the same afternoon he shoved someone.

Travis: *Dammit. Is he okay?*

Me: *Getting gum out of hair is Liam's special talent, and if he can't do it, I'll give Ollie a haircut. I give a mean haircut.*

Me: *What I'm saying is that either way, I've got this.*

Travis: *Thank you.*

Travis: *Should I cancel practice tonight?*

Me: *Nah. Go. You need it.*

Then I text Liam, asking if he could help, and he immediately responds. Probably because I haven't suggested any hangouts for weeks.

Liam: *Yup. Bring him over. I'll get out the oil and peanut butter.*

I've missed my brother. Longed for him.

But I'm still figuring out who I am as just Hannah, not half of the unit who helped raise Connor.

I'm also working through the rest of my anger about what happened at Big Catch. I hadn't thought my friends would abandon me like that. Like I was nothing to them. It brought back a lot of hard memories. Maybe it's also made me feel more attached to Ollie. Because we've both learned the hard way that people can just walk away from you. They can be there one day, a bitter memory the next.

Of course, my brother carries that same burden, so I've made sure not to completely cut him out of my life, even temporarily. I've been texting with him, and whenever he calls, I answer.

I wait until Ollie and I are in the car to ask what happened with Mickey.

"He said something mean about Travis."

"It was nice of you to stand up for your dad," I say, feeling a swell of emotion in my chest. "But we can't just walk around shoving everyone who annoys us. If someone aggravates you, you give them a piece of your mind, without any violence. Besides...I think this whole war with Mickey might be based on a misunderstanding."

"Oh, there's no misunderstanding. He's made it very clear that he doesn't like me."

"What if that's because he thinks you don't like him?"

"I *don't* like him, Hannah."

I hold back a laugh. Truthfully, I'm biased and think anyone who messes with Ollie is automatically a twat, but I've been reading a few nanny blogs about teaching valuable lessons, and unfortunately they've rubbed off on me.

"I have an idea," I say. "Why don't we watch some *Teenage Mutant Ninja Turtles* at Liam's place while he works on your hair problem?"

"The movies aren't very good. The special effects make them look like monsters."

"Sure. But the ones you're talking about aren't the original version. There was this great cartoon from the eighties, and a live action movie they made in 1990. I watched them when I was a kid. Your dad probably did too."

"That's really old, Hannah," he says in a serious tone. "I don't think it will hold up."

Look at that, he's using an expression he picked up from me *against* me.

"You'll see, mister. You're going to like those turtles, and next week Mickey's going to think you're the coolest dude in the school."

"What if I hate them?"

"Then I'm going to suggest that you avoid future interactions with Mickey."

TEN MINUTES LATER, we're standing outside of my brother's apartment. I have his spare key, but I knock on the door. He opens it and engulfs me in a famous Liam bear hug. As his arms wrap around me, I take in his familiar scent of lemon and hops, and a feeling of profound relief envelops me.

God, I really missed him.

Distancing myself from him is one of the hardest things I've ever done, but it felt necessary, like we both needed to learn how to function on our own. To figure out how to craft strong relationships with people who aren't blood related and bonded by trauma.

He squeezes me before releasing me and crouching down to offer one of his huge hands to Ollie. I almost laugh at the sight of them: small, dark-haired Ollie next to my huge beast of a brother with his reddish-brown hair, too long right now because I'm probably the only one who cuts it for him, and trimmed beard. At least he's been taking care of his facial hair. But I also feel close to tears, because I love them both so much, and they're meeting for the first time. It feels like a big moment.

"I'm Liam," my brother says. "I'm told you're Ollie."

Ollie nods as he shakes Liam's hand, peering up at him with wide eyes. "You're *very* big. Much bigger than Hannah."

"Eat your vegetables. You'll get big too. Unlike Hannah, who never met a green bean she liked."

I push his massive arm and get nowhere.

"I don't know if I want to be that big," Ollie ruminates. "Can you touch the ceiling? My dad's tall, but he's not as tall as you, and he can't touch it. I know because he tried to get a bug off the fan and he couldn't do it."

"Depends on how low it is," Liam says with a laugh. Then he gets up on his tiptoes and touches the ceiling of his apartment, instantly earning him points in Ollie's scorebook.

"Are we done with the masculine posturing?" I groan. "Because we need a specialist in gum removal and the best ever version of *Teenage Mutant Ninja Turtles* to help Ollie bond with his nemesis."

My brother grins at Ollie. "Does she always threaten you with a good time?"

"I don't know what that means," Ollie says, "but Hannah

does like to have fun. She gets bored a lot, though. Sometimes we do, like, five activities in an afternoon."

Liam laughs and gently pats him on the back. "She does, but guess what? She's never bored with you. She told me so."

I smile at him and mouth, *Thank you.*

"Here, let me get the *Turtles* on for you," he says, and within five minutes, Ollie has a pretty sick little setup in front of the living room TV with toons on, a glass of Gatorade, and a bowl of Goldfish crackers that's not long for this world.

Once the little guy is situated, I catch Liam's eye. "Can I talk to you privately for a minute?"

He gives me a wary look, probably because I yelled at him the last time we talked "privately for a minute."

I drag him into the bedroom and shut the door.

"Should I have given him a juice box instead?" he asks, lifting his brows.

"Ha ha. No, I just wanted to tell you that I'm ready to get over this rift between us. I'd like to put it behind us."

"Good," he says, a person of few words as always, which usually leads to me having to translate him to the world.

"But—"

"I knew there would be a but."

"You're not making a good case for yourself right now."

He nods. "Go on."

"But you owe me one good favor. A really freaking juicy one. I'm going to ask you to do something, and you're going to do it, no questions asked." I pause, then shake my head. "No, screw that. You owe me *two* good favors. One for dating my friend, and the other for putting me in an impossible position."

He considers this, then nods. "That's fair."

"You'll do anything I ask, twice."

He nods again. "Anything you ask. Twice."

"And you'll never, ever, in a thousand million years date another one of my friends."

"Nice to know you think so highly of me, Han."

I glare at him, and he laughs.

He looks like our mother when he laughs. He knows this, which is one of the reasons why he doesn't do it much.

"Okay, have it your way," he says. "I'll never, ever, in a thousand million years date another of your friends. You know, you're supposed to put the bigger numbers first, the smaller ones second. Besides, the human lifespan is—"

"I don't care, you agreed. Now, let's shake on it and then get that gum out."

He grins at me and holds out his big mitt, and I feel something settle inside of me. It's been harder than I realized to keep this distance between us. Liam and I didn't even tell our brother we were at odds, because it would only worry him, and he's got enough to worry about, running his own kitchen.

I shake hands with Liam, then pull him into a hug.

"Whoa, have you been working out more? Don't become one of those gross bodybuilder guys. I'd have to pretend I don't know you."

"I've had lots of time on my hands, since I haven't been running your pointless errands," he says.

I shove his arm, and just like that, we're good with each other again.

It doesn't hurt that everything turned out okay after the huge fallout from the Margaret situation. Sure, I lost some friends, but Travis was right: if they'd been true friends, they wouldn't have turned their backs on me for something that wasn't my fault. And, yeah, I stepped away from a job I loved, but if I hadn't done that, I wouldn't be working with Ollie. I wouldn't have gotten to know him and Travis as well as I have, and I probably never would have met the powerhouse that is Eugene Peebles.

We head back out to attend to little King Ollie, who's enjoying his setup.

Liam's good with him, not that I expected anything less. He probably sees Ollie as a version of our little brother, or maybe even me—another kid abandoned by the people who were supposed to care. I used to see Ollie that way, too, but that has changed over the last couple of weeks. I don't just care about him because he's in the same position we were in all those years ago. I love him because he's Ollie.

CHAPTER EIGHTEEN

TRAVIS

Drake, the guy we just auditioned, gives us a two-fingered salute, grinning like he thinks he's God's gift to the guitar, and heads out the door without looking back, offering us a perfect view of his party-in-the-back hairstyle. I'm guessing it would give Hannah hives.

None of us say anything for a few minutes—our usual habit after the colonic cleanse guy overheard Bixby bitching about him. Good thing, too. I've got the feeling this guy is probably listening in at the door, waiting for us to sing his praises.

I start wiping down my gear. I have a different kit here, so I don't need to pack it up, but a drummer takes care of his drums.

When it finally feels like enough time has passed, I glance over at my friends. "He wasn't a good fit."

"Are you kidding?" Bixby protests, pissed and making no attempt to hide it. "He was awesome, Trav. You're the one who wasn't playing right."

His words hit me like a fist to the gut. He's right. My heart wasn't in it today. I'd gotten to practice late after heading home to hide the presents, and I'd arrived in a shitty mood. Drake was already jamming with the guys, and it had felt like I was interrupting something—like they were the unit, and I was the outsider.

A dumb feeling, because it's *my* band. They're *my* buddies, and he's a stranger none of us know. But there it is.

The truth? Drake *is* good.

He knows all of our songs, and he blended well with Rob and Bix, but I wasn't able to tap into the energy of the practice. I was always a second behind or ahead, wrong-footed.

Before Drake left, the four of us had a drink and a conversation, and Drake practically fanboyed over Rob's connection to Bad Magic, saying Rob's the one who wrote all their best hits (true), and that we were just as good (also true), and that within a year, we'll be going on tour too.

Which was when it hit me...

I don't *want* to go on tour. I *can't* go on tour. I'm trying to get full custody of Ollie, and even if Hannah by some miracle agrees to go full time, it wouldn't work. But Rob and Bix both grinned at him as if this were good news and they'd been waiting for it. Working toward it.

My mood took another hit—like a ship that's torpedoed after hitting an iceberg—but I just nodded. Willed Drake to reveal he was the kind of closet psychopath who collected guitar picks from all the musicians he'd murdered. Anything to keep him from joining us and pushing Garbage Fire in a direction I didn't want it to go. But the only skeleton he revealed was his slightly douchey personality, and now it's obvious I'm the only one he bothered.

I tell myself it's not only because of his comment about touring, but I can't deny it didn't help his case.

"Rob?" Bixby says, turning toward him. "Talk some sense into this guy."

Rob claps him on the back. "It's a group decision, Bix. All of us say yes, or it's a no."

"Shouldn't it be two against one?" he asks darkly.

"No, man, because we're the three musketeers. We all go up or down together. That's how it's always been."

"But not how it's always got to be," Bixby says, glaring at me. "You don't want us to get bigger, Trav. You're happy playing at the same old bars and breweries. Getting up every day knowing it's going to be the same old shit. But I'm not. I want to go places."

"So go," I say hotly. "Choose some guy you just met over your best friends. See how that works out for you. Maybe you can be the first bassist to successfully go solo."

He shakes his head, his lips forming a flat line. "You're an asshole."

Then he packs up his bass—Bessie, he calls her—and takes off, nearly getting smacked in the ass by the door on his way out.

I run my hand through my hair, feeling like the asshole he accused me of being. Bixby's not like me. He'd probably be over the moon if someone stalked him in a toy store because they'd watched footage from a show that never got made.

Rob doesn't say anything. He just looks at me, inviting me to talk. He's already stowed his guitar.

"I know Drake's good," I finally admit, my voice hoarse. "And Bixby was right. I didn't play well tonight."

Rob nods. "He's hot-tempered. Bixby will be fine by the time we set up at New Belgium tomorrow. But how about you tell me what's going on?"

Where to start?

"Someone posted about me in a *Ships Ahoy* forum, and now a bunch of my dad's superfans are coming to our show tomorrow afternoon," I say, feeling a dull ache in my head. "If Lilah finds out about my dad, she's going to think I have a shit ton of money. She'll be on the next flight out of Australia to try to extort me, and we both know she won't think anything of using our son as leverage. I'm trying to get full custody, and she'll fight it if she thinks he's a bargaining chip she can use to get money out of me."

"Fuck," Rob says.

He doesn't ask if I'm sure about fighting for custody, even though he knows I've struggled with fatherhood, and I'm grateful to have a friend who sometimes has more faith in me than I have in myself.

I sit down heavily. "I don't mind paying her off if that's what she wants, but she's going to think I inherited more than I did. She's not the trusting type."

"So we've got to shut these superfans down without pissing them off."

I snort. "It's too late for that. One of them ambushed Hannah and me in a toy store today. I told her to mind her fucking business or something along those lines. I can't remember. I was seeing red."

Rob grins at me. "Something broke through your Travis cool?"

"Lately it feels like everything does," I admit. "Ollie's been having some trouble at school, most of these people we've tried out for the band are shit, and then there's Hannah…"

I trail off, thinking about Hannah in that dress. Hannah laughing as we made a melody on that floor piano. Hannah tracing my birthmark. Hannah kissing me back like she didn't want to stop…

He gives me a sidelong look. "How's it going with her, anyway? Sounds like you've been spending a lot of time together."

"She's great with Ollie," I say with a sigh. "She's in our lives for his sake, and that's how it's gonna stay."

"All right," he says with a smirk. "If that's how you want to spin it."

"It's not how I want to spin it," I say, feeling unreasonably pissed at him, especially since I'm the architect of all of my own problems. "That's how it is. She's Ollie's nanny."

"And single dads never end up with the nanny," he says wryly, with a knowing look that has me seeing red for probably the fiftieth time today.

"Funny."

"Come on," he says. "I'm guessing your mother hired an elderly nanny. I'm thinking thick glasses, floor-length dresses even in the summer. Maybe a knee brace or two. Someone your father's actual age."

I have to laugh at this, because it's like he just drew a picture of Nanny Grace.

"So did Lilah," I volunteer. "Ollie and I have FaceTimed his old nanny a few times. She looks like Mrs. Doubtfire."

"But not you, you crazy bastard," he says, laughing. "You had to hire the only woman you've wanted this bad in years. Maybe ever."

I drop the cloth I was using to wipe down my kit. "What are you talking about? I never said that."

"It's all in what you haven't said, brother. I know you. Just like you knew I was in deep with Sophie before I had any idea."

I swear under my breath. "Sure. Fine. I should have gone with Mrs. Doubtfire. Hannah drives me crazy. Everything in the house smells like her, and worse, I want it to smell like her." I drop my head before admitting, "And, yeah, I kissed her the other day, which was a huge mistake, but I can't stop thinking about it."

"I know a thing or two about that," he says, a sparkle of humor in his eyes.

"I want her, but I'm not going to give into it. I have enough on my plate, and Ollie needs her more than I do."

"There's no denying you have a lot to deal with," he agrees.

"Should we give your fan base a thrill and wear *Ships Ahoy* T-shirts? Maybe learn some yacht rock?"

"Very funny."

"Do you want to cancel the show tomorrow?" he asks, and I know he'd do it for me. He'd send Drake away for me too. Which is exactly why I can't let him do it.

I shake my head. "No, Bixby's already pissed, and if I cancel, they'll probably just show up at my door with popcorn and ask for a special airing of the movie."

"Sophie and I would join you," he says with a grin. "She hasn't watched them since she was little."

"I'll pass." I swallow, then admit something that hurts. "Drake's good. I guess we should give him a shot. He can play with us for Frank next week. See what he thinks of the sound."

He gives me a crooked grin. "You don't like him, though."

I shrug. "He's cocky."

"But that's not your only problem with him."

I should tell him I don't like where this is going. That I can't envision myself going on tour, ever. That I'm not even sure I want to level up, because it might mean people start recognizing me as Travis Thomas, not Ships Junior, and I'm not sure how I feel about that.

But if Rob wants the tour and the fame, he deserves them. He's worked his ass off for this band, and it's his music we're playing, even if we work together on the arrangement and melodies.

If I need to step down when the time comes, I will, as much as the thought destroys me.

"Yeah, it is," I say. "Bixby's cocky enough—he doesn't need the encouragement—but let's give this guy a go if he's interested. He's by far the best we've seen."

Rob laughs. "I mean, if it's between him and the other people we've seen, I'm going to have to agree with you."

"I'll make it good with Bix," I promise. "I'll Uber him some nachos."

It's an in-joke from the first night we met Bixby, when he ate two orders of nachos during a ten-minute conversation.

Rob pats me on the back, but he doesn't leave yet. He watches me for another long moment, then says, "Be a little easier on yourself. You're doing the best you can."

"What if it's not enough?" I ask, giving voice to the fear that's been growing inside of me like a sun-drunk weed. "What if I fuck Ollie up?"

I leave the second part of that fear unvoiced—*like our fathers fucked us up*. Rob's had a time of it too. His dad's a piece of work, same as mine. He always favored Rob's dipshit little brother, Jonah, who I now have very personal reasons for loathing. It gets to me that he had the privilege of touching Hannah and didn't value it. It makes me want to ruin him, although Hannah, Sophie, and Briar already did a pretty thorough job of that. It gives me particular joy to know that he had no choice but to leave his chosen profession and go work for his father, an embarrassing prospect for any man.

Rob smiles at me—a sad, knowing smile. "The fact that you care makes it much less likely to happen."

"I can't let Lilah take him away from me," I say, my voice cracking. "I can't lose him."

"You won't. You've got a lot of people on your side."

I nod, trying to keep the worry from taking over. "Thank you."

"Go home to them," Rob says, and I don't miss the "them."

CHAPTER NINETEEN

TRAVIS

When I get home, I take off my shoes and socks and round the corner into the living room. Some cartoon I don't recognize is playing, and Hannah is on the couch with her arm around Ollie, both of them fast asleep. I approach them, intending to carry him to his room, but I hesitate at the sight of them curled up on the couch.

Hannah's bright hair surrounds her face like a halo, and my son's face is at peace, his long eyelashes fluttering softly against his cheeks.

Ollie's hair is shorter, so presumably Liam's not the gum wizard he used to be. A sense of loss hits me hard. I have no idea when he got his first haircut, or whether his hair initially grew in a different color. More details that have been denied to me, details Lilah would never share, if she even remembers. Suddenly I need that information in the way a body needs food, the way I need music.

The haircut makes Ollie look a little older, but he's still so vulnerable looking. So breakable.

But Hannah's holding him firmly, her strength so obvious I can feel it. I want to savor it. She's still wearing that yellow dress from earlier—a bright spot. A beaming light. A glimmer of pure beauty in a world full of darkness.

They're *both* beautiful, and it hurts to look at them.

Everything hurts lately, as if every wound I've ever been dealt has begun to bleed at once.

Trying to shake off the thoughts, I close the distance to the couch and gently caress Hannah's arm, not wanting to wake her with a start. Her lashes flutter open and then her green eyes settle on me, stirring a warmth that fills my entire body and the soul caged within it.

"I'm going to carry him to his room," I say, my voice thick.

She nods, but I notice she hugs him before relinquishing him to me. She cares about Ollie. She understands this fierce feeling inside of me, the painful need to protect someone smaller and in need of care.

I stare into her eyes, almost hypnotized, but Ollie makes a little snuffling noise, and I gather him up in my arms. He snuggles against my chest, and the protective feelings swell into a tidal wave that nearly bowls me over.

I lay Ollie down on his bed and pull the covers over him, then give in to the need to run a hand over his hair before leaving the room.

When I return to the living room, Hannah's sitting up on the couch, waiting for me. There's a smear of makeup under her right eye, but otherwise she looks immaculate, just like always, whether she's dressed down or like this.

"Thank you for today," I say. "For all of it." I remain standing, because I don't know if I can be that close to her right now without reaching for her.

She smiles sleepily. "Is my makeup all over my face?"

"No. Just a little bit near your eye."

"Help a girl out?" she asks, tipping her head up to me.

A painful yearning consumes me as I sweep a finger

beneath her eye, rubbing away the makeup smudge. I can't resist caressing her cheek. Her skin is soft and warm and so touchable my fingers don't know how to stop.

Her lips part, giving me a glimpse of her tongue, and the need to kiss her is almost overwhelming. I've been wanting to kiss her all day. All week. *Longer.*

But I can't do that. I can't.

"Will you sit down with me a minute?" she asks, her eyes lingering on me.

"I can't sit right now," I say, pacing a little to make the claim more believable. "You had to cut Ollie's hair?"

She snorts. "It took Liam half an hour to finally admit he'd lost his magic gum-removing touch, but the trip wasn't wasted, because Ollie actually really likes the OG *Teenage Mutant Ninja Turtles* cartoon. So it's possible he and Mickey Mouse won't be enemies for life. Liam was really annoyed with himself, but I cut his hair too as a consolation prize."

"I'm glad you and Liam are getting along better." I know it was weighing on her, being at odds with him. "And thank you for handling all of that. Ollie's hair looks good."

"I'll cut your hair if you'd like."

My mouth goes dry at the thought of her moving her hands through my hair, her fingers tugging slightly. That shouldn't be an erotic thought, but right now everything's erotic. "No, thanks. I have a feeling you'd go a little too short in the front."

She grins. "What makes you think I'd want to share your birthmark with the world? Maybe I like that I get to see it more than most people."

I suck in a deep breath, count to three, then slowly let it out. It doesn't nothing to dull my reaction to her. "Still no."

"Fair enough." She picks up a coaster idly, then puts it back down before meeting my gaze again. "Thanks for hiding all the stuff from the toy store. Is it in here? What'd you do with it?"

"Maybe we'll have a scavenger hunt sometime," I say with a smile. "I assume you've already looked?"

"I checked under the bed and in your bedroom closet and gave up. I'm disappointed to admit I never would have made it as a spy."

So my bedroom's going to smell like her again. I'm glad about it, and the thought also makes me burn.

I must be staring at her too intently, because she glances away, her gaze finding something on the wall—probably marker, judging on past experience.

"How was the guy you auditioned?" she asks.

"Good... I think I hate him."

Not something I meant to admit, and probably an unfair remark, but I realize it's true. I *don't* like him.

She laughs. "Isn't it my job to form irrational opinions about strangers?"

"Maybe we can both have a turn," I say, grateful for the coffee table between us. That's good. I can't exactly pull her to me if there's a coffee table between us.

"So why do you hate this guy?" she asks.

"You're going to laugh."

"Maybe I could use a laugh."

I shrug one shoulder. "He's full of himself."

"Isn't every musician?" She waggles her eyebrows, looking cute as hell.

"Sure, but I don't get a bad vibe from every musician. I got one from him."

She fulfills my prophecy and laughs. "Look at you, being surprising again. You seem too organized and practical to believe in vibes."

"I've learned to trust my gut," I say with a shrug. "I've had to. When I first met Lilah, I could tell we'd be a disaster together, and I still let it happen."

"So you think this guy's going to Yoko Ono your band?"

I laugh. "Not unless Bixby starts dating him. But..." I pause, considering. "Yeah, I'm worried he's going to cause tension. I guess he already is. Bixby stormed out earlier."

She studies me for a moment, sucking on her bottom lip. "I'm worried this will piss you off..."

"Not a great beginning."

She smiles. "It's just...is the problem that this guy and Bixby want the band to get big, and you don't?"

Well, damn. Leave it to Hannah to cut right to the heart of things. "Now you're the surprising one," I say. "I didn't say any of that."

"No, but I've seen how you react to aggressive fans. I know you're not the kind of guy who wants to be asked to sign bras in the produce section at the grocery store."

"I can't let Rob and Bixby down," I insist.

"Maybe you should think less about what other people want and more about what *you* want."

"You're encouraging me to be a narcissist?" I ask, arching my brow. "Why does this feel like a trap?"

She laughs, her whole face getting in the game. No one else smiles like Hannah. "It's not. I'm not telling you to go for what you want no matter what it costs anyone else. But you should *know* what you want. Everyone should know what they want."

I take a step toward her, and my leg knocks into the side of the table I temporarily forgot was there. "And what do *you* want?"

She gets up, her eyes fixed on me. "I want to be there for Ollie, and to help the staffers at Big Catch. And I really want to help Eugene get laid."

I laugh. "And here I was hoping you might want to help *me* get laid."

Fuck, I didn't mean to say that.

But she starts laughing too and taps her full lips with her finger. "I don't think that was in the job description, but I *have* already gone above and beyond to help keep this place clean. I suppose I could help you with that too."

She's only teasing, of course, but I feel the line I crossed. "I shouldn't have said that."

"No, you probably shouldn't have," she says. "Because now I'm going to expect you to do something about it."

The next thing I know, she's standing in front of me and holding my arm, her fingers wrapped as far around it as they'll go—not very. I stop in my tracks, my whole body shifting its focus to her.

At this particular moment, she might as well have wrapped her hand around my cock.

"Hannah," I breathe out.

"Are you going to take what you want?" she whispers, her voice curling around me.

Her hair is in luscious soft curls around her face, and I let myself run my fingers through one.

Instead of answering her question, I lower my face toward hers, our mouths a whisper apart. Her lips are so touchable, the dare in her voice obvious.

My mouth answers for me as I press my lips to hers, the contact instantly sending a shudder through me. I'm disappointed in myself—I only held out two days, *two days*—but I'm so relieved to be touching her again that I can't make myself care. My hand weaves into her hair, drawing her closer, and I kiss her as if it's the only thing keeping me going.

She's the first to pull back. "Why, Mr. Sir Travis..."

"Oh, for the love of God," I groan.

She grins at me, her eyes full of mischief. Then she leans in to kiss me again before saying, "The couch. I want to straddle you. I've been thinking about it ever since we watched that movie together."

"Hannah, we shouldn't..."

"I don't care," she says, holding my gaze. "Not tonight. Let's let ourselves have tonight."

She said *tonight*, which means the offer might be off the table tomorrow. That should give me pause. Ever since I kissed her, I've been thinking about her obsessively. It's only going to be worse if I kiss her again. If I touch her. Take her. But I'm powerless to say no. Worse: not a single part of me wants to.

I lift her into my arms and carry her to the couch. When I sink back against the cushions with Hannah on my lap, the warm weight of her against my needy cock is so good, so right, I can barely resist the urge to dry-hump her.

She weaves both hands into my hair as she kisses me hard and rocks against me, and fuck it, I *am* dry-humping her, my hand guiding her hip as we move against each other. Right now, nothing feels real for me other than Hannah. It's like we're in a void, existing only for each other. Her sweet mouth, the gorgeous, delectable swell of her breasts...

What the hell is happening to me? I have absolutely no control with her, none. But it doesn't make me anxious. It makes me feel euphoric.

I just got done telling Rob that I couldn't have her. That I couldn't even kiss her, and here I am with my tongue in her mouth and my hands moving all over her. Learning her. Cupping her breasts and holding her butt and caressing every available inch of her.

I know this is madness, and all madness has to end eventually, so I want to absorb as much of the moment as possible so the memory can last.

She moves her hips, grinding against my cock, and bites down on my lower lip.

"You feel so good," I groan.

"So do you." She grins impishly at me. "I just knew you had a big stick."

I grip her hip, holding her to me, and kiss her deeper as she presses down on my cock, moving those hips. She's still wearing that tempting yellow dress, so I reach under the skirt, skimming my hands over her rounded thighs and ass as my mouth consumes her. She's perfect here too. Soft and warm and strong.

I break the kiss to stare at her, soaking in the way her lips are swollen from me. "I'm going to touch you, Hannah. Are you wet for me?"

"Yes," she says, rocking against me again. "And I can tell you're *very* hard for me."

I dip my fingers under the waistband of her panties as I bury my head in her chest, kissing the swell of her breasts—so soft and fragrant I want to lose myself in there and never find my way out. My fingers find a place she likes, and she bucks against me as I slide one of them into her. She's wet. So wet and tight, and the thought of taking what I want consumes me. It's all I can think about as she moves against me, my cock caught between us, straining as she rides my hand.

"So beautiful," I murmur against her breasts. "I want you so bad."

I kiss her, then bite down softly, and she likes that, quickening the movements of her hip. Pressing my palm against the spot where I know she needs it, I keep moving my fingers inside her, desperate to feel her take her pleasure from me. Desperate for it to happen at least this once.

She gasps. "I'm going to come."

"Thank God," I murmur.

She moves faster against me and starts to moan, the sound curling around me, enveloping me. I lift my head from her breasts to catch the sound in my mouth. We can't make too much noise because we might wake Ollie.

Ollie.

Oh shit.

I pull back slightly, panting, my fingers still curled inside of her because I can't bear to take them out yet, even though I know she already came.

She smiles at me, then very pointedly lifts my hair and traces her tongue over my birthmark.

My dick instantly gets even harder, and she tugs back to look at me in the dim light of the apartment, her eyes gleaming like emeralds.

"Am I allowed to go into your bedroom now?" she asks, her voice throaty. "Or is it still *off-limits.*"

"You already went in there tonight," I reply like a real idiot. I *feel* like an idiot, like my dick is the only part of me with more than half a thought, and all it's thinking is, *Take her now, you idiot. Don't ask too many stupid questions.*

"It was *very* naughty of me to break the rules. I'll let you spank me."

Oh, fuck. From the gleam in her eyes, she actually wants me to.

I swallow dryly. "The music room."

"Why?" she asks. Then her eyes gleam with understanding. "Oh, because it's mostly soundproof? Do you think that highly of your skills, Travis?"

"You were right. All musicians are full of themselves."

"Do I get to be full of you too?" she whispers.

"If you don't kill me first. Let me up, and I'll be right back."

She climbs off my lap, and my dick is already anxious for her to come back.

I make a mad dash to grab a condom from the bureau in my bedroom, but when I get back to the living room, she's gone.

For a moment, I think the universe has restored order by keeping us apart, but then I stride to the music room, my heart in my throat, my dick hard as hell. I open the door—and feel the air whoosh out of my lungs at the sight of her. She's sitting at my drum kit, completely naked, her yellow dress and underwear in a pile by the door. Her hair is a curly halo around her head, her full breasts revealed to me, her nipples pink and perfect. She's holding my drumsticks, turning them around in her hands.

It's the sexiest thing I've ever seen in my life. It's so hot, it immediately incinerates the memories of any woman who isn't her.

"Are you trying to trick me into giving you a lesson?" I ask as I step into the room, locking the door behind me.

She hits the snare. "I figured I'd play with your other sticks while I was waiting."

This woman...

"Besides," she adds. "Maybe I wanted to get into your headspace."

"The only thing I'm thinking about now is you," I say, walking over to her. She swivels on the drum seat so she's facing me, still clutching my drumsticks, sliding her hands suggestively down the length of them.

I lean down to kiss her hard, burrowing my hand into her hair. Her lips invite me in, and it feels so good to lose myself in her. So good to lay down the weight of the day and just be with her.

She pulls back slightly, breaking the kiss, then smiles at me. "You're wearing a lot of clothes, Travis. It's kind of rude."

I start in on the buttons of my shirt, nearly tearing off a few of them in my hurry to get the damn thing off. When I get far enough, I tear it off over my head and then pull off my undershirt, before attacking the buckle on my jeans.

She uncrosses her legs, giving me a view of the short thatch of red curls between them before crossing them again.

Yes, she's definitely going to be the death of me, but I'll enjoy every minute of it.

I grab the condom out of my pocket, then push down my jeans and boxer briefs, giving her everything.

I know I don't have anything to be ashamed of, but the look on her face is satisfying to me on a deep, primal level, maybe because it would seem unfair to want a woman this much and not have her want me in return.

"Is this better?"

"Much," she says, releasing the sticks. They hit the floor with a thwack, and I don't hide my wince.

"That's no way to treat a man's sticks," I say as I reach down and lift her up from the seat.

"What are you going to do about it?"

Her voice is full of innuendo, and I remember what she suggested in the living room.

"Put your hands on the chair and turn around."

She grins at me and does as I asked, lifting her perfect round ass to me. I let myself palm it, running my fingers over her soft skin, then dip a finger in to feel her again. Even wetter than before.

I run my hands over her ass again, before spanking it on one side—not hard, but not nothing.

She glances over her shoulder and lifts her ass up further. "You can do better than that."

My dick throbs painfully, plaintively, as I caress my hand over her, dipping into her with my finger before I pull back and spank her on the other side, harder.

She hums under her breath and pushes back into my hand as I slide my fingers between her legs again, pausing to rub her most sensitive area.

Then I run my hand down the slope of her delicious back and place a palm at the base while I spank her ass again on the first side, this time dipping in deeper between her legs afterward.

"I'm going to fuck you. If you want me to stop, this is the time to tell me, Hannah."

"God no," she says. "If you stop, I'll never forgive you, and I'm a woman who holds a grudge."

I tear open the condom wrapper with my teeth, then slide it on and line myself up.

"I believe in keeping things even," I say before I smack the other side of her ass and then thrust into her.

CHAPTER TWENTY

HANNAH

My first thought as Travis thrusts into me, his big dick stretching me perfectly and my ass stinging slightly, in a perfect, heady mixture of pleasure and a drop of pain: *Yes. Yes. One thousand times yes.*

My second thought, in the back of my mind: *This definitely wasn't supposed to happen.*

But I can't think about that now. Not when he's rubbing me in all the right ways, in all the right places.

The stool I'm leaning on screeches a little as it gets shoved a half inch across the hardwood floor. I push back into him, and he gathers my hair with one of his big hands, pulling but not yanking, as the other reaches between my legs and rubs me.

He bends forward, going impossibly deeper with his next thrust and says, "You feel so damn good."

His voice rumbles through me, and it's as if I'm being engulfed by him in all the best ways.

He pulls nearly all the way out, then thrusts back in, tugging slightly on my hair as he does, and I nearly come on the spot. Pleasure spirals through me, blurring the edges of my vision, as I hold onto that stool for dear life. I look over my shoulder at him, taking in the intensity of his expression as he fucks me, but when he sees me looking back, he bends over and kisses me passionately, his dick buried inside of me.

He's still kissing me as he pulls out and thrusts back in, his fingers working me. It feels so intense, I let out an inhuman moan that he swallows with his kiss.

The stool gives another sound of protest as it jolts across the floor, closer to his drum kit. Are we going to fall into the drums? Knock them over?

He thrusts in again, his mouth finding my neck, and I forget about the drums, and where we are, and anything other than the way he's making me feel.

His hair brushes against me as he moves inside me again, and then the stool topples over. In a split-second reaction, he swings an arm around me and tugs us back, maneuvering our bodies as we're falling so I land on top of him, his dick still buried in me from behind.

"Oh my god," I say, pulling up off him and getting up. "Are you okay?"

He groans, taking a few deep breaths, but then says, "I will be if you keep fucking me."

I don't question him. He undoubtedly banged his head and his back, but the man knows what he wants. And right now he wants me.

I climb onto him, lowering down onto his dick, and his hand finds my hip, curling around it as I set my pace, taking him in deep at this new angle, staring intently into his eyes as I take his dick.

He leans up and sucks one of my nipples as I move over him, grazing his teeth over it slightly before moving on to the next. And it's that slight rasp of his teeth against my nipple that makes me come again without warning, clenching against him.

I cry out, the sound reverberating through the room.

His hips jerk up once, twice, and then he buries himself deep inside me and sighs into my neck before kissing it.

I feel dizzy with pleasure, but after a moment I pull off him. I start to get up, but he tugs me back down to lie with him on the floor of the music room.

"Let's not let reality intrude yet," he says gruffly, running a hand over my hair and my shoulders as I settle against his chest.

"Did you get a concussion?" I ask, half meaning it. "Are these the ramblings of a contused mind?"

"Probably." He laughs as he continues gently caressing me, and my heart feels drunk and woozy in my chest. I remind myself that we agreed to only one night, and Travis is, unfortunately, a man of his word, but my heart doesn't want to listen. It's a greedy bitch, and it's taken a liking to this man. Alarmingly, I don't just like him when he's like this, at the edge of chaos and spilling over, but also when he's planning his meals and making ridiculous rules. I like all the little parts that form the puzzle that is Travis Thomas.

I tilt my head up so I can get a better look at him. "Seriously, are you okay? You must have gotten hurt when we fell down."

"I'm better than okay," he says, tugging me closer. "This was exactly what I needed."

Not quite the same as *Hannah, you are perfection itself and the only person who could help me get my groove back*, but then again, I'm the one who said this was just for the night, and I'm not blind to the fact that Travis has his own issues.

He angles his head to look me in the eye. "Will you stay a little longer? If it's only going to be like this between us tonight, I want it to last as long as possible."

"Yeah," I say, feeling my heart do strange things in my chest. Trying to grow maybe. Or break. Or figure out if it's the Olympic gymnast of hearts and can do both things at the same time.

He takes off the condom and knots it, and I pull my dress back on and take the condom from him.

"You shouldn't have to do that," he says, as if I'm going to be disgusted by the condom we used together.

"I need to pee afterward, or I'll definitely get a UTI, and I have terrible insurance."

Guilt ghosts across his face. "You need insurance? Maybe I can—"

"I have to pee," I say, my heart thumping hard in my chest, because this conversation is driving in the wrong direction, ready to crash against a wall.

I don't want to be a messed-up crash test dummy.

So I hurry to the bathroom and hide the condom beneath a mound of other trash, then take care of business and wash up. Before I go, I change my mind and knot the trash bag so I can take it out. The last thing we need is for Ollie to find the condom and ask what it is. With our luck, he'd probably bring it up to Mrs. Applebaum, who already thinks we're deviants.

Travis is waiting outside for me in a T-shirt and some athletic shorts, looking thoroughly undone. I did that, and for a second I let myself soak him in, even though I can already tell he's freaking out.

"Are you okay?" he asks, scratching the back of his neck.

"I'm not the one who fell onto his back with an actual person on top of him."

"I'm fine," he insists, but there's something in his eyes that suggests he's *not* fine.

"You think this was a mistake," I say flatly.

His eyes are full of regret, and my body starts trembling slightly, which makes me furious with myself.

"Not a mistake," he says, shaking his head. "But I feel like a selfish prick for putting my own needs before Ollie's."

"What?" I ask, my temper heating up. "Why is this a problem? You think I'm going to get so addicted to your dick I'm going to start stalking you like those *Ships Ahoy* people? Or are you worried that I'll take off and leave Ollie? Disappear from his life? You really think I'd do that?"

He looks over at me, his eyes impossibly sad. "His mother did."

I wrench my hand from him as an old pain threatens to split me open "I would *never* do that to him. Especially not over a man. You'd have to fire me to keep me away from him. I am nothing like Lilah."

He swears. "I know you're nothing like her. Not in the ways that matter. I just..."

"What are the ways that matter?" I snap.

He looks pained. "You know that line between control and chaos?" He pauses, as if he expects me to nod. I don't. "Both of you are on the chaos side."

"Oh, does she not clean to your satisfaction either?"

"I don't mind doing the cleaning. I like it."

For some reason this infuriates me even more. Possibly because it makes him a unicorn of a man, and he basically told me he doesn't want me.

I hold his gaze. "You said you knew Lilah was going to wreck your life when you first met her. What did you think about me? What was *my* vibe?"

Emotions I can't read pass through his gaze, until regret settles in as if it's comfortable there. "That you were a hurricane that could blow my life apart."

He might as well have slapped me across the face. I take a step away from him, hurt radiating through me.

But I'm no coward. I learned long ago to slap back when someone hurts me. To hit them before they can hit me again or turn their back and leave forever.

Lifting my chin, I say, "I've never met someone so afraid of living. Now, I'm going to take off before I do something *else* I regret. But guess what? I'll see you tomorrow, because I don't flake on people I care about. I'm talking about Ollie, obviously. Not you."

"I understood," he says, his jaw flexing. "Let me walk you out."

"To make sure I leave? Are you worried I'm going to hide in your bushes so I can sneak in and take photos of you sleeping?"

"I want to make sure none of my dad's scary superfans are waiting out there," he says. "I've been worried about that all day. Believe it or not, I care about you. *A lot.*"

"Let me guess. Do you feel that way against your better judgment?"

"Yes," he replies tightly. "Because you. Work. For. Me." He sucks in a slow breath. "Tonight was incredible. *Beyond* incredible. But yeah, it was a mistake. I'm already enough of a failure as a father. I don't want to mess up the one situation that's actually making Ollie happy."

Some of my anger cools, leaving me frustrated and uncomfortable in my own skin. Anger, I can live with—it's actionable—but sadness and confusion just plain suck.

"You already did ruin it," I say.

He reaches for me, but I shake my head. "Like I said, I won't be leaving him. But this thing we've been doing...we need to keep our distance from each other."

"Hannah."

"You know I'm right. By the way, I'm bringing my friends over with me tomorrow. My real friends."

Hurt burns in his eyes, but he nods once. "Ollie told me."

He doesn't say anything else. He just walks me to the door. I don't object when he follows me out, but I do take a little pleasure out of completely ignoring him.

I drive home with stinging eyes, but I take some pride in the fact that I don't cry until I'm at home alone in my bed.

CHAPTER TWENTY-ONE

HANNAH

Babes of Brewing chat

Sophie: So I know you told us this was NEVER going to happen just two weeks ago, but let's be honest, I knew it was going to happen. YOU probably knew it was going to happen. I think Briar did too.

Briar: Definitely. The lady doth protest too much.

Me: You're focusing on the wrong thing. Did you somehow miss the part where he said sleeping with me was a huge mistake?

Me: And today he didn't say a damn thing about any of it. He just told me to have fun, like he was some boring TV dad.

Me: And he had on a polo shirt for a freaking show.

Me: I'm grateful he didn't pop the collar, but honestly…

Me: I don't even know why I hooked up with him. He's not at all my type.

Sophie: Do you want me to pretend I believe you?

Briar: Why are we texting? This is dumb.

Briar: Can someone pass the popcorn?

I pass Briar the bowl of popcorn, rolling my eyes.

We're sitting on Travis's couch—the very couch where he dry-humped me last night. Ollie and I are in the middle, with Briar to my left and Sophie to his right.

I should never have broken my vow to keep things platonic with him. But the pull between us was so hard to fight that even Travis, who's way more self-controlled than I am, gave into it. If he couldn't tight the riptide, how was I supposed to?

It had started at the toy store, when we'd nearly kissed over the piano, and then he'd been so sweet and gentle when he'd put Ollie to bed, only to come back and prowl the living room like a panther, his dark eyes undressing me.

I'd wanted him to do unspeakable things to me, and he had *delivered*. Truthfully, I'd fantasized about him taking me exactly that way while I was at their concerts.

I'd been entirely lost in the moment, especially because he'd seemed so lost in it too...

But then he'd said the thing about me being a hurricane.

I've been told I'm too much by nearly every man I've had the misfortune of getting tangled up with. Most of the time I don't care about the people who accuse me of that. I figure they only think I'm too much because they're too little—like Jonah, whose ego was so fragile, he had to have at least four women around at any given time to stroke it. Or my first serious boyfriend, who said I was too "embarrassing" to introduce to his parents. They were jerks, but it hadn't mattered, because I'd known they were jerks. We were using each other. I'd chosen them because I'd known they didn't have the power to really hurt me. The most they could do was bruise.

But it had hurt like hell for Travis to treat me like that, because I respect him. Because I *like* him.

Over the past couple of weeks, I've started feeling close to him, like the two of us were teammates on Team Ollie. Co-matchmakers for retirees. But now...

I'm bitterly disappointed, even though I'd promised myself a long time ago that I was done getting disappointed by men. Because sex with Travis had felt like a kind of...awakening. It had made me realize how different it felt to be with a man I actually respected and cared about.

But that feeling was obviously one-sided.

Travis is at his afternoon show with the guys, and even though I still feel a lot of righteous anger toward him, I hope it goes well.

I texted Ships Ahoy Alice earlier, asking her to keep me apprised of how the performance is going, both to make her feel important and because I'm worried, and she sent me fifteen texts back in response, all of which boil down to: it'll be her privilege and honor to keep an eye on him.

"Will you guys *please* stop it with the phones," Ollie says, rolling his eyes. "It's not fair that I'm not allowed to use one ever, and you use yours whenever you want."

"Life isn't fair," I say darkly, waving my hand at the TV screen, where one of the teenage mutant ninja turtles is executing a sick takedown. "Imagine. They were normal little turtles before all that ooze turned them into mutants."

"Isn't it better that they're mutants?" Ollie asks. "Now they fight crime and know cool fight moves. Real turtles don't really do anything except eat lettuce and poop."

"I'm sure they do other things."

"No, I think he's right," Briar says, pausing her popcorn consumption. "I researched turtles before I got a cat. They're a bit dull, honestly, unless it makes you feel relaxed to watch things happen very slowly. I guess that does it for some people."

"So the ooze was good for them, Hannah," Ollie insists. "Can we make some ooze after the show?"

"Only if we keep it away from the cushions. There are only so many ways that I can fail to clean them."

"Are you talking about slime?" Sophie asks. "I know how to get that stuff out. You should have asked me."

I sigh, feeling my foul mood at a soul-deep level. Maybe I should go pick someone up at a bar so I can erase Travis from my mind, or at least have the satisfaction of knowing he's no longer the last person I slept with. But the thought of sleeping with someone else makes me feel like my stomach is coated with turtle ooze, which brings me back, in a vicious cycle, to being pissed at Travis. How dare he affect me like this...

"You're frowning again," Briar points out unhelpfully, then thrusts the bowl of popcorn at me. "Have some popcorn. It always makes me feel better. Popcorn goes through a pretty miraculous transformation to go from hard, gross little kernels to this majesty."

Briar's in a weird mood, but I don't call her on it, because I'm in a weird mood myself.

I start to reach for the bowl, then nearly tip it over when my phone buzzes. Briar wraps her arm around it as if she's protecting a baby.

"Here we go again," Ollie murmurs, giving me a dark look, as I pick up the phone to check it.

"I have to look," I say. "It may be your dad's stalker."

"Dad has a stalker?"

"Sort of," I say. "I'll let him explain." The thought of Travis's discomfort gives me momentary satisfaction, but I don't want Ollie to worry that there's some weird man hiding in the bushes outside of the house, so I add, "But what you should know is that she's not dangerous. She's more like a really desperate wannabe friend."

"Okay, whatever," he says, less interested in this than he is in real turtles.

I glance at my phone and see a message not from Alice but from Eugene, asking if we can meet up to discuss the Big Catch party.

"It's Eugene," I announce happily.

My friends give me tolerant looks, because they've heard all about him and care less about interruptions to *Teenage Mutant Ninja Turtles*. Ollie ignores me.

I glance down at the screen again.

I remember the dearly beloved hedgehog Mrs. Applebaum lost and write back:

> Why don't we paint some pottery together to discuss everything? It's supposed to be very relaxing. I think your number one goal should be to learn how to relax.

> I'll research some days and times.

> Let's go tomorrow.

> Sunday seems like a good day for pottery. We can do it at noon, maybe. I'll text you the location tomorrow morning.

He seems like a man who probably has a color-coded calendar, so I'm guessing this on-the-fly planning will drive him crazy —and possibly be good for him.

He responds more quickly than expected:

> One of the Wise Elders has a granddaughter who runs a clay studio. Perhaps we can go there.

Oh, Eugene, all grown up and making friends with adorable older ladies.

> I'm glad you joined their club.

> Did you have fun discussing the dispersal of your remains?

> They had some informative opinions. Did you know that human ashes can be pressed into a record?

> No, and I could have gone without knowing that.

> I had coffee with them this morning, too, and they had some interesting ideas for tactics I can try at Big Catch.

> Oh?

> I'm going to attempt some of them today.

> Dottie offered to help facilitate.

> I was thinking we could plan a staff party for December. That'll give us enough time to make a thorough plan. I already started the spreadsheet.

> A holiday party! Holiday parties are epic. We can discuss the details over pottery.

Oh, by the way, could your tech genius son figure out who made this post?

I send him the link Alice gave me the other day, and he responds with admirable speed:

I love assignments.

Nothing about that surprises me.

I'll ask him immediately, but he's traveling for work, and it's possible he won't respond in a timely manner.

Thank you, Eugene.

I hope to have an answer for you soon.

"Hannah," Ollie groans. "You've missed everything."

I glance up, and sure enough, the end credits are streaming.

"No, I didn't," I lie. "They fought someone, and then at the end everyone's friends again, and they ate a pizza. Speaking of which...do you guys want pizza later?"

"Yes," Briar says. "I've been stress-eating. My mom and dad are scouting locations for his new business. I don't even know what it's going to be anymore."

"So you're going to become Mrs. Silver Star *very* soon, "I say.

She sighs and sets the popcorn bowl down on the coffee table. "Seems likely, but he wasn't kidding about Briar Boot Camp. I think he's been watching too many game shows."

"What's he up to now?" I ask, drawn in.

"He challenged me to find out which of the staff members are talking about him. They're *all* talking about him. Even around me. I'm not about to tell him that, of course, so I panicked and told him the brewer praised his work ethic. He knew it was a lie, though. Then he told me I had to remove all of the chairs from the break room because people were spending too much time in there. He asked me to do it in the middle of the day, when everyone was watching, so now they're probably talking about me." She heaves a sigh. "And he's driving the brewer crazy about the tropical IPA. Nothing satisfies him. And yesterday, he asked me to drive all around town to find twenty different tropical IPAs for him to taste test."

Sophie cringes. "His tropical IPA obsession might be my fault."

She'd famously tossed back some of his tropical IPA and then informed him that Buchanan Brewery's was better. Briar's dad is nothing if not competitive.

"At least the staff will be happy when you take over," Sophie adds. "You'll be an amazing boss."

"We'll see," Briar says with another sigh. "I'm a little nervous about the transition. I couldn't manage a single staff member with the jewelry business. How am I supposed to run a whole brewery?"

"Can we do something fun?" Ollie asks. "This isn't really a kid conversation."

I wrap him in a hug before releasing him. "More turtles?"

"Nah, how about we play with some of the toys you and Travis got yesterday?"

I laugh. "How'd you know about that, you little gremlin?"

"Travis isn't nearly as good at hiding things as he thinks he is."

I'm not so sure I agree with that. I looked and found nothing, but I guess I wasn't very strategic about my snooping.

"Do you have painting supplies?" Sophie says. "What if we paint turtles?"

"Yeah!" Ollie says. "Maybe I'll give mine to Mickey. Hannah thinks we won't hate each other so much if we can talk about the mutant turtles. I don't know if it'll work, but I'm willing to try for the sake of peace."

I ruffle his hair, feeling my heart expand, as if it's growing around him. "That's because you're a good kid. A real A-plus child over here."

My phone buzzes again.

"Hannah," Ollie groans. "*Please* don't look at that. People can get addicted to their devices, you know. That's what Travis told me. I don't want you to have an addiction, Hannah. They're really bad. You might have to go to a halfway house."

I frown at him. "What have you been reading?"

"You're the one who gave it to me."

Oops. I found some middle-grade-looking books in the Little Free Library in my building and brought them over.

"I'm going to ungive it to you. Don't worry about the phone, though. I'm not going to be glued to it. I just have to make sure it's not the stalker."

I check the screen and see that it *is* Alice.

The first thing she sent is a photo of the crowd at New Belgium Brewery gathered around the outdoor stage. Right near the front, there's a group of women of variable ages wearing sexy sailor dresses totally inadequate for the chilly November air, carrying signs that say *Rip It, Baby Ships* and *I Ship Ships Junior*.

It's followed by a long text:

We didn't do this, Hannah. I have no idea where these other fans came from, but they're VERY disrespectful. One of them just threw her unmentionables at Travis, and they got caught on his cymbal. He had to remove them with a drumstick. We'll try to encircle them to contain the problem, but I wanted you to know that we played no part in this disaster.

I'm still furious with Travis, but I care about him, and I know what this must be doing to him. They're ripping him apart. Making him feel like that little kid again, lost and in need of control. A commodity to be packaged and used.

"Just a second, Ollie," I say. "Your dad is a damsel in distress."

CHAPTER TWENTY-TWO

TRAVIS

It's a chilly day, but sweat drips down my neck as the group near the front of the crowd starts up a chant: "Ships, Ships, Ships Ahoy!"

It's like they stepped out of a nightmare. Six of them are in sailor dresses. A couple of these women are older, maybe in their sixties, probably fans of the original movies when they aired. All of them have their hair in pigtails. Maybe it's my imagination, but one of the older women looks like she has a *Ships Ahoy*–themed tattoo sleeve. My father seems to be winking at me from her arm, promising me I can never move beyond his legacy.

Why are they here? When I checked the forum this morning, the post I'd asked the moderator to remove was gone. I assume the woman from the toy shop took my message to heart, too, because she's not with them.

And yet, here they are anyway, making a spectacle. A few minutes ago, one of them threw her bra at me. It skidded across my arm before landing on my cymbal.

I picked it up with my drumstick and made a show of

twirling it around before throwing it back into the crowd, but my pulse was pounding in my ears.

Worse: I jacked up my back last night when Hannah and I fell, so I'm in mental and physical pain.

I don't like this.

I don't like it one bit.

Especially since I've seen plenty of cameras in the crowd, and I know this will end up all over social media. The more posts there are, the more likely it is that Lilah will see them.

My custody of my kid could be threatened by a bunch of grown women dressed in skimpy sailor dresses in November.

More sweat drips down my hair, plastering it to my head as Rob sings "Hot Honey."

Neither he nor Bix seem too bothered by the sailor crew, but then, these women aren't here for them. They came for me. To watch me. To catcall me. To photograph me.

This is hell, but maybe I deserve a place in it for what I did to Hannah last night.

I couldn't sleep last night, tossing and turning as I thought about the way she'd felt and tasted. I smelled her on my pillow, on *myself*, because I couldn't bear to take a shower and wash off the scent of her.

So after a while I got out of bed, poured myself a drink, and stayed awake, stewing in my dissatisfaction with myself.

I've never met someone who was so afraid to live.

Hannah's right.

I'm a fucking coward.

I didn't tell her the whole truth last night.

When I first met her, I stayed away because I sensed she could destroy my world the way Lilah had, but it hadn't taken me long to realize it needed to be destroyed.

I crave Hannah's chaos.

Before Ollie and Hannah came along, my house was cold

and clinical, neat and organized but about as exciting as a museum honoring wallpaper.

For so long, I'd kept my world controlled and predictable, a world that couldn't break me. I would never again have to feel the way I did when my father pushed me in front of those producers, or when Lilah sat down on Roland's lap in front of me, twenty-four hours after telling me she loved me. I'd never have to depend on anyone other than myself.

But that life was lonely, and I don't want it anymore. Hannah made my world come alive again, and now I can barely turn a corner without being surprised by something.

Even if nothing else ever happens between Hannah and me, a man shouldn't be afraid of the truth.

I don't just crave Hannah's chaos—I need it.

I need *her*.

"Row, row, row your boat!" one of the women sings, her scratchy, off-pitch voice warring with Rob's deep baritone.

One of the younger women shouts, "You can row my boat anytime, Ships Junior!"

I miss my mark, screwing up the song.

"Can it!" someone hollers at them.

There's a sudden shift in the crowd, and I watch as the Ships ladies are swallowed by another group pushing their way to the front, one of whom turns directly to me and gives me a smart salute. *Alice.*

She's dressed in regular clothing, no signs of *Ships* paraphernalia.

I'm relieved...until one of the sailor-suit ladies throws a toy boat at my head, clocking me right in the birthmark.

"What the fuck?" I say, stopping midbeat, the words clearly audible over the sound system.

"Hole in one!" someone shrieks.

So they're drunk, too. Fantastic.

"Well," Rob says with an easy laugh, although I can tell this is Rob, front man, speaking, not Rob, my best buddy. "Looks like we've got a wild crowd this afternoon. Please refrain from throwing anything else on the stage. We've got everything we need up here, my friends."

"Ships, ships, ships ahoy!" one of the women screams.

"You might be lost," Rob says firmly. "No ships here. Only rolling blue mountains."

Our stage is right next to the river, and a bunch of people lounging on inflatable floats roll by lazily even as he says it.

"But his heart is in the ocean," another of the sailor-suit women rebuts, pointing at me. "He's ocean royalty."

While Alice's group has the drunken troublemakers surrounded, they're just standing around them like hall moni-tors with disapproving frowns. They can't actually stop them from heckling me.

Nope, I can't finish this set.

I need to get out of here. But abandoning my drums would be only slightly less unimaginable than abandoning Ollie.

So I start packing up without another word.

"What are you doing?" Bixby hisses at me, but I ignore him, set on my task.

The crowd murmurs and pulses. The energy has shifted, as if there's blood in the water.

Dammit, now they have me using maritime metaphors.

"We're going to play the rest of the show as an acoustic set," Rob says. "Every now and then we like to do something differ-ent, friends. Keeps us on our toes."

He's doing it for me, being a good friend to try to keep the *Ships* bullshit down to a minimum.

I carry on packing up, my hands shaking.

I pick up the toy boat, then figure screw it, it looks like something Ollie might like in his bath. Whoever threw it at me automatically forfeited it, so I pack it away with the rest.

Rob starts playing again as I carry the first of my cases down, feeling sick in the pit of my stomach. I've got at least two or three trips ahead of me, and there's no way Alice, however motivated, is going to be able to get her people to hold the sailor ladies back. I'm not afraid of fans, even *Ships Ahoy* fans, but I don't want to have to physically defend myself against them if they get aggressive.

As soon as I reach the ground, I see them pushing toward me in my peripheral vision. One woman's hand closes around my bicep. "*Ships Junior*," she croons. "I'm here. I can't believe it's really you. My mom and I came to see you from Massachusetts! I'd do anything for you, Travis. I mean *anything*."

I tug her hand off, but it doesn't faze her. She looks like she's about to launch herself at me. She's small and blonde, and I seriously don't want to have to push her.

A huge block of a man steps out of the crowd and acknowledges me with a nod as he steps between us.

It's Hannah's brother. Liam's hair is freshly cut, short and glinting red in the sun.

"He's got a bodyguard!" the woman shrieks. "Come on, man. We just want his autograph. We were *promised* his autograph. The last thing we'd do is hurt him. We love him."

"Who promised you?" I ask gruffly, ignoring the professions of love from a group of people who've never met me.

"He talked to me!" she shouts to her friend, her voice rising above Rob's acoustic version of "Hot Honey."

"He asked you a question," Liam says, his voice gruff.

"It was MaritimeLaw69. They said you'd be giving autographs. Can you sign my bra? I wore the blue one just for you, Ships Junior."

"No," Liam says flatly. "Never gonna happen."

I curse inside my head. MartimeLaw69 is the same person who informed Alice's online group where they could find me.

Did I really piss off Rachel enough that she'd wage some vendetta against me? I had a five-minute conversation with the woman. No one likes getting rejected, but this would be a pretty extreme reaction.

Liam grabs the cases I'm holding and nods toward the stage. "Can you grab the rest in one trip?"

I'll have to.

I nod to him, then head up onto the stage and muscle up the remaining cases. Bixby is watching me with narrowed eyes, probably still pissed that I'm jumping the shark (dammit, again with the maritime metaphors).

Liam's waiting for me with the other cases, and when I reach him at the side of the stage, he starts walking me to the lot.

Is it embarrassing to have a de facto bodyguard? Absolutely. I take pride in being able to take care of myself, but it's obvious these women won't stay away if I ask nicely. Unless I wanted them hanging off me like limpets, I'd have to shove my way out. That would be ruder than I'd like, and there'd be photos. The odds of this mess making some local paper would skyrocket.

I show him where I'm parked, and we get the kit packed up in my truck. Rob and Bix drove separately, so at least I don't need to wait for them to leave.

Thankfully, no one has tried to approach the truck, but when I glance up, the group of sailor-dressed ladies is standing at the edge of the parking lot, surrounded by Alice's hall monitors, all of them staring at us as if they're stalkers in a horror movie.

"You okay?" Liam asks with a nod.

"Not really," I admit, my gaze on the ladies as a few of them start waving and blowing kisses. "Did Hannah send you?"

She must have. It's the only reasonable explanation for him showing up when he did.

He nods. "I didn't get the full story. She talks really quickly when she's worked up, but some woman named Alice texted her about what was happening."

Toy Store Alice. I feel like I've been struck down with a sudden and possibly terminal case of chest congestion. Hannah's pissed at me, deservedly, but she's still taking care of me and my child. Of course she is. She likes to hide it, but she has the biggest heart of anyone I've ever met.

I'm a complete asshole. A waste of life. I feel like Ships Fucking Junior.

"You look pretty beat up about a few chicks in sailor dresses wanting you to sign their bras," he observes, raising his eyebrows.

"It's a long story."

"Why don't you come back to Big Catch with me, grab a drink before you go home? No offense, but you don't look ready to face your kid."

He's right. I'm not ready to face anyone.

"Yeah, okay," I say. "Thanks."

I get behind the wheel, take a few deep breaths—inhale, hold for three seconds, exhale—then I follow his beat-up red truck to Big Catch, almost in a trance.

He leads me into the brewery, nodding to the hostess, who has a name tag that reads: *I'm Rae, ask me about my crocheting!* The "I'm" and "ask me about" are printed, her name and hobby handwritten in. Liam says, "We'll sit in the kayak booth."

"Sure." She pauses, scratches her nose. "You're supposed to wear one of these name tags too. Eugene came in with them a few hours ago, and he was really adamant about it."

"I work in the back," he says flatly.

"Everyone on staff."

Liam groans but nods. "Fine, you have them?"

She grabs a sticker from under the hostess stand and hands it to him, along with a red Sharpie.

He writes in *Liam* and *beer*.

"Uh, it's supposed to be a hobby other than beer," she says, offering him another label.

This time he writes in *Liam* and *hitting people.*

"*Liam.*"

"What? The only other thing I do is box. It's accurate. Eugene always says accuracy is important."

She rolls her eyes and hands him a third label. "I don't even know how to crochet. Write something socially acceptable."

He sighs, and this time writes in *Liam* and *boxing* before sticking it to his shirt.

"Thanks, he'll be really pleased," she says, even though the look on Liam's face says he doesn't give much of a shit about pleasing most people, and particularly doesn't give a shit about pleasing Eugene.

"Yup, I aim to please," he says dryly, then leads me to a booth beneath a couple of kayaks mounted to the wall—hence the kayak booth, I guess.

"Take a seat," he says. "I'll bring you back something better than what they're serving."

"Yeah? Hannah gave me something you made the other night. It was really good..."

I trail off, filled with a sinking feeling. Thinking about Hannah fills me with fresh shame.

I need to figure out a way to make it right with her, without succumbing to the deep pit of need that's opened up inside of me. I could give her a raise, but I already feel sleazy about sleeping with a woman who works for me. Paying her more after that would feel like adding insult to injury.

"Yeah, that was a good one," Liam says, and it takes me a second to register that he was talking about the beer. "I'll get you something else this time. Mix it up."

He claps me on the shoulder and then disappears, leaving me to wonder if he's actually going to poison me this time. Maybe he knows what happened with Hannah last night. Maybe he can tell all the things I did to his sister in the music room just from looking at me.

I drum my fingers against the table, feeling miserable in a way that I could only put into music. God, there has to be a way to fix things between Hannah and me. Right now, I'd even settle for just making them better.

I take a bracing breath, then pull out my phone to text her.

> Thank you.

> I'm so fucking sorry about last night.

> I should have said so this morning, but I was ashamed and embarrassed.

Three dots appear, disappear, and then she writes:

> Were you embarrassed about the polo shirt?

My fingers rise to trace the collar of my now-sweaty shirt.

> What's wrong with polo shirts?

> Are you planning to go out for a jaunt on a horse with a mallet?

> Maybe.

> I don't think I could feel like more of an ass, but I'm willing to try.

You seem to succeed without trying.

Hannah, I should never have said all of that last night.

I don't know what I would have done without you.

Ollie would probably still be hiding sweet gum balls in my bed.

Yes, and you're welcome.

I was trying to push you away last night because I thought it was the right thing to do.

You did a good job of it.

Say, is there a nanny HR department I should report you to?

Probably. Maybe you can just report me to one of those Ships Ahoy fan forums. That seems to be the best way to circulate information.

Where are you?

Liam asked me to have a drink at Big Catch.

Is he about to murder me?

Not on my behalf. So if you get murdered, we can blame your personality.

Odds aren't good for my survival, but if I make it, I'll be home in an hour or two.

We'll be here. We're having a paint-off in your living room without a drop cloth. Whoever gets the most acrylic paint on the floors wins.

Have fun ;-)

I'm about to write something else—hopefully something deep and meaningful—but Liam sets a beer in front of me.

"Talking to Hannah?" he asks as he gets settled into the booth with his own drink.

I itch to pocket my phone, as if Liam might develop X-ray vision and see our conversation, but I settle for setting it down on the table.

"Yeah. I let her know we're here."

He raises his eyebrows, leaning back in the seat across from me. "Are you going to tell me what that was all about?"

"You mean with Hannah? I—"

"No, I meant with those women at the show," he says, frowning, and gestures to the kayaks on the wall. "Those people have as much of a hard-on for ships as the guy who started this place."

I laugh and nearly choke on my sip of beer. "I figured Hannah told you all about my past."

He holds my gaze for a moment before saying, "Hannah might seem like an open book, but she doesn't share other people's secrets."

"So I'm discovering," I say, feeling an ache of longing.

I don't need to tell Liam about my dad. I get the feeling he won't insist on it, but at this point, the secret isn't much of one. People will be talking. People will be *posting*. My only hope is that Lilah's still in the middle of her internet desert or that the local news is the only place this will end up. After all, my dad is old news, and I shouldn't be news at all.

So I tell him about Ships Junior. Meeting Alice in the toy store. The social media post.

"Well, damn," Liam says, cracking his scarred knuckles. "Someone's got a grudge against you. Who have you pissed off other than my sister?"

I laugh uncomfortably. "She said something about that, huh?"

"I've known her since she was born," he says, giving me a look that informs me he could kill me without trying. "She didn't need to say shit."

"I think very highly of Hannah." I immediately feel like an idiot. It sounds like the kind of thing an HR professional would spout off, but I can't exactly tell him how I really feel about her. How I felt perfectly happy for the first time in years last night, only to screw it up. Because there's a part of me that doesn't believe I get to be perfectly happy—that I could have my son and a woman who cares about both of us.

A silence settles between us, not exactly comfortable, because I can feel him sizing me up.

Finally, he says, "You should know that Hannah asked me for two favors, to be granted at a time of her choosing." He allows for a dramatic pause before finishing. "She could have asked for anything, but she used one of them to send me over to New Belgium to get you. So it seems like she thinks *very highly* of you too."

Fuck. *Fuck.*

I need to make this up to her somehow. I have to show her how much I value her, how much I care, even if I can't show her the way I'd like.

"Thanks for telling me that," I say with a tight nod.

"Needless to say, if you mess with my sister, she won't have to use her remaining favor to get me to defend her. I'll—"

"You'll use my balls as a boxing bag," I say, gesturing to his name tag. Feeling the sweat beading again at my hairline. "Got it. I'd deserve it. Like I said—"

"You think very highly of her," he says with a smirk. "Yup, got it. So, do you have any enemies?"

There's a rustling sound, and then Eugene turns the corner,

coming into view holding a big aluminum pan filled with tiny cakes frosted with curlicues.

"Would you like to try a free sample?" he asks with a tight smile that shows too much teeth.

"I work here," Liam says.

Eugene sets the container down on the table with a huff. "So what are you doing—"

"*Eugene*," says a calm, serene voice from behind him. Dottie Hendrickson appears behind him, giving him a supportive smile. "Go ahead and stroke your crystal. It'll help you remember the buzzwords we talked about. *Collaboration. Community. Connection.*"

A sigh whistles out of Eugene like he's a tea kettle full of boiling water, but he nods his head three times and reaches into his pocket, presumably to stroke his crystal. Then he gives Liam another rictus grin. "I see you're wearing your name tag. Good job, Liam."

"Where's yours?" Liam asks, lifting his eyebrows.

Eugene looks startled, and he glances down at his own shirt as if expecting it to appear. "I'll be right back," he says, before turning and hustling away.

Liam shrugs and slides the box of cakes toward him, popping one into his mouth.

"Oh, a spicy one," Dottie says with a smile.

He starts coughing immediately, and she pats him on the back soothingly, as if he's Ollie's age.

"How's your dear boy doing?" she asks me.

"He's having a bit of trouble at school."

"Has he been placing those crystals around the house like we discussed?"

I glance at Liam, who's now guzzling his beer.

Turning my attention back to Dottie, I ask, "Uh....were they supposed to be hidden all around the house? I thought he and Hannah were playing hide-and-seek with them."

She clucks her tongue. "Oh, no. We developed a sound strategy for their placement. Well, no harm. I'd be happy to come over and help him relocate them to their rightful places."

"Was there supposed to be one in the cereal box? Because I have a very strict 'no rocks in our food' policy that I'm not willing to bend on."

She cocks her head. "Oh, yes, I see. I *did* tell him to put the citrine in the kitchen, but perhaps he felt he needed to keep it hidden." She gives me a serious look. "I don't want to alarm you, but he might be under the impression you're closed-minded."

Liam makes another choking sound, but this time I'm pretty sure he's trying not to laugh.

"I'm surprised he's so 'open-minded,'" I say. "He loves science."

Dottie presses a hand to her chest. "So do I, my dear. It's science that creates the beauty of all of those stones, but it's something else that gives them their power—a force not even science can explain. Would you allow me to spend some time arranging them with Ollie?"

"All right," I say. "I'm sure he'd enjoy that."

It'll mean granting yet another person access to my home—worse, a person who intends to hide sharp little rocks every-where to potentially hit me in the head and stub my toes, but I don't feel anxious about it. This is something Ollie obviously wants. Something that might make him feel happier and more confident. More at home in our house.

If that means a little more upheaval, so be it. It's a time of revelations, and I'm not above admitting that the biggest way I've messed up with both Ollie and Hannah is by being too rigid. Too stuck in my opinions about how things are supposed to be.

Eugene bustles back to our table with a fresh name tag on his sweater vest. *I'm Eugene, ask me about my spreadsheets!*

"What kinds of spreadsheets do you like to make, Eugene?" Liam asks, crossing his arms.

"First tell me why you're not working."

Dottie tips her head at Eugene, a sweet, encouraging smile on her face.

He sighs and rewords his reasonable question. "Is there a reason why you're not working now, Liam?"

She beams at him, nodding in approval.

"I'm creating community by talking to Travis." Liam gestures to me. "And we're *connecting* because my sister works for him. It's possible we could *collaborate* on a new beer, because Travis has an extensive background in boating."

I laugh despite myself. "Well, Hannah did warn me that you're an asshole."

Liam gives me a small smile. "Funny, she said the same to me about you."

"I think that's just wonderful," Dottie says. "Don't you, Eugene? Creating connections is what community is all about."

Eugene looks like he's about to blow a gasket, but he still nods several times like a bobblehead before saying, "Yes. Of course. It's wonderful for people to call each other names." Turning to me, he adds, "I hope you don't mind, but Hannah asked me to pass that Maritime individual's post along to my son so he could do some research. Cormac said he'd look into it, but he's traveling, so it might take a couple of days."

Another favor Hannah's done for me without being asked.

I steeple my fingers and nod. "Thank you. I'd appreciate it if you could keep it quiet."

Liam laughs. "Good luck with that. Those women created a scene. Everyone in town's going to be talking about it before long." His expression turns fierce. "They were clearly meant to.

Which brings us back to my earlier point: who would hold a grudge against you?"

At this particular moment, it feels like *everyone* resents me. But I share Hannah's theory about Rachel.

Liam shrugs. "Seems a little more personal than that. If she barely knows you and thinks you could bust her, I don't know why she'd go to the trouble. Who else?"

I rub my forehead. "I don't know. My ex-girlfriend, maybe. Or..." I pause, my mind sluggish. Then an idea pops into my head, surprising me. "Maybe Rob's brother Jonah." I know both Liam and Dottie are aware of the Jonah situation, but for Eugene's sake, I add, "My buddy's dating Jonah's ex-fiancé, so he might feel like he has a score to settle."

"You young people," Eugene says, shaking his head, "sleeping around like you're playing musical beds."

Liam's hand tightens around his beer. "Nah, I don't think it's him."

"Why?"

"I told him I'd beat his face in if he went anywhere near my sister again, and he knew I meant it. He nearly pissed himself."

I believe Jonah would be afraid of Liam—he'd be stupid not to be—but at the same time...

"I wouldn't put it past him to try. He might not know she's working for me. Maybe I'll pay him a visit."

"Anyone else?"

I glance at Eugene, then add, "The only other person who seems to dislike me is Mrs. Applebaum."

"Moira Applebaum has more integrity in her little finger than either of you," Eugene says with feeling.

I shrug, thinking about the sour look on her face after she told me I'd shown her class *quite enough fun, and surely it was time for me to move along and entertain someone else.* "Wasn't saying she'd do it, but she definitely doesn't like me."

That's when it hits me. Hannah wants to play matchmaker for Eugene and Mrs. Applebaum. Helping her with the matchmaking would be a way of showing her I care, wouldn't it?

"Does Moira like music?" I ask.

Eugene frowns, as if thrown by the abrupt change in topic, but something in him shifts, maybe at the thought of Moira Applebaum listening to music. With a dreamy smile, he says, "She *did* tell me she has a certain fondness for acoustic music. 'Blue River' is one of her favorite tunes."

I barely repress a grimace. "Well, we can certainly work with that."

He flinches. "I'll have you know Moira Applebaum is *not* open to bribery. She has the strictest moral integrity." A mournful sigh seeps out of him. "I have personal reasons for knowing that."

"Oh?"

"It's a long story," he says, fiddling with his mustache.

"Let me get us some drinks to go with our little cakes," Dottie says, seeming to abandon whatever original plan she had for the free samples. "I *do* love a good story. We'll get you all sorted out, Eugene. Don't you worry."

My phone buzzes, and I pull it out, expecting Hannah, but it's a string of messages from Rob.

> Where are you, man?

> Bixby had to go home, but we need to talk.

> This got way out of hand.

"Looks like our party's about to get bigger," I say, glancing around at the others.

The thought of talking about this afternoon's performance has me downing the rest of my beer. I abandoned Rob and

Bixby, and even though I didn't have much of a choice, I feel like an ass for that, too.

Liam gives me a censuring look as I set the empty bottle down. "That's a sipping beer. You want a beer to chug, get something they serve in the taproom."

I knock my knuckles against the side of the table. "I'm going to do that. Should I get a pitcher?"

CHAPTER TWENTY-THREE

We each painted one of the four ninja turtles, but my mind was so fixed on Travis that mine came out looking more like a snail. Ollie took a liking to it, though, since Leonardo is his favorite, and asked to hang it in his room.

It was the easiest yes I've ever given.

Finally, Travis texts me from the bar, and some of my worry and angst floats away. He hasn't been murdered by insane fans, and he's with Liam, so I can stop agonizing over whether Alice will really hack it as a bodyguard. (I'm guessing the answer's no.)

Once we've cleaned up our painting supplies, Briar lets Ollie braid her hair, which is extremely generous since it'll probably take her half an hour to get the knots out. He ties a rubber band at the end, nodding to himself as if he's satisfied with his work.

"Will you look in the mirror?" he asks. "I want to make sure I did an okay job."

He's so adorable, I can barely stand it.

We all shuffle into the bathroom together to inspect Briar's hairdo. She's a good sport and manages to not look horrified when she sees her bumpy braid.

"Good job, Ollie." She turns her head back and forth, checking out the long sort-of braid. "It's a treat to have someone else do my hair."

"Maybe we can use those face masks now," he says hopefully. "Mom didn't like it when I used hers, but sometimes she would let me use one to make me be quiet."

As if I needed another reason to dislike Lilah. My list is already several pages long, partly because I think she did more damage to Travis than I realized at first.

"Of course, Ollie," I say tightly, already planning on buying him an even bigger box of skincare masks. "We'll all do one together, and you can talk as much as you'd like. We're all talkers here."

Except for Briar, who's usually more of a listener than a talker. Grinning, she says, "Please talk over Hannah, Ollie. You'd be doing us all a favor."

Sophie, bless her, has tears in her eyes as she offers Ollie "first pick" of the masks, and soon we all look delightfully ridiculous. Ollie, of course, selects a turtle, and we pile onto the couch to watch another episode of *Teenage Mutant Ninja Turtles*.

Briar is still wearing her unicorn mask when she gets an all-hands-on-deck text from her dad.

Rolling her eyes, she says, "He's been doing this for weeks. They're never about anything. It's one of his tests for me—to see if I'll drop everything and show up when I'm needed. But all he's doing is making everyone mad."

"Tests make me mad too," Ollie says with a shrug. "Mrs. Applebaum keeps giving them to me to test my grade level. It's no fair because everyone else gets to do fun stuff like make art out of trash."

Sophie beams at him. "That *does* sound fun. Maybe we can work on a trash-into-treasure project for The Crafty Monster."

"Yeah," I say. "I'm sure parents are aching to hang up a bunch of cereal boxes on their walls."

Sophie shoves my shoulder good-naturedly. "You'd hang up Ollie's cereal box."

Well aware that Ollie's watching me with a hopeful look beneath his turtle face mask, I reply, "Of course I would. I'd hang up all of them. My wall would look like a grocery store, and I'd love it."

Briar leaves, keeping her mask on, because we convinced her it would be more fun to show up at the meeting that way.

Ollie, Sophie, and I watch a final episode of *Teenage Mutant Ninja Turtles*, which is surprisingly addictive, and then my phone buzzes with texts from Travis.

Sorry.

I'll be home later than planned. Rob's here, and Dottie and Eugene and your brother. Would you be able to put Ollie to bed?

Sure.

Use my credit card to order some dinner. Whatever you want.

So we have pizza, and then dessert (thank you, Travis), and afterward Sophie and I get Ollie to bed.

After he snuggles up with his stuffed sloth, I kiss him on the forehead and leave the room. The sight of my turtle painting on his wall makes me smile. He wanted it up, so up it went. I figured Travis was hardly in a position to get mad at me for putting a hole in his wall.

Sophie is waiting for me on the couch with a couple of sodas. She hands one to me, her eyebrows raised. "Well, they've all had too much to drink, apparently. So Rob's playing taxi driver for all of the drunks. He should be here soon with Travis."

"They're *all* drunk?" I ask, wide-eyed, thinking of Eugene and his bottlebrush mustache, sweet Dottie, and even my brother, who has an infamously high tolerance for alcohol. I'm a little bit annoyed that I missed their epic night out, especially since it was at Big Catch.

"Sounds like it."

"Is there any chance we can convince Rob to stop here first so we can get a look at them?"

"He *is* stopping here first. I volunteered to give Dottie a ride home to help him out." She laughs. "Why are you this excited at the thought of seeing a bunch of drunk people? I'm surprised you didn't get sick of it at Big Catch."

"I mostly want to see Eugene, but Dottie's also a delight when she's shit-faced. Liam's mostly just silent and broody. I wonder what Travis is like when he's drunk."

"You can look your fill and then head home. After Rob drops Eugene off, he's coming back. He said he'd stay over here tonight."

"No way. I'll stay with Travis and Ollie. He'll probably even pay me overtime."

"Hannah," she says in an undertone.

"Oh, please. I'm not going to take advantage of him when he's wasted. He made it very clear that he doesn't think we should hook up again, and drunk guys don't do it for me."

"It's not that." She blows air into her cheeks, then lets it gust out. "He doesn't want to see you."

Fucking ouch.

She must see the hurt on my face, because she grabs my hand. "Rob said he was embarrassed. Travis is probably worried he's going to throw up on you. And after last night..."

"Well, too bad. There's no reason for Rob to stay. Get your man to come home with you, and I'll take care of my boys."

She gives me a look that says she noticed what I said and we'll be talking about it later, but she nods. "Okay. I know better than to argue with you when you use that tone."

She darts conspicuous glances at me as I settle down next to her on the couch to wait. I'm guessing she's trying to spur me into conversation, but I'm not going to make it easy for her.

"So you really like Travis, huh?" she finally asks.

"He's a mess."

I feel guilty for saying it, but right now it's true. I don't hold it against him. I'm a mess too. Always have been, always will be.

There's beauty in messes, but if I know one thing about Travis, it's that he won't be a mess forever. He'll figure out all the things that need figuring, and when he's done, I'll still be a mess.

"So?" she challenges.

"I told you I'm not getting involved with one of your boyfriend's friends. It's a terrible idea."

She gives me a flat look. "My boyfriend's my ex-fiancé's brother. A lot of people thought that was a terrible idea too."

"It was. You're just lucky."

"Seriously, Hannah?" Sophie used to believe wholeheartedly that she attracted bad luck, and she still looks incredulous at the thought of fortune smiling on her.

"Yeah, I said what I said. You *are* lucky. You just took a while to realize it. Besides, you don't work for Rob."

"No," she says. "But it's not like this is some random job for you. You love Ollie. I can tell."

"You're right. Which is why Travis is right. We can't risk our situation blowing up in some awful way just because we're attracted to each other."

She shakes her head slightly but says, "Sure, it's definitely a risk. But I have to admit I'd like it if we were dating best friends."

"It would definitely be an upgrade from dating the same person."

We both laugh, and I expertly shift the conversation in a different direction, asking about her craft business.

Then a knock lands on the door, and I grin at her. "The Drunk Express!"

"The rest of them will be in the car," she says with a smile.

"Party pooper."

I follow her to the front door, which she opens to reveal Rob with his arm around Travis. Travis's polo shirt, which was crisp earlier, looks kind of seedy now, like he's a drug dealer who snuck into a polo match to sell weed behind the stables. His hair is all mussed, and there are hollows under his eyes, and I feel an awful urge to hustle him inside and take care of him. To smooth his hair down and help him pull on a clean shirt. To wrap my arms around him and bury my face in his neck.

Of course, the first thing he says to me is: "What are you doing here?"

He has an alarmed, hunted look on his face.

Ah, he must have asked Rob to make sure I left before he arrived. Smooth.

"Funny you should ask," I say. "I work here. And you'll be paying me overtime. You can leave him on his bed, Rob. I'll get him some Tylenol and water, but there's something I have to do first."

"Hannah," Rob starts. "That's not—"

I'm sure he's about to say something regarding his plan to spend the night here with Travis, but I've already made my decision.

Sophie can fill them in.

I head over to the car in the driveway, laughing when I see

my six-foot-six brother folded into the back seat. Dottie's in the front passenger seat, looking bright-eyed and cheerful in her soft sweater dress and dove-gray overcoat. I know Liam did the gentlemanly thing, as he should.

I get into the driver's seat so I can talk to them.

"Oh dear," Dottie says. "I felt certain Rob was driving."

I grin at her. "He was. I'm just visiting. I want to hear all about your drunken exploits." I glance back and am disappointed to see that Eugene has all the hallmarks of being asleep against the window.

He has a name tag on his sweater vest that reads: *I'm Eugene, ask me about my spreadsheets!*

"I'm not drunk," Liam insists.

"I certainly had a few too many tipples," Dottie says. "But it *was* an interesting evening, wasn't it, Liam dear?"

Eugene starts snoring in a way that suggests sleep apnea.

"Why are you in this car if you're not drunk?" I ask my brother.

"One of the *Ships Ahoy* groupies knifed my tire. Must have been a slow leak. We got to the brewery safely, but it was flat by the time we left."

Hot damn. That second group of fans wasn't messing around.

"What happened at the brewery?" I ask, glancing between them.

"We all shared the essence of our souls," Dottie tells me with a broad smile. "It was beautiful."

Turning back to Liam, I say, "Please tell me you didn't have an orgy."

He gives me a lopsided smile. "It was tempting, but I promised not to sleep with any more of your friends. You know I keep my word."

"Oh, it wasn't an orgy, dear," Dottie says, tapping my arm.

"It was a more beautiful kind of connection. By the end of the evening, our auras had melded together."

Kind of sounds like an orgy.

"Eugene's gonna flip when he wakes up," Liam says with a low laugh. "He was drunk in front of everyone on staff. But the real horror was that he was nice to everyone. He asked them all about the BS they wrote on their name tags."

"The name tags were such a success," Dottie says with a soft smile. "I learned so much about crocheting and NASCAR, and your dear brother offered to teach Eugene how to box."

I raise my eyebrows at Liam.

"He's not going to take me up on it when he's sober." He sounds irritated, like he's annoyed he was caught being nice to someone. "He did a lot of things he's going to regret." His lips tip up. "He gave the guy who always wears that hat a fifty percent tip and told him not to spend it all in one place."

"Jesus, Liam," I groan. "You've worked there for years, and you still don't know his name? Wasn't he wearing a name tag?"

"Sure," he says blandly. "I don't remember his name, but I know he enjoys playing Dungeons and Dragons."

I bite my lip, considering everything he's said. "Is it possible they like Eugene now?"

"Let's be honest," he says. "There was nowhere to go but up. At least they know he's human enough to get drunk. That's something. Also, he has a new staff nickname."

Everyone has one. Liam's is Beast, mine was—cue eyeroll—Big Red.

"What is it?" I ask with interest.

"Spreadsheet."

Appropriate. Eugene might even like it.

"He also told us all about his long, sordid history with Mrs. Applebaum."

"I missed that?" I ask mournfully.

"I'm sure your 'friend' can fill you in."

Someone taps on the window, and I look over to see Rob standing outside the door. Right, it's his car. I roll down the window. "Yes?"

"Come on, Hannah," he says with a sigh. "It's been a long day, and I'd like to get this over with as quickly as possible. Sophie says you're okay with staying with Travis and Ollie?"

"Yup," I say. "Duty calls," I announce to the others.

"And you're going home with Sophie," Rob tells Dottie. "She's waiting in her car for you."

"Oh, what a delight!" Dottie grins at him, then turns to the others. "Have a wonderful sleep, my dears. I'll see you soon."

Before she gets out of the car, she reaches into her purse, which must truly be bottomless, and emerges with a couple of thumb-sized crystals. She tucks one into Eugene's balled hand, getting no response from him other than a twitch of his mustache, and hands the other to Liam.

"You hold onto that," she says, tapping Liam's hand. "It'll all become clear to you in time."

"That's good to know," he says dryly, but I can tell he's fond of her. It would be pretty impossible not to be.

Dottie climbs out of the car, and I'm about to follow her when my brother calls my name. I glance back at him, lifting my eyebrows.

"Be careful," he says.

He's talking about my situation with Travis. I wouldn't have called in that favor for just anyone, and he knows it.

I salute him and exit the car.

"Thanks for bringing Liam home," I tell Rob in an undertone after shutting the car door behind me.

"No problem."

Before getting into Sophie's car, Dottie waves to us so energetically she almost topples over. Sophie waits for Dottie to settle into the passenger seat, and then she blows us a kiss and then drives off.

Once they're out of sight, Rob hugs me and nods toward the house. "Go easy on him. I don't really know what's going on between you two, but he's going through some heavy shit, and he had a hard day. I'm sure he'll tell you the rest in the morning."

"Thanks, Rob. You're a good guy to have around."

"I wouldn't leave him with anyone else when he's like this," he tells me seriously.

I nod, feeling a little choked up—because if that's not a sign of trust, what is?—and go inside.

I head into Travis's room, expecting to find him passed out on the bed, but he's standing at his dresser, taking his shirt off with one hand held against the furniture for balance.

I come to standstill, as if someone just paused me.

His back is to me, and oh what a back...

It's toned and still tan from the summer, and the muscles bunch as he tugs the shirt up over his head and throws it. I should probably leave, or maybe help him get another shirt. But I stay motionless as he stands bowed over the dresser, his hair tumbling down in the front where it's longer. His hand is white-knuckling the edge of the wooden dresser.

This is one of those times when he needs music, but right now he's in no condition to wield his sticks.

I move toward him, one step after another, the need to go to him overwhelming every other doubt.

I place my palm on his lower back, feeling his taut muscles and the delicious heat of him. "Whatever you're doing to yourself, you need to stop. *Now.* Hannah's orders."

He turns toward me, but there's no sign of surprise when he

sees me there. Even though I'd never do anything with him when he's like this, I feel a rush of awareness. There's something primal about him tonight, just like there was last night. All of the gentlemanly nuances have been stripped away.

"Please don't be nice to me right now," he says. "I couldn't take it."

I almost laugh, but I can't, because there's a dark, haunted look in his eyes. He stumbles a few steps toward the bed, then sits down hard at the foot of it and bows his head, his hands spearing into his dark hair. He's wearing nothing but a pair of dark jeans, belted at the waist, and those loafers I've teased him about.

He looks like a fallen god.

I sit on the floor in front of him and remove his loafers one at a time. When I look up, he's staring at me with that same fevered intensity.

"I asked you not to be nice," he says.

"God forbid I help a drunk person take their shoes off. You know I spent years working at Big Catch. Helping drunk people with their shoes is basically second nature. Would you like me to take your pants off too? I know from experience that I'll appreciate the view."

He smiles for half a second, which I consider a victory. "No, this isn't how I'd like that to happen again."

Heat flashes through me, because at least some part of him wants it to happen again. And he's looking at me in a thirsty way that suggests I'm the only thing that could possibly satisfy him.

"Then you should take them off," I say, making no move to leave. "I'll stay to make sure you don't fall over and hit your head. Now, *that* would be an embarrassing ER visit."

"You want to watch me take off my pants?" he asks, more of a challenge than a question.

"Yes. I watched you last night, and I really enjoyed it."

He lowers his hands to the belt and unfastens it with careless ease. I can hardly breathe as I watch him, desire prickling across my skin. His hand misses the button on his pants on his first try, and I turn away, because suddenly it feels wrong for me to be here.

"I thought you were going to watch," he says, his voice ragged.

"And I suddenly remembered you're drunk. It would be inappropriate, even for me."

I hear the fabric rustling as he pushes his pants down. I want to look, I'm desperate to look, but I say, "Get under the covers, Travis."

"Are you going to tuck me in?" he asks with a husky laugh.

"Yes, but first I'm getting you Pedialyte and Tylenol. What kind of beer did you drink?"

He moans. "The lager."

"That's good. Hangovers from the dark beers are much worse. Especially Liam's. He doesn't like porters, so I think he does it on purpose. I'll be right back."

There's another rustling sound, so hopefully he's pulled up the sheets, and I leave the room to get the goods.

When I return, he's lying nestled in those dark silk sheets, his head resting on the pillow, his hair pushed back to reveal the heart birthmark.

My own heart swells.

I set the Pedialyte and pills down on his bedside table, then sit on the edge of the bed and run my fingers down the side of his face.

He opens his eyes and lifts his hand toward me, playing with one of my curls as it spills down toward him. "Thank you for staying with Ollie. I knew he'd be safer with you than with me today." He pauses. "I'm a bad father."

"You would have been a bad father if you'd come home and

gotten wasted in front of him. Plenty of dads do. My dad's a good guy, mostly, but he drank plenty of that beer he and Liam made while he was at home watching the three of us."

"I don't know what I'm doing, Hannah. Being Ollie's dad is the most important thing to get right, and I keep messing up."

"He's doing great," I say, tracing his face again, letting my fingertips get lost in his hair.

"Because of you. You're so good with him. I could watch you together all day. You make it look so easy to make him laugh and smile, but I don't know how to do it. I'm no good at this."

"Okay, stalker," I tease as I keep running my fingertips through his hair. "You seem determined to be hard on yourself. Even more so than usual. Feel like telling me why?"

"There have already been lots of social media posts about the *Ships Ahoy* fans at the performance today," he says, glancing away, a far-off look in his eyes. "A reporter called me. Everyone knows." He pauses. "Frank, the producer who's interested in the band, knows too. He told Rob and Bixby we should lean into it. He says he'll pick us up if we go with it. He doesn't even care how Drake plays with us."

"Oh fuck," I say, because he doesn't need to tell me how much he hates that. I know it in my bones. This is Travis's worst nightmare, descending on him in a bunch of poorly matched sailor dresses.

He turns back to face me. But when he meets my gaze again, he says, "Lilah's going to find out and take him away from me."

My heart goes supernova in my chest. This man's worst nightmare is coming to pass, but he's not thinking about himself —he's worried about how it will impact his son.

I didn't want to feel this way about Travis. I've tried very hard not to. But he's making it difficult tonight, damn him.

"You're a much better father than you give yourself credit

for," I say, smoothing his hair back. "And she's already been gone for nearly sixty days. You have a stronger case than you think. Even if she steps off a plane in Asheville tomorrow."

I'm not sure that's true. I know next to nothing about the law, but I'm nothing if not determined. And I will *not* let Lilah use Ollie as some kind of bargaining chip to enlarge her bank account.

"Now, drink some of that Pedialyte so we can both go to sleep."

"I'll sleep on the couch," he says, trying to get up.

I wrap a hand around his thick bicep. "Nope. Not happening."

His gaze darkens. "I'm not going to let *you* sleep on the couch. This is my screwup. You might as well sleep in here anyway. The pillows already smell like you. They always do."

"They do?" I ask, surprised. "I've only been in here a couple of times. But I did hide under your covers once for hide-and-seek."

"It's been driving me insane," he says with a groan. He reaches for the Pedialyte and takes a swig, following it up with the Tylenol I set out for him. The satin sheet pools at his waist, showing off his chest and arms.

I swallow against my suddenly dry throat, then take the Pedialyte from him and take a big gulp, very aware that his lips were pressed there before mine. Maybe it's the closest I'll get to kissing him again—a depressing thought if ever I've had one.

I set the bottle down. "If it's driving you insane, why do you want more of my scent all over your bed?"

"Sometimes a man wants to be driven insane," he says thickly. "I can't sleep anyway. Stay with me, Hannah. I won't touch you. I'll just dream about it."

"Shouldn't I be promising you that?" I smile at him. "You're the one who's compromised."

"Stay," he says, his gaze holding mine. "I don't have any virtue for you to keep safe."

I don't believe that for a minute, but I get up and circle around to the other side of the bed before pulling the covers down and climbing in next to him.

"I thought you were leaving," he says, shifting to face me.

"As if I'm not perfectly well aware that you're one of those people who has a preferred side of the bed," I say as I plump my pillow.

"What kind of maniac wouldn't?"

"I don't. The whole bed is mine. Why settle for less?"

He smiles at me, and there's such hidden depths in that smile. I wish I had the ability to put it into words.

"You should never settle for less than you deserve."

"I know. That's why I'm working for someone who pays me an insane hourly rate for playing with a kid I'd play with anyway. You are aware that you're basically paying me double the going rate, aren't you?"

"You deserve it. You're incredible. A natural with him. With everyone. Look at what you've done for Eugene."

I laugh. "Yeah, I got him shit-faced, just like you."

"You weren't even there," he says, giving me a small smile in return. "You may be the most badass woman I know, but I don't think you have magical powers."

"You say that like a man who wasn't inside my magical pussy last night."

Oops. Didn't mean to say that.

He swears and rubs a hand over his eyes. "Maybe it was a bad idea to ask you to sleep in here."

"Too late. You can't ask me to leave now. It would be rude."

"Pillows," he mutters. "We need a pillow barrier. There's at least two extra pillows we can use."

I laugh, then laugh harder because I can tell he's serious.

"You don't trust me?"

"I don't trust myself," he says raggedly, grabbing an extra pillow from the floor and starting the barrier. I add another, our fingers brushing in a way that sends electric heat right to my magical pussy, and then we settle back into our places.

"Did your pillow barrier help your self-control?" I whisper, turning toward the very short wall.

"No." His tone is morose. "I don't think anything would at this point. I know what it feels like to kiss you. To be inside you. I can't forget that, and I don't want to."

"Yeah, it would have been much better if you'd tasted like onions. Next time you kiss someone you're not supposed to, eat a blooming onion first."

"I don't want to kiss anyone else."

There's no hesitation, no doubt, in his voice.

I tell myself that's only because he's drunk. But I'm pleased anyway. I want him to want me, because despite everything, I want him. I want him in a deep, desperate way, and attraction is only part of it.

I peek over the pillow barrier and prepare to ask him what's probably an unfair question, because I suspect he'd never do this sober. "Travis?"

"Yeah?"

"Would you sing me to sleep?"

"You want me to sing to you?"

"I've never heard your voice."

An inscrutable look crosses his face, and then he starts softly singing. The song is unfamiliar to me, but his voice wraps around me in an embrace as sensual as the black silken sheets.

"What song is that?" I ask after a minute.

"I wrote it about you."

I reach across the pillow divide, my heart gushy and soft in a way that scares me, and he clasps my hand in his big, callused fingers.

"You scare me," I admit.

"You terrify me."

"Will you finish the song?"

I fall asleep to the sound of his voice, my hand nestled in his as if I'm something precious.

CHAPTER TWENTY-FOUR

TRAVIS

"Travis? Travis?"

A tiny finger pokes my chest.

"Travis?"

I open my eyes, regret it, close them, regret that too, and sigh.

"Yes, Ollie?"

"Why is Hannah in bed with you? Does Hannah live here now?"

My heart starts racing.

I sit up, my head protesting loudly, my back still sore and radiating pain, and for a second all I can do is stare at Hannah. She's stretched out on the other side of a pillow barrier I don't remember making, her bright hair a gorgeous pop of color against the black sheets.

Did she make that pillow barrier because I came on to her while I was drunk? Normally, I have a higher level of self-control than that, even when I've had one too many. Then again, I've never had much control around Hannah.

My heart racing, I run my hands through my hair, then look

around for a T-shirt I can throw on and find nothing but my dirty polo shirt from last night on the floor.

Ollie's standing beside the bed expectantly, waiting for my answer. I don't want to walk out half naked while there's a woman in my bed, pillow barrier or not, so I stay put. "She doesn't live here, Ollie. She just stayed over last night because I wasn't feeling well. She was helping us out."

"Okay," he says, seeming to accept my answer at face value. "It's a little late, though. Don't you think we should be starting our day?"

I glance at the wall, cursing in my head when I see it's already ten thirty.

"Yeah, I'm sorry, buddy. Did you have breakfast?"

He rolls his eyes. "I can pour myself cereal, Travis. I'm not a baby."

"Never doubted it."

"Want me to pour some for you?"

I don't want to eat anything, possibly ever again, but it's one of the first things he's ever offered to do for me, and I'm not about to deny him. Maybe Hannah will want to eat it.

"Yeah, that would be great. Thanks."

He leaves the room, and I shuffle over to the dresser, feeling ten years older than I did last night, to grab a clean T-shirt and athletic shorts. I tug them on, then head into the en suite to brush my teeth.

If Hannah's going to tell me off for being a presumptuous prick, I'd prefer to have clean teeth for it.

She must sleep like the dead, though, because she's still out cold when I sit down on her side of the bed.

My heart thumps painfully in my chest as I look at her. She's so beautiful. She must have gotten up and washed her face at some point in the night because her eyelashes are that gorgeous red-gold color again. I stroke her cheek, and instead of sucker punching me, like I half expect her to, she stirs and makes a sound that's half murmur and half sigh, which shoots straight to my cock.

She's not yours.

But I'm ready to admit that I'd like her to be.

I've never wanted anyone like I want her. She's funny, bold, and very opinionated. I want to hear all of her opinions. I want to argue with them because I know she loves arguing back. I want to fuck her, but I also want to talk to her, dance with her, and play music with her—and I know that's more dangerous. If it were just about sex, I could sleep with someone else, but the thought of doing that is as repellant as running a cheese grater over my dick.

"Hannah," I whisper, needing to ensure I won't be overheard. "Hannah, I'm sorry about last night."

Her eyes open slowly, their vivid green sucking me in.

"Sometimes you sound like a broken record. What exactly are you sorry for this time?"

I gesture to the stupid pillow barrier. "Did you do that because I was being inappropriate?"

She smiles at me. "You don't remember?"

"Obviously not."

"I feel like I should lord this over you for at least a day, but no, you weren't being inappropriate. You were just worried you might be tempted, because I made a...colorful comment. Sorry about that."

"I wish I could remember."

"Probably best if I don't repeat it now that the pillow barrier is no longer between us."

Now I *really* wish I could remember. But I'm also glad that I don't, because I'm sure I made an ass of myself.

"It's past ten," I mutter.

"Are you asking me to leave?" she asks playfully.

"I mean, you've been working for over twenty hours."

Hurt flickers across her face. "I didn't stay here because I was hoping for a big payday."

"I didn't mean it like that. I—"

"Say no more," she says, climbing out of the bed, her expression closed down. "You're right. I'll just go say goodbye to Ollie. Do you have band practice or anything later?"

"*Hannah.*"

"Let's keep this professional," she says, crossing her arms.

"I don't think we know how to do that."

She smiles for half a second before it ghosts off her face.

I did that. I took her smile away.

"Oh, for fuck's sake," she says in a hissing undertone, stomping her foot. "I see that look on your face. Stop blaming yourself for everything. It's so tiresome."

"Don't leave," I say, getting up too quickly and jarring my head. "Please don't leave. We need to talk."

She pauses by the door and puts a hand on her hip. "Fine, but only because I need you to tell me about Eugene and Mrs. Applebaum."

I scratch the back of my head, feeling slow-witted. "What?"

"My brother said Eugene poured out his heart about the whole Mrs. Applebaum situation. I'm supposed to meet up with him for pottery painting at noon, and I need to know everything."

"Oh," I say. "He told us about his golf cart mishap at the school. I guess it happened after Mrs. Applebaum turned him down. She and her husband were broken up at the time—Eugene was very clear about that. He said he didn't want us thinking she was some kind of common strumpet."

"Oh crap," she says with feeling. "She wasn't interested?"

I shrug. "It doesn't mean she'd turn him down now. They

don't work together anymore. He seems to think that mattered to her."

I let myself imagine what that would look like for Hannah and me. Maybe we could give this a real shot if I could find another nanny for Ollie, someone he'd like. I probably should have kept looking; I've always known this couldn't last forever. Hannah's not a nanny, and eventually she'll want to get back to living a normal life.

But losing her would feel like losing a limb, which is insane, because she's only been with us for two weeks. The second nanny was with us for almost as long, but I barely remember her name or what she looks like. Hannah would be a tough act to follow. The thought of some other person taking her place nearly sets off an anxiety spiral.

"What's going on with you?" she asks, uncrossing her arms. "You've got that worry line between your eyebrows."

"I realized that I should have kept interviewing nannies. You're not going to want to stay forever."

She crosses her arms again. "I thought I made it clear that I'd *never* leave Ollie in a lurch. Or you, you jerk."

"I know you wouldn't. I just...part of me doesn't want you to leave at all. You're the only person I fully trust with him."

She looks at me with disbelief. "Suddenly you trust me?"

"Remember the pillow barrier? I'm the one I don't trust."

Her expression softens. "Oh, Travis."

I laugh, then press a hand to my head at the sudden stab of pain. "Come on. Don't look at me like I'm some hairless dog you found wandering by the side of the road. I'm no harder on myself than most people."

"I know you're not a hairless dog," she says, rolling her eyes. "You've got very nice hair and the perfect amount of chest hair. Has anyone ever told you that? Never mind, I don't want to know. The bottom line is that I don't think you're pathetic. But I *am* taking that polo shirt to save you from yourself."

I smile at her. "And my button-downs?"

"I like those. You look weirdly hot in them."

"Weirdly hot? I'll take it. Would it be unprofessional for me to tell you that you look entirely hot in everything you wear?"

"*Very*, but you're right, obviously."

Smiling, I go to her. I tuck her hair behind her ear. It wasn't sticking out or anything. I just wanted to have my hands on her.

"I don't think I can stop wanting you," I admit.

"Good," she says, her lips tipping up at the corners. "What are we going to do about this?"

"I don't know," I say with a frustrated sigh. "Ollie needs you, and—"

"I understand why you're anxious about that, but I'd never walk away from him," she protests, sounding pissed by the idea of it. "*Never*. Even if I wasn't his nanny anymore, I'd still bring him to Dottie's or to one of Sophie's craft things. It wouldn't matter if you and I had a falling-out and I wanted to cut your balls off. I'd still do it."

I nod, because I don't doubt her. It would be foolish of anyone to doubt her. I've never met anyone so sure of herself. So full of the need to make other people feel sure of themselves too.

"I want to see where this goes, Hannah. I..." I pause, then admit, "When I told you about the hurricane thing ..."

She groans. "Can we please never talk about that again?"

I capture her hand before she can walk away. "I could tell you were going to tear my life apart, and I was resistant to that. But part of me already knew that I was going to like it. That everything needed to be undone so it could be rebuilt into something better. I wasn't doing a lot of living before you and Ollie came along. You were right about that." I press her hand to my heart. "I'd like to try...with both of you. But I don't think we should do this while you're working for me. It feels wrong."

"Like you'd be paying me to sleep with you?" She gives me a wicked grin. "I'd be worth every penny."

"I know that," I say, feeling the needy ache of my cock, from the memory of being deep inside her and feeling her clench against me. "So...I think I really do need to find a new nanny. Someone he'd like."

"Don't you dare pull my job out from under me." She pauses. "Not yet. You were right about a few things too. It's not a good time for another big change for him."

My throat feels thick with emotion, so I swallow. "We're at a stalemate?"

"For now," she says with a sly smile, her hand still pressed against me. "But the games continue."

"I need to get my shit together anyway. I'm a mess."

She lifts an eyebrow. "Lucky for you, I have terrible taste in men."

She probably doesn't mean for her words to affect me like they do, but they hit like a gut punch. I don't want to be that guy. The boss who screwed her when she was supposed to be taking care of his child.

"I don't want to be your next mistake, Hannah."

"So don't be," she says, lifting her eyebrows. Her hand is still on my chest, pinning me in place, and my eyes lower to her lips. She's got beautiful lips, a Cupid's bow with the top perfectly curved and the bottom lush and begging for my teeth.

I lean in and kiss her once, softly, so she knows I mean it. "I want to do something for you."

"Other than leaving money on the dresser?"

I sigh, but this is the game we're playing, and I know my part. "I always use Venmo."

"You don't need to do anything for me. You already overpay

me. Just figure out your shit. If you do that, you'll be doing something for me."

"What's your favorite flower?"

"I hate flowers."

"I'm going to come up with something good."

"I look forward to seeing what you come up with," she says with a grin.

"Your cereal is getting soggy!" Ollie calls out.

I nod toward the door. "Duty calls."

"You didn't answer earlier. Do you have practice later?"

I shake my head. "I want to spend the day with him. It's past time I explained some things to him. People will be talking. He needs to know what to expect."

I was about to say *before Lilah comes back*, but I can't bring myself to acknowledge it. Still, I'll be on the phone with my lawyer first thing on Monday to prepare for a potential custody battle.

"Good," she says with a nod. "Do you want me to stay? Off the clock, I mean."

Yes.

Right now, I feel like I need her to stay forever, but I don't want to be one more person who needs her, like Eugene. Like Liam, even.

I want to support her the same way she supports me.

"I have to do this part alone," I say. "But I would appreciate it if you could stay late on Wednesday. I have a meeting with the guys."

"Of course," she says, way too polite for my taste. "Is this about that producer?"

"Yeah," I reply with a sigh. "We've got to form a united front. One way or another."

She grips my arm, surprising me. "You're not going to say yes to be agreeable."

"Yeah, that's me," I joke, "Mr. Agreeable."

"You can't say yes, Travis."

"I'm not going to." Glancing at the door, I lower my voice. "I wouldn't agree even if I wasn't worried about Lilah finding out. I'd quit the band first."

I open the bedroom door, then nod for her to precede me through it.

"You don't have to treat me like I'm a queen," she says with an amused smile.

"You're the queen of this household. It's time I started treating you that way."

She plucks the polo shirt up off the floor and runs out like she thinks she's gotten away with something. Fine by me. I like the thought of her wearing it, not that she ever would.

I follow her out, and a couple of seconds later, I find Ollie sitting at the kitchen table. There's a soggy bowl of cereal at one place setting, and the rest of the table is occupied by the packages we picked up at the toy store, minus the art supplies he and Hannah used yesterday.

He found all of them.

Hannah and I exchange a look, and we both start laughing, sharing our appreciation for my son's hustle.

"What if I bought all of that for myself?" I ask.

"You didn't." Ollie pauses, a worried look filling his eyes. "You didn't, did you?"

"He *is* a child deep down." Hannah gives me a weighing glance. "Deep, deep, deep down. But no, that's all for you."

"When can I open them?" he asks, bouncing a little from foot to foot.

"Go for it, kid," I tell him, walking over and ruffling his hair. "I figured we could get a better handle on what you're interested in. Maybe we can find something we both like to do."

Hannah gives me a pointed look that reminds me of something I hadn't forgotten. *Show him what you love, and teach him to play.*

"Okay, but eat your cereal," he says. "Hannah told me it was important to eat a complete breakfast."

I glance at the soggy mess in the bowl, raise my eyebrows at Hannah, then sit and scoop up a disgusting spoonful.

"That's love," she says, grinning at me. Then her eyes widen, and she snaps her fingers. "Oh, before I forget. I promised Alice I'd get you to sign some headshots of yourself that I could send to her and the other Ships Junior bodyguards."

"Headshots?" I ask blankly. "I don't have headshots."

She takes out her phone and snaps a photo of me. "You do now. I'll get them printed out."

I groan but nod. Alice was helpful yesterday, and I appreciate that she and her friends didn't try to mob me.

Hannah hugs Ollie goodbye and then turns to leave us. Once she's gone, the house instantly feels darker. Drabber.

"This place feels different without her," I say, because my filter is apparently broken this morning.

"It does," Ollie agrees.

I expect him to start tearing into the boxes, but he sits down in the chair across from mine. "Do you like Hannah in an adult way, Travis? Mom only shared a bed with people she liked in an adult way."

Way to stab me in the chest from thousands of miles away, Lilah.

I try to breathe out my anger over her exposing Ollie to her cheating ways. "I think a lot of Hannah, but that's not something you need to worry about right now, Ollie."

"Hannah's my friend, but I don't mind if you and Hannah are friends too," he says. "You smile a lot more when she's around."

I rub my hands over my temples. "Thank you, Ollie. I think you're right about that."

"Will you date her? Aunt Dottie said you might want to date her. Like when people kiss each other."

Jesus Christ, I'm way too hungover for this conversation. I make a mental note to have a talk with Dottie about what is and isn't appropriate for children.

"Maybe, but I can't do that while she works here, buddy. It wouldn't be appropriate for us to date."

"If you say so." He pauses, his expression thoughtful. "But Hannah would still be around here a lot if you were dating each other, right?"

"Yeah, I guess."

"Well...we might need to think about interviewing a few other people to be my nanny."

"Seriously, Ollie? You didn't want anyone else to take care of you. You drove them all away."

"I think you've learned what a good nanny is like. You needed someone to show you." He shrugs. "Are you going to tell me about *Ships Ahoy* now?"

I drop the spoon into the mushy cereal. "Did Hannah tell you about that?"

"No, but she talks really loudly to Sophie and Briar sometimes when she thinks I'm asleep. Your dad was in some old movie, wasn't he?"

"Yeah," I say woodenly. "There are six of those Ships Ahoy movies. He was in them before I was born, and he was really proud of himself. I'm telling you this because some of the other kids might start talking about it. You deserve to know from me."

"That's pretty cool. I'll bet Mickey's grandfather wasn't a movie star."

"Probably not, but you should know my dad wasn't a nice man, Ollie. We didn't get along. He was always pushing me to be someone I wasn't. Both of my parents were." I take a deep breath. "I had a nanny, too, when I was a kid, and my parents didn't spend much time with me. I'd like things to be different for us, but I haven't done a good job of showing you that."

"You haven't played the drums with me," he says, watching me closely. "You don't want to."

I spear my hands through my hair, practically hearing Hannah whisper, *I told you so.*

"And you don't want to introduce me to the kids you teach or the rest of your band. I haven't even met the third guy who plays the weird guitar."

"He's not too happy with me right now," I say. "But I'll introduce you to him eventually. And if you want to come meet the kids at The Missing Beat, Hannah will bring you. She's already offered. I just..." My mouth feels dry. My heart is pounding. "I didn't want to push you to do something only because *I* like it, Ollie. My father wasn't interested in figuring out who I was. He wanted me to be just like him. I don't want to do that to you."

He gives me one of his serious looks, his face so like mine I'm taken aback. "But Hannah said I should watch the turtle show so I could see if Mickey and I had anything in common. Isn't that the same for us? How am I going to know whether I like playing music if I never learn how?"

"You really are smarter than me."

He just grins expectantly.

"I'd love to teach you the drums, Ollie. I'll teach you on my own kit. And if you like it, but only if you like it, I'll get you one too. Or maybe you'll like playing the guitar. I know Uncle Rob or one of the kids at the Beat would love to teach you."

"Can we start now?" he asks, ignoring the whole table full of toys in their packages.

My head feels like it's being mined for gold, but there's only one possible answer.

Hell, yes.

I take him into the music room, and we start with a lesson on how to hold the sticks and alternate hands while drumming. Keeping a steady beat.

He regards me with wide eyes. "This is harder than it looks."

"But it'll become easier. Once you're used to it, you become the beat. You feel it down to your bones, and it feels good. It feels right." I pause, embarrassed. "If you like drumming, obviously. It's not like that for everyone."

"Can you feel it when you're not at the drums?" he asks, watching me with an interest that surprises me.

"Sometimes. Sometimes when I'm feeling anxious or spun up, I can slip into it. I can get into the same state I'm in when I'm playing, and it makes me feel better."

"That sounds cool, Travis. I want to learn how to do that."

We're still at the drums when Rob comes over an hour or so later to check on me. Perfect timing, I figure, and ask him to show Ollie how to hold a guitar and play a few chords. I could have done that, too, since I play passably enough, but it feels right for "Uncle Rob" to be the one.

"He's a natural musician, just like his old man," Rob says with a grin.

"I'm bringing him to the Beat this week," I tell him. "He wants to come."

"They're going to love you, Ollie," Rob says. "Our students are going to compete for the right to play with you."

Ollie beams at him, and my chest hurts in a new way, because damn, I should have seen what Hannah did. I should have let him decide how much he wants of my world.

Before Rob leaves, I ask Ollie to go play in his room for a few minutes so his uncle and I can have an adult conversation.

"So this producer," he says once we're alone together, cutting right to the point. "We're going to tell him we're not interested in any *Ships Ahoy* publicity, obviously."

I laugh and instantly feel my headache from earlier reassert itself. "Bixby's already writing some yacht rock songs, isn't he? And I'm sure Drake has probably put in an order for some sailor hats for all four of us. If he gives one to me at our next practice, I reserve the right to shove it up his—"

"This is our band," Rob says. "Ours. We started it. We wrote the music. This is *our* garbage fire, and we're telling them no Ships Junior shit. End of story."

Emotion rises in my throat. "You mean that."

"I fucking do. You're my brother. My *real* brother. I'd do anything for you. You saved my life."

"We saved each other's lives," I say. Because it's true. He'd been struggling when I met him, deep into drinking, trying to drown out the pain of what he'd lost when Bad Magic moved on without him. I'd been struggling in my own way, too, still reeling from getting thrown off the roller coaster Lilah and I had been on. Rob and I had found purpose together, and for a long time, he was the only person I trusted, and I was the only person he trusted.

That's changed, but the connection we formed back then is as strong as ever.

"Thanks, man," I say. "You know how it is with all of that shit."

He nods to show he does indeed know.

"But Bixby's going to want to do it," I point out.

He laughs, then gets serious, saying, "Look. This is your personal business. You get to keep that quiet if you want to, no matter what anyone else has to say about it."

I hug him, because no amount of back patting could express how grateful I feel for our friendship.

"Bixby will understand," he says.

"And Drake?"

"If he doesn't understand, fuck 'im. He's been in the band for a week. He hasn't even played a show with us yet."

We both laugh.

I feel like I should tell him about the rest of it too, how I won't be going on tour. How I want to be home most nights so I can say good night to my son. We'll have that conversation soon, but I can't handle anything else today. There's been so much change piled on me at once.

Rob doesn't press me about Hannah, probably because he's already said his piece. He isn't one to push. We talk for another few minutes, and then he hugs me again, says goodbye to Ollie, and leaves.

Dottie Hendrickson texts me almost immediately after Rob steps out the door.

> Dear, I was wondering if I could come over to help with the placement of the crystals.

The timing is so impressive I know it must have been choreographed. Rob is passing the baton, but it's kind of nice that they care.

CHAPTER TWENTY-FIVE

HANNAH

"So the tension is pretty crisp with Travis right now. Not gonna lie, I'm starting to think we're at the beginning of an epic love story. You know, like Elizabeth Taylor and Richard Burton."

Eugene looks up from the hedgehog pencil holder he's painting and regards me through his double-bar glasses. "They broke up. More than once."

"Huh. That's probably not a good sign."

We're at The Clay Place, Constance's granddaughter's art studio, situated in a big warehouse in the River Arts District. The whole building belongs to this awesome art collective called The Waiting Place, filled with small studios that offer specialized classes and sell art. It got washed out by a hurricane a while back, but they've rebuilt, and some remarkable artist painted a mural outside captioned, *Stronger than the storm.* I wouldn't willingly admit this to most people, but it makes me tear up every time I see it. It's an impressive space with all the studios lined up around a gorgeous atrium capped with a sunroof, complete with a coffee shop and café tables.

"I'm not sure why you're telling me all of this anyway," Eugene says. "It's *decidedly* none of my business."

"This is what friends do, Eugene. They shoot the shit. Besides, I *do* have a point. You're being impatient."

He sighs and carefully dabs black eyes onto the little hedgehog pencil pot I badgered him into choosing. His painting skills are impeccable. The squirrel sculpture I'm painting for Ollie looks like microwaved roadkill.

"And the point?" he asks.

"You're not the only one who's had some workplace tension, my friend. There are no easy answers. But I have to be honest. Travis shared what you told everyone about Mrs. Applebottom—"

"Applebaum."

"Sorry, it's hard to get that right. Anyway, he told me, but I'd already guessed. I could tell how much you respected her. In any event, if you've still got it bad for her after all this time, I think you should do something about it, you know? She's officially divorced, and you no longer work at the school, so the time is right to pursue something real."

He sighs and adds a dab of red, a surprisingly jaunty color, to the hedgehog's collar. It seems pretty unrealistic for a hedgehog to have a collar, but art's gotta art, I guess.

"I don't know," he says after a moment. "She must have several more appropriate men pursuing her."

I stifle a laugh.

He glowers at me. "Moira is a lovely woman."

"Sure, of course. But she's no better than you. You're Eugene Freaking Peebles. *Spreadsheet.*"

He scowls at the nickname.

"Trust me, they only give nicknames to people they tolerate. You've moved up in their esteem."

He shrugs. "Well, Moira didn't get terminated for crashing a golf cart into a vending machine. That automatically makes her better than me."

"The teachers did seem salty about the broken Cheetos button, but no one's perfect. I'm sure she has some kind of embarrassing incident buried in her past.

"Oh, I doubt that very much."

He executes a little flourish with his paintbrush that makes me smile.

"Don't put her up on a pedestal, Eugene. No one likes being on a pedestal. It makes for a pretty crappy fall."

"Wouldn't it be highly unusual for me to give her a call after all this time?"

"Okay, here's our plan. Step one, give her the pencil cup."

"Why?" he asks, his brow furrowing.

"I wanted you to make this because the one you originally gave her broke. You're making the replacement as a grand gesture."

He glances down at it, his brow still furrowed. "I never gave her a pencil cup."

Oh, shit.

"Well, she had one just like this, and she said another teacher gave it to her in the Secret Santa exchange, and you said—"

He sets down his brush, looking panicked now. "It was the gym teacher, Mr. Rodney. He can bench-press sixty pounds."

"That's not as impressive as you seem to think it is."

He takes off his glasses and starts wiping them manically on his shirt. "Of course. I don't know why I never saw it before. She's in love with Mr. Rodney."

"Snap out of it, Eugene," I say, snapping my fingers in front of his face. "The person who gave it to her is immaterial. She didn't say she wanted to jump the guy or anything. What matters is that you're giving her a new one."

"She'll think I'm a stalker."

"I'll explain that you and I are friends, and when you found out about the broken pencil pot, you insisted on personally replacing it. That's the first step."

"And the second?" he asks, giving me a hopeful look.

"We'll cross that bridge when we come to it."

He sighs and forlornly applies some gray paint to his hedgehog. It's still excellent, bless him, even now that he's feeling deflated. I add some jagged white teeth to my squirrel's mouth.

"Is that a vampire squirrel?" the purple-haired studio owner asks, walking past us with a grin.

"It is now."

"Excellent." She checks out Eugene's work and nods. "Wow, that's really good."

Eugene huffs another sound of dissatisfaction as she walks away, joining her tattooed boyfriend at the front desk.

"Yes, Eugene? Was that sigh for me?"

He sighs again, pushing his glasses up. "I can't imagine going into the brewery this afternoon after the display I put on. I'm tempted to call in sick."

I feign shock. "Playing hooky? What have I done to you?"

"Moira would be disgusted with me," he grumbles. "She would never play hooky."

"Well, don't worry," I say. "We're going together, after we go clothes shopping, and we're going to announce our supercool holiday party. Everyone's going to want to slap you on the back and buy you a drink."

"No more drinks."

"Have it your way, Spreadsheet."

"Are my clothes inadequate?" he asks, glancing down the front of his checkered brown shirt.

"They're fine. You should always wear what makes you comfortable. I just think we could explore a few different colors. We'll go brown adjacent to make things easy on you. Some gray maybe. Dark green. We might get crazy and layer in dark red."

He runs his finger over his mustache.

"You like having that mustache?"

He touches it again. "My ex-wife told me I have a weak upper lip."

"If you like it, we keep it. If you don't, it's coming off or getting trimmed. Screw what she thinks. I'm guessing you two broke up for a reason. How about the glasses?"

"I enjoy seeing, Hannah," he says wryly. His cheeks flush as he adds, "And Moira told me she appreciates seeing men in glasses."

"That's a yes for some slutty little glasses. Let's try out a few other frames, though. You should have a backup."

He gives me an amused look. "You're very unlike anyone else I know."

"I'm going to take that as a compliment."

"It is one," he says, his expression turning serious. "Hannah. I owe you."

"I like the sound of that, but you don't owe me anything. We don't even know that any of this will help."

He surprises me by reaching out and touching my hand. "You've already helped, just by wanting to help. If there's anything I can ever do for you, all you need to do is ask."

Heat wells behind my eyes, catching me off guard.

My instinct is to make light of what he said to deflect the way it's making me feel. But I've done that for years, keeping the world at arm's length by making everything a joke, and I think I'd like to be done with that. No more bullshit for me, thank you very much. So I just nod. "Thanks, Eugene. You're all right."

His phone buzzes, and he takes it out of his pocket while I paint a cape onto my squirrel, only realizing after the fact that I shouldn't have used red paint. Now it really does look like roadkill. Vampire squirrel roadkill.

Movement in my peripheral vision draws my eye to the

window—a couple of women are strolling down the hallway outside the studio, moving at a snail's pace as they look from left to right. The moment I get a clear look at them, I drop my red-dabbed paintbrush onto my dress, because I know them. The woman closest to the window is Rachel, "childcare professional" who tried to screw up Travis's life. I recognize her from her profile pic. And the woman she's walking with is none other than Karen, Travis's ex-girlfriend.

I bristle at the sight of the two of them together. I'm guessing it's no coincidence that Rachel knew all about Travis's past. Are they in cahoots? Are they trying to tear him down?

"Uh, Eugene," I say. "I think I'm ready for that favor."

He looks up in surprise. "That was fast."

"We need to spy on those women." I nod toward the front window, where the two women have paused to chat.

I fully expect him to balk, especially since I've given him no reason for my interest in them, but he lifts a finger, makes one final dab on his piece of artistry, then says, "I think it would be better if I spied on them by myself, Hannah." He waves at my bright hair and the purple sweaterdress I changed into after getting back from Travis and Ollie's house. "I can go through any crowd without being noticed."

"They don't know me."

He smiles. "But they *will* notice you."

"I don't want to miss out," I insist. "Let's go together."

He cleans up his station, and then we stop at the front to pay and turn in our masterpieces, which we're told will be ready for pickup on Wednesday.

"We'll pretend we're power walking," he says as we hurry after Rachel and Karen, who have resumed walking are now far ahead of us but still within view. "There's a power walking club that meets here a few times a week, so they won't be suspicious."

"Were you in the club?"

"I saw a flyer by the front door."

I give him a teasing smile.

"It looked interesting," he adds defensively.

"Of course it did."

"You can pretend I'm your father."

"How do you power walk?"

He starts moving his arms in a hilarious pantomime that cuts off as he gives me a sidelong look and says, "You need to do it too."

Dammit.

But I paste on a smile and power walk right beside him until we start getting close, which is when I realize there's a problem. If we keep power walking, we'll power walk right past them, and while we're nearly at the end of the atrium and can double back, passing them again, we won't overhear anything.

"Fake a muscle cramp," I hiss as we get closer.

"What?" he asks, way too loud.

"A muscle cramp. *Fake one.*"

He taps his ear, indicating he still didn't catch what I said.

We're close enough to Rachel and Karen that I can hear them now. Rachel is saying something about a kid in her daycare class who picks his nose and fling the boogers.

"God, I could *never* work at a daycare," Karen says.

"Because you hate kids," Rachel replies with a laugh.

"What's to like? I guess I should be happy Travis broke it off again." She pulls a disgusted face. "I don't care how loaded he is, I don't have it in me to be a stepmom to some snot-nosed brat."

Crap! I'm coming up on them too quickly. In a couple of seconds I'll be practically next to them. I was so focused on listening to their conversation, I didn't pay attention to our speed.

I stagger to a stop. "Oh, no. My leg. I've got a really bad muscle cramp, Dad. I was going at it too hard."

"You should have eaten that banana," he says in a tone I'm guessing his son is very familiar with.

"Yes, you were right. You're *always* right."

Karen glances back at us with a small smile, then does a double take.

"Hey, I know you," she tells me, stopping in her tracks and turning to face us.

"No," I say, "I'm pretty sure you don't. I remember faces."

"So do I." Her face creases into a deep frown. "You're that redhead who's always at the Garbage Fire shows checking out my ex-boyfriend."

Okay, fine, the power walking gig is up. Time to take a direct approach.

"Oh, yeah," I say, standing up straight. "That *is* me. I'm surprised you noticed, since you're always so busy eye-fucking him yourself." I smile at Eugene. "Sorry for my language, *Dad.*"

"That guy is Karen's ex-boyfriend," Rachel says, putting a hand on her hip. "She has rights."

"*Ex*-boyfriend. I figure she doesn't have rights anymore. I'm guessing you agree with me since you made a pass at him a couple of weeks ago."

Rachel gapes at me.

"Oh yeah, I know all about that."

Karen steals a glance at her friend, clearly confused. "What's she talking about?"

"It's no big deal. You know I hate my job, so when I saw Travis was hiring a nanny, I took an interview with him. But he was a jerk, not that I'm surprised after everything you've told me, and—"

"*Everything you've told her?*" I ask, glancing between them before letting my gaze settle on Rachel. "Like the fact that he's Evan Thomas's son? You're the one who blasted that little chestnut all over the internet, aren't you?"

"I don't know anything about that," Rachel says, pink in the face now. "All I said online was that he was very rude to me, which he was."

Karen looks ready to...well, pull a Karen.

"What did you do?" she hisses at her friend. "I told you not to tell anyone."

"I *didn't*. I wouldn't. You told me in confidence. I just..." She shrugs. "I tried to get a job with him. Why do you care, anyway? You just finished saying you hate kids, and the guy has a kid. A *rude* kid."

"A fantastic kid," I snap. "I'm his nanny. And neither of you deserve to have him in your life. Actually, you don't deserve either of them."

Maybe that's unfair. For all I know, Travis really was a dick to Karen. But if he says he didn't mislead her, I believe him, and she's been making him uncomfortable, showing up at show after show. She's also sharing his secrets with other people, which sucks, even though it's starting to look like Rachel may not be MaritimeLaw69.

Travis isn't my boyfriend, exactly, so maybe it's not my place to defend him, but he basically declared himself to me this morning. Maybe it's time for me to do the same.

"In fact, stay away from *both* of my guys," I add. "No more shows. No more skulking around him in low-cut dresses, hoping he'll fall and face-plant onto your boobs. Trust me when I say you'll both want to listen to me. I'm unhinged."

"She is," Eugene says, nodding easily. "She stabbed the slowest member of our power walking group after we lost our last competition. If he heals fast enough for the next one, I'm sure he'll walk like the wind."

"I can't leave Travis at the mercy of some obsessive psycho," Karen sputters. "I'm going to warn him about you."

"Let's not throw stones in glass houses. But please do tell

him." I give her my best naval salute. "I'm sure he'll double down on what Dad here told you. Just wait until you hear what happened to the person who ignored the no-soliciting sign on the door."

"You're nuts!" Rachel says, taking a step back.

"Yeah, that's kind of the point."

They turn and hustle away, their heels click-clacking on the floor.

"That was invigorating," Eugene says, his eyes shining.

I pat him on the back. "Taking a stand usually feels that way. Now, let's go spend a lot of money on you. That always feels good too."

Some of the glow seeps out of him. "Those kids at the brewery are going to laugh at me. They'll think I care what I look like."

"Eugene, my friend, there's nothing wrong with caring what you look like. And, trust me, if they want to laugh, they'll find a reason. Better for them to poke fun at you for having a kick-ass mini makeover than for being a jerk."

He has to concede I have a point.

CHAPTER TWENTY-SIX

TRAVIS

Conversation with Karen

Travis, your nanny is fucking crazy

She threatened me

You need to fire her and get a restraining order

Let's meet up and talk

Conversation with Hannah

I hear you made friends with Karen?

Look. I'm sorry, but she was hanging out with that nanny who bad-mouthed you. The whole situation stank. So Eugene and I decided to follow them.

You roped Eugene into this?

He was a willing participant.

Turns out Karen's the one who told Rachel about your dad, but we don't think either of them is the snitch.

And, fine, I told Karen to stop coming to your shows.

Are you pissed?

You claimed me, Hannah?

I guess I did.

No, I'm not pissed.

Karen is definitely pissed.

Good.

Were you jealous?

I'm not telling you that until you admit you're jealous of Jonah.

I'm not jealous of Jonah. I'd like to crush him. There's a difference.

So, maybe I wanted to crush Karen.

Good. But we probably shouldn't crush either of them. Liability and all that.

Buzzkill.

I'm sending him a glitter bomb, though.

I've created a monster.

[Monster emoji]

Guess what? I gave Eugene a mini makeover, and we're heading over to Big Catch so I can make sure the other kids play nice with him.

Tell him his friend Dottie says hello.

Dottie's over there?!

I didn't even give her my number, but I guess Rob did. She texted me half a dozen times asking if she could come over to hide some crystals, so I finally caved.

Sounds like her.

She said it's going to take 'several hours.' Ollie is surprisingly into it.

Conversation with Karen

I'm giving Hannah a raise

"The house already feels more serene," Dottie says, patting my hand. "The energy is exactly what it should be."

I smile at her, wishing it were true rather than believing it might be. "Thanks, Dottie."

"Can we make cookies?" Ollie asks, practically bouncing on his feet.

It's hard to believe he's the same kid who wrote mathematical equations on the wall to get a rise out of me. I'm starting to realize that he may have just needed more people in his court.

I think I did too.

It's been a real up-and-down day. A surprisingly good one, though. I'm glad Dottie came around. I don't even mind the basket full of crystals she brought with her. Hell, I helped her and Ollie "strategically place them," although that wasn't something I'd care to admit to Hannah. Or to Rob.

And then I got that text from Karen.

The thought of Hannah laying claim to me got my blood hot. It made me want to do the same.

Soon, I promise myself. I've already posted a few ads for nannies, using different sites than last time. Unfortunately, the only response I've gotten so far is this comment: *We don't forget. Justice for Rachel!* So it's not off to a great start.

"Why don't you go have a little lie-down, dear?" Dottie suggests to me. "You look tired. Ollie and I will make some cookies, read some tea leaves, and then maybe we'll draw our spirit animals. Mine is a llama."

"I think mine's a fox," Ollie says, doing his little happy dance again.

"Just don't turn him into one, and I have no objection," I joke.

Ollie shocks me by throwing his arms around my middle and hugging me. "Today was a good day."

I wrap my arms around him, feeling choked up. "Yeah, buddy, it really was."

Other than the off-and-on headache from my hangover.

"And you're on the path to great things," Dottie say to me meaningfully. Glancing down at Ollie, she adds, "Can I have just a second alone with your dad, sweet boy?"

"Sure," he says with a shrug and heads toward the kitchen.

Dottie pats my arm, giving me a serious look. "I want you to know that I'm here to support your love journey."

I cough. "Excuse me?"

"You probably don't get much time alone with Hannah, but I would always be *delighted* to spend time with little Ollie. I know for a fact that Sophie and Rob feel the same way, and I have other friends who would be thrilled to volunteer their time. I also have a few great-grandchildren his age who would *love* to play with him. You have a village, my dear."

My heart swells at this confirmation of what I was feeling earlier. We're not alone anymore. Maybe we never were, and there were always people ready to step in, waiting for me to let them.

"Thank you. I appreciate that, Dottie." I pause. "How did you know I'm interested in Hannah?"

No point in denying it.

She laughs. "It's clear from the way you look at her, my dear, and in your aura when you speak to her. My goodness, I could tell weeks ago, when you were both in my tea shop."

"I don't think we should date while she's working for me. It feels...wrong."

"Oh, poppycock," she says, surprising me. "I worked for Beau Buchanan for years while we were together, and it was the loveliest partnership imaginable."

I pause, trying to pinpoint what my holdup is. "But I don't want to pay her for looking after Ollie. I want..."

My chest tightens as I consider what I really want. What I've been afraid to put into words, even in my own head.

I want the three of us to be together because we all want to be there, not because there's money on the table. I want her to be...

Fuck, I've only known her a few months, and I've only known her well for two weeks. I can't already be thinking...

But I am. I'm thinking about the three of us sharing holidays and birthdays. Celebrating with party poppers and glitter bombs that will make an unholy mess. I'll complain about them, of course, while secretly loving the way those things make both of them smile.

I heave a deep breath. "I don't know," I hedge.

"I do," Dottie says with glimmering eyes that say she's seen everything passing through my head, the snapshots of the life I want. The life that feels too far away to touch. "And maybe you're so focused on the problems, dear boy, that you're missing the solution sitting before you."

"You?" I ask.

She laughs, then pats her chest. "It's in *you.*"

That sounds more like verbal gymnastics than an actual answer, but she's so earnest it's impossible not to like her. I'm touched that she cares enough to try to help me. My mother wasn't an affectionate woman, and Nanny Grace was practical and no-nonsense. Caring but hardly warm and fuzzy.

Dottie reaches into her pocket and pulls out yet another crystal. "This one is for you. It's for letting love back into your life. I've been holding onto it awhile, but I can tell you're ready for it now."

Another crystal? She must have spent a fortune on the ones she's seeded throughout the house. Still, I'm grateful when I take it from her. Because she's saying she believes in me. She thinks I'm capable of being the kind of man Hannah and Ollie deserve.

"Thank you, Dottie. You seem to take everyone you meet under your wing. Hannah's a bit like that." I run my fingers over the crystal. "I'm surprised you don't run out of space."

"Oh, dear, here's the secret. You just grow bigger wings."

Then she taps me once on the arm, almost like she's casting a magic spell, and maybe she actually is. Because as she strides out of the room, I feel remarkably energized.

Instead of taking a nap, I place a few special orders for Hannah on my phone and then head into the music room and pick up my guitar to practice "Blue River." While I'm playing, I let my mind drift, and it naturally lands on Hannah and the problems before us. I want to be with her, and she maybe wants to be with me, but it won't feel right if it happens while she's working with me, and I haven't been able to find another nanny Ollie likes.

Dottie said my solution was right in front of me. *In* me...

Maybe it's the music, or maybe Dottie really did cast a spell on me—either way, I suddenly know what I need to do. And it *feels* like magic.

When I emerge from the music room, the house smells like cookies. I follow the sweet scent to the kitchen, where Ollie and Dottie are smiling together as they sample the cookies.

"Want one?" Ollie asks, grinning at me. "They're maple spice. Dottie says they're full of love and they really taste like it. I already ate five."

"Then I'd better take at least two," I say with a smile, wrapping them in a napkin.

"Are you on your way out?" Dottie asks with a meaningful look.

I don't ask how she knows. She may not be clairvoyant, but she's definitely intuitive, a person who sees beneath the seething surface.

"Yeah, if that's okay. I was wondering if you could stay for another hour or so."

"Of course," she says, acting like I'm honoring her by asking. "I was hoping to tell Ollie a story before bed." Her smile broadens. "Do say hello to Hannah and dear Eugene for me. Liam too."

"Of course," I say with a smile, not all that surprised that she guessed where I'm going.

"Are you giving Hannah one of those cookies?" Ollie asks, looking delighted by the idea.

"I am," I confirm.

WHEN I GET to Big Catch, the guy manning the host stand says, "Heyyy, it's Drummer Boy." He's wearing a beanie over his dark curly hair and has a name tag that says, *I'm* [ink smeared], *ask me about Dungeons and Dragons!*

I smile and nod, at a disadvantage, because I honestly don't remember him. Maybe I should be embarrassed about getting so drunk last night—I don't usually let myself overindulge like that—but I'm sick of beating myself up over things I can't change. I came here last night, got tanked, and that's that. No need to dwell on it.

"Good to see you again," I say with a nod.

"How's your head, man?"

"It's been better. Is Hannah here?"

"Yes!" he says, beaming. "And she brought Spreadsheet. You won't believe it when you see him, man. They're in the back. I'll take you there."

He promises the group people in line behind me that he'll be right back, then walks at a completely unhurried pace past the familiar tables and booths, including the kayak booth. I vaguely remember trying to climb into one of the kayaks last night, which is another thing I'm determined not to be embarrassed about.

We head into the back, and then he leads me through another door into a wide, warehouse-style space, where Hannah is holding court. She's wearing a purple sweaterdress that brings out her red hair and green eyes. She looks almost unreal—too bright, too pretty, too good for me, to be certain. She's standing with Spreadsheet, the man formerly known as Eugene Peebles, next to a bunch of kegs.

His mustache is history, his hair has been restyled, and he's wearing a button-up shirt, a pair of jeans, and loafers.

Fuck, she dressed him up to look like me.

A laugh bubbles up inside me just as Hannah catches sight

of me. She grins, then announces to the people gathered around her, including Liam, who gives me a weighing look: "We're gonna have a banger of a holiday party this year, friends. Eugene here is going as Santa Claus." She ignores the surprised look he gives her. "Trust me when I say you don't want to miss that."

They start talking amongst themselves, and Hannah gives Eugene a little push, as if he's a baby duckling she's casting into the pond. My smile grows larger as she makes her way to me.

"What are you doing here?" she asks, sounding surprised but not upset, thank God.

"I had to see you, and Dottie offered to stay with Ollie for a little while." I hand her the cookie I brought her. "She made some love cookies."

She gives me a searching look as she accepts the cookie. I half expect she's going to lob a barb at me, but instead she asks, "Does this have weed in it?"

I laugh. "I hope not. Ollie ate five." I glance at Eugene, who's talking animatedly to someone, hopefully not about spreadsheets or self-discipline. "You chose a weirdly hot look for him," I say, quoting what she said about my button-downs earlier.

"I was inspired," she says with a smile, tucking the napkin-wrapped cookie into her purse. "But, really, what are you doing here?"

"Is there somewhere private we can talk?"

She searches out Liam—who's been watching me like a hawk since I walked in and would definitely make a hat out of my face if I screw up—then nods to him and takes my hand. The gesture is so natural, it fills my chest with hope.

She leads me into a small, cramped storeroom, then shuts the door. There's a bunch of kegs stacked up behind us, another row of them on the floor in front of us, and the walls are covered in floor-to-ceiling racks crammed with cardboard boxes of alcohol and barroom supplies.

"Well?" she asks, turning toward me. "You're being very mysterious."

"I wanted to thank you in person," I say. "I gave Ollie a drums lesson today. It felt..." I'm surprised by the welling of heat behind my eyes. "It was awesome. And if you're okay with it, I'd love it if you could bring him to The Missing Beat tomorrow."

She gives me one of her gorgeous whole-face smiles. "I'm so happy I'm not even going to say I told you so."

"You can if you want," I say. "You were right. You did tell me so."

"I did, I really did," she says, practically bouncing in her excitement. Her excitement for us. For what this might mean for my relationship with Ollie.

I hesitate, afraid to say this next part but needing to. I take a deep breath. "Before I met you, I was afraid of being a dad. I figured the best thing I could do for Ollie was find someone else to raise him. Someone who knew what they were doing. Maybe that sounds ridiculous because I spend my afternoons working with other people's kids, but it's different. They're older, and they're there to learn music, not life lessons. So the first thing I did when he got here was try to look for someone else to spend time with him. But I'm done doing that. I want to be his father, Hannah. I'm not going to hire another nanny. *I* want to do this. I'm going to bring him to the Beat with me every afternoon, and Dottie helped me realize that I can just get sitters for when I have shows."

"This is the nicest way I've ever been fired," she says with a laugh, her eyes shiny with tears. She wraps her arms around me and pulls me close, burrowing her face into my neck. "I'm so fucking proud of you."

"I'm *not* firing you," I say, holding her close, savoring the scent of her, the feeling of her in my arms. I sent her away the other night like an idiot, but I never want to do that again. I want to hang onto her for as long as she'll let me. Until my fingers break. "You can keep the job for as long as you want. It'll help in the beginning to have you with him at The Missing Beat. But you need something else, too, Hannah. Something bigger. You're good at working with people, at bringing them together." I pause before admitting, "And I want you to be with us because we're yours, not because it's a job. You're the person I'd choose to be with, out of everyone in the world, and I want you to choose me back. I want to prove I'm worthy of it."

She pulls back to look at me, and I'm gutted by the tear sliding down her cheek. I don't need her to tell me she's not the crying type. She probably sees tears as weakness. I always did, growing up. Whenever we would cry, Our mother would hand us over to Nanny Grace for "acting out," and Nanny Grace would rap our knuckles.

I trace the tear with my finger. "I didn't mean to make you cry."

"I think they're happy tears," she says, laughing softly. "I honestly don't have enough experience with tears to be sure."

I lean in and kiss her softly, reverently.

"You're really blowing my mind right now, Travis," she says. "But you've been a bit hot and cold. I don't know what to make of it. I thought you didn't want to be with me until I stopped working for you."

"Maritime law is different," I say, wanting a smile from her.

"Okay, Ships Junior. Enlighten me."

"When you're on a ship, you don't know how much of a future you have ahead of you. Pirates might attack, or everyone might get scurvy. So it's all about living in the moment. You've made me value that. I was hoping we could try living in the moment together."

"I'd like that," she says, then lifts onto her toes and kisses me. "I'd like that a lot."

"Then will you sit down on that keg, so I can get down on my knees and worship you?"

She smiles up at me, and I kiss her slowly, wanting to savor it. To prove to myself that she's going to be mine. When we finally part for a second, panting, she says, "I've had fantasies about this room too."

"You've had fantasies about my music room?"

"Oh, yes, *Mister Sir*," she says, her expression full of mischief. "You wouldn't believe it. My mind is an unclean place. It's even worse than my apartment."

"Good. We're going to make all of your fantasies come true." Grinning, I urge her back on to the keg, and she sits down on it, spreading her legs for me. My cock is instantly hard, but it doesn't get to play a role in what's happening tonight.

I step between her legs and very slowly, very deliberately get down on my knees before her. Then I push up the skirt of that pretty purple dress and pull her panties down with my teeth—and she throws her head back with delighted laughter. The panties snag on her shoes, and I pry them off. They fall to the floor, but I pick them up, and after making sure she's watching me, I tuck them into my pocket.

"I'll be taking these," I say.

"Will you mount them on the wall like a trophy?"

"Ollie would ask too many questions. I'll have to hide them in my drawer like a pervert."

She starts laughing again, but her laughter hitches as I spread her legs wider, pulling her toward me, and start kissing my way to her center. Her skin is soft and warm beneath my mouth, and I can feel her whole body arcing toward me, wanting my touch. My kiss.

I want her taste.

So I hook her legs over my shoulders and go right for what I want, burying my face in her as she grips my hair. I suck and lick, losing myself in her soft moans, in the slight pain of her fist clenching in my hair, in the way her body responds to my tongue and the graze of my teeth.

Her hand tightens in my hair, and I can feel her trembling now, her release close. My body begs me to stand up and thrust into her now, when she's nearly there, so she can come all around my dick instead of against my mouth. But that's not what tonight's about. Tonight, I'm showing her that I want her pleasure even more than my own. I want her to know how *highly* I really do think of her.

"I'm coming," she says finally, and I suck harder, move my tongue faster, wanting to give her the best orgasm she's ever had. Wanting each orgasm I give her to be better than the last.

I feel her tense around me, and I keep worshipping her with my mouth until she tugs me up to her.

"You're very good at that," she says. "Even better than in my imagination."

I smile at her. "Good."

I pause, weighing what I'm going to say next. "I need to go home soon, but I was wondering if you could show me around. I've been here a bunch of times, but never with you. Not since we've gotten to know each other."

"You really want a tour of a brewery you've been too dozens of times?"

"Yes. I want it with you."

Maybe it'll kill the mood, since she obviously hasn't moved on from this place, but I get the sense that it hasn't totally moved on from her either.

"We're going to do that," she says, her eyes shining. "I'm glad you want to. But first you're going to fuck me on this keg."

"Hannah." My voice is ragged with my need to do just that.

My cock aches. "I didn't bring a condom. I wanted to...this was about showing you how much you matter to me."

"If you really want to show me, you'll fuck me. Besides, you don't need one. I'm on the pill, and obviously I got tested after the Jonah fiasco."

A fresh longing to kill Jonah rolls through me, but I grit my teeth and focus on what she's trying to tell me. "You don't want me to use a condom?"

"I want to show you around Big Catch while your cum is dripping down my leg. How does that sound?"

I get my pants shoved down so quickly it probably breaks some kind of speed record.

She opens her legs wider, inviting me in. Without hesitation, I line myself up and thrust into her hard, the feeling so overwhelming I nearly come on the spot. Especially when she wraps her legs around me and bites the lobe of my ear.

"Don't go easy on me, Travis," she whispers. "I want it all."

I thrust in harder the next time, gripping her thighs on either side of me so I can get deeper, and she throws her head back, her curly hair streaming behind her, making a deep moan of pleasure that has me pushing in even harder, deeper.

The need I feel for her stuns me with its intensity. I've never wanted anyone like this. Never felt like this with anyone.

I burrow my head into her dress, seeking out her nipple, and she tugs the material down for me as I thrust in again, my hands flexing on her thighs.

Then she digs her fingernails into my back, the slight pain driving me wild as I push in faster, quicker, knocking against the keg so hard I wouldn't be surprised if it fell down and caused a chain reaction of all of them falling down. Even if it did, I still wouldn't stop fucking her. I don't know if I could. But then she clenches down on me, a guttural groan escaping her lips.

"Yes, yes," I say, my voice raspy and uneven. "Come for me,

Hannah." Even as I say it, I feel my own orgasm rolling out, taking hold of me. I give myself over to it, losing myself entirely to the wave of pleasure.

Once it recedes, I pull her even harder against me, collecting all of her in my arms, needing every part of myself touching every part of her, and kiss her neck and lips before finally pulling back.

She beams up at me, her dress in complete disarray. "Do I look like I just got fucked in the storeroom?"

"Yes," I say, grinning back at her. "Do I look like I just fucked you?"

"Absolutely."

I pause, wanting to ask but not wanting her to react poorly. "I need to see it. I need to see my cum dripping down your leg. I know you're going to clean up, but first I want to see it."

"Look at you being a secret pervert," she teases, getting to her feet.

"A pervert for you, definitely," I say as she spreads her legs and leans back, letting me see the cum trickling down the top of her thigh. The breath whooshes right out of me.

"Let's stop at the bathroom and then go on that tour," she says.

I nod in agreement, still incapable of speech. I help her straighten her dress, and only once she's fully covered again do I regain the ability to speak. "But why don't we make a point of avoiding your brother."

CHAPTER TWENTY-SEVEN

HANNAH

It's Wednesday morning—*late morning*, full disclosure—and I'm about to go meet Sophie and Briar for breakfast, but when I go to leave, a knock lands on my door.

I look through the peephole and frown. It's Mick, the big guy from down the hall who goes to the same boxing gym as my brother. He's a total asshole half the time, so the joke is that he's Mick half the time, Dick the other half. But occasionally he and my brother grab a beer because they both enjoy punching people.

My heart starts thumping faster. Did something happen to Liam last night, and this guy figured I didn't need to know until morning?

I whip the door open, but once I get a close-up view of him, I cock my head. Because Mick/Dick is covered in glitter, and he is *not* the glitter type. "New look for you?"

"It was meant for you," he says gruffly, sounding pretty pissed off. He shoves a small cardboard box at me, and I start laughing hysterically when I realize what must have happened.

Travis tried to glitter-bomb me, but he accidentally glitter-bombed Mick/Dick instead.

"It's not funny," he insists. "It got me in the eye."

"They can do that," I say through laughter. "Why'd you open my package anyway?"

He scratches his head and unleashes a cloud of colorful sparkles. "Oh, c'mon, Hannah. I wasn't trying to steal it. I just didn't look at the label."

"Well, thanks for taking one for the team."

"Do you know who sent it?"

He clearly means to do the sender harm, and there's no way I'm throwing my guy under the bus, so I shake my head, feigning ignorance. "Guess I must have pissed someone off."

He grumbles and stomps off, leaving faint glitter footprints along the hall.

I'm laughing so hard I'm barely breathing now, but after a few seconds, I gather myself enough to close the door behind him. I carry the little box in with me and sift through the remaining glitter, finding a note.

All it says is:

Now, it's even.
With love from your guys

If that doesn't make my heart swell...

He's sent me something every day this week so far. On Monday, it was a box of donuts that would have given me early-onset diabetes if I'd eaten them all, followed by another huge stuffed dog on Tuesday because my first dog might be lonely. And then the glitter bomb today.

Grinning, I get out my phone and text him.

Did you send me something?

I believe in plausible deniability.

> So, it would mean nothing to you if I say that instead of exploding on me, the glitter bomb exploded all over my huge heavyweight boxing champion neighbor.

> Now I really want some plausible deniability.

> Do you have any more fantasies for us to work through later?

> Always

> Any more articles about [nautical emojis]?

> Not today. Seems to be dying down a bit. [Fingers crossed emoji.]

There was an article about Travis in the local paper on Monday, but the story hasn't gone national...not yet, at least. A few videos about the Ships crew have gone viral on social media, but no one has shown up on Travis's doorstep, thankfully.

I lock up my apartment, which is delightfully clean of glitter but not all that clean in any other way, and head over to Tea of Fortune to meet my friends.

When I arrive, two minutes late, I spot Sophie and Briar in the back, but I pause to greet the Wise Elders Group, which is still in session at the front of the tea shop. Eugene's with them, and he actually gets up and hugs me! Talk about presto change-o. I secretly think getting drunk with Dottie was the best thing that ever happened to him. It's like she magicked her laid-back philosophy into his head. Of course, when I told her that, she clucked her tongue and said that "awakening" Eugene to his better nature has been a group effort and that it wouldn't have worked at all unless he was ready for it.

She's probably right. She's right about most things, aside from her crystal fetish, which I'm willing to overlook.

"The hedgehog is ready," I tell Eugene with a meaningful look. "Project Applebottom Jeans is on."

I wanted to give Eugene and Mrs. Applebaum a celebrity couple name, but this is the best I could come up with, and as an upside, it makes Ollie laugh hysterically whenever he hears me say it. He has no idea what it's in reference to, other than that it has something to do with his teacher.

The project kicks off today. After breakfast, I'm going to pick up the hedgehog pencil cup, and then I'll give it to Mrs. Applebaum when I pick up Ollie after school later. It'll have a note inside. Not one of those middle school notes with checkboxes for DO YOU LIKE ME, YES OR NO, but an invitation to the brewery on Friday afternoon for a "tipple," which is apparently her old-timey word for having a drink with a pal.

If she shows on Friday, Travis is going to serenade her—he even learned her favorite song on the guitar!—and Eugene's going to tell her how he really feels.

If it all goes to hell in a handbasket, Dottie says she knows at least five potential relationship candidates for Eugene who could soothe the sting of Mrs. Applebaum's rejection. I'm thinking we could set up some kind of geriatric *Bachelor* situation for him.

I explained the whole thing to Travis, and he said, "If you ever doubt my feelings for you, remember that I willingly had this conversation."

Eugene sits forward in his chair, giving me the stoic nod of a man going into battle. "I'm ready."

"Yeah, you are. I'm going to pick up the cup after breakfast. I already have the invite you prepared."

"You handwrote it, didn't you, Eugene?" asks Ann. "Handwriting is a *very* sensual act. She'll appreciate that."

Constance snorts. "You think *everything* is a sensual act."

"I'd be happy to make you a ginseng tea blend too, dear," Dottie tells her.

I grin at Eugene, pat him on the back, and wave to the rest of the elders before heading to the back to join my friends.

"You're here," Sophie says, popping up from her chair to hug me. Briar hugs me too, and then I lower into the chair next to Sophie.

"You two were totally talking about me, weren't you?"

"We want to know what's going on with Travis," Briar says, lifting her tea for a sip.

It's not like they're not in the know. I've been group texting them about the whole situation in a long stream-of-consciousness babble.

I grin at Briar. "For someone who's so entirely done with love, you're sure interested in it. You should be begging me to stay away from Travis, because as soon as Dottie decides she's done working her magic on me, she's coming for you next. She said we were all going to find our great loves. Nora too. It sounded like a threat."

"So you're admitting Travis is your great love?" Sophie says, her eyes sparkling.

"I don't know," I say, which makes her look like I just tore a puppy out of her hands, so I admit, "I'm happy, though. Really happy. And last night we told Ollie we're seeing each other, and *he* was happy. But you and I aren't having a double wedding no matter what happens. I figure I should say that right now to get it out of the way."

"Who says I want a double wedding?" she asks, glancing at Briar with a mischievous look in her eyes. "I'll settle for nothing less than a triple wedding."

"Not a four-way?" I waggle my eyebrows. "Dottie insists that Nora is going to pop up when we least expect her."

"I don't blame her for not wanting to talk to us," Briar says, setting her teacup down. "I wasn't sure I wanted to be friends with you two in the beginning."

Sophie gasps as if she just slapped her across the face.

"Don't get me wrong. I'm happy I did," Briar says quickly, setting her hand on top of Sophie's. "But Jonah made me feel so dumb and blindsided, just like I did after my business partner took off with all our money. I didn't want to keep my stupid mistakes. Maybe that's how Nora feels."

"Like hanging with us would mean reliving a horrible memory over and over again?" I ask.

"Yeah, but either way, I say we let her live her life while we live ours." Briar sighs and fidgets in her chair. "I could really use some good news right now, though, so tell us more about Travis."

I hesitate, not wanting to gush when she's clearly dealing with something right now, but I know she believes in even exchanges, so I tell them about the last few days: Travis's little gifts. The way he's been helping with Project Applebottom Jeans. How he signed those printed photos of his face so I could send them to Alice and her friends even though he hated doing it. (I made up for it by giving him head beneath the table, which goes without saying.) How he agreed to switch to tacos on Monday night even though it's supposed to be spaghetti night. (To be fair, the tacos were terrible, so we ended up making spaghetti anyway.)

"You're glowing," Briar says with a smile that doesn't meet her eyes.

"What did your father do to you this time?" I ask suspiciously.

She cradles her head in her hands.

"Briar?" Sophie asks, reaching across the table to put a hand on her arm.

"My dad's making me fire people," she says.

I'd ask why she's playing along with his games at all, but I know the answer. She wants the brewery. To him, it's a disposable project, one he never really liked that much in the first place. But she's been working there for the past couple of years with the dream of running it, spending each day visualizing how it will go. It's hard to let go of a dream like that. Especially since her other dream is six feet under.

"Oh no," Sophie says. "What did they do wrong?"

"Nothing," Briar says flatly. "He thinks we have too many bartenders now that we scaled back the food menu to just appetizers. So he wants me to pick two people to fire by the end of November. Then he's going to make me be the one to break the news. It's part of Briar Boot Camp."

"Wow, no offense, but your dad's a piece of work," I say. "Are you sure he's not just messing with you to see what it'll take to get you to say no?"

She releases a heavy sigh and leans back in her chair. "I *did* say no. He threatened to fire five people unless I got on board. If he let five people go, the rest of the staff would be stretched so thin. They'd hate me anyway."

"Should we introduce your dad to Dottie?" I ask. "She seems to have magic powers to transform assholes."

"Even she couldn't save Jonah," Sophie says, and we all take a moment to savor memories of the asshole's downfall. Sure, he's still gainfully employed, but he had to change careers, go work for his daddy, and now every woman in town knows that he's a philandering creep. That's got to sting.

"I think I'm going through with it," Briar says after a moment. "I overheard my dad talking to my mom about his new business. Sounds like they already closed on a space, so it seems like that's getting closer. This might be one of the final hoops I have to jump through."

"I don't think you should have to jump through any hoops," Sophie says, frowning.

"I can probably convince Travis to send him a glitter bomb," I offer. "He's turning into a loose cannon."

"And you love it." Sophie smiles at me.

"I do," I confirm. "He's this amazing blend of predictable and unpredictable. I can't get enough of him."

"I'm probably the one who's going to be getting glitter bombs soon," Briar says morosely, playing with her long braid. "Everyone at Silver Star is going to hate me."

"No one could ever hate you," Sophie says, with all the confidence of someone sweeter than me.

"Don't fire the people who are the worst at their job," I warn Briar. "Fire the ones who are liked the least by the other staffers. Trust me on this."

She doesn't answer right away, just keeps playing with her braid, and after a moment changes the subject to scheduling our next viewing of *Matchmaking Small Town America*. Sophie hasn't been watching it with us because she says dating shows stress her out. I privately suspect that they stress Briar out too, and that she only likes watching it because it validates her decision to stop dating. But I haven't called her on it. She's under enough stress.

"WHAT'S IN THE BAG?" Ollie asks as we wait in the corner of the school auditorium. I asked the tweed-wearing teacher, who must be in charge of dismissal, if I could have a private meeting with Mrs. Applebaum about a "very important matter," and he sighed heavily to show his displeasure and then asked me to wait in the corner with Ollie until dismissal was finished.

Judging by the forty or so kids still pushing each other, shouting, and running around the auditorium, this might take some time.

I pull the little pencil pot out of its paper bag to show Ollie.

"What *is* that?"

"You've never seen a hedgehog before?"

"They don't really look like this, but it's cool. You said your friend made it for Mrs. Applebaum?"

"Yeah," I say. "I have high hopes for it."

"Can I take a look?" he asks, his eyes wide.

I hand it to him—just as a big kid pushes past him to get to the door. A gasp escapes me as the perfectly painted hedgehog tumbles to the vinyl floor. It's vinyl. It won't break. It totally won't—

It cracks in half, spilling out Eugene's very nicely hand-written note.

"Dammit," I say, loudly enough that a teacher hushes me.

"I'm so sorry," Ollie says, crouching down to pick up the pieces.

I sweep his hands away, not because I'm unhappy with him, but because I don't want him to get hurt on any jagged edges.

"Hannah, I'm so sorry," he says louder, his eyes filled with unshed tears.

"Oh my gosh, Ollie, it's okay," I say, sticking the pieces and the note in the paper bag and wrapping an arm around him. "It was just an accident. You have nothing to be sorry for."

He's crying now, and I hold him close, my heart breaking. This isn't over the hedgehog (although RIP, you perfectly painted bastard). He's worried he'll be punished or that I'll turn my back on him, all because of an accident.

"It's okay," I whisper to him again and again. "It's okay."

A little boy with brown hair approaches us, his eyes wide.

"Is Ollie all right?" He pats Ollie on the shoulder. "Ollie, are you all right?"

"Yes," Ollie says, tears running down his cheeks. So, clearly he goes to the Travis school of emotional repression.

"Don't worry," the little boy says. "Leonardo's not really dead. It's a fake-out. I know the end of season two is scary, but he'll be okay."

My eyes practically pop out of my head. Holy guacamole, this is Mickey? Did the turtle bonding actually work?

"Thanks," Ollie says. "I'll see you tomorrow. Hannah has to talk to Mrs. Applebaum."

"Mickey? Mickey?" Tweed Teacher calls in a harassed tone. "Come out, come out, wherever you are."

Mickey rolls his eyes at us. "I gotta go."

He runs off, and I gape down at Ollie. "That's Mickey? I was envisioning a super villain. He's just...a kid."

He shrugs carelessly, as if he and this kid haven't been getting on each other's cases since day one. "He's okay. We've decided to try to be friends. Mrs. Applebaum said she'd give us some leftover candy on Friday if we have a good week."

Mrs. Applebaum is bribing them with candy now?

Mind. Blown. I'm instantly desperate to tell Travis about all of this, but he and Rob are taking their Missing Beat students on a field trip to a concert this afternoon, so Ollie and I aren't joining them. I won't see him until after his band meeting tonight.

"I'm going to need a minute to process all of this," I say, "but I want to ask why you reacted like that about the broken hedgehog. You know I wouldn't get mad at you over an accident."

"But it was important to you," he says, fidgeting with the hem of my shirt. "I was worried you'd want to leave. I know you're not going to be my nanny for much longer."

I crouch down on my haunches so we can be eye to eye.

"No, probably not," I admit. "But that doesn't mean you'll stop seeing me. I'm sorry to tell you that you're stuck with me. We're going to be friends forever, you and me."

"Do you mean it?" he asks with those serious brown eyes, so like Travis's. I feel like I'm answering both of them as I say, "Yes," emotion burning behind my own eyes.

He hugs me tighter, and then the sound of someone clearing their throat behind me signals me to turn around.

Tweed Teacher is gazing at me expectantly. He is one of the few people left in the auditorium, which has virtually emptied out other than a few teachers.

"Mrs. Applebaum has agreed to see you," he says.

Ollie holds my hand as I follow Tweed Teacher back toward Ollie's classroom. Crap, what am I going to do now? The hedgehog present is ruined.

"..." Tweed Teacher clears his throat as we walk. "How's Peebles doing?"

"He's doing great. We call him Spreadsheet now."

"Uh, okay."

And an awkward silence floats between us before he comes to a stop at Mrs. Applebaum's door.

I knock and then enter at her officious, "Come in."

She raises her eyebrows as I step into the classroom with Ollie.

"Hey, Ollie, can you sit over there for a minute while I talk to Mrs. Applebaum?" I point to a desk in the back, and he nods, squeezing my hand before he lets go.

I approach the front of the room, where Mrs. Applebaum is seated at her desk. Can't say I'm really feeling the spirit of welcome, considering the doom-and-gloom stare she's giving me.

"What is it now, Miss Hannah?" she asks, then glances back at Ollie. "I thought everything was going quite well this week.

I'm not sure if Ollie told you, but he and Mickey have finally found some common ground."

"I've watched an unreal amount of *Teenage Mutant Ninja Turtles* to help make this happen," I say with a smile.

She surprises me when she admits, "And I offered them candy at the end of the week if they were willing to work it out. I'm not proud, Miss Hannah, but I do think good work should be awarded, and Ollie has been *very good*."

My heart swells with pride, but I admit, "I'm actually not here about Ollie."

She gives me a strange look. "Do you have an odd relationship with some other child in my class?"

I laugh. "No."

Oh, what the hell. It's the thought that counts, right?

I thrust the bag forward, and she looks at it doubtfully.

"It's for you," I say.

"I don't accept gifts from students," she says, glancing at Ollie again.

"It's not from Ollie. Or me. Or Travis. A...mutual friend found out about the broken pencil cup, and he immediately decided he was going to make another one for you." I remember Eugene's worry about the gym teacher. "But it wasn't the gym teacher."

Her frown deepens. "I never said the gym teacher made it for me."

Oh crap, mayday, mayday...

"Uh, yeah, well, why go for a gym teacher, when you could aspire to have a principal, am I right? Anyway, my friend Eugene Peebles made this for you."

She gasps and takes the bag from me, and I'm so blown away by her very encouraging reaction that I actually forget that I'm giving her yet another broken pencil cup until she reaches inside and picks up one of the halves.

Giving me a puzzled look, she says, "Is this some kind of joke?"

I very nearly swear in front of her before getting a handle on myself.

I'm about to explain what happened when a quavering little voice behind me says, "No, Mrs. Applebaum. It's no joke."

I glance over to see Ollie has walked up to us. He looks nervous, but there's a sweet determination flowing from him as he says, "I broke it. I'm sorry. I wanted to look at it in the auditorium, and Hannah let me, and it fell down and cracked. I felt so bad, but it was too late to take it back."

"Oh," she says softly, then reaches inside the bag and picks up the note, reading it in front of us, which surprises me.

I'm even more surprised when her eyes well up.

Hot damn, this is a day of turbulent emotions. I'll have to ask Dottie if Mercury is in retrograde or something.

"You're friendly with Eugene?" she asks, glancing up, the note fluttering in her hand.

"I am. He replaced me at Big Catch Brewing. I started hanging out with him to help with his transition, but we've become friends."

I'm surprised by the truth of that.

"He had nothing but good things to say about you," I say, wanting to make his case. "We're sorry we screwed up his present, but I have to tell you, I was with him when he painted it, and I've never seen anyone take so much care with a gift."

She sniffles a little, then nods. "Yes. Tell him I'll be there."

I reach out to take the bag with the hedgehog pieces, but she tightens her grip. "I'll keep it. My daughter is good at fixing things. I'll see if there's something she can do."

"You have a daughter?" Ollie asks in disbelief.

To my utter shock, Mrs. Applebaum laughs. "Yes, but she's not a young child anymore. She's thirty."

"I didn't know you were that old," he says with the complete innocence of youth. Then he tugs the bottom of my shirt with all the subtlety of Travis when he wants to lodge a complaint. "Well, can we go, Hannah? I want to watch the *Turtles*."

"My condolences," Mrs. Applebaum says to me, letting her mask drop again. "But I admire your devotion."

It's as if I became a real person the moment I brought Eugene's gift to her. It hits me that she's probably dealt with hundreds if not thousands of parents and guardians making demands of her over the course of her career. She'd probably have to be good with boundaries to survive as a teacher.

I nod in acknowledgement. "I'll tell Eugene you'll be there." I start to steer Ollie toward the door, but then stop and turn back. "By the way...you're going to see a few changes in him."

Better to warn her now, in case she was super attached to his awful mustache.

"Oh?"

"Yeah, his mustache is gone, and I helped him with some wardrobe updates."

She smiles. "You remind me of my daughter. She's always trying to help me the way she sees best. If she had her say, I'd be on every dating site on the internet. Of course, she's had a hard time with dating too," Mrs. Applebaum says, suddenly chatty. "But that's to be expected. I don't mind telling you, because Eugene knows, of course, but my ex-husband was a philanderer."

"You deserve better," I tell her.

"Perhaps I do." She smiles at me and actually ruffles Ollie's hair before we leave the classroom.

"That was weird," Ollie says in the hall as we make our way toward the building's main entrance.

"Adults are weird," I agree.

We head back to Travis's place, make some popcorn, and

fall right into *Teenage Mutant Ninja Turtles* for a few episodes before we head over to Sophie's place to help her test the craft for her next pop-up event.

Making cereal box houses.

Apparently, we were her inspiration.

We're back at Travis's place eating pizza when my phone buzzes in my pocket.

"My phone," I say through a mouthful of pizza, pulling it out of my pocket.

"You're definitely getting addicted to that thing," he says in a sad voice, like he'll miss me when I'm in phone rehab. "Shouldn't we have a no-electronic-devices-at-dinner rule?"

"Probably," I agree, swallowing. Then I look at the screen and gasp, because it's a message from Eugene.

Mercury *has to be* in retrograde.

> I'm with my son, and we've found something interesting.

> To be clear: this is my evening off. I'm not shirking my duty at Big Catch.

> I'd NEVER accuse you of that.

> Will you come over to Cormac's house so we can show you?

> YES. Send me the address, and we'll be right there.

> I'm with Ollie. I'm guessing it's okay if he comes?

There's a pause, three dots appear, disappear, reappear, and finally a message comes through.

> Yes, if you must.

CORMAC'S HOUSE is a little old bungalow in West Asheville with a surprisingly large fenced-in yard.

"Do you think he has any toys?" Ollie asks.

"Probably not the kind he wants kids playing with. But I'll let you use my phone."

We unlatch the fence and approach the front door, and before I even knock, a dog starts in with a deep, resonant bark.

"It's okay," a voice says from the other side. "She likes kids."

She doesn't sound like she enjoys much of anyone.

I smile tightly at Ollie. "Get behind me, Ollie. Just in case."

He listens, his little fists gripping the back of my shirt, and the door swings open to reveal a small but muscular corgi, who stops barking and bounds across the threshold to sniff my feet.

I put out my hand, but the dog ignores it, her body going rigid, and then bursts off after a squirrel, barking again.

A tall guy with curly brown hair, gray eyes, and glasses stands in the doorway next to Eugene. "Sorry," he says. "Cookie's failed obedience school twice. My neighbors love me. Let me just set up the ball thrower to keep her busy."

He squeezes past us and pulls something out from behind

the porch. It's some kind of metal box, one side filled with at least two dozen green tennis balls, and to my shock, when he flips a switch, the device starts moving around on hinged legs. A few seconds later, it spits a tennis ball.

"Did you make that?"

"Yeah," he says dismissively, as if it's no big deal. "That's my hobby. I make things."

Everyone makes things. I like to make messes. Not very many people make ball-throwing robots. But I let it go. Right now, I'm more interested in what he found.

"That is *so* cool," Ollie says, watching the robot with fascination.

Eugene makes a *hmph* sound under his breath as he steps aside and waves us in. We enter the house, followed by Cormac, who shuts the door.

"You haven't introduced yourself, Cormac," Eugene says gruffly, as if he still thinks he needs to teach his son manners.

An image pops into my head of Travis doing that when Ollie's thirty, and I smile.

Will I be there laughing at him?

I'm surprised by the tug of longing in my chest.

I *want* to be there. I don't know what the future will look like, or how we'll get there—Travis and I have been living firmly in the present for the last few days—but I'd like us to have one.

"Uh, yeah, I'm Cormac," the curly-haired guy says, smiling at us. "You must be Hannah and Ollie."

"Yeah," Ollie says. "Can I check out your other creations?"

Eugene surprises me by saying, "How about I show you, young man? And Cormac can talk to Hannah for a minute."

I'm grateful he doesn't want to keep me in suspense. I don't want to keep him in suspense either, so I say, "Our mutual friend is excited to see you again."

"Wonderful," he says with a broad smile.

The house is tidy, with a big sectional couch by the door and a TV across from it. Cormac leads me past it, down a short hallway, past a room with a bright red guitar displayed on the wall, and into an office with two computer screens and a swiveling desk chair. He sits on the singular chair, seeming unaware that I'm awkwardly standing behind it.

"All of this suspense is killing me," I admit.

"Well," Cormac says, swiveling to look at me. "First..." He glances at the door. "Would you mind shutting that?"

I do, and he continues in a hushed voice. "I wanted to thank you for helping my dad. He's been fighting off a pretty bad depression, but everything seems to have changed now that he's hanging out with you and your friends. I owe you one, Hannah."

People are offering me favors left and right lately. I smile at him. "Seems to me we're already square if you figured out who was posting those messages."

He nods. "But I'll still owe you one. Because your favor only took me half an hour."

That makes me feel pretty inadequate, since I spent way more than half an hour trying to research the problem, but he clearly knows what he's doing. "Thank you."

He nods again, then moves on, saying, "There were half a dozen identical posts across different discussion boards, all posted by the same username over a span of three days in mid-October. October twelve to fifteenth. They were all deleted on Saturday evening, but they had already been cached.

I gasp, because I'd only known about two posts. The one found by Alice and the one that had attracted the more aggressive Ships fans. The timeline also suggests means it wasn't Rachel.

"I'm pretty sure I know who did this," Cormac continues, pushing his glasses up.

"How?" I ask eagerly. "Was it the photos? Did you strip the metadata? Oooh, or figure out the IP address?"

He smiles. "That wouldn't have told me much. You can only get within ten to fifty miles of the physical location if you have the IP address."

Well, that's disappointing...and possibly reassuring.

"Then how?"

He pauses. "This person created a fake Gmail account to connect to the fan sites, but Gmail requires you to provide a first and last name and a birthday. I was able to figure out the information used to create the account. Either someone set this person up, which feels like a stretch, or he did it himself and was incredibly sloppy."

That means a man was behind this. My first thought is that it must have been Jonah after all, trying to get even with Rob by destroying his band.

But that still doesn't totally feel right.

"All right," I say tightly. "Enough foreplay. Who did this? Was it Jonah?"

He purses his lips and shakes his head. "I don't want to cause any trouble."

"Too late."

"You're right. But I'm a little familiar with your friend's band, so I know this is a big deal. That's why I wanted to tell you in person. I wanted to explain that it could still be someone else using this person's name."

My mind darts to Rob, finds it impossible, and then settles on...

"The name on the account is Chance Bixby. I can show you, if you'd like."

I don't want to see the evidence of his betrayal, but I'm the kind of person who believes in bringing receipts, and Travis needs to know this immediately. Like, yesterday.

CHAPTER TWENTY-EIGHT

TRAVIS

"The answer's no," Rob says firmly. He, Bixby, Drake, and I are sitting in a circle of chairs in The Missing Beat, discussing the *Ships Ahoy* crap. It feels like we're a bunch of toddlers having circle time, and given the energy flying around, I wouldn't be surprised if it ended in a brawl.

I nearly got into one yesterday, although I haven't told anyone. When Ollie was at school, I swung by Jonah's office to ask him if he was behind the *Ships Ahoy* BS. He was outside, smoking a cigarette of all things—a new habit—so I got to sneak up on him and catch him off guard.

He'd stood up to the interrogation about as well as a rain-soaked cardboard box.

"It wasn't me," he said. "What makes you think I care about you or your stupid band? Every woman in town thinks I have herpes, and I'm working for my father. I've got enough fucking problems."

"No, not enough," I sneered. "You deserve for your dick to fall off for what you did to Hannah and her friends, you spineless piece of shit."

I had plenty more to say, but it wouldn't help anyone if I

stood around taunting him, so I left him there to dwell on his poor decisions.

Bixby makes an incredulous sound, and I return my focus to arguing with my bandmates. "Why does it matter how we get attention, as long as we do? If they want us to wear sailor suits and sing about maritime law, I say we do it, and once people know about us, we can do whatever we want."

"I've got no problem with that," Drake says, shrugging. "My rent bill that doesn't give a shit about personal integrity." He and Bixby bump fists.

Guilt takes root in my gut, because money's not a problem for me. Hasn't been for most of my life.

It doesn't matter, though. Even if I wanted to give them what they want, I can't.

"It's not happening," I say. "If my ex finds out about this, she'll fight me for custody of Ollie and use him as a bargaining chip."

"Which is why this discussion is at an end," Rob says curtly. "Now, this Frank guy was interested in us before all of this crap, and he'll still be interested if we play well at our next concert. We don't need some gimmick. We're good enough without it."

"But does it really matter if Lilah gets custody?" Bixby asks, giving me a hard stare.

"Yes, it fucking matters."

"You didn't even know this kid existed a couple of months ago, Trav, and you were better off not knowing. How are you supposed to go on the road anyway, if you have a kid at home? You've already stopped staying late at the shows, and the fans expect us to interact with them."

He might as well have punched me in the gut, because it's nothing I haven't thought of myself.

"I think you do plenty of interacting for all of us," I grumble.

He laughs as if it was a compliment—it definitely wasn't—

and nudges Drake's shoulder. "Travis is dating that redhead now, and Rob's got Sophie, so you and I will get all the women."

"Fine," Rob says. "But you won't be doing it in a sailor suit."

"We need this," Bixby objects hotly. "I need this, Travis. I think I'm about to get laid off at work."

More guilt gnaws at me.

Rob gives me a hard stare and shakes his head, silently telling me not to cave. He wants to protect me, obviously, but he doesn't know everything about my situation or what my plans are for the band.

It's time he did.

"I need to talk to Rob for a minute," I say.

Bixby snorts. "Oooh ho, Mom and Dad need to have a talk."

"Grow the fuck up," I say, then storm out the door.

Not my usual move, but I don't like the bad vibes filling up the room.

Rob shuts the door behind us, then walks several paces down the corridor to the large picture window. I join him, and we stand there for a moment, gazing down at the scenic parking lot. We've always joked that it adds to the curb appeal.

"I'm going to quit the band," I say.

Rob sighs. "I knew you were going to say that, but why does that make any sense? If you quit, then we wouldn't be able to do the stupid Ships Junior publicity anyway."

"It's not that. Bixby made a good point." I sweep my hair out of my face. "I don't want to miss Ollie's childhood. I don't want to hand him over to other people to take care of him. If we go on the road, I'd need to leave him. I'm not going to do that...and if I'm being honest, I'm not sure I want it anyway. After what happened last week..."

I trail off, not sure where I'm going with that, just sure that it sucked.

He whistles, shaking his head slightly. "Do you really want to quit, or are you worried you can't handle the attention?"

I rub the bridge of my nose. "I don't know."

"I don't want to endlessly be on tour either," he says, turning me toward him. "There are plenty of bands that do just fine without it." He pauses. "I'm going to marry Sophie, Travis."

"You proposed?"

"Not yet," he says with a smile. "So maybe don't tell her before I get around to it. But I'm going to. I want to have a family too."

I try to process this, to consider what the future might look like for us. But there's a sound of approaching footsteps—running footsteps—and then Hannah turns the corner, her hair a mess around her face.

My heart stops. She looks devastated, and there's no sign of my son.

"Where's Ollie?" I ask, fear filling up every molecule of my body. Did Lilah grab him? Is he lost? Was he hurt? The possibilities spiral through my mind my whole existence on pause until I know the answer.

"He's okay," she says, lifting a hand, panting slightly. "He's okay! I'm sorry. I left him with Dottie. I didn't want to scare you, but I have to talk to you alone." She shifts her attention to Rob. "Actually, this concerns you too."

"What's going on?" I ask, crossing the remaining distance to her, my heart racing now.

She glances at the closed door bearing our sign—*The Missing Beat,* with a musical note replacing each I. "Are Drake and Bixby in there?"

I nod, reaching for her hand, needing the reassurance of it under mine. "What's going on? Did Lilah come by?"

"No," she says, shaking her head so hard her curls spin out. "No, not that. Eugene's son is some kind of genius computer expert, remember? And he figured out who MaritimeLaw69 is..." She captures her bottom lip in her teeth, and I already know it's bad. If it weren't, she wouldn't hesitate to tell us."

"Just say it," Rob says quietly.

"He's not one hundred percent sure, but the person who set up the email address linked to that MaritimeLaw69 account used the name of someone we know." She glances at the door again and whispers, "Chance Bixby."

Rob swears loudly.

I press my palm to the wall, whether to help myself stay upright or convince myself not to punch it, I'm not sure.

This is what it felt like that night in Nashville, when Lilah climbed onto Roland's lap. This is what it felt like having my father tell me I was a genius, the best son ever, only for him to tell me I was the worst disappointment of his life when I refused to do the show. This is what it felt like every time my mother handed us over to Nanny Grace the second we acted like we might need something.

I want to sit down and grip my hair and rock back and forth, and I also want to storm in there and beat the shit out of the guy I thought was one of my closest friends.

Bixby's always been immature and impulsive, but I believed he cared about me. I thought he, Rob, and I were a unit. A band. Brothers.

But he did something that could risk my custody of my son, and that's unforgivable.

I'm practically vibrating with rage, so deeply immersed in it that it's the only thing I feel. The only thing that matters. But then Hannah burrows herself into my chest, wrapping her arms around me, and the worst of it fades away.

"We don't know that it's him," she whispers. "We don't know yet. It's still just a possibility."

Part of me wants to walk away so I can preserve the hope that it's not true for a little while longer.

Hannah has made me stronger, though, and I don't want to run from uncomfortable things anymore.

"So let's find out," I say, bending to kiss her forehead before I release her. Then I turn to Rob, who looks like he'd enjoy bludgeoning Bixby with his own bass guitar.

"We're going to ask him," I tell him. "Talk it out."

"I'm going in with you," Hannah insists hotly.

I meet her gaze, smiling. Feeling lucky that this incredible force of a woman thinks I'm worth her rage. "Are you going to listen if I say no?"

She lifts her chin. "I think you know the answer to that."

"Don't kill anyone for me, Hannah." I reach for her hand and squeeze it. "Ollie and I don't want to have to visit you in jail."

"I make no promises."

"All right," Rob says, nodding to the door. "Let's get this over with."

"I can't play with him anymore if he did this," I tell Rob. "His reasons don't matter."

"No," he says, looking sad. "They don't."

The three of us walk in together. I'm still holding Hannah's hand, partly because I'm not certain she won't stalk over and kick Bixby in the balls if I let her go. Partly because I don't want to let go. Ever.

They stop talking the second we walk inside, then Bixby lifts his chin, indicating Hannah. "Can't go a minute without your new girlfriend, Trav?"

She gives him a furious look that makes me glad her hand is still tucked in mine.

I consider what to say, then figure fuck it, might as well pull a Hannah and not try to dress up a flaming bag of shit and call it a sundae. "Were you the one who posted in those *Ships Ahoy* forums, Bixby?"

Guilt flits across his expression, but he glares at Hannah. "Did she tell you that?"

"Did you do it?" Rob asks. "We need the truth."

Drake looks uncomfortable, but I don't care about him. My attention is on Bixby.

The look on his face says it all. I still need to hear his side of things, though. I want to understand.

"We just needed a little attention," he says after a few seconds. "A little press. I knew that's all it would take for us to level up. Get some national attention."

Rob swears loudly.

"You know how I feel about my father," I say coldly.

"Yeah," he says, shaking his head, summoning some anger of his own. "And what I would give to have my shitty dad leave me a fortune *and* a platform. You act like you're so high and mighty, Travis, but you're not above using your money. You basically bought this place for Rob, so he'd have a purpose, and I know you poured money into it."

"We offered you a job here," I say evenly.

I can feel Rob staring at me, but that's a conversation for a different time.

"I didn't want a job at this stupid fucking place," Bixby says, standing up. "I wanted our band to go places. That's why I did it. I knew all it would take was a little push, and—"

"We didn't need it," Rob says, his tone hard. "Frank was interested in us before all this dumb stunt, but now he wants us in sailor suits. You made us a joke."

"I didn't know that would happen." He starts pacing. "I did it before we met him, and then I forgot about it. I erased the posts after the show."

"You forgot that you betrayed me?" I say dryly. "Well, at least you did it for the good of the band."

"Yeah." He stops pacing. "That's all I care about, and I used to think that was all you cared about too. But you obviously have different priorities." He turns his glare on Hannah again. "Ever since that kid got dropped off at your doorstep and this bitch started working for you—"

That's all it takes. I'm no longer thinking about the fact that this guy was my friend until fifteen minutes ago. I'm not even thinking of the way he buried a knife in my back. All I'm thinking is that he just insulted my son and the woman I care about. The woman I *love*. I rush forward and bury my fist in his face. His nose gushes blood.

"You don't fucking talk about them like that. You don't talk about them at all."

I haven't punched anyone since I was twenty-one, and it feels awful, but I don't have time to cradle my hand, because Bixby punches me back hard, clipping me in the shoulder.

I see Hannah coming toward us with a look of intent in her eyes—a distraction that gets me punched again—but then Rob physically lifts her and plants her behind him before rushing forward.

He's yelling something, but I don't hear him, because the blood is beating hard in my ears as I punch Bixby again. He tries to get his arm around my neck, hitting me in the side this time, probably nearly taking out a rib, and then suddenly Rob's pulling me back. "Not worth it, man."

Drake pulls Bixby back, too, though Bix is staring murderously at me. Still just as pissed off as I am, even though he's the one in the wrong. The one who used me.

"You're out of the band," Rob tells him.

Bixby actually laughs. "Out of the band? There *is* no more band. Screw this."

He shrugs out of Drake's hold and storms out of the room.

Drake stands there for a second, rocking on the balls of his feet. "Uh, does that mean I'm out, too?"

"Yes," Rob says as Hannah steps out from behind him and runs over to me. "Obviously."

I almost laugh, but I don't. I can't.

I wrap my arms around Hannah, needing her warmth. My blood feels like ice in my veins. Because Bixby's right. Without a rhythm guitarist and a bassist, we've got no band. We're cooked.

CHAPTER TWENTY-NINE

HANNAH

Travis is quiet as we get into my car.

I insisted on driving both of us. He protested and said it was stupid because he'd have to come back and get his car later, and I said I didn't care if it was stupid, I was damn well driving him. Then he just shrugged and got into the passenger seat like he didn't care about anything, which made me think that maybe I should have let him drive after all.

Before Rob left, he told Travis that they were going to take a breather but they'd work something out. But from the look on Travis's face, he doesn't believe it.

"Do you wish you were driving?" I ask.

"I don't care, Hannah," he says, but he layers his hand over my thigh. So at least he's not pissed at me for being the bearer of bad news.

Before I can turn on the ignition, he asks, "Do you think Dottie could watch Ollie for a little longer? I don't think... I need a little time to process this."

"On it," I say, already hopping onto my cell phone.

Dottie responds immediately:

I sensed some trouble in the air, my dear.

Yeah, right. More like Eugene texted her the intel. I've seen their super active chat window. Honestly, I don't know how Dottie finds the time.

You take the time you need. Bear and I would be delighted to have him stay with us tonight— what a treat! If that would be acceptable, let me know, and I'll plan on it. We have some pajamas we keep here for my grandchildren's visits.

I ask Travis, and he nods. "Yeah, that would probably be best."

I fill Dottie in on the situation, and she sends back a photo of some crystals. I'm not sure whether they're supposed to be inspiring to Travis in his time of emotional upheaval, or if she's doing some craft with them, so I send back a thumbs-up.

"Sounds like they're having fun," I say to Travis.

"Good," he says. Then, as I turn on the ignition, he says, "Let's go to your apartment. I want to see it."

"Uh, it's a bit messy."

He smiles at me. "I had every expectation it would be messy."

"Are you sure you don't want me to bring you to a doctor? What if you have internal bleeding?"

"I don't have internal bleeding," he says tightly. "He didn't hit me hard enough."

"It sure looked like he did," I say, feeling the righteous burn of anger.

"He threw weak punches on purpose," he insists. "I hit him harder."

I'll have to take his word for it. It looked like Bixby hit him pretty damn hard.

I drive to my apartment, feeling my nerves prickle, because I honestly don't remember what it looked like before I left this morning. At least the glitter bomb didn't go off in my place, but I'm pretty sure there are some clothes strewn across the floor, and a half-finished fashion project on my mannequin.

Not that Travis is going to care. He's obviously in the middle of a mind storm. I know what it's like to have someone you love turn on you. Margaret and I were close before things went south between her and Liam. I'd thought it was the kind of friendship that would stick.

I keep stealing glances at him as I drive, and finally he cracks a smile and says, "I'd feel a whole lot better if you'd keep your eyes on the road, Hannah. Every time you do that, the car veers."

At least he's making jokes.

I park in the lot in front of my building, feeling a little ashamed, because I'll be honest, the place is a total dump.

"It's not quite what you're used to," I say wryly.

He sits back, not getting out yet. "I forget sometimes," he says thoughtfully. "A lot of things haven't been great for me, but I've never had to worry about money. I should have been more understanding with Bixby. Maybe it wouldn't have come to this if I had been."

I give him a look of pure disbelief. "Are you kidding me? You don't need to be understanding. He's a tool. He—"

"He's right. I started The Missing Beat because I thought it would give Rob and me purpose. I told Rob I got some grants that never came through. I paid for a lot of it myself."

"How dare you," I say, deadpan.

He smiles, shaking his head. "But I didn't do anything like that for Bixby. I could have. We've been friends for years."

"The only thing he wants is to be famous. You can't make

him famous. If you guys did the whole dumb sailor suit thing, you'd be a joke. It would make the news for a week or two, but then no one would care."

He nods, but his jaw is still tense. "He called you a bitch. I'm not going to forgive him for that."

"How about not forgiving him for stabbing you in the back?"

"Yeah. That too."

"He's a total shithead. Who cares if he doesn't have a lot of money? I don't have a lot of money, and *I'm* not a total shithead."

"You're not a shithead at all," he says, smiling softly at me, but with eyes so sad I almost tear up myself.

I force a return smile. "You're so romantic."

"Show me your apartment, Hannah," he says, unbuckling his seat belt and taking my hand. "You already showed me the place where you loved to work. I want to see your home."

Tension coils in my chest, because even though I know he cares about me and wants to be with me, I'm worried he'll reject this side of me. The full manifestation of my chaos.

He must see it in my eyes—the fear that I might be both too much and not enough—because he says, "I want it all."

Then he leans in and kisses me so sweetly it lessens my worry.

When he pulls back, eyes on me, I nod. "I want to show you. But it's a mess."

"I love your messes. Every time I find slime on a pillow, or a balled-up piece of paper, or one of your abandoned art projects, it's like you've laid your claim on me. Declared that I'm yours."

I gasp, because that's the sweetest thing anyone's ever said to me. Lifting my hand to cup his face, I trace my fingers over the heart on his forehead. "You *are* mine, dammit. I'm glad you finally admitted it."

He leans in and kisses my neck, the press of his lips leaving a mark on my soul. "And will you be mine, Hannah?"

"I already am," I say, feeling tears in my eyes, as I pull away to meet his gaze again. "But you should really come in and see my apartment. You might change your mind."

"Why?" he asks. "Is there a dead body in there? I'll help you bury it."

I laugh. "What if I'm a hoarder?"

He makes a disgusted face but shrugs. "No one's perfect."

I laugh harder, shoving his arm. "You're lying. You would totally dump my ass if I were a hoarder."

"No, I'm sure there's a crystal for that. Dottie would help me rehabilitate your hoarding ways. And Eugene would pitch in. That man looks like he'd enjoy a good purging." He pauses and tucks my hair behind my ear. "Nothing up there could change my mind about you. I know this is early, and you're probably going to laugh at me, but I love you, Hannah."

Shock barrels through me, but I know he means it. He's a man who says what he means. I take a second to study my own heart—and know what should have been obvious.

"Ugh. I can't make fun of you for that. I love you too," I say. Then I'm laughing and crying as I kiss him, and he kisses me back like my mouth is his only available source of oxygen.

When we pull apart, I'm still crying a little, and I say, "I'll never forgive you for making me cry twice in one week. It's like I'm a leaky faucet."

"You're not a leaky faucet." He leans in and kisses my cheek, my mouth. "You're my beautiful, sexy girlfriend. Don't think I missed the way you were ready to step into battle on my behalf."

I feel myself flushing. "I totally could've gotten him in the balls. Rob should have let me try."

"Rob did what any good friend would. He protected my girl."

He leans in and kisses me again, his lips soft and reverent. For a moment, I let myself get lost in the soft press of his lips and his hand against the side of my face. But he wants to come upstairs and see the parts of me that I usually hide, and I'm surprised by how much I want to show him.

"Come inside before we get arrested for indecent exposure," I say.

"Sounds fun."

I poke his arm. "You don't get to be the crazy one. *I'm* the crazy one."

He just smiles and gets out of the car, then comes around to meet me, as if he's going to escort me into some fancy dinner and not my rundown, messy apartment.

His shirt is untucked, and there are a few flecks of blood on the collar. It must be Bixby's, from his busted nose, or maybe Travis's, from his abraded knuckles. There's probably a special place in hell waiting for me, because I think it's sexy.

I'm worried about his injuries, though, about the future of the band, and about Lilah too. But I can tell Travis doesn't want to talk about any of that. He'd prefer to escape into this connection between us for a while, and I'm letting him, because I want that too.

I guide him into the building, and then up to my third-floor apartment, which is third down a long hallway of identical warped doors, the carpet an always-damp maroon.

I pause when we reach the door, giving him an uneasy look.

"Should I close my eyes to make the most of the surprise?" he asks dryly.

I nudge him with my shoulder, then nearly have a heart attack when he flinches. "You're bruised."

"That's what happens when you get into a fight," he says with a lopsided smile that's not that convincing.

"Well, this should take your mind off it." I unlock the door and swing it open.

He smiles more genuinely as he walks inside, stepping over a blouse I considered wearing this morning and then tossed over the back of a chair. Or at least I meant to toss it over the back of a chair.

"Will you give me the grand tour?" he asks.

"Yes." I follow him in and shut the door. "And it's going to take all of a minute, because there are only three rooms in this apartment. This beauty." I gesture around to the combo living/dining/kitchen area. "My bedroom, and a bathroom that you probably won't even fit in."

"Let the tour commence," he says, his eyes skating over the full-body sewing mannequin in the corner of the living room with my pin-studded, half-finished creation on it. "You gave it a smiley face."

"Most of them don't have heads, but this one did," I say. "It felt a little cruel not to give it a face. Her name is Thea Thread-salot, and I love her."

"I'm jealous."

"Are you going to take a swing at her too?" I ask. My gaze drops reflexively to his busted knuckles. I make a face and rush over to the freezer, grabbing the first thing I find that will work as an ice pack. I stride back to him, nearly tripping over one of the adorable dog stuffies Travis got me, and hand him the bag of frozen strawberries. "For your knuckles."

He grins at me, some of the heaviness leaving his face. "Don't you have a resealable plastic bag?"

I start to wilt, feeling dumb, and take a step toward the freezer, but he stops me with a light hand on my wrist and takes the bag from me.

"Thanks for taking care of me, Hannah," he says gently. "Let's finish the tour."

"There's a pile of clothes in a basket on my bedroom floor, but they're clean," I say. "I just haven't gotten around to folding them yet."

"Understandable. Is that why you invited me over?" He gives me a lopsided smile. "To fold your clothes?"

"You invited yourself." I weave my arm through his again. "Now, let me show you to Clothes Mountain."

"Please do," he says. "I've heard great things."

I open the door, feeling a creeping self-consciousness as he takes in the small, cramped space, so different from his huge bedroom with the massive king-sized bed. The mountain of clothes sits at the foot of the bed, barely contained by a broken laundry basket. Usually, I pay attention to the things in here that I like, the colorful quilt and prints on the walls, but that laundry basket is like a stain on my existence. A sign that I could use a few crash courses on adulting and maybe an ADHD diagnosis and some Adderall.

I dart a nervous look at him.

"I told you I like cleaning," he says with a smile that suggests he knows exactly what's going through my head. He surprises me by reaching down to lift a shirt out of the laundry pile—his Garbage Fire shirt. "Do you have my polo shirt in here too?"

"Yeah," I say, feeling a pinch of self-consciousness. "I like wearing them. They're comfortable."

"Good."

"Let's move on from the laundry. It's embarrassing."

"It doesn't bother me," he says, folding the Garbage Fire shirt and setting it on the bed. "And I like that you've been wearing my shirts. But I'm going to fold all of this before I leave, because I want to leave my mark on your space, the same way you've left your mark on mine."

I push up onto my toes and kiss him.

"I like it in here," he says, grinning. "It smells even more like you than my bedroom. And the last room in your apartment?"

"You seriously want me to escort you to the bathroom?"

"I want the whole Hannah's apartment experience."

Laughing, I swing the bathroom door open and wave him in.

He enters the tiny room, and his gaze catches on the vanity. My big makeup kit is stowed in the closet, but I keep a few other toiletries out for daily use. They're untidily set out on the sink, of course—some mascara, concealer, powder foundation, eyeliner, and lipstick, plus my hair-cutting scissors.

He turns to me, filling the space so utterly the breath leaves my lungs. It's a heady experience, having him here in my space. Letting him into this part of me.

His gaze finds mine. "I want you to cut my hair."

I gasp. "You mean..."

"I'm not hiding anything anymore. I've decided I'm done with that. It's only caused me problems and grief. I want you to do it. If you're willing."

I comb my fingers through the longer fringe in the front, then push it up. "You want to show everyone your heart?"

He smiles slowly. "Yeah. I think I do."

"Good, we're doing this. Take off your shirt."

He sets down the strawberries to unbutton and remove his shirt. Then he pulls off his undershirt. I gasp at the sight of the swollen red marks on his skin where that asshole punched him.

"Does it hurt?" I ask, gently running my fingers over it.

He laughs as he folds both shirts and sets them on the towel shelf next to the tub-shower combo. "It does when you do that. Are you going to cut my hair in here?"

There's barely room to move, let alone create a masterpiece. "No," I say, grabbing my scissors, a straight comb and a spray bottle I use for my hair. "Let's go in the living room."

He returns the strawberries to the freezer, then helps me set out a clean sheet. I put a chair on it and close the shades. There's barely enough room for the setup, and I have to move my stuffed dogs and a few stray shoes.

"Looks like you're setting up a murder room," Travis teases as I guide him into the chair.

"I take my haircutting very seriously," I say, running my fingers through his hair.

He closes his eyes for a second at my touch. "That feels good."

I decide to make it feel even better and pull off my shirt.

"Fuck, Hannah," Travis says, grinning at me. "Please tell me you don't do this every time you cut someone's hair."

"Lucky you, you get special treatment." I throw my shirt, and then my bra, onto the couch. He leans forward to kiss the side of my breast, then takes my nipple into his mouth, teasing it with his tongue and his teeth before moving to the next.

It feels mind-bendingly good, even more so because we're out here in my living room. My space, just like when we were at Big Catch the other night. I like having him in *all* of my spaces. I weave my hands into his hair, holding him close for a moment, and then I make myself step back.

"You're going to have to look but not touch," I say in my best sultry voice. "Do you think you can be a good boy?"

"No," he says, grinning.

I put my hand on my hip. "What if I accidentally cut your ear off?"

"You're the one who has to look at me."

Rolling my eyes, I run my hands through his hair again, lifting it up. Plotting. Then I realize I'm going to need a step stool. He's taller sitting than I am standing.

"Are you going to make fun of me if I take out my step stool?"

"No, I think I'll enjoy the view."

I bring it out, and seconds later, I make the first cut.

Travis watches with something like disbelief as the first lock of black hair falls down.

"Are you sure about this?" I ask, even though it's obviously too late.

"Your tits are pressing against the back of my head. Right here, right now, I'm completely happy."

CHAPTER THIRTY

TRAVIS

The hair continues falling down onto the sheet. I didn't know I had so much hair. But it's hard to pay attention to it, because I can feel Hannah's tits pressing against me, her fingers gliding over me. Even the feeling of her scissors slicing through my hair, cutting off the deadweight, is almost sensual.

Right now, I need her more than I need air.

Bixby's betrayal keeps stabbing into me, bringing back those other betrayals. All the reasons I'd wanted to live my life quietly. But I don't want that anymore. It was a desperate wish made by a hurting man.

I want to live my life loudly—to be someone Ollie and Hannah can be proud of.

No more hiding.

While I'm not about to wear a sailor suit and sing about the Good Ship Lollipop to get people interested in my band, I'm not going to cringe from who I am anymore. If I'd accepted that sooner, this would never have happened.

She climbs off her stool and circles back around to the front again, her breasts on display, and I can't miss the opportunity to bury my face in them. I feel her laughing before she gives me a little push. "Come on, I need to see it from the front."

A grin stretches across her face as I lean back, letting her look her fill.

"You are *ridiculously* good-looking," she says, letting the scissors fall onto the sheet, and then climbs into my lap. I groan as my already-half-hard dick gets all the way there.

She kisses me and then kisses the birthmark on my forehead before rocking against me, her delicious heat hidden from me by her yoga pants and my jeans. Too many layers.

"I'm going to have to lay down the law at your shows, because there's no way I'm letting women throw their unmentionables at you."

"Last time it was a toy boat," I say. "They clocked me in the birthmark, which you just made a clearer target."

"If anyone tries to use you for target practice of any kind," she says, moving her hips, "they're going to have to get through me first."

"Lucky for you, there probably won't be any more shows," I say darkly, still not wanting to think about it. I want to savor her for as long as I can. Until the reality of what happened bites me in the ass.

She grips my chin, lowering it so my gaze is glued to hers. "You listen right now. There will be."

"Two people don't make a band," I say, wrapping my hands around her hips.

"So you'll find two more."

"We weren't having much luck finding one more before we dropped Bixby."

She sighs, burying her face in my chest, above the area where a massive bruise is forming, thankfully, and says, "Liam plays guitar, and I know he jams with his friends sometimes. He might be willing to sit in for a while."

"What?" I ask in shock.

"He's pretty good," she says. "You know I like to sing..."

"Yes..."

"We used to have this super lame family band when we were kids—Liam, Connor, my dad and me. We were the Moroney Movers and Shakers. It was my dad's other way of bonding with us...you know, besides the beer thing. I almost hate to admit it, but there are videos."

"Seriously?!" I say, laughing as I glide my hand up and down her back, pulling her closer. "Why have you been holding out on me? Don't tell me you were embarrassed. You saw the Ships Junior videos. What could be worse than that?"

"Honestly? I figured you guys might be interested in bringing Liam into the band if you knew, and I was still pissed at him. But I'm not mad anymore, so yeah, I can talk to him. I bet he'd be willing to help you out for a while. Or point you toward someone else."

"That's great, but I also want to see these Moroney files," I say, gripping her close. "I need them. It's the only thing that will make me feel better."

She bites my chest playfully, and I laugh, then stand up with her and swing her up over my shoulder. She shrieks as I carry her into the bathroom like that.

"What are you doing?" she asks, laughing.

"You cut my hair. The least I can do is wash you off."

I stop in my tracks when I glimpse myself in the mirror.

"Wow," I say.

I set her on her feet, barely recognizing my reflection in the mirror. My hair's not overly short, but it doesn't hang in my face anymore. The birthmark I've spent my entire adult life trying to hide is on full display. I'm surprised by how much I don't hate it. By how good it feels to embrace the change.

"Do you like it?" she asks, her tone a little self-conscious.

I turn toward her, lowering my hands to the waistband of her pants. "I love it," I say, pushing her yoga pants down. "But I love this even more."

I turn the shower on, testing the spray with my hand, and Hannah gives me an indulgent smile. Probably because she always leaps in without testing the water first. So fuck it. I pull her under into the tub and under the still cold water, and she laughs and dances in it, even as it soaks us.

She's breathtaking. Easily the most beautiful thing I've ever seen.

"Oh my God," she squeals, "it's freezing."

But it's already warming up, and I pull her to me, kissing her as the water rains down on us. Kissing her like she's my salvation. I slide my hand between her legs, feeling her there as the cold water heats up, steam clouding around us, and she gasps into my mouth even as she reaches down and finds my hard cock. The feeling of her hand around me, squeezing my tip, is almost enough to make me come on the spot. But I hold off. I need to come inside her.

She practically leaps up onto me, wrapping her legs around me, and I laugh into her mouth and back her into the wall. There's barely enough space in here for one person, but if we can make that storeroom work, we can make this work too. She reaches down to adjust my angle, and I thrust into her as the water beats down on us. My shorn hair is soaking wet, and her drenched curls are plastered to the sides of her face as she leans her had back, giving me the perfect angle to trail kisses down her neck as we move together.

My need builds, and I move faster as she tightens her legs around me, her fingers exploring my shorter hair and tracing the line of my back.

I feel her come around me, and I follow her two thrusts later, kissing her face, her lips. Overcome with ecstasy not just because the sex is so good with her, but because I'm with her. Because she loves me. My body hurts where Bixby bruised me, and my soul hurts worse, but she's helping me heal it. I already feel a thousand times better than I did at The Missing Beat this afternoon. I feel hopeful. With her love, I feel like I can do anything.

"I promised to wash you," I say.

"I can definitely wash myself," she replies, her expression amused.

"Obviously, but I'm asking for the privilege."

The wry humor fades from her face. There's something bare and open about her expression as she nods. "Yeah, okay."

I slowly wash her body, getting half hard already, and then her hair, following her instructions, making her laugh with my ineptitude with curly hair.

"I'll learn," I say.

And she looks up at me with love in her eyes and says, "I know you will."

We follow the trail of our discarded clothing back to the living room, getting dressed as we go. Once we're put back together, I pull her against me, meeting her gaze. "It's probably too late for me to go pick up Ollie. I'd like it if you'd spend the night at my house with me. It's closer to Dottie's house, and we can go pick him up together in the morning and drop him off at school. Maybe you'll get a chance to say hello to your new favorite teacher."

She wraps her hand around my arm, her eyes lighting up. "Travis, I didn't tell you."

I smile, because I love her enthusiasm about everything. "What?"

"Mrs. Applebaum is meeting Eugene on Friday at Big Catch. She seems excited about it."

"I'll play them 'Blue River' until my fingers bleed."

"God, I love you," she says, getting on her toes and wrapping her arms around me.

"I love you too."

"What will Ollie think about us?"

"He already knows how I feel about you," I say with a grin, "and he told me he doesn't mind if we're friends too. I think he'll be happy. But there's something I have to do first."

"Oh yeah?" she asks, giving me a quick kiss.

"I'm going to need to watch those videos of the Moroney Movers and Shakers while I fold your clothes."

I FORWARD the videos of the Moroneys to Rob, who needs a reason to smile too. It's both adorable and hilarious to listen to Hannah sing about the importance of brushing your teeth daily. They were genuinely talented, and it makes me want to meet Connor and her dad. Thanksgiving's coming up quick, but maybe we can find a last-minute flight to Boston to join them for the holiday too. Maybe Liam will come, too, and it can be a Moroney reunion.

We text Dottie, who confirms "dear Ollie" is already asleep after drawing star charts with her. She insists she'll have him ready for school in the morning, because fate "knew" he'd be staying over. It turns out her grandson is exactly the same size, so he won't need to wear today's clothes tomorrow.

Hannah and I head back to my house and make love in my bed, slowly, thoroughly before falling asleep in each other's arms. It's been a turbulent day, full of really low lows, and impossibly high highs, and I'm toast.

But before our alarms are set to go off, someone rings the front doorbell—four times.

Hannah and I both sit up, immediately alert, and exchange a worried look. It's a look probably all parents know: what if something happened to him? What if he's not okay?

"I'm sure it's nothing," she says. "It's probably a rude neighbor." But she gets out of bed and opens my dresser drawer, throwing me a thermal shirt before she starts whipping on the change of clothes she brought.

I pull on the shirt, then tug on a pair of shorts. "I'm going," I say, kissing the top of her head as she pulls on a skirt. "I need—"

"Go."

I run to the front door and throw it open, and instant horror buckets through me. It's Lilah, holding a stuffed koala and a bunch of balloons as if she's throwing herself a party. She looks fresh and dewy, like she didn't just step off a plane, so she probably got in last night.

"What the fuck?" I say before I can stop myself.

She gives me a scathing look. "Have you been swearing in front of my child?"

Her child.

Her child?

Rage grips me first, followed by fear. Because she's obviously here to take Ollie away from me.

I remind myself of the emergency custody order. My lawyer walked me through this. He said I don't have to let her leave with Ollie, and in this case, I can't.

"No, and he's not here," I say as Hannah emerges from the back of the house wearing the outfit she brought—a soft blue-green sweater and a flowing white skirt. "He's staying with a friend for the night."

It would probably be smarter to pretend Hannah's just a friend, or to introduce her as the nanny, but I don't owe Lilah any explanations. I wrap my arm around my woman.

"I see," Lilah says icily.

"You didn't tell me you were coming," I say with an equal dose of frost. "You said you'd be impossible to contact for the next few weeks."

"Are you going to invite me in?" she asks, brushing her hair back over her shoulder. It's an old move, meant to show off her neck and long, glossy hair, but I'm completely immune to her now.

I step aside and gesture for her to enter.

Lilah walks in, glancing pointedly at Hannah. After I shut the door, she says, "Don't you think it would be better to send her on her way? We have to talk about Ollie's future."

I tighten my grip on Hannah. "Then I can think of no better person to be here. Hannah's been helping me with Ollie. School lets out right when I go to work. She's been spending afternoons with him."

"I thought you got him a nanny?" Lilah scoffs.

"He did," Hannah finally says, sweet as sugar. "I *am* the nanny."

"You're sleeping with your nanny, Travis? How cliché." Her comment is directed at me, as if Hannah doesn't exist, and I clench my jaw, trying to get myself back under control. I don't want this to devolve into some ugly court battle that goes on for months. Maybe years. If I can't avoid it, I will absolutely go that route, but it would be better for everyone if we can settle things peacefully.

"Yeah," Hannah says, her tone still like syrup. "That's what they call a bonus. Why are you here, Lilah?"

She thrusts out the stuffed animal. "I got this for Ollie."

"Super," Hannah says. "He hates koalas. His favorite animals are turtles."

"Are you going to let her talk to me like that, Travis?" Lilah snaps, turning toward me.

"I don't tell my girlfriend how to talk," I say. "She's protective of Ollie, and I'm grateful for that. So am I." I pause, trying to collect myself, then say, "*You kept him from me*, Lilah, for nearly seven years." My voice rises, so I take a deep breath. "I didn't know I had a son. I missed so much. His first steps. His first words. The first day he went to school. I'll never get any of that back."

Surprise ripples across her face, like it never occurred to her that she was taking something away from me. She tries to set the koala down on the coffee table, but it tumbles to the floor, the balloons detaching and floating up to the ceiling. Annoyance flickers in her eyes, and I'm not surprised when she tries to turn it around on me. "You lied to me too," she says. "Your father was famous, and you never said a word."

"What, you think you missed out on your big chance with him?" I ask. "You know, he probably would have been thrilled to get attention from you, just like Roland, but he was already dying. I didn't find out until later, when I got to Asheville. My dad and I weren't talking anymore. I had no reason to think he'd ever want to talk to me again."

There's a worried look on her face now, like it's occurred to her that he might not have left me anything after all. But she snaps out of it, clearing all emotion from her face. "You've always liked your secrets, Travis."

"I did," I say, feeling the birthmark on my forehead as if it's a brand. "But not anymore. That's not who I want to be. I want to be Ollie's father."

Hannah squeezes my hand.

"Well, he can't stay here forever, obviously," Lilah says.

Bitter rage nearly shatters me, and it's only Hannah's hand in mine that keeps me from coming apart. That allows me to say what needs to be said in an even tone. "You left him here for almost two months as if he were some kind of handbag you weren't sure you wanted to bother claiming from the lost and found. He didn't deserve that. He's a good kid. So smart and funny and talented. He's in school here, and he's doing well, and I love him. *I love him*, Lilah. I have emergency protective custody, and you've almost been away for sixty days, which is the state's standard for abandonment. If you want to take him away from me, you're going to have to fight for it in court. And then you'll have two court cases underway."

She looks shocked, maybe because I've never spoken to her like this before. Not even the day she left me.

"You're being unreasonable, Travis," she says, glancing at Hannah. "I think we should have this conversation privately."

"Anything you have to say to me, you can say in front of Hannah."

"Well..." She glances at Hannah again, nervously, which is probably wise, because Hannah's giving her a death glare. "There's no reason we can't settle this out of court. If you start paying me child support, I can send him to Gentleman's Crest. It's this boarding school in Nashville. My friend has some connections with the admissions—"

"Over my dead body," Hannah snarls.

"He's not going to boarding school," I say, holding Hannah close. "I want him here. Living in my house. Sleeping in his room. I don't have any objection to you seeing him or spending time with him, but I want him to live here."

She plants a hand on her hip. "Travis, he *didn't* want me to leave him here. I doubt he wants to stay. This is the best solution for everyone."

"No shit, he didn't want to stay," I say, some of that awful, bitter rage slipping out. "He didn't know who I was until you left him at my door. A stranger's door. You and I hadn't talked more than once in seven years. You didn't know anything about me. But you left him here anyway. Even though he begged you not to. And you called him all of three times. One of those times he was *asleep.*"

"I knew you were a good guy," she says, flushing slightly. "I knew nothing would happen to him."

"You *hoped,*" I say. "That's not enough for me. I need to know he's safe and cared for. I need to know you're not going to leave him with someone else you're sure is a good person because you hung out with them a few times nearly a decade ago. Now that I know about him, I can't erase that knowledge, and I don't want to. He's my son. I want him here."

Lilah's expression softens a little. "I had no idea you felt like this."

"Because you didn't give me a chance to process everything before you took off."

The doorbell rings, and Hannah and I exchange a look, because I can't imagine who it could be. Rob, maybe, but it would be strange for him to show up this early without calling, especially since he knows I drop Ollie off at school in the morning.

"Just a second," I say, then stalk through the room to the foyer and open the front door.

I open it, and to my shock, Ollie and Dottie pile in. Ollie's wearing an outfit that makes him look like a Boy Scout, complete with a small, collared shirt and brown pants with a belt, and it would probably make me laugh under other circumstances.

"I thought we were supposed to pick him up," I say, panic shooting through me. *He's going to want to leave with her. She's going to take him. Everything we've been building will be lost.*

I wrap my arms around him, and he lets me. Thank God, he lets me.

"Oh dear," Dottie says, laughing. "We must have gotten our wires crossed. I woke up this morning positively certain that I needed to come here. I felt it down to my bones, even though our messages said something different, but you know my bones *are* getting older these days. Well, no harm done." Her gaze settles on my hair, and she grins. "You have a heart on your forehead, my dear. I never saw the shape of it before. How marvelous."

"I like it," Ollie says. "I can see your face better." Then he squints up at the ceiling and points his little finger. "What's that?"

One of the balloons has strayed into the foyer from the living room like something out of a horror movie.

"Ollie," I say, releasing him and crouching down so we're on the same level. "Your mom—"

Lilah steps into view through the archway to the living room, Hannah hot on her heels. And I'll be damned, Lilah is holding that stupid koala again.

"I'm back from my trip!" she announces sunnily, as if it's no big deal. As if she went to the corner store. "Here's the koala I got you. Isn't he fuzzy?"

My heart hurts so much worse right now than it did yesterday, when the band Rob and I had built from nothing was on the verge of breaking and I thought it might be forever. He's going to run to her. He's going to ask to leave.

I'll still have to tell him no, but it'll break my heart.

But he doesn't. He pushes the koala away and bursts into jagged sobs. "I don't want it. I hate koalas, and I hate Australia. I don't want to go anywhere with you. Please don't make me leave. *Please.* I want to stay with Dad."

It's the first time he's called me that. A sense of wonder steals over me, but Lilah looks like he just struck her. "Did *he* tell you to say that, Ollie? Did Travis tell you which words to use when I came back?"

"No," Ollie says through tears. "Dad's never told me what to say. I like it here." He turns to me. "Don't make me leave. *Please.* I know what I said when I first got here, but it's not true. I don't want to go. *Please* don't make me go."

I'm still crouching down, so I pull him close and hug him, feeling his tears against my neck. Something breaks inside of me and is rebuilt stronger. No matter what happens, I won't allow him to leave my life again. I won't allow him to be ignored or mistreated by anyone, including myself.

"Don't you want to hear about my trip?" Lilah asks, still holding the koala.

"No," Ollie shouts. Directly into my ear. I nearly fall over, but I'll happily risk the hearing deficit, because my son's clinging to me now. "I want to go to school," he says quickly in an undertone. "Mrs. Applebaum doesn't like it when I'm late, and I have to talk to Mickey. I don't want to disappoint him."

"They're friends now," Hannah says softly, watching us with a reassuring smile. I know she's putting on a front for me, though. I can tell she's scared too. Scared and pissed off.

"How about you stay here and spend time with me, Ollie?" Lilah says.

"I don't want to miss school."

Lilah gives a bitter laugh. "Well, he certainly sounds like your son, Travis."

"I'm going to take him to school," I say, not letting go of him. "We'll talk when I get back."

"Splendid," Dottie says, clapping her hands, and I'm taken aback by the reminder that she's still here. "We'll let Travis bring Ollie to school, and I'll make some tea for us girls. Won't that be a lovely restart to the day?"

"Who are you?" Lilah says coldly.

Dottie gives her a surprisingly stern look. "I'm someone who cares very deeply about the well-being of both of these young men. And Hannah, of course. But something tells me that my confused old bones aren't the reason for my visit this morning after all. I was drawn here because I'm needed."

I'm not so sure I believe in that. But I do believe in her.

I glance at Hannah. "Are you okay with this, or would you like to come with us?"

"I'm staying," she says, but she walks over to Ollie and gives him a hug. "You say hey to Mrs. Applebaum for me, okay? Let me know if she has that hedgehog back up and running."

Ollie casts an anxious look at Lilah, then detaches from Hannah for a second to walk over to his mother. He gives her a quick hug, but his face is full of a pain I can feel in my own chest.

"Goodbye, Lilah," he says.

Maybe I'm not a good man, because I hope that fucking hurts.

CHAPTER THIRTY-ONE

HANNAH

"Well, aren't *you* a pretty young thing," Dottie says sweetly to Lilah, who gives her first genuine smile of the day.

I grit my teeth.

We're sitting at Travis's kitchen table, drinking tea from a china set I can only assume Dottie brought over herself or purchased for Travis on an earlier occasion, because I've never seen it before.

"Thank you," Lilah says, throwing a haughty look my way as if she expects me to repeat the compliment.

It'll be a cold day in hell.

Logically, I know I can't bitch-slap Ollie's mom, but that doesn't make me want to do it any less. I don't just hate her for that little boy's sake. I also hate her for what she's done to Travis. This woman has caused him so much pain—first, for throwing him out like discarded tissue paper, and second, for hiding his son from him. She's got a permanent place on my shit list.

"Dottie says that to literally everyone," I say. Because if I can't bitch-slap this woman, I can at least prick her ego.

Lilah glowers at me.

"Now, it's natural for Hannah to be protective of her man," Dottie says, nodding to me. "She should be. And she's taken such good care of your son. He's blossomed over the last few weeks. It's been lovely to see." She sets a hand over Lilah's, and to my surprise Lilah doesn't pull away. "We all want what's best for Ollie. That's what joins us together at this table."

"I do want what's best for him," Lilah says. Her eyes look dewy with emotion, and I'm guessing she hopes there's a hidden camera in the wall.

"Of course," Dottie agrees. "And you also need to look out for yourself." She takes a contemplative sip of tea. "Because if this goes to court, and the judge sides against you, you might have to pay child support to Travis. That could be a financial strain."

"I don't have an income," Lilah says, pulling her hand away, her tone frosty again.

"Oh, you poor thing. Do you need help finding a job?"

I look at sweet Dottie in wonder, because damn, this woman is a force of nature. I already knew that, but here she is proving it to me again, in a different way.

"No," Lilah says. "I'm in the middle of a divorce. My soon-to-be ex-husband is a very wealthy man."

"I hope he gives you your fair share," Dottie says, clucking her tongue. "I've been through a divorce myself. Did you sign one of those agreements?"

"Yes," Lilah says. "But we were married for over seven years, so the settlement will be substantial."

"That's lucky, but when you're doing your budgeting, my dear, make sure you consider that any assets you have will be considered by the court if they grant Travis primary custody. Their decisions aren't solely based on income. One of my dear friends is a family law attorney here in town, and she has all kinds of stories. You wouldn't believe some of the things I've heard."

"He won't get primary custody if I ask for it," Lilah snaps, pushing her teacup away. "They always favor the mother."

I snort. "Tell that to my father. My mother abandoned us too, for over a year. She came back, but the judge sided with my father. It's a good thing, too, because she instantly took off again."

"I've been gone for less than two months."

I tilt my head, studying her. Seeing the uneasiness in her gaze. "Maybe," I say, "but you also left him with someone he didn't know. My mother left us with the man who'd raised us. I'm guessing a judge will have thoughts about that."

"Oh, dear," Dottie says, tsking. "Yes, you were lucky that Travis is such a good man. Plenty of the men I dated in my youth couldn't be trusted with a houseplant, let alone a child. If he were less of a man, he might have treated the boy poorly as a kind of revenge."

A hint of guilt flickers in Lilah's eyes.

"Being a parent isn't an easy job," Dottie says ruminatively. "The work is never-ending, day in, day out, week after week, month after month. My niece wasn't suited for it, and it hurt my heart watching her struggle to give her little boy what he needed. She left him with me, eventually, and I raised him with my whole heart. My boy has a family of his own now. I couldn't be prouder of him."

Lilah doesn't say anything. She just takes a sip of her tea, her expression far-off.

"Now, drain that down, my girl," Dottie says. "I have a talent for reading tea leaves."

"You do?" Lilah says, and I can already tell she's ready to be a true believer.

"Oh yes, it's my calling."

I watch Dottie closely, certain she has a plan, while Lilah gulps her tea down to the dregs and hands the cup over.

"I sense this is a very significant cup," Dottie says, which is BS, but Lilah, who clearly thinks she has main character energy, perks up.

We both watch with interest as Dottie does the song and dance of turning the cup over, rotating it, and then flipping it again. She does it with the finesse of a magician—and then gasps theatrically as she peers into it.

"I knew it," she says.

"Knew what?" Lilah asks eagerly.

"Do you see those two shapes?" Dottie asks, pointing into the cup. Curiosity has me sliding out of my seat so I can check them out too. I have to swallow the laughter that bubbles up. The "shapes" look like two blotches, one larger and more stretched out than the other.

"This one"—Dottie points to the bigger blotch—"is a bird, my dear. It symbolizes freedom and a coming voyage. The smaller one, there, is a suitcase." She shifts her finger to point at the dregs flecking the edges. "And those are waves. All of these shapes represent travel. I'm sensing there will be adventure in your future. Oh, how glorious. Of course, the cups only show me possibilities—one path you could choose among many."

"A suitcase and waves?" Lilah asks, pointing to the smaller blotch. "Are you sure?"

Her energy has changed. She's practically humming with excitement now.

"Oh, yes. It's very clear to me," Dottie says authoritatively, "and I've been doing this for years. Does this mean something to you, dear?"

"Yeah...yeah, it does." She beams at Dottie, her smile annoyingly gorgeous. "You're a genius. This is...this is going to work."

I seriously hope not, because whatever her plan is has her

practically jumping up and down with glee. Then again, if this plan drives her away from us, I'll begrudgingly let her have it, no matter how happy it makes her. It's definitely better than if she hangs around creating problems for Travis and Ollie.

"Thank you," she says to Dottie, grinning. Then she squeezes her hand and gets up from the table. Ignoring my existence (which is just fine by me), she tells Dottie, "Tell Travis I'll be in touch. We have a lot to discuss, but I have a few calls to make, and I have some spa treatments lined up for the afternoon."

No mention of Ollie. No suggestion about coming over later to try to make things right with him.

I tighten my jaw. My initial judgment of her character was spot on: Lilah is Cunt-acula, Queen of Cunts.

"Do you need somewhere to stay, dear?" Dottie asks.

"Are you offering? How quaint. But no, I'm staying at the Grove Park Inn."

Of course, she is. The Grove Park Inn is a gorgeous, sprawling hotel that looks like a huge gingerbread house and has sick mountain views. It's also where every rich person who comes here stays. How original. I hope the Pink Lady, the Grove Park's famous ghost, haunts her ass.

She waves at Dottie and then walks off, like she didn't just torpedo our day. Seconds later, the front door opens and closes, and she's finally gone.

"What the fuck was that all about?" I ask as Dottie gets up.

I watch her grab two juice glasses from the cupboard, then start laughing when she pours a finger of bourbon into each of them.

"We're drinking?"

"Not me, dear. I have to go to the tea shop for a few hours, but I suspect Travis will need it when he gets back." She returns to the table and hands one of the glasses to me. "And to answer your other question, I don't know. But I felt certain she'd respond to those particular images."

"Why, Dottie Hendrickson," I say, grinning at her even though my heart is still thumping hard. "Did you just admit tea-leaf reading is a crock?"

"I'd never," Dottie say. "But I may take a few liberties on occasion if I feel it's important to get a certain message across."

Well, I'll be damned. I lift my glass to salute her before taking a sip.

We hear the front door open, and moments later, Travis hurries into the room, stopping beside me and glancing around wildly.

"Satan's gone," I say. "She told us she'll be in touch later. She has *spa treatments* this afternoon."

"This is for you, my dear," Dottie says, pushing the bourbon toward him. It's very unlike Travis to break the rules, even unwritten social rules like *don't drink in the morning*, but he downs it in a gulp and sinks into the chair next to me, running his hands through his freshly shorn hair. I'm not sure I'll ever get tired of seeing that.

"What happened?" he asks, sounding dog-tired.

"Dottie pulled out all the stops and mind-melded her like a champ."

"Now, I wasn't trying to manipulate her," Dottie says. "Manipulation is an ugly word. I wanted to help her see the greater good."

"You're a master manipulator for the force of good," I tell her, "and we love you for it."

"I have to go, my dears," she says, clasping her hands together, "but let me just say how happy I am that you've come together. I hoped for it, of course, and Ollie and I did plant a good many pink crystals around this house. Now, I can't wait to see who the universe has in mind for dear Briar."

"Are you going to try to dowse out an answer again?" I ask.

She smiles knowingly at me. "I just might."

Then she leaves us alone, closing the door behind her.

I turn to Travis and wrap my arms around him, burying my face in his neck. "Go play in your music room," I say. "It always helps when you've had a bad day."

He kisses me on the lips, pulling me onto his lap. "Who said it was a bad day? I knew she was coming back. She was always going to come back sometime. But Ollie called me Dad, Hannah," he says, his voice shaking. "He said he wants to stay here with me, and I already called my lawyer to talk about my next steps, and he sounds confident. So no, I can't write it off as a bad day."

I run my fingers across his cheekbone, then kiss him—again and again, needing the rasp of his stubble against my cheeks and the hard press of his soft lips.

"I still think you should go play," I say after a minute, forcing myself back. "This has been a lot."

He nods and tucks a curl behind my ear. "I will. But I'm not going to lay down a beat. I'm going to play 'Blue River' on the guitar." He grins. "And you're going to sing with me. Tomorrow too. The Moroney Movers and Shakers need to ride again."

"Are we bringing Liam in on this?" I ask, grinning, my heart full of him.

"Yes. We're going to make a group effort to get Eugene laid."

"God, I really love you."

CHAPTER THIRTY-TWO

TRAVIS

I call Rob to tell him about Lilah's visit and ask if he'll bring in a sub for me. There's no way I'm up for teaching kids after the last twenty-four hours. I also give him a heads-up that I'll have to leave The Missing Beat early on Friday so I can be there for Eugene's big moment.

By the end of the day, Lilah still hasn't shown up. She doesn't call either, and after Hannah and I put Ollie to bed, I find the koala in the bathroom trash can.

I take it out and brush it off. He might want it later, and the last thing I need is Lilah showing up and accusing me of throwing out her unwanted gift.

Friday morning passes in a blur of working out and talking to my lawyer. Hannah spends it with Dottie and the Wise Elders Group, who called an emergency meeting to help Eugene prepare for his date. They're also going to babysit for Ollie during the big moment, and I have every expectation that he'll be returned to me afterward with a sugar high that lasts half the night.

Hannah's acting the way I did before my first big public performance, and it's cute as hell. Part of me thinks she and the

Wise Elders should just let Eugene do his thing, but then I remember the Eugene I first met—crotchety and alone—and I realize this is probably exactly what he needs. Friendship and encouragement. The knowledge that if he stumbles, he'll still have friends to break his fall.

Hannah told me weeks ago that Eugene reminded her of an old version of me, and she was right in a way, because that's what I needed too. For someone to pull me out of my solitary bubble and get my head out of my ass. And that someone was Hannah. She's worked her magic on both of us. With any luck, Eugene's date will go well tonight.

For now, however, I have other things to focus on. It's time to go back to The Missing Beat.

I head there early, needing to make peace with the space before the kids show up, but I'm not surprised when I open the door and see Rob already here, standing at the window.

"Enjoying the view?" I ask, walking up and slapping him on the back.

He laughs and shakes his head. "Only a real dumbass would buy a place like this." He looks me in the eye, his smile fading. "You really set all this up with your own money?"

I hold his gaze. "We're talking about this now?"

"We're talking about it."

"It was my father's money. It never felt like mine. Only a way to make a different life."

He lifts his brow. "And those grants you told me you'd gotten?"

"The first one I made up, but I got better at applying for them. There was a learning curve."

He shakes his head, but he doesn't look pissed, at least. After a moment, the corners of his lips curve up in an amused smile. "Dammit. I wish you'd told me."

"You wouldn't have agreed." I pause, but he doesn't dispute

it. "And I didn't do it just for you. I needed this too. But...yeah, I should have told you sooner."

He gives me a sidelong look and then turns to face me more fully. "The band's not dead. It's not dead until we say it is. Do you want it to be dead, Travis? Because we'll piss on its grave if you say so. I can find another band to join."

Until this moment, I wasn't totally sure.

But now I know. This is what I want. I want my son, and I want Hannah, and I want my band. And I want Garbage Fire to do well, whatever that ends up meaning.

"Let's put it on life support. I think there's some life in this garbage fire yet."

He grins at me, I grin back, and I feel a weight lift off my chest. "Besides," I add, "I may have a lead on a rhythm guitarist.

I tell him about the Moroney Movers and Shakers and Liam, who came over to practice "Blue River" with Hannah and me. He's not interested in joining the band long term, but he has a couple of buddies who play, and he's willing to fill in until we find someone permanent.

"No shit?" Rob says, shaking his head. "We were short a rhythm guitarist, and now we're short a bass player."

"Maybe the universe has more surprises in store for us."

"I know you're joking," he says, "but I've learned that stuff's no joking matter."

I nod, because it's the truth, and I feel in my bones that the universe isn't done with me yet.

"I feel awful about what went down with Bixby," I admit.

"So do I, but he made his own problems. If he'd told us he was struggling, we could have worked something out. All of this could have been avoided. Frank wanted us for us, dammit."

I shrug. "Maybe Frank will still be interested. You know, once fate magically drops a bass player onto our laps."

"I'll put up the ad," he says. "We'll get on it. But we'll have to cancel our next few shows. I've already called the brewery we were supposed to play at on Saturday."

I nod, still feeling sick at the thought of Bixby. Yesterday morning, when I threw on my shirt before answering the door, I noticed the red marks had darkened into deep purple bruises, but it felt right for the hurt to show on the outside. "We're never going to be friends like that again. I can't trust him, and that sucks. He's been with us since the beginning."

He nods, and I can tell from the circles under his eyes, he's been losing sleep over it. "But he didn't act the way a friend does. He was selfish, and it cost all of us."

"Should we exchange friendship bracelets now?"

"We can," he says, laughing. "I've got about two dozen of them back at the apartment. Sophie's planning a new class."

I bump his shoulder, feeling an intense swell of emotion. "I love you, man."

"Back at you," he says, then forces a grin. "And, hey, we're best friends dating best friends. They make TV shows about that kind of thing."

I feign a dramatic shudder. "No, thank you." I pause before telling him what's in my heart. "But something tells me we're going to be best friends married to best friends someday."

This time his grin is so big his face creases with it. "From your mouth to God's ears, my friend."

"I love Hannah," I say. "I don't feel like I deserve her, but I'm not about to complain."

"I know how that feels."

We hug spontaneously, and then we start setting up for the kids. Just like that, this space feels like mine again. It feels safe.

CHAPTER THIRTY-THREE

TRAVIS

Lilah being Lilah, she texts me just as I'm leaving The Missing Beat for Big Catch.

> I need to talk to you right away.

> We can get everything settled this afternoon.

> Good.

I bristle a little that she still hasn't asked to see Ollie again. It's like she's punishing him for not running to her with open arms.

> Give me an hour.

> I'd prefer to meet now.

> I'm busy now. I'll see you in an hour. We can meet here. [Drops pin for Tea of Fortune] Ollie's there with Dottie.

> Oh, good. I was hoping to see her.

> And our son?

Of course. That goes without saying.

It doesn't, but I don't want to get into a long, drawn-out passive-aggressive argument with Lilah. I have some "Blue River" to play for my girl.

When I get to Big Catch, I laugh at the printed sign on the door—CLOSED FOR A STAFF EVENT—and beneath it, written in one of the crayons they hand out with the kids' menu—

Welcome, Mrs. Applebaum!

I try the door and find it open. I don't have to look very hard for Eugene, because he's the only person sitting in the dining room, looking nervous as all get out in a button-up shirt, a blazer with elbow patches, and what I'm presuming are Hannah-selected horn-rimmed glasses.

I glance around to search for Hannah, but there's no sign of her, so I head over to the man of the hour.

"Hey, Eugene," I say as I get closer. "Looking sharp."

"Good gracious, young man. You finally got a haircut."

I laugh. "Yeah, It was about time. Where are Hannah and Liam?"

"Over here," Hannah calls out in a whisper-shout that's more of a shout than a whisper. I glance over and find a fake lighthouse, surrounded by decorative rocks.

"They're hiding behind the lighthouse," Eugene confirms. "They thought it might be more romantic if the music filtered out from behind it."

I scan the bar for other staff. "You got anyone here to grab Mrs. Applebaum a drink, some food?"

"Liam offered to give us a tasting after you play the song." He sighs heavily. "This is probably a terrible idea, though. I haven't romanced a woman in years. The last time I went on a date, the woman tried to sneak out through the back door. They stopped her because they thought she was trying to dine and dash."

"That's exactly what she was trying to do." I glance at the lighthouse, smiling, and look back at him. "If the chemistry isn't there, you can't fake it. But when you meet the right woman, it's not hard at all. It sounds like you've had that feeling about Mrs. Applebaum for a while now.

"I think we can call her Moira off school grounds," he says.

"Moira," I say, nodding. "A beautiful name for a—"

Frankly, I still haven't had a single pleasant interaction with the woman, so I'm going to have to take Hannah's word for it.

"—warm, loving woman. It sounds to me you've already made a good impression on her, Eugene. Just be yourself. Be open to possibilities."

He gives me a severe nod. "I think my first impression of you was wrong, son. You're not a long-haired hooligan."

I open my mouth, realize I don't have much to say to that, and give him a nod. "Thank you. I'm going to go hide behind the lighthouse now."

A few seconds later, I start to round the corner, and I'm pulled the rest of the way by a small, surprisingly strong hand. Hannah pushes me up against the lighthouse and kisses me. Which would have been way hotter if her brother weren't crouching next to us.

"Jesus, Hannah," he mutters under his breath as I pull away to grin at her.

"That's a hell of a welcome," I say, hugging her close before I let her go.

"You sounded like a greeting card when you were talking to him," she whispers. "It was so heartfelt I nearly started crying again."

Liam grunts and rolls his eyes. "Let's get this over with."

He hands me my guitar case. He's already got his out. The plan is to start with a performance of "Blue River," and then Liam will use his phone to put on a playlist over the sound system.

"I talked to Rob about you," I tell him as I pull my guitar out.

"Yeah?"

"We're grateful you're willing to stand in. Can you practice over the weekend?"

"Probably. Unless Hannah tells us we have to follow this old guy around and sing to his date," he whispers gruffly. "Let me see your fist?"

I flex it, then show it to him, flinching a little at the pain that radiates through it.

"I'll have to teach you how to throw a punch," he says with a grunt.

"I'm hoping I won't have to put that knowledge to much use."

"Maybe not, but it's something a man should know."

"How about blocking a punch?" I ask. "Can you teach me that in case you decide to beat me up some day?"

He grins at me. "If I decide to do that, my friend, all the angels in heaven couldn't save you."

Hannah stamps her foot. "Come on, guys," she whisper-hisses. "Stop this posturing nonsense right now. She's going to be here any minute."

Speaking of...

"Hey," I say, grabbing her hand. "I have to leave soon to meet Lilah at Tea of Fortune. She says she's ready to talk."

She raises her eyebrows. "But you still came here?"

"I wasn't about to let you down. I know how much this means to you. Besides, if she's serious about having a real conversation, I want to have it, but it can't just be on her terms."

She squeezes my hand. "Thank you."

The front door creaks open, signaling a new arrival, and all three of us freeze like deer caught in the headlights. Hannah peeks around the lighthouse and then starts doing a little dance on her feet, her eyes full of excitement.

"Eugene?" I hear Mrs. Applebaum say with wonder. (Sorry, Eugene, I don't have it in me to call her Moira.) "Is that you?"

"It is," he says. "You look breathtaking."

Hannah turns to us urgently, holding her hands in a heart shape over her face and pulsating them.

I grin at her, because she *should* be proud of her work.

There's a sound of a chair being pulled out, and then Eugene says, "I realize this invitation probably seems like it came out of the blue, but I've...admired you for years, Moira. Of course, I never would have said anything about it while you were married. I shouldn't have said anything while we were working together. I've been beating myself up about it for years. But the truth is, I've always thought very highly of you."

Liam gives me an amused look, because I said the exact same thing to him about Hannah a week ago, in this very room.

"And I've always thought very highly of *you*," she says. "I didn't say no because I wasn't interested. I have tremendous respect for you, Eugene. You're a man who believes in attention to detail. Why, the hedgehog you gave me was immaculate. Much better than the one Mr. Roberts gave me. It's too bad it was broken, but—"

"Broken?" Eugene asks, his tone piqued.

Hannah gives us an urgent nod, her eyes wide, and Liam and I break into our rendition of "Blue River."

There's a gasp, followed by the sound of a chair being

pushed back, and just before Hannah starts singing, I hear Eugene say, "Would you do me the honor of dancing with me, Moira?"

"Oh, Eugene," she says, and it sounds like a good *oh, Eugene*. Then Hannah starts singing, still crouched behind the lighthouse with us, and her voice is so pure and deep and soulful, it makes it impossible to think about anything else. All I can do is play alongside her, completely in her thrall, and think about the things I'd like to do with her later. Which is uncomfortable with her brother wedged right next to me, but I can't control my thoughts.

Finally, the song ends, and Hannah peeks out from behind the lighthouse. Her eyes widen with shocked delight, and she gestures for us to come closer.

We do, and wow, I didn't know he had it in him. Eugene and Mrs. Applebaum are making out like teenagers.

Hannah looks like she's going to explode into one of her happy dances, Liam looks uncomfortable as hell, and I mouth to them, *Can we go?*

"What about their drinks?" Liam whispers.

"They're busy," I respond.

Hannah nods adamantly and adds, "Having secret sex in Big Catch is like a rite of passage for new employees."

Liam makes a sound of disgust, and then the three of us tiptoe out from our hiding spot, moving along the side of the dining room. I could swear Eugene gives us a thumbs-up as we sneak past him and out into the crisp, cool air.

I HADN'T PLANNED on bringing Hannah to the tea shop, let alone Hannah and Liam, but I'm glad they're with me. My nerves are humming now that the conversation is getting closer. Because I know Lilah's not just going to give in. If she offers me what I want, it'll be because she thinks I have something she wants.

Something tells me it won't be a small ask.

When we get to Tea of Fortune, we're a few minutes early, so I'm surprised to see Lilah's already here, seated a few tables from the entrance, with Dottie and Ollie.

Liam glances at me. "How about I take Ollie for a walk?"

I nod. "That'd be great. Thank you."

Ollie jumps up when he sees us, then runs toward us and wraps his arms around me.

"Mom said I can keep living here," he tells me.

I glance at Lilah as Ollie moves on to Hannah, giving her a bear hug. Lilah smiles sweetly, and I'm struck with the certainty that she *does* want something—something specific. If it's money, fine. I'll pay. It's my father's money anyway, mostly, and I never asked for it in the first place.

"I'll go with Liam and Ollie," Hannah says, grabbing my hand and squeezing it.

I meet her gaze, shaking my head. "Stay."

"You've got this."

"I know I do. But I want you to stay. This concerns you too, or at least I'd like for it to."

She nods several times, then waves at Ollie and Liam as they head for the door.

Hannah and I approach the table together, hand in hand. Lilah looks annoyed by that, but fuck Lilah.

"I'll just go get you two some refreshments," Dottie says, getting to her feet.

I smile at her in gratitude and take the seat she's vacated while Hannah sits down beside me. Dottie leans in to squeeze my shoulder and then leaves for the kitchen.

"You told Ollie he was staying?" I ask Lilah, cocking my head as I size her up. Hannah puts her hand on my leg, silently telling me she's on my side.

Lilah bites her bottom lip. "He said he wanted to, and you practically begged me, so yeah...but there was something I was hoping you could do for me, too. Your friend Dottie is the one who helped me think of it, and it's going to solve everything. We'll all get what we want."

"That sounds pretty unlikely," I say.

"It's not," she insists.

Hannah casts an annoyed glance at her. "How about we cut to the point?"

Lilah pouts her lips, though she's clearly excited about something—it's dancing in her eyes—and she wants to tell someone else about it. "Well, there's this reality show I heard about, and I really wanted to get cast on it. I'm an actress, you know."

"I heard your single," Hannah says flatly. "Wise decision to move on from music."

Lilah ignores her, continuing, "It's called *Dr. Lovin' Boat*. Anyway, there's going to be a captain, and then a bunch of women will be competing to see who he chooses as his first mate."

"Sounds like they slayed the naval analogies even worse than the *Ships Ahoy* movies," Hannah tells me with a small smile.

But I'm not smiling. Because I think I already know where Lilah's going with this.

"So I sent in my application video a while back, right? But I hadn't heard anything, so I figured it wasn't happening, but then Dottie read my tea leaves the other day, and she saw travel in the leaves and a wave. I made the connection because I was sitting in your house, Travis. *A wave.* That's when it hit me. I mean, here I was acting like I had no special qualifications for the job, when I had Ships Junior's baby." Her eyes bright, she continues, "So I called them up and asked if they'd be more interested in casting me if I went on as your baby mama."

Hannah's staring at me with big eyes. She must know how much I want to say no. How deeply I loathe the idea of the whole country hearing Lilah talk about me and my supposed legacy. Of having my privacy obliterated in the name of must-see TV.

"And they said yes!" Lilah cries out. "I had a video interview with them yesterday, and I'm a number one pick for them." She bites her lip again and does the hair flip, which spreads nothing but revulsion through me. "Now, you wouldn't need to be on the show, but they'd want to air a recorded statement from you. Just a couple of minutes, and I'd need to be able to talk about our past relationship, of course."

I breathe in slowly, then exhale slowly. "I don't want you telling them any details about Ollie or sharing his picture. They can know his name and his age but nothing else."

"They'll want more than that," Lilah says, as if I'm being unreasonable. She toys with a slinky strand of her hair. "They'll want to know what he's interested in, and—"

"Make it up," I say. "Tell them to say whatever tracks best with audiences."

She considers this and then nods.

"If I agree, you'll sign the papers granting me full custody?"

Hannah inhales sharply and squeezes my leg. "*Travis...*"

I meet her gaze and give her a reassuring nod.

I mean, obviously I'm not okay with this—I'm not a lunatic—but I want Ollie, and I don't want to hide anymore. Isn't that what cutting my hair was all about? It's like fate is rolling out the opportunity for me to prove I'm not a hypocrite.

If Lilah gets on this show, it's going to be uncomfortable and annoying, but it won't kill me. Losing my son *would* kill me.

"Yes," Lilah says. "I'll sign them. But you'll need to put your agreement into writing too."

"I'll do it," I say, then look at Hannah again and find her eyes full of tears.

"We need to go talk for a minute," she says, then fires a murderous glance at Lilah. "Alone."

Lilah rolls her eyes. "I don't see what this has to do with you. But if you want to be on the show, I'm sure they can work in a cameo or whatever. Maybe flash your photo across the screen."

"That's not what this is about," Hannah seethes as she gets up, tugging me with her.

She leads me out of the back door of the tea shop, into a little alley space that Dottie or someone who works for her has dressed up with a little garden that's mostly dead but was probably very nice a few months ago. A park bench sits in front of it.

"Travis," Hannah says, turning to me and taking my hands. "You can't do this. This is your *nightmare*. This is exactly the kind of BS Bixby tried to back you into, and his evil plan worked, dammit, because she never would have found out if it weren't for him."

I pull her into my arms, wrapping her up tight. Breathing her in. "It's okay," I say softly into her ear. "If this is how I keep Ollie, it's okay. It has a sort of full circle feeling, doesn't it?"

She leans back to peer at me. "You shouldn't have to do this."

"No, maybe not," I say, "but it's not going to be the end of the world. You helped me realize that." I pause, trying to order my thoughts. "For the longest time, I thought I had to leave behind the person I was to become who I want to be, but it's all connected. I'm Evan Thomas's son. If people want to talk about it, that's fine. Besides, I get to vet whatever they say. Maritime law is mine."

"I love you so much," she says, her eyes glimmering as she lifts up to me for a kiss.

I kiss her once, twice, probably a dozen times, before I draw back and say, "I'm going to marry you someday, Hannah. You just watch."

EPILOGUE
HANNAH

Just over a month has passed since Travis signed those papers, and oh, what a month…

Lilah took Ollie on a single outing before flitting off to Florida, where she officially joined the cast for *Dr. Lovin' Boat*. It's going to film next spring, and we'll be graced with its hot garbage nonsense in the fall. I'd be lying if I said I didn't plan on watching every last episode with Sophie and Briar. (Travis wants no part of it, but he agrees it's probably a good idea for one of us to keep an eye on it.)

I've slowly phased out of official nannying, but I still pick up Ollie after school on Fridays to go on adventures—and I stay over at their place at least three times a week. I'd be there more often, honestly, but I'm giving Travis and Ollie space to figure out their relationship. It's been beautiful to watch. They play music together, they've plotted out a garden for the spring, and apparently they're conspiring about what to get me for Christmas. I'm so proud of Travis that I've become one of those women who talks about her boyfriend all the time. I'd slap myself if I weren't so happy.

The three of us went to Boston for Thanksgiving, and I introduced Travis and Ollie to Connor and my dad, who instantly asked if they wanted to make beer with him. Like, as soon as they walked through the door of my dad's condo. All of the supplies were already sitting out too.

Travis looked like he was suffering instant and crippling constipation, so I explained that my dad was just messing with him and is willing to go *very far* with a joke.

"Oh, so that's where she gets it from," Travis said. My dad got him a beer and clapped him on the back, and that was that. They were fast friends, which made my heart happy.

When we got home from the trip, Travis and Ollie made me dinner and then asked if I wanted to revive the Moroney Movers and Shakers with the two of them, saying my brothers and dad had all given them permission to carry the family torch.

I said *yes*, obviously.

Our first performance is going to be at a Christmas market next weekend.

In addition to this very important new band gig, I just accepted a job as the daytime floor manager at Big Catch. When the woman I'm replacing quit, Eugene called me before the door hit her ass on the way out. Everyone knows the daytime shift is dull as dirt, but I love this brewery, and the hours are better for spending time with my guys. So I accepted, even though I'm wary of stepping back into my old role with Liam. He's already in Travis's band—temporarily, at least—and as much as I love my brother, I don't want to slip back into codependence.

But that's something I can worry about next week, when I start.

It's Sunday afternoon, the day of the big holiday staff party Eugene and I have been planning for weeks, between his many dates with Mrs. Applebaum.

Speaking of Mrs. Applebaum—those two are madly in love, and I don't at all mind taking credit for it.

The other day, when Eugene and I were power walking through The Waiting Place, something we do on purpose now, he told me he was thinking of getting a promise ring for her.

"Come on, Eugene," I said, halting. "Promise rings are for kids who don't know the joy of getting into each other's pants."

He harrumphed and told me I just didn't get it.

I don't, but I'm still happy for him.

Travis and I agreed that a staff party at a brewery, Christmas themed or not, is not a great place for a kid, so Ollie is staying over at Dottie's tonight. But Travis, Liam, Sophie, Rob, Eugene, and a couple more recruits are here getting the place ready for the shindig.

Briar was supposed to help out too, but she's late.

Briar's *never* late.

Then again, she's definitely going through something. She picked two Silver Star staffers to fire at the end of last month, and her father informed her that she had to do it before the holidays. She refused, and he responded by telling the staff they weren't getting their holiday bonuses, and that Briar was to blame.

I glance at the door a fourth time as I set down another of the table decorations Sophie made—gorgeous arrangements of dried flowers in decorative gourds.

"Maybe there's traffic," Sophie suggests as Travis adjusts the mistletoe he hung on the lighthouse for the tenth time.

"For the love of God, Travis..." Liam mutters, which only prompts Travis to move it again, this time with a smirk on his face that almost makes me laugh.

"She *is* a very sensible driver," I tell Sophie.

"More young women should be," Eugene says, glancing up from the spreadsheet he's reviewing on his iPad two tables away.

"Very funny, Eugene. You think five over is a crime—"

"It is, technically speaking," he says, just as Travis sputters a laugh.

"Five miles over?" my guy smirks at me. "I wish."

I defend my honor, and we all laugh. But as the minutes tick past and there's still no sign of Briar, Sophie and I start to really worry.

We worry more as people start trickling in, and then gushing in. I introduce Eugene's son, Cormac, to Travis and Liam, and all three of them instantly launch into a discussion of some band I've never heard of and have no interest in. So I pick my way over to Sophie and Rob, who are drinking Liam's gingerbread beer and talking in undertones.

I point my thumb at the guys. "They're having a music discussion, Rob. I think that means your presence is mandatory."

He laughs. "Is this your way of getting rid of me?"

"Maybe."

He starts saying something but cuts off abruptly and gestures to the front entrance. I look over as Briar enters the bar without a coat, dressed in a short-sleeved T-shirt and jeans.

Sophie and I hurry over, nearly knocking into Eugene and Mrs. Applebaum, who are making out under some of the mistletoe Travis hung. They barely seem to notice as we charge past them to get to our friend.

As I get closer, I can see Briar is trembling and her eyes are red-rimmed.

"Oh my God, what happened?" Sophie asks as I tug Briar away from the door.

"Wait," I say. "She'll want to tell us somewhere private."

I lead Briar toward the back, grabbing a Big Catch sweatshirt off the merch shelf on the way back and handing it to her.

She takes it but doesn't put it on. She's still shaking, and after I open the door to the back room, I nudge her through.

Sophie follows us in, shutting the door, and the noise from the party becomes a muted murmur. I dress Briar in the sweatshirt as if she's a child, and Sophie gently tugs Briar's long hair out from under the back of it so it's not trapped.

"What happened?" I ask again, leading her over to a picnic table that's kept back here. She practically falls onto it.

"I did it. I fired them this morning, because my dad said that if I didn't, he'd carry through on his original threat and fire three other people. And then my dad ..." She wraps her arms around herself, trembling harder even though she must be physically warm now. "He gave me Silver Star Brewery. He said it was my Christmas present." She pauses. "It's mine."

She starts laughing, but there isn't a hint of amusement in it.

Sophie and I exchange worried looks.

"Right, I'm going to get you a drink," Sophie says.

She hurries off while I rub Briar's arm, but Briar just keeps laughing so I give her a light tap on the cheek. "You need to stop that and tell us what happened."

The laughter cuts off, and she looks up at me, her soft brown eyes filled with tears. "I messed up so bad, Hannah. I don't know what I'm doing."

"None of us know what we're doing," I say, rubbing her arm again. "You're going to be fine. You're going to kick ass."

"You don't understand," she says as Sophie hurries in, carrying a bottle of—

"Seriously, peach schnapps?" I say as I take it from her.

She shrugs and hands out the paper cups she brought with it. "Eugene had it in his desk. My aunt gave a bottle to everyone in the Wise Elders Group as an early Christmas present."

Yes, peach schnapps, the gift that keeps on giving.

I uncap it and fill Briar's cup practically to the brim.

She takes a gulp, flinches—understandable—and then says, "Everyone quit. Everyone. They all walked out while playing 'You Better Watch Out' over the speakers." She releases a jagged sob. "They hate me. No one's ever hated me like that since boarding school."

Sophie and I exchange knowing looks before Sophie says, "Of course they don't."

It's a sweet lie, to which I add a dash of truth. "They don't hate *you*, Briar. They hate this person your dad's made you out to be for the past few months. That person's a lie."

"I don't know what I'm going to do. How am I supposed to run a brewery without a staff? I...I went along with my dad's tough-love nonsense because that's what I've always done—fallen into line—and I figured I could fix everything once I took over, but now..."

I stroke her hair. "So when you're saying *everyone* quit..."

Silver Star is a much smaller outfit than either Big Catch Brewing or Buchanan Brewery, but that's still a lot of people to replace.

"*Everyone*. All twenty. The brewer was the first to go. He told me I was never going to make it. That no brewer in their right mind was going to work for me or anyone in my family. He said he was going to put the word out to make sure of it."

Crap, he pulled a Rachel.

"I'll work for you," I blurt. "I'll tell them I can't take the job here. It's fine. I haven't even started yet."

But Briar's already shaking her head. "The daytime manager position here is perfect for you. If you don't take it because of me, I'll be miserable. Please, Hannah."

"My cousin," Sophie says. "Our crafting business is still only part time. He'll work for you. I'm sure he'll want to."

"Thanks, Sophie," Briar says sadly, but she knows what I do —a brewery isn't a brewery without a brewer.

A brewer.

That's when it dawns on me...

I can't fix all of this for her, but I can fix one thing. Maybe the most important thing.

"I'll be right back," I say, rising.

Sophie looks up in alarm. "Where are you going?"

"To hire more staff for Briar," I say with a smile.

I return to the party with purpose powering my steps, dodging friends, acquaintances, and strangers, until I run directly into a dark-haired woman.

I rock back. "Sorry. I'm just looking—"

She turns, and I go momentarily mute. Because it's Nora Leigh, GingerBeerBabe herself.

What is *she* doing at our staff party?

"Did Dottie invite you?" I ask, shocked. I wouldn't put it past Dottie to invite someone to a party she's not attending or throwing.

"No, I'm here with her..." She glances nervously into the crowd, then points to the last person I would have expected: Moira Applebaum. "Moira's my mom."

Moira *did* tell me she had a daughter.

A daughter who I reminded her of.

I stare at Nora in shocked disbelief, my mind struggling to process any of the big news I've gotten in the past few minutes.

"I've been wanting to email you," Nora continues, "but I figured it would be better to talk in person. I'm so grateful for what you've done for my mom. She's happier than she's been in years."

"*You're* Mrs. Applebaum's mother?"

"Her daughter," she says with a smile.

Oops.

I rub my temples. "Sorry, I just got some big news, and this is blowing my mind."

She rocks a little where she stands. "Yeah, it kind of blew my mind too. Mom told me about your boyfriend's little boy before she mentioned you by name. She said she's never had such an advanced student."

I nod, because flattering Ollie will get her everywhere. "He's the best."

"I'm not," she says with a directness that surprises me. "I've dealt with everything badly. I'm just... I've always been a private person, and the last thing I wanted was for everyone to be talking about..."

"Your boyfriend having a fiancée and two other girlfriends?" I ask with a laugh.

She lifts one corner of her mouth, nodding. "Something like that. It was complicated and super messy, and I'm hoping we can put it all behind us and maybe be friends. But if there's anything I can do for you. Anything at all—"

I beam at her. "I'm going to be calling in that favor really soon for my friend Briar. She's taking over her family's brewery, and she's going to need all the help she can get. You'll meet with her?"

"Briar as in..."

"One of Jonah's other ex-girlfriends. You can't escape us, can you?" I say it with a smile, because there's something magical about this night suddenly. A few minutes ago, it felt like all hope was lost for my friend, but now possibility floats in the air like little golden motes of light. I plan on grabbing as many as I can and shoving them at Briar.

Nora smiles back at me. "It's enough that I escaped Jonah."

"Agreed," I say, distracted by the sight of Travis walking my way.

"I have to go take care of a few things," I tell Nora. "Have a good time, and I'll be in touch."

I practically run to Travis. He wraps his arm around me, and I lean into his neck, needing to breathe him in. I can sense everyone murmuring around us, but I ignore them. For a second, the two of us exist in a bubble that's just ours. Then he kisses my forehead, and I say, "Liam—I need to have a private talk with Liam. Let's get him and go to the storeroom."

"Uh..."

I can sense him remembering what we did in that storeroom, but there's no better place to go. It's important for this conversation to be totally private, and it's freezing outside. "Don't worry, I won't tackle you until after he leaves."

He smiles, shaking his head softly. "Is Briar okay? We saw you bringing her to the back."

"No, but she's going to be," I say firmly. "Let's get Liam."

My brother's deep in conversation with Cormac, but as soon as I signal to him, he cuts it short.

Striding over, Liam asks, "What's up? Something wrong with your friend?"

"Yes," I say. "You and I are having a super-secret meeting in the storeroom. Right away." I glance around, making sure no one's listening, because I would one hundred percent get into trouble if anyone finds out about this.

"What about Travis?" he asks, raising his eyebrows.

"He's coming as my Emotional Support Travis."

"Are you good with that emasculating description?" Liam asks him, still joking around as if everything isn't about to change.

"Yup," Travis says, squeezing me.

"Well, by all means. Let's pack into a tiny space together, because that's not suspicious."

Travis laughs, and I jab him playfully with my elbow and

say, "Just be cool, and it'll be fine. If anyone asks, we'll say someone puked in the bathroom and we're getting supplies to clean it."

Liam nods, giving me a searching look, and I start toward the storeroom, worried I might chicken out if I don't get this out soon.

A couple of minutes later, the three of us are shut inside, Travis's arms still wrapped around me. I'm breathing hard, my heart racing, but I force myself to calm down as I face my typically stoic big brother.

"That other favor you promised me," I say. "You meant it, didn't you?"

His eyes darken. "You know I did."

My mind races at the thought of what I'm about to say. But the truth is, I wouldn't ask my brother to do this if I didn't think he could handle it. If I didn't think the challenge would thrill him—and that he'd rise to it—and that it would be the making of both him and Silver Star Brewery.

I wouldn't be saying this if I thought it was a bad idea.

Especially since it could get me fired from my brand-new job if anyone found out.

But doubt bites into me suddenly.

I'm asking Liam to leave his job just because I say so. It's an enormous ask, way beyond the normal scope of a favor.

I glance at Travis, needing his take on this. If he thinks it's a horrible idea—another instance of Hannah Overreach—I'll back off. But he's watching me with a look of such deep faith, I'm blown away. He smiles and squeezes my hand, and even though I didn't run this by him before dragging him in here, I know he's behind me one hundred percent. That he'll always be behind me, whatever crazy scheme I concoct. Just like I'll always have his back.

"Hannah?" Liam all but growls. "I didn't come in here to watch you make out with your boyfriend."

"Too bad," Travis says. He lifts my hand to his lips, nodding. Giving me his silent go-ahead.

Filled with strength and fresh conviction, I straighten, looking Liam in the eye, and I say, "I'm calling that favor in."

Don't miss Briar and Liam's story next in *Best Kind of Trouble*!

ABOUT THE AUTHOR

ANGELA CASELLA is a romcom fanatic. Writing them, reading them, watching them—she's greedy, and she does it all. In addition to her solo releases, she was lucky enough to collaborate with Denise Grover Swank on three complete series.

She lives in Asheville, NC. Her hobbies include herding her daughter toward less dangerous activities, trying to trick her corgis into behaving, the aforementioned romcom addiction, and dreaming of having someone else clean her house.

Visit her website at www.angelacasella.com or Angela and Denise's shared website at www.arcdgs.com.